W9-AKC-802

Rickety Stitch

AND THE GELATINOUS GOO

Created and Written by

BEN COSTA & JAMES PARKS

Illustrated by

BEN COSTA

ALFRED A. KNOPF

New York

We would like to supremely thank Jason Shiga, Dan Lazar, Stan Sakai, Rima Singh, Evin Wolverton, and, of course, Jenny Brown, Stephen Brown, and the entire team at Knopf.

We would also like to thank our families for the love and support over the fifteen years that Rickety Stitch and the Gelatinous Goo has been in our lives, especially Kieu Nguyen and Ellen Ma.

THIS IS A BORZOI BOOK PUBLISHED BY ALFRED A. KNOPF

This is a work of fiction. All incidents and dialogue, and all characters with the exception of some well-known historical and public figures, are products of the authors' imagination and are not to be construed as real. Where real-life historical or public figures appear, the situations, incidents, and dialogues concerning those persons are fictional and are not intended to depict actual events or to change the fictional nature of the work. In all other respects, any resemblance to persons living or dead is entirely coincidental.

Text, cover art, and interior illustrations copyright © 2017 by James Parks and Ben Costa

All rights reserved. Published in the United States by Alfred A. Knopf, an imprint of Random House Children's Books, a division of Penguin Random House LLC, New York.

Knopf, Borzoi Books, and the colophon are registered trademarks of Penguin Random House LLC.

Visit us on the Web! randomhouseteens.com

Educators and librarians, for a variety of teaching tools, visit us at RHTeachersLibrarians.com

Library of Congress Cataloging-in-Publication Data is available upon request.
ISBN 978-0-399-55613-5 (trade) — ISBN 978-0-399-55615-9 (ebook) — ISBN 978-0-399-55614-2 (trade pbk.)

The illustrations were created digitally.

MANUFACTURED IN CHINA
June 2017
10 9 8 7 6 5 4 3 2 1

First Edition

Random House Children's Books supports
the First Amendment and celebrates the right to read.

This book is dedicated to all those summers spent with the best of friends, dreaming up heroes, embarking on backyard adventures, and slaying imaginary dragons.

It is an age of ashes. The gleaming empires of old have faded into obscurity, leaving a tired world riddled with dungeons and ruled by fiends. With trade roads host to brigands and mighty castles neglected, goodly folk are left to huddle in remote villages, where the tales of a golden age lie all but forgotten . . .

Chapter 1
Awake

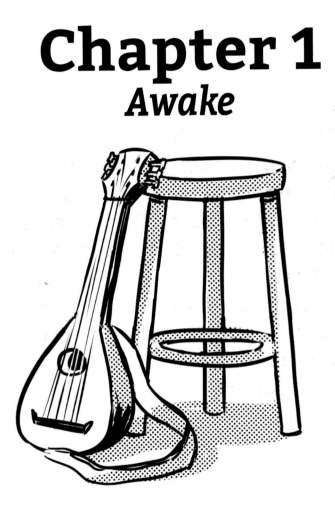

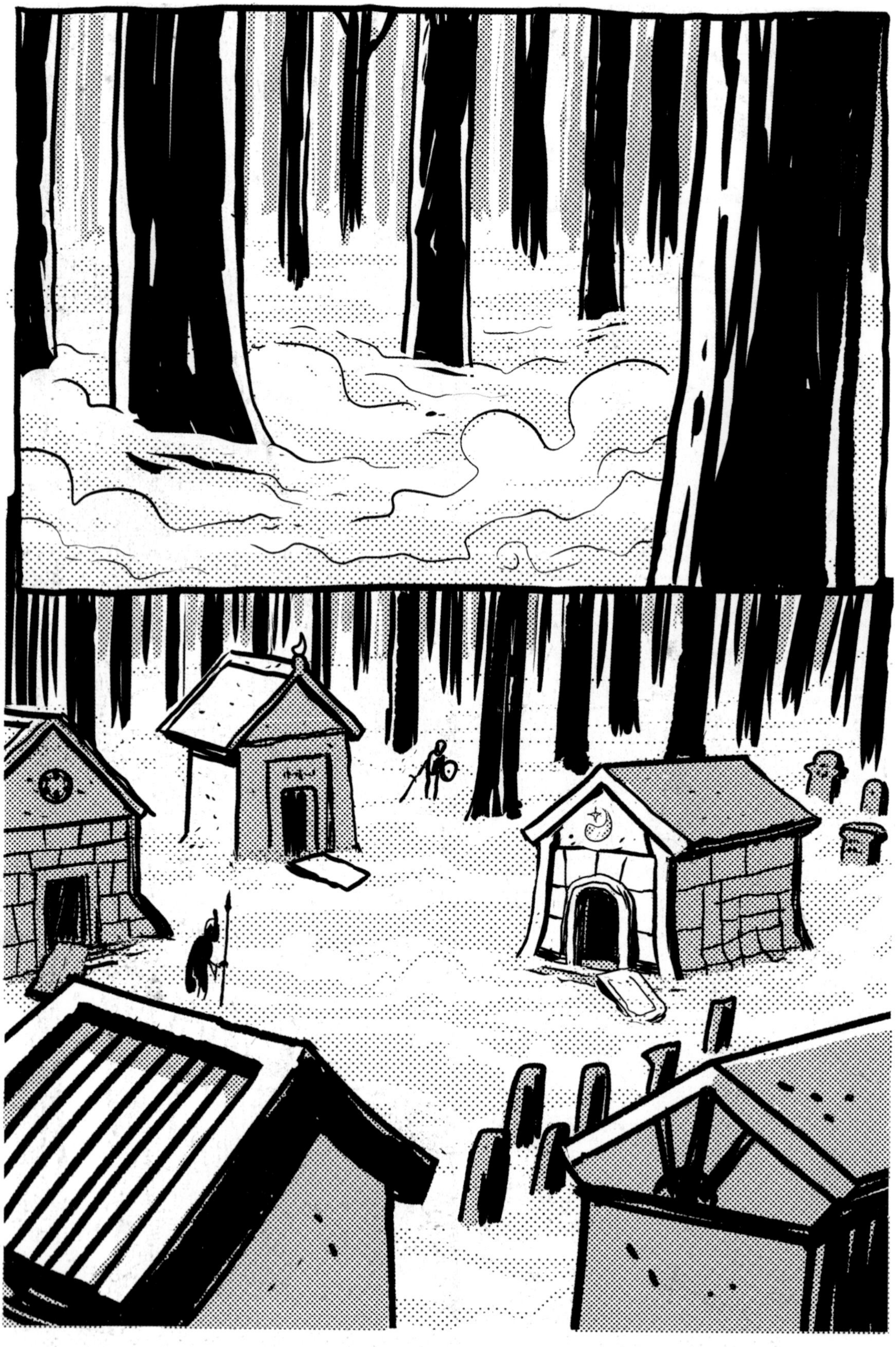

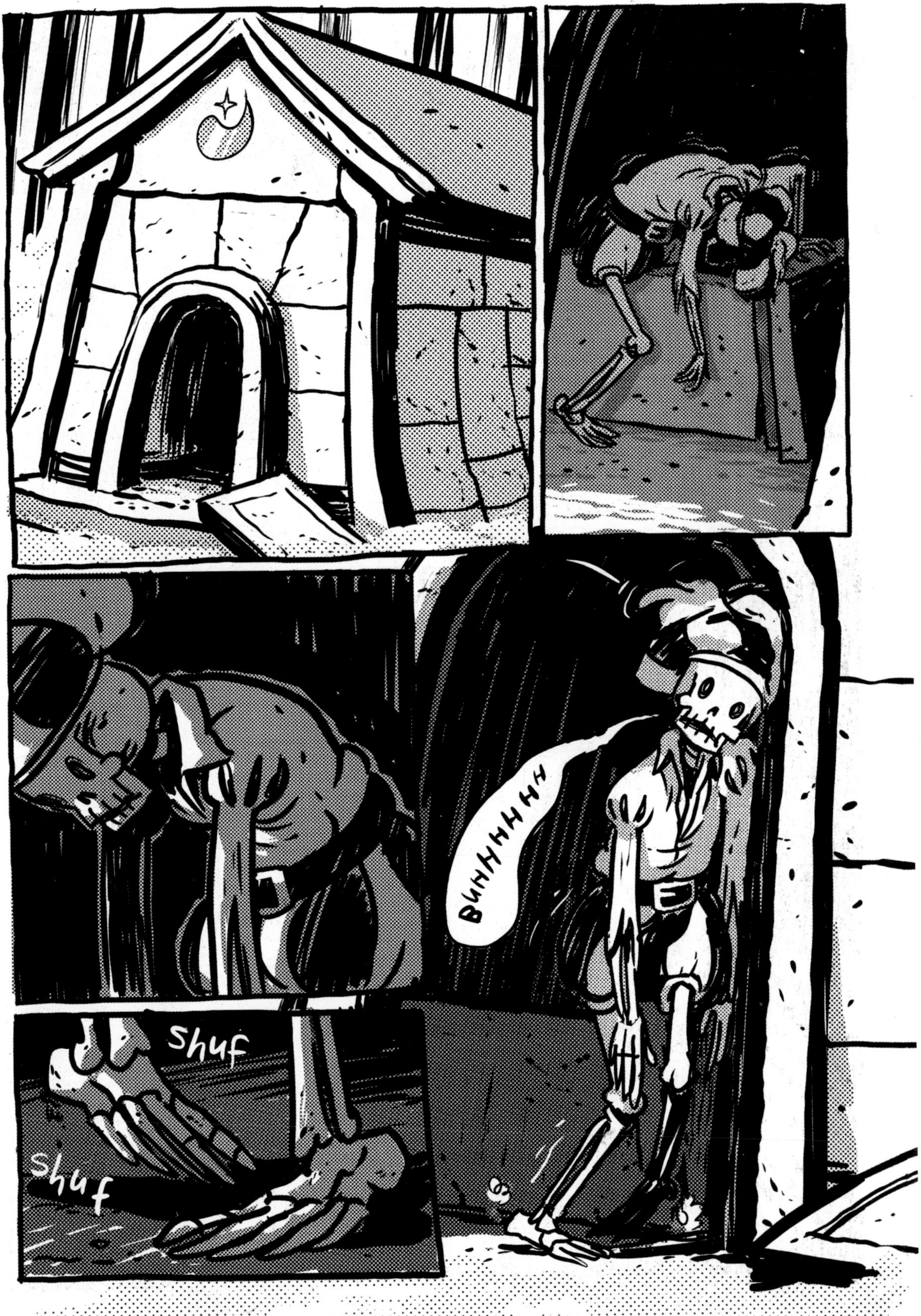
BUHHHHHHH
shuf
shuf

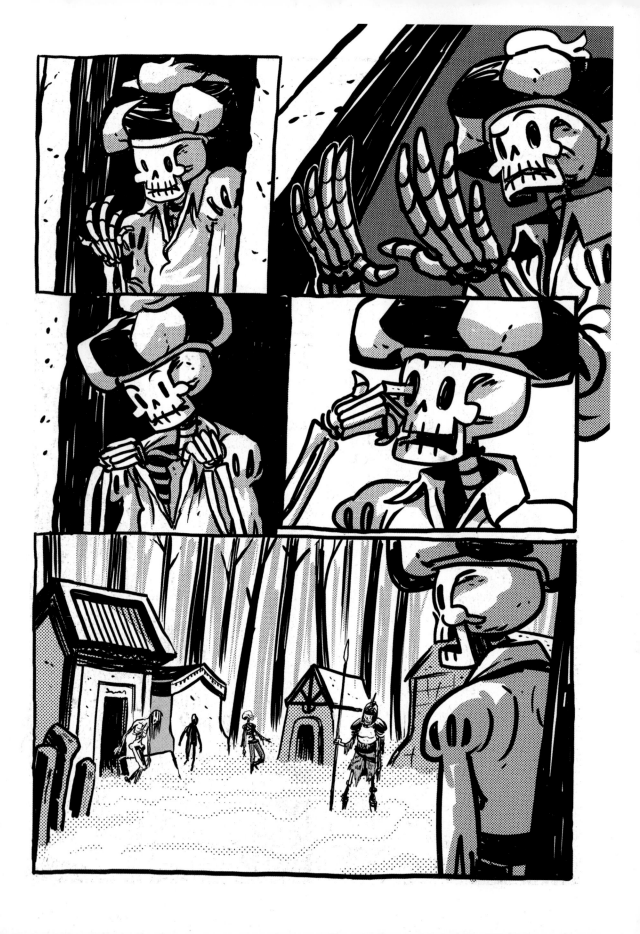

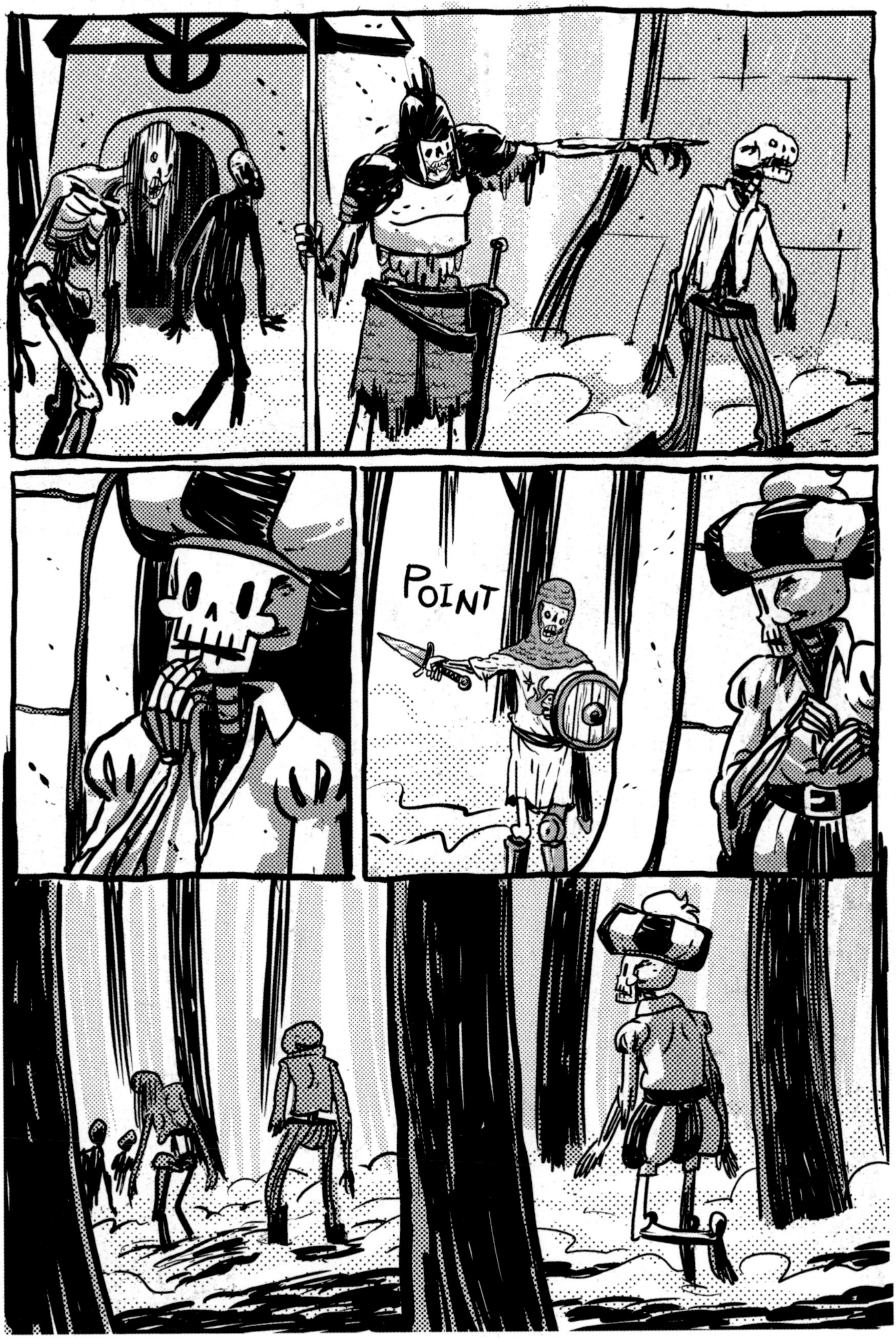
POINT

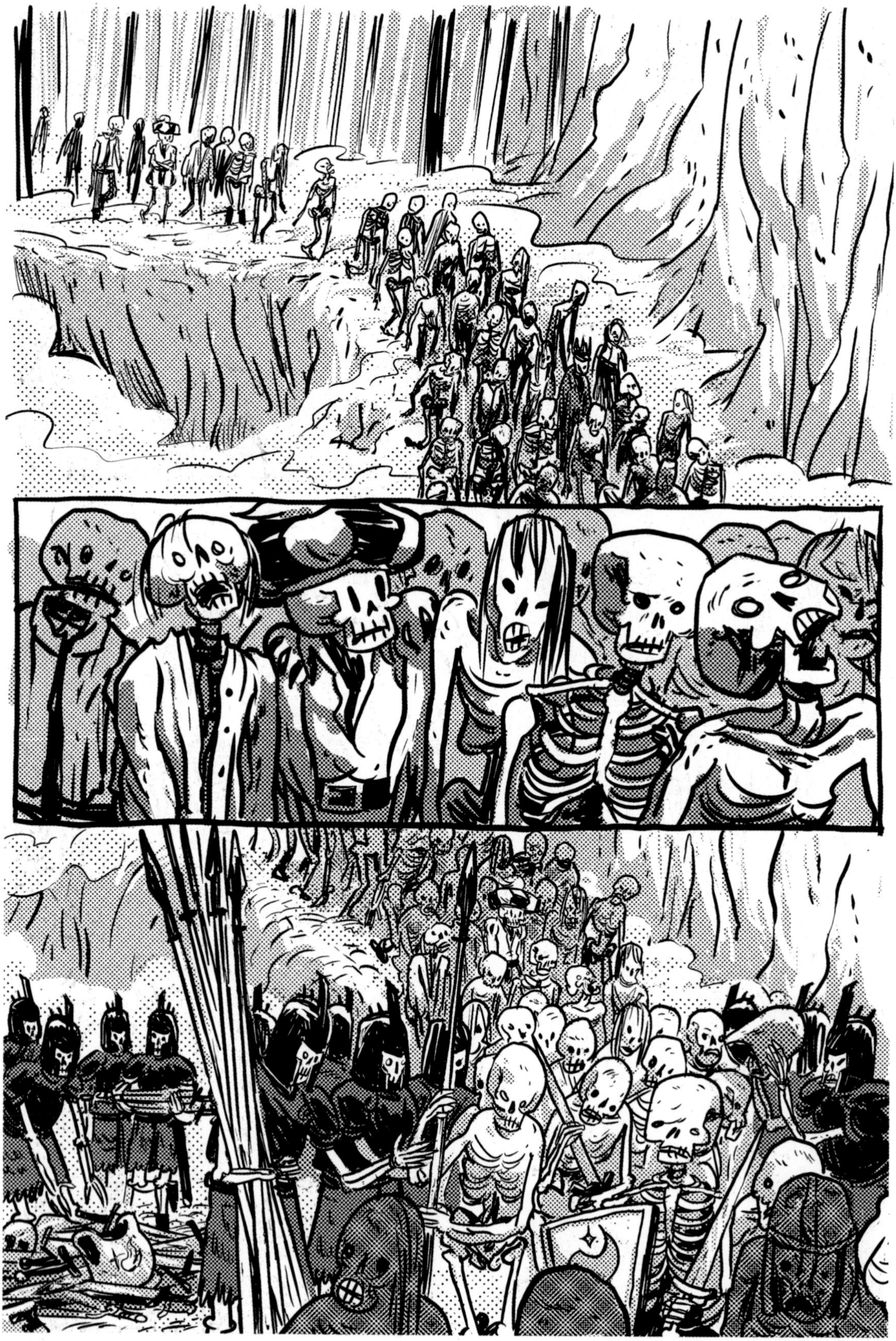

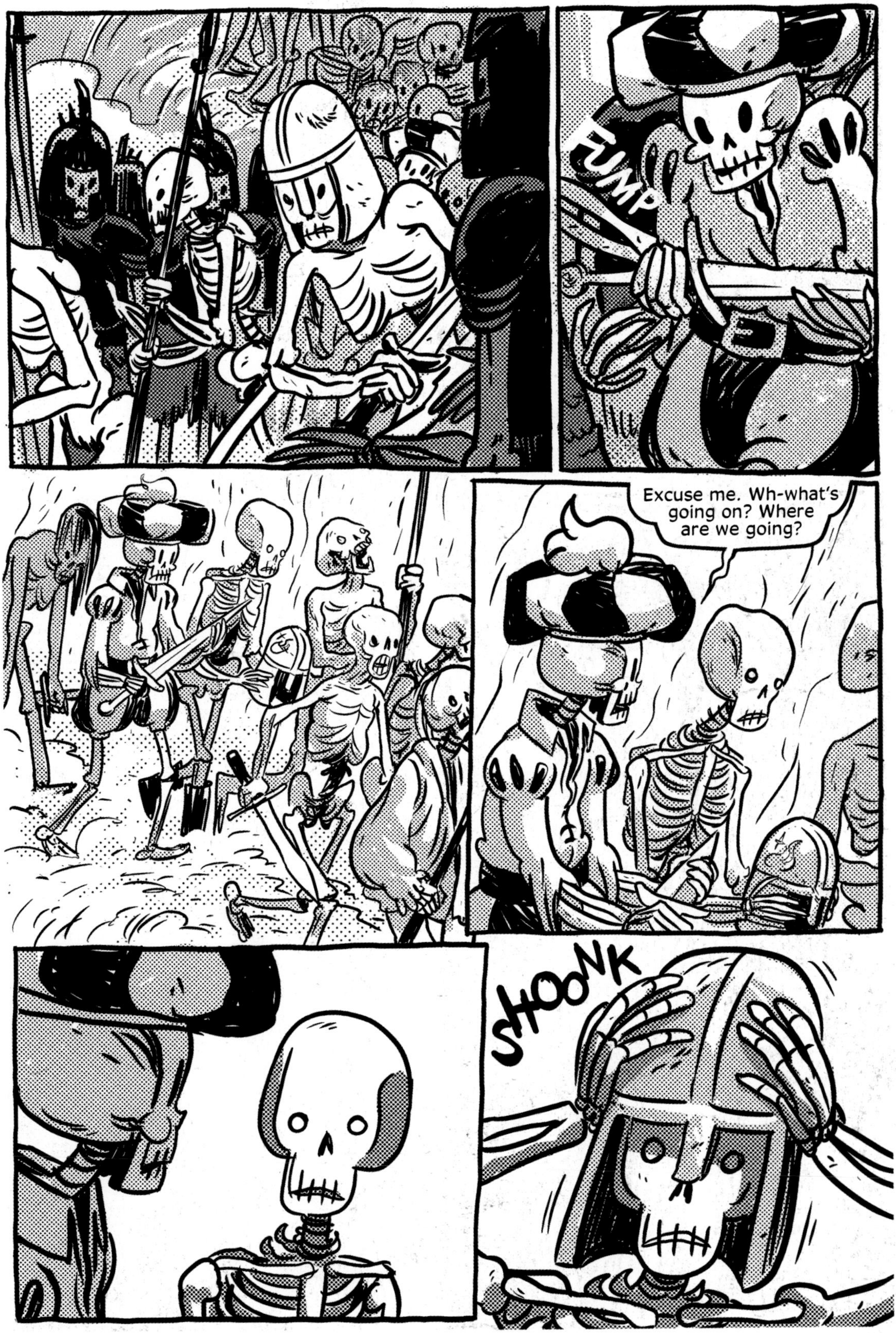
FUMP
Excuse me. Wh-what's going on? Where are we going?
SHOONK

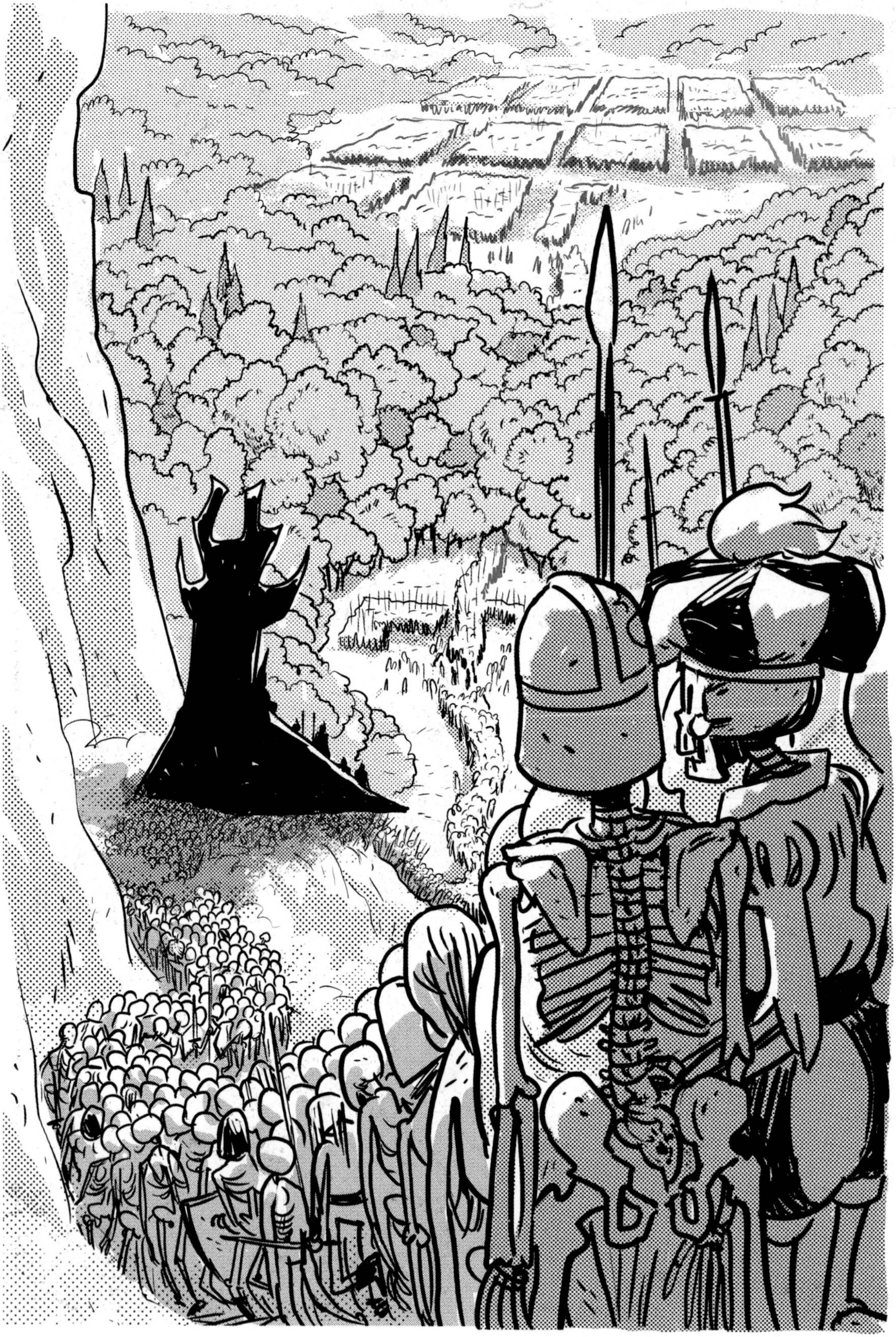

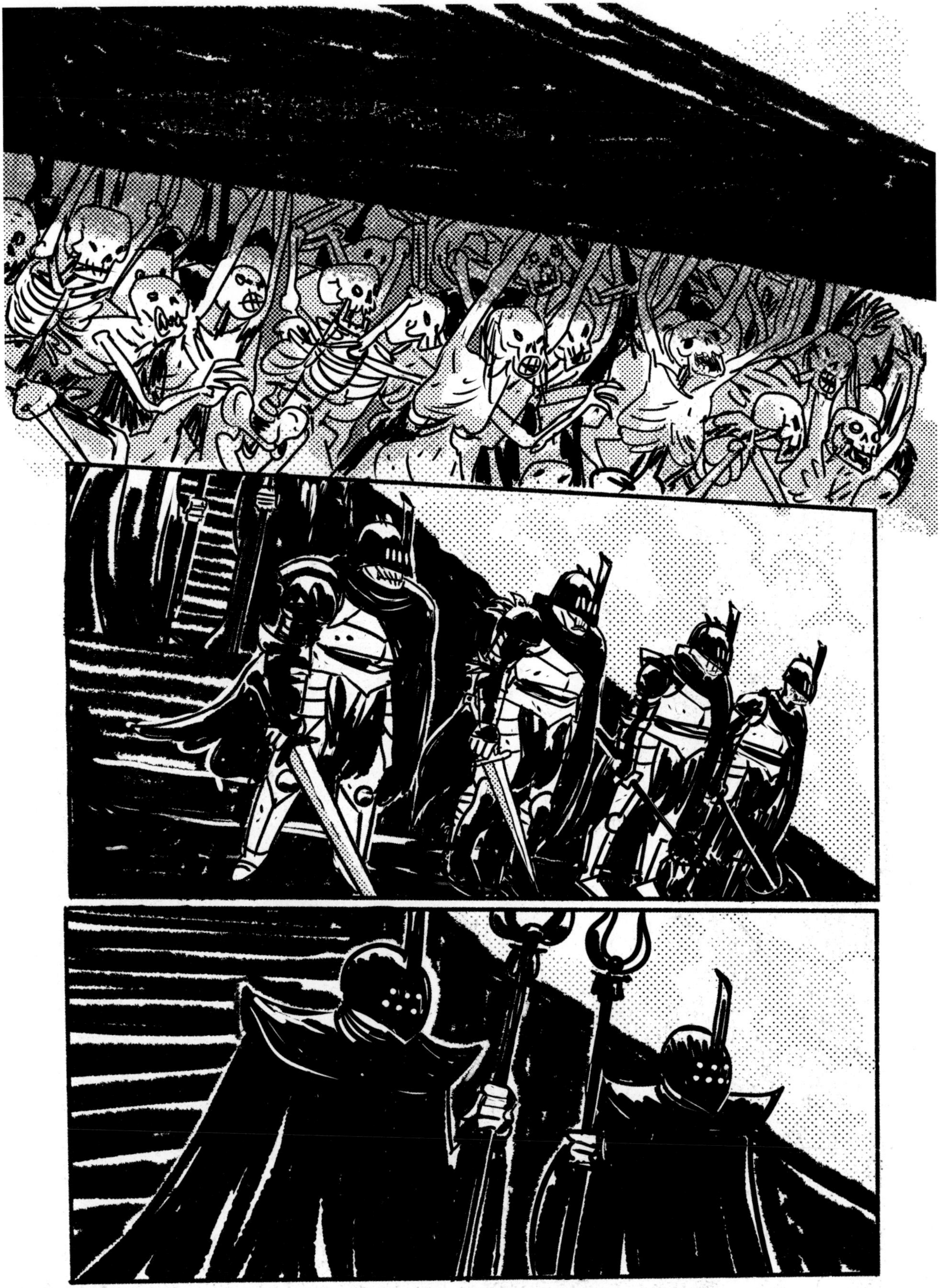

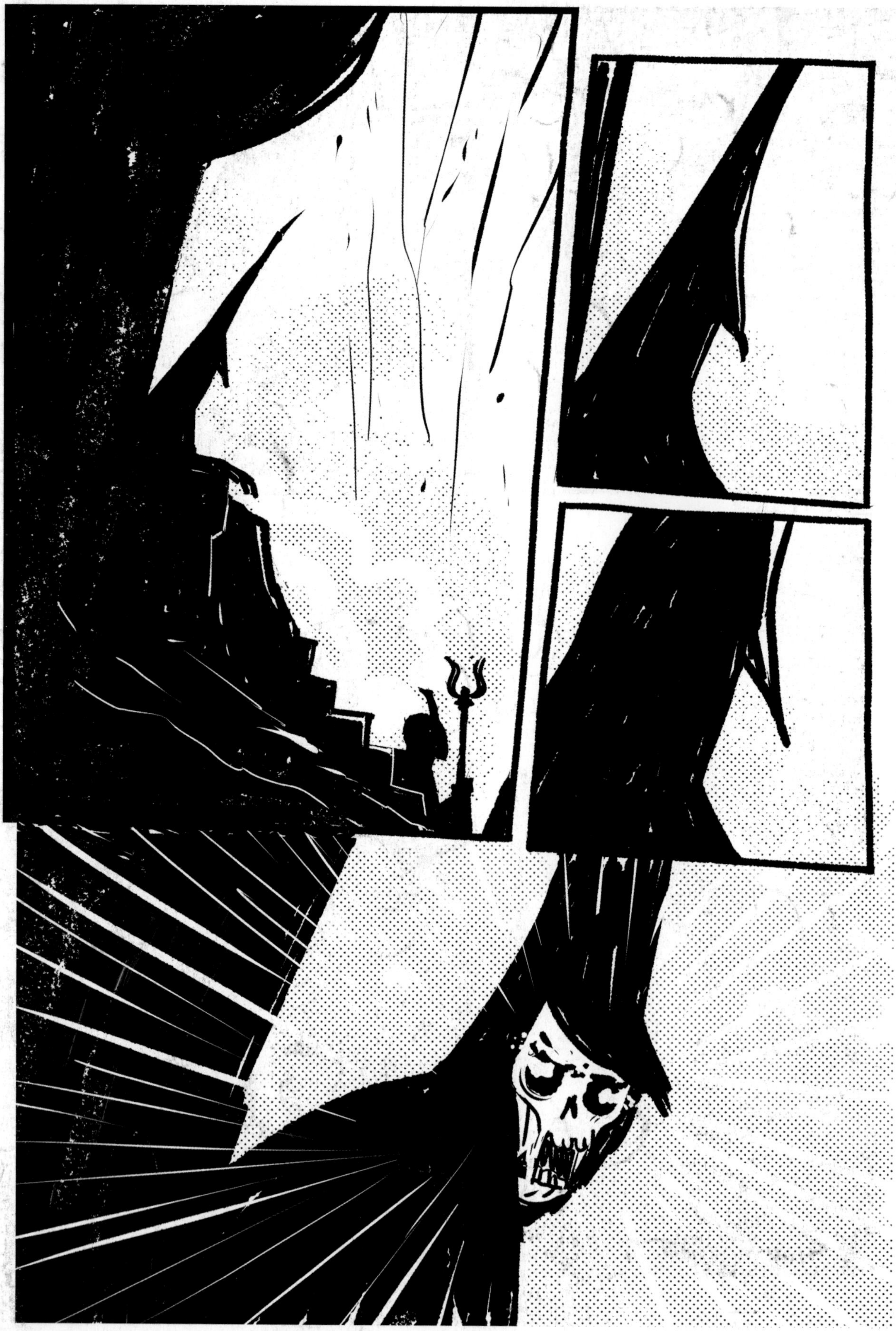

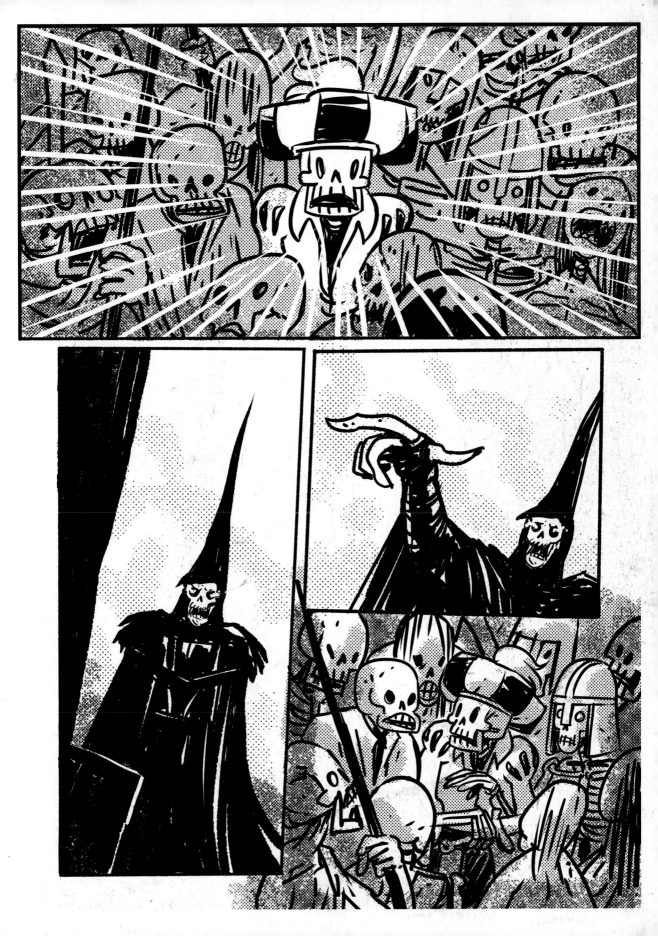

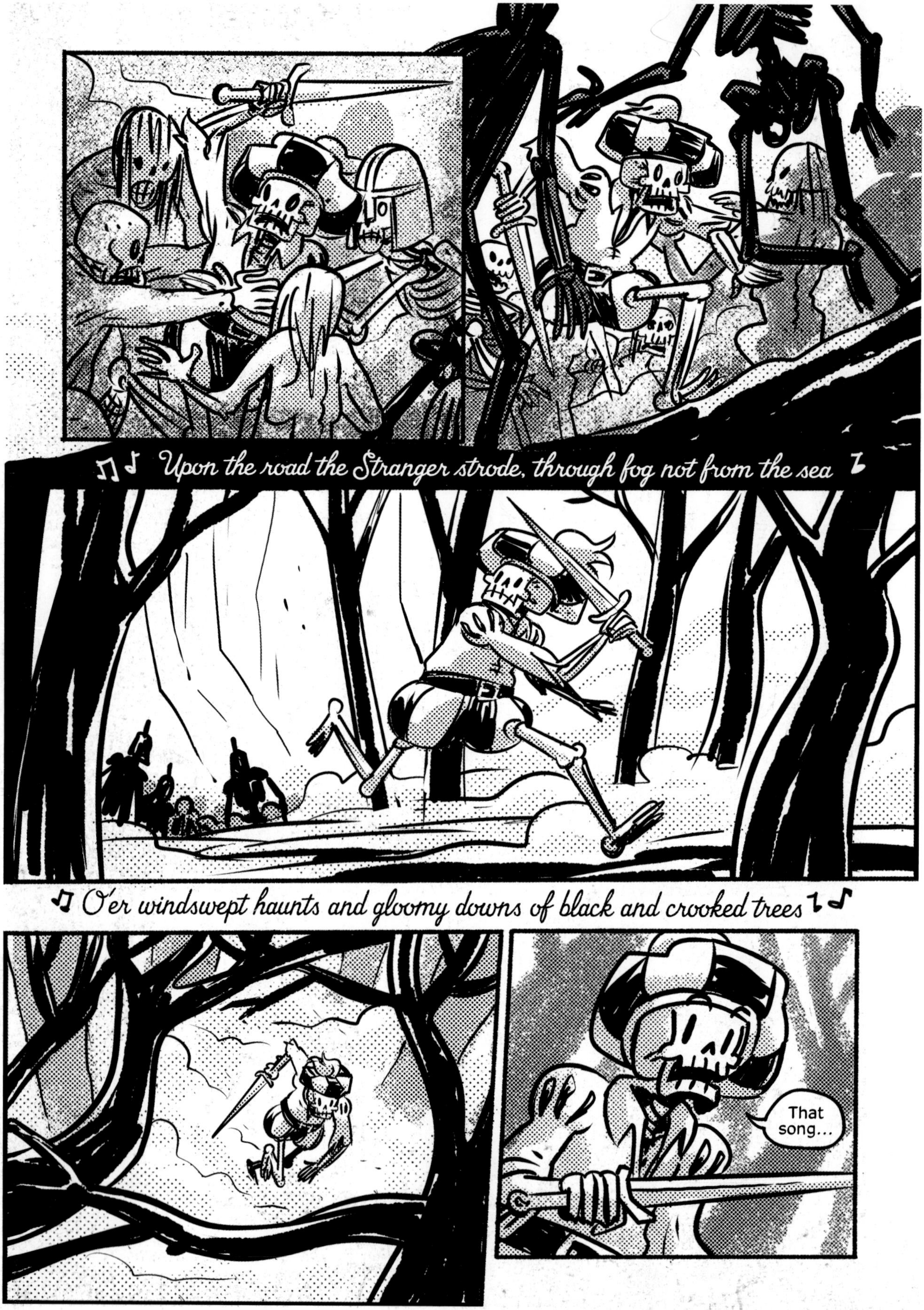
Upon the road the Stranger strode, through fog not from the sea
O'er windswept haunts and gloomy downs of black and crooked trees
That song...

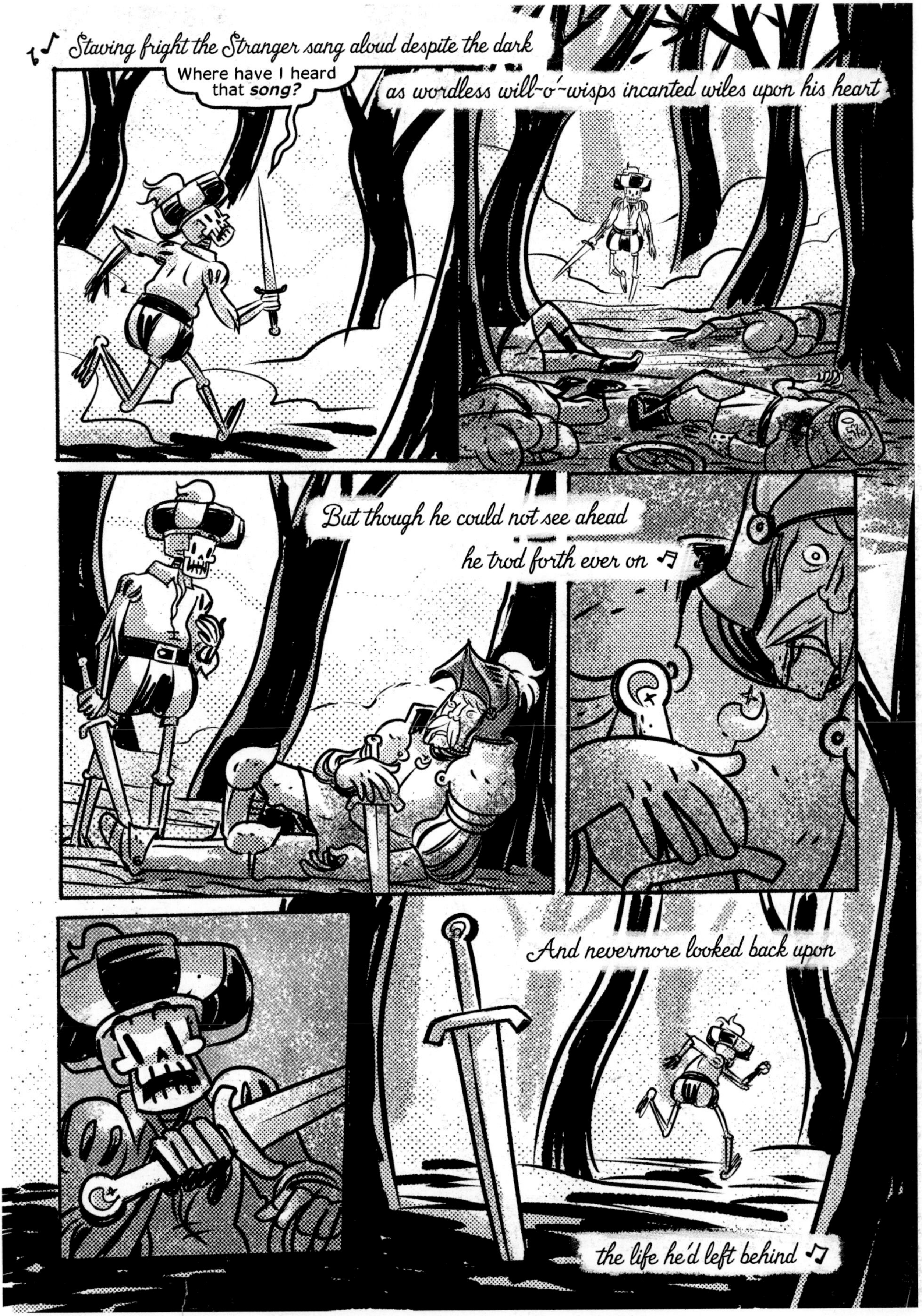
♪ Staving fright the Stranger sang aloud despite the dark
Where have I heard that song?
as wordless will-o'-wisps incanted wiles upon his heart
But though he could not see ahead
he trod forth ever on ♫
And nevermore looked back upon
the life he'd left behind ♫

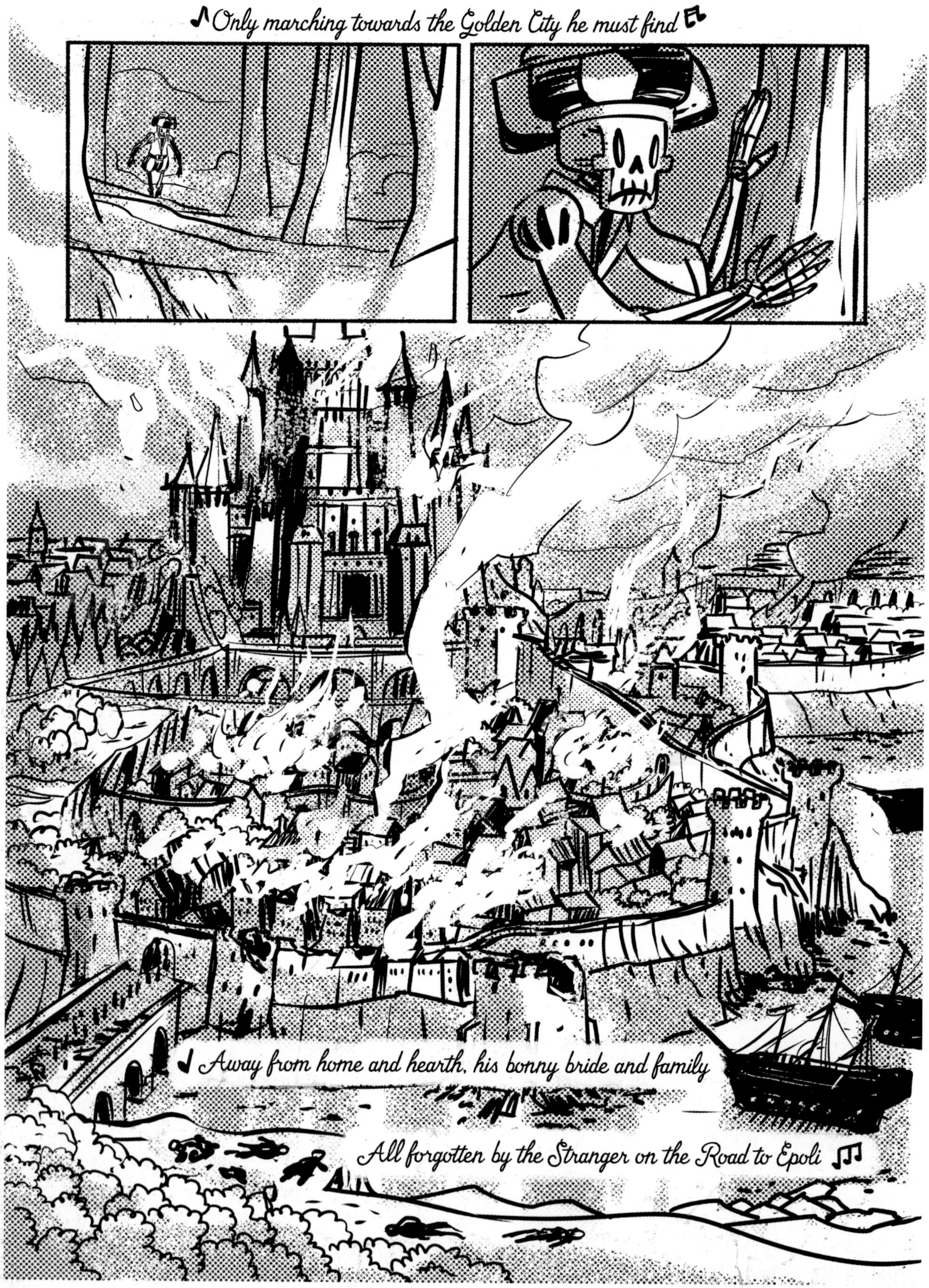
Only marching towards the Golden City he must find
Away from home and hearth, his bonny bride and family
All forgotten by the Stranger on the Road to Epoli

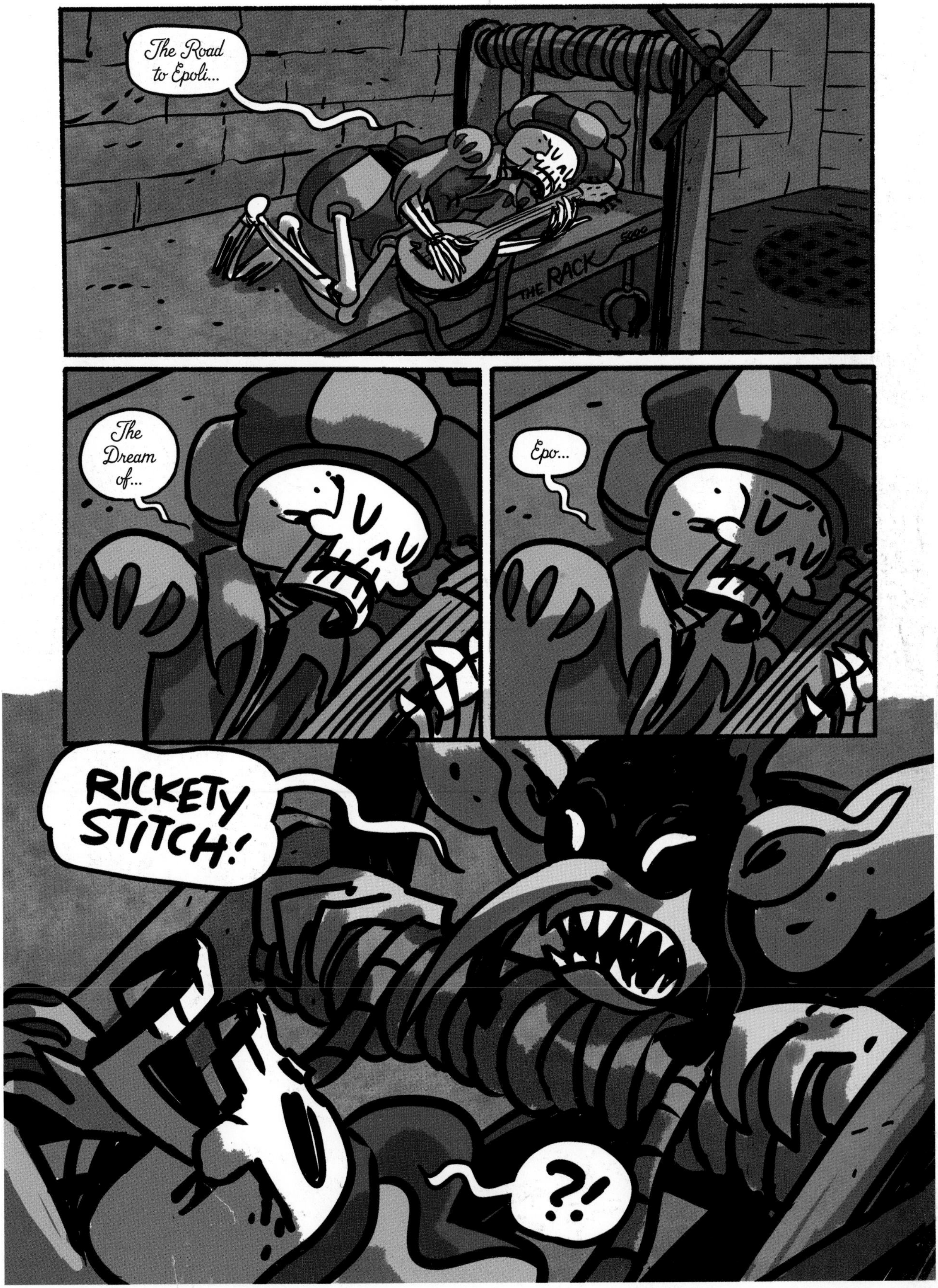
The Road to Epoli...
THE RACK 5000
The Dream of...
Epo...
RICKETY STITCH!
?!

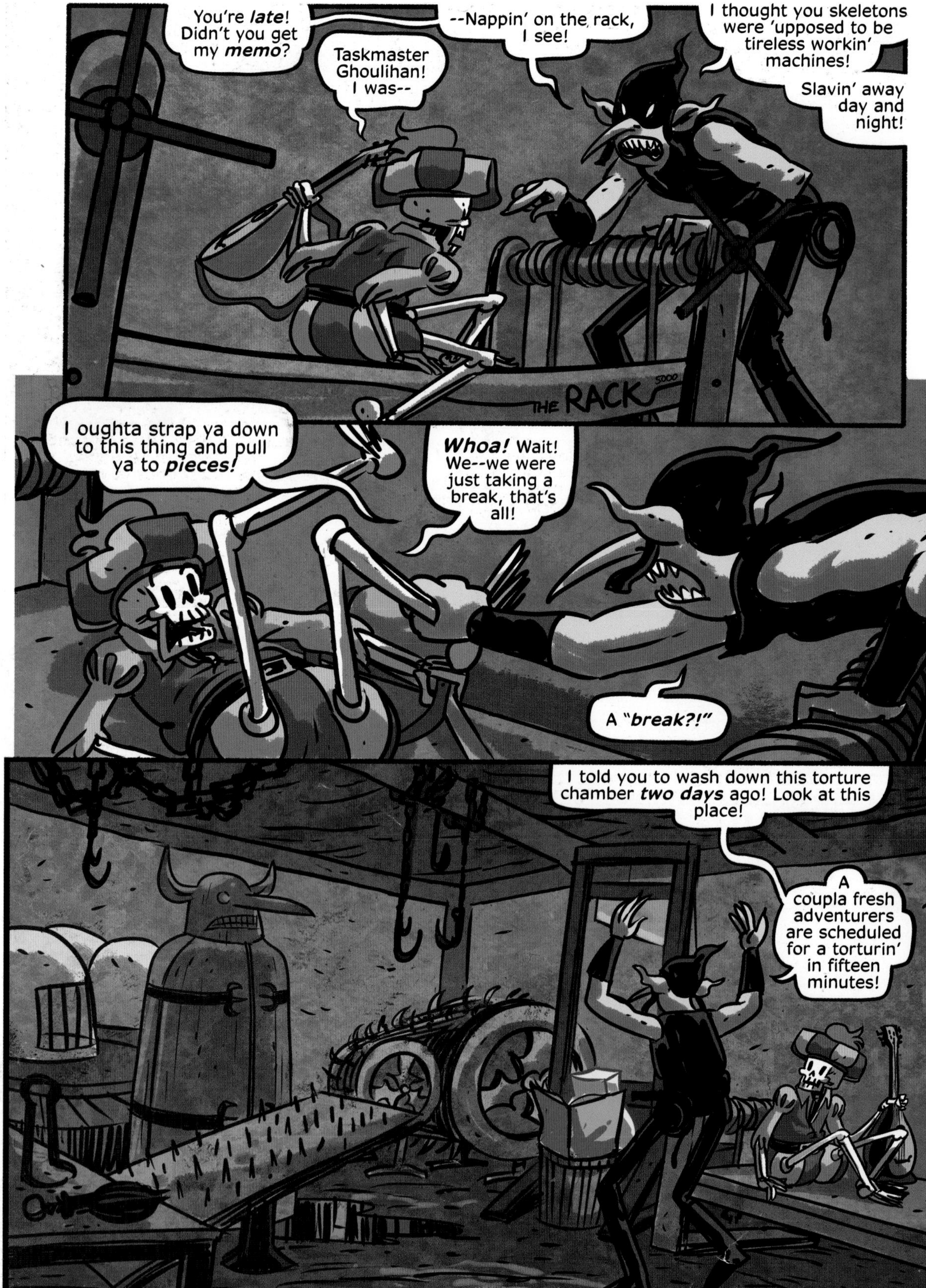

You're *late*! Didn't you get my *memo*?
Taskmaster Ghoulihan! I was--
--Nappin' on the rack, I see!
I thought you skeletons were 'upposed to be tireless workin' machines!
Slavin' away day and night!
THE RACK 5000
I oughta strap ya down to this thing and pull ya to *pieces!*
Whoa! Wait! We--we were just taking a break, that's all!
A "*break?!*"
I told you to wash down this torture chamber ***two days*** ago! Look at this place!
A coupla fresh adventurers are scheduled for a torturin' in fifteen minutes!

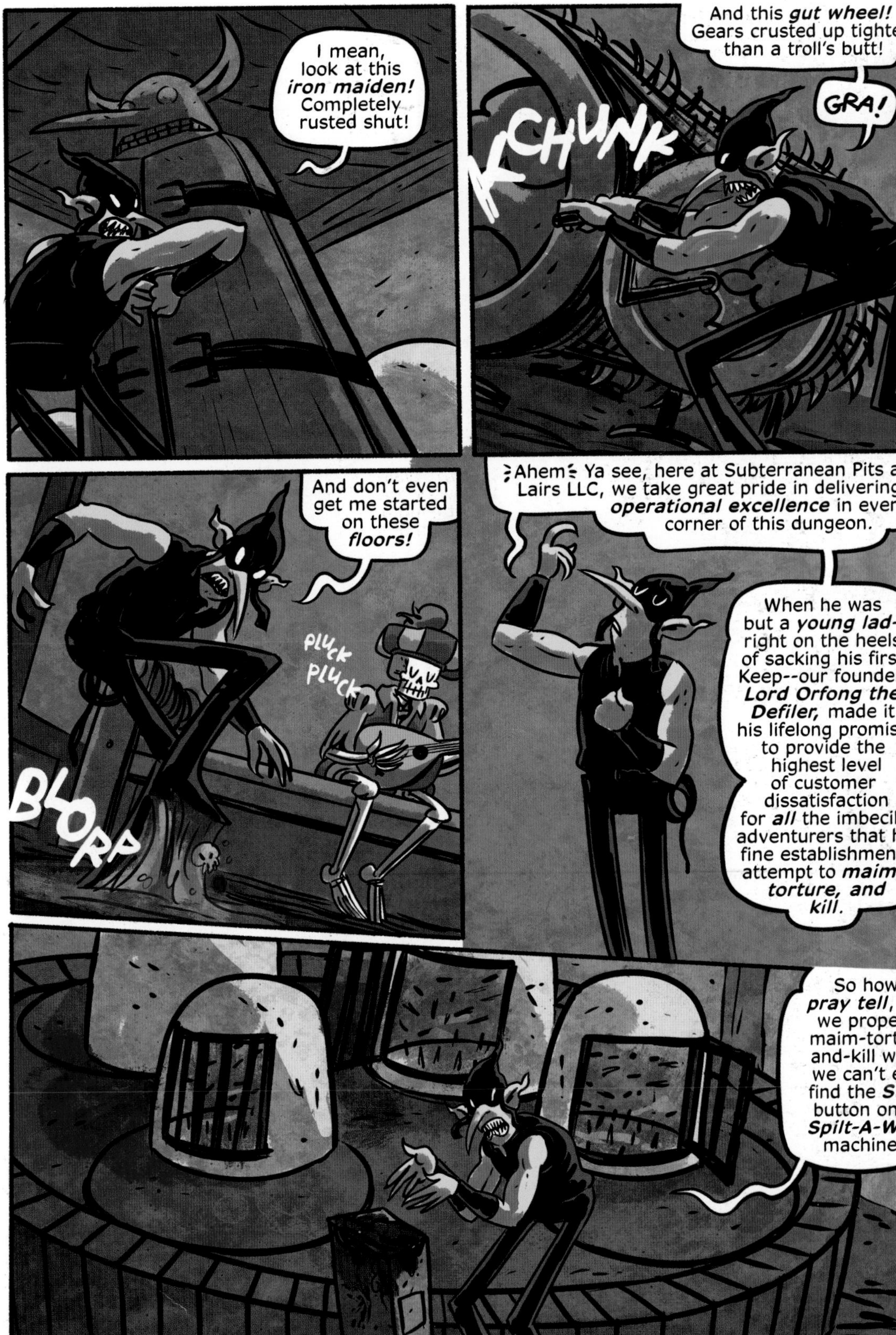
I mean, look at this *iron maiden!* Completely rusted shut!
And this *gut wheel!* Gears crusted up tighter than a troll's butt!
GRA!
KCHUNK
And don't even get me started on these *floors!*
PLUCK PLUCK
BLORP
Ahem Ya see, here at Subterranean Pits and Lairs LLC, we take great pride in delivering *operational excellence* in every corner of this dungeon.
When he was but a *young lad*--right on the heels of sacking his first Keep--our founder, *Lord Orfong the Defiler,* made it his lifelong promise to provide the highest level of customer dissatisfaction for *all* the imbecilic adventurers that his fine establishments attempt to *maim, torture, and kill.*
So how, *pray tell*, can we properly maim-torture-and-kill when we can't even find the *Start* button on the *Spilt-A-Whirl* machine?!?

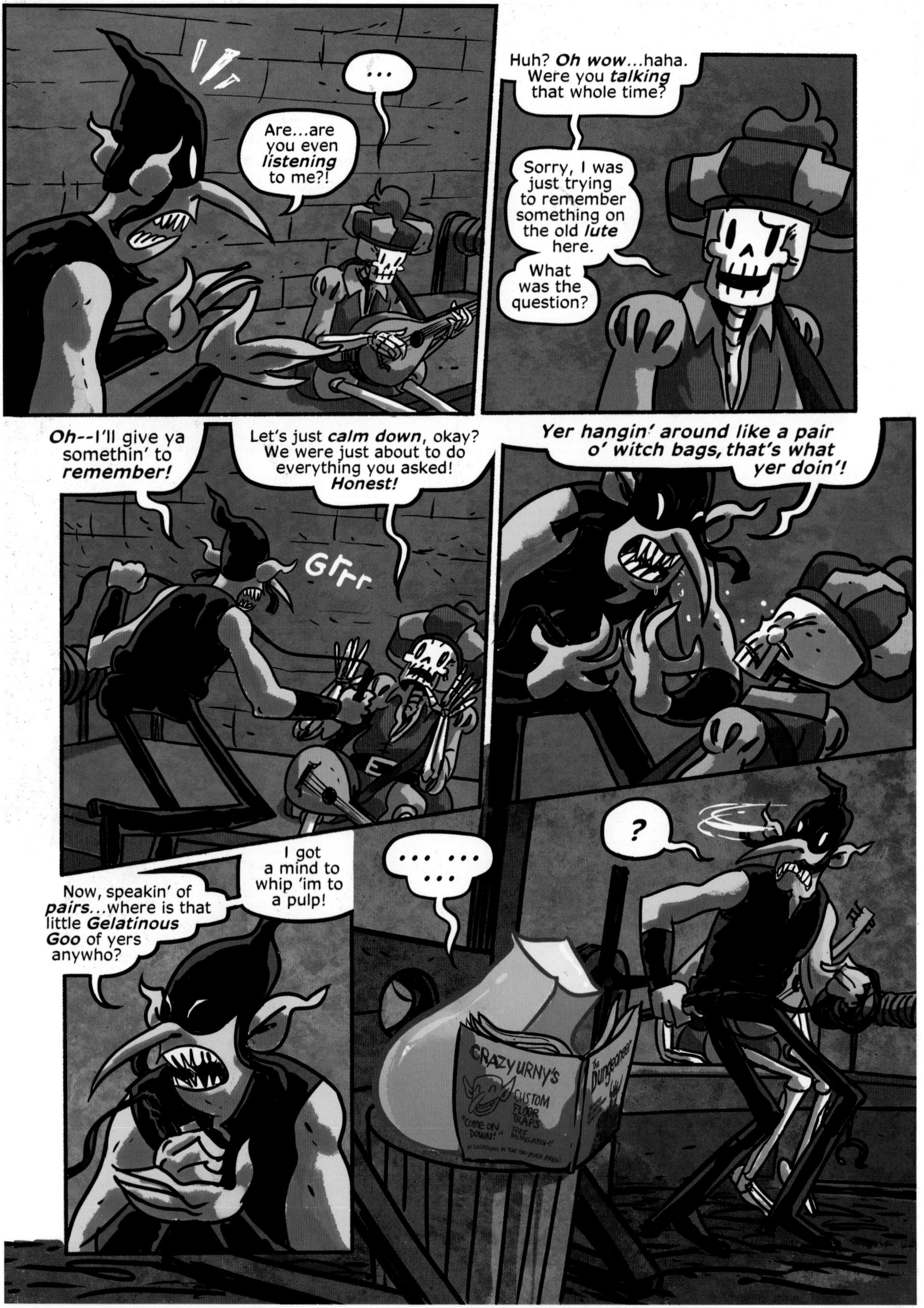
...
Are...are you even *listening* to me?!
Huh? ***Oh wow***...haha. Were you ***talking*** that whole time?
Sorry, I was just trying to remember something on the old *lute* here.
What was the question?
Oh--I'll give ya somethin' to ***remember!***
Let's just ***calm down***, okay? We were just about to do everything you asked! ***Honest!***
Grrr
Yer hangin' around like a pair o' witch bags, that's what yer doin'!
Now, speakin' of ***pairs***...where is that little ***Gelatinous Goo*** of yers anywho?
I got a mind to whip 'im to a pulp!
... ...
?
CRAZY URNY'S
CUSTOM FLOOR TRAPS
"COME ON DOWN!"
FREE INSTALLATION!
The Dungeoneer

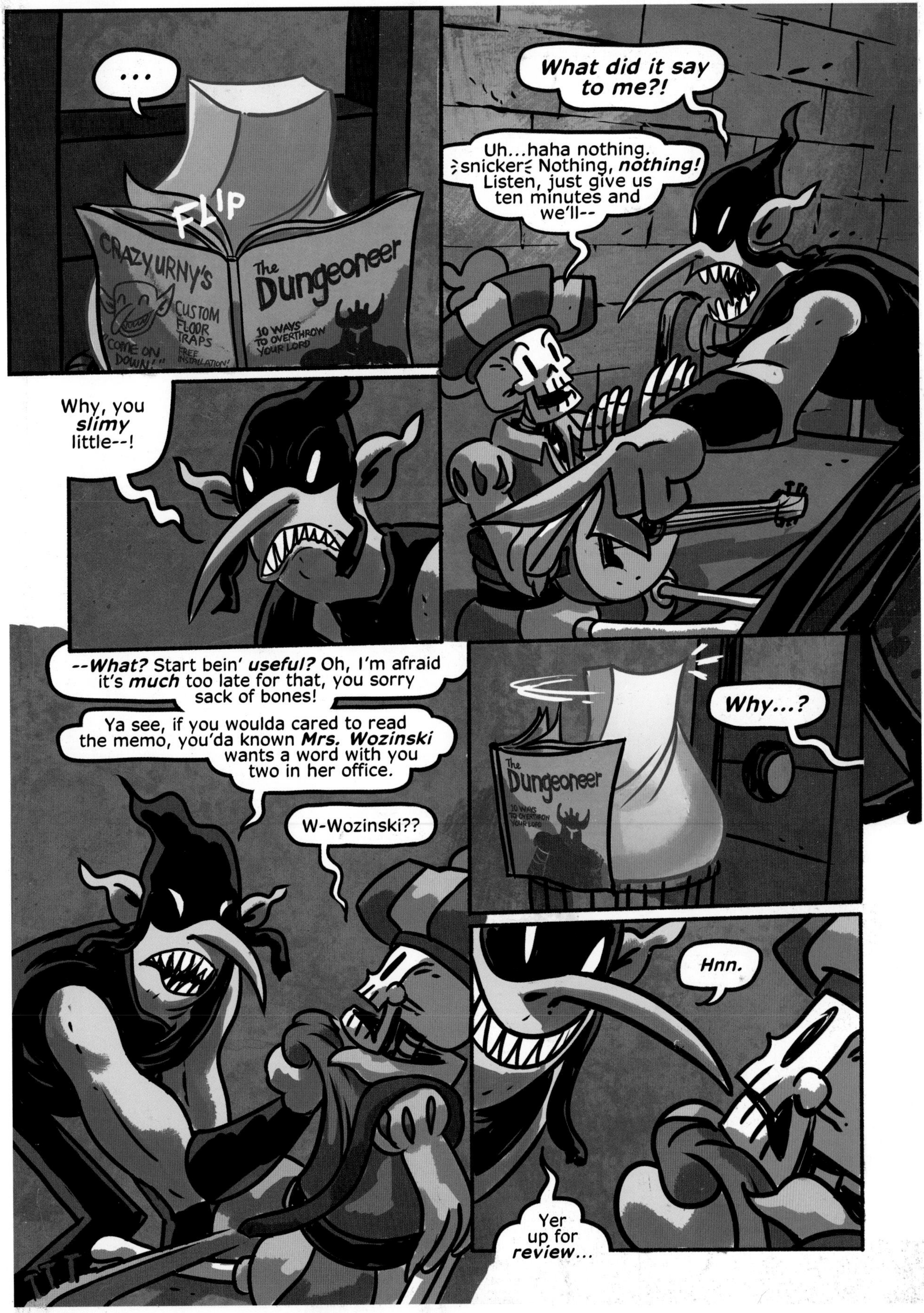
...
FLIP
CRAZYURNY'S CUSTOM FLOOR TRAPS
"COME ON DOWN!"
FREE INSTALLATION!
The Dungeoneer
10 WAYS TO OVERTHROW YOUR LORD
What did it say to me?!
Uh...haha nothing. ⪢snicker⪡ Nothing, *nothing!* Listen, just give us ten minutes and we'll--
Why, you *slimy* little--!
--*What?* Start bein' *useful?* Oh, I'm afraid it's *much* too late for that, you sorry sack of bones!
Ya see, if you woulda cared to read the memo, you'da known *Mrs. Wozinski* wants a word with you two in her office.
W-Wozinski??
Why...?
The Dungeoneer
10 WAYS TO OVERTHROW YOUR LORD
Hnn.
Yer up for *review*...

Chapter 2
Out of the Dungeon

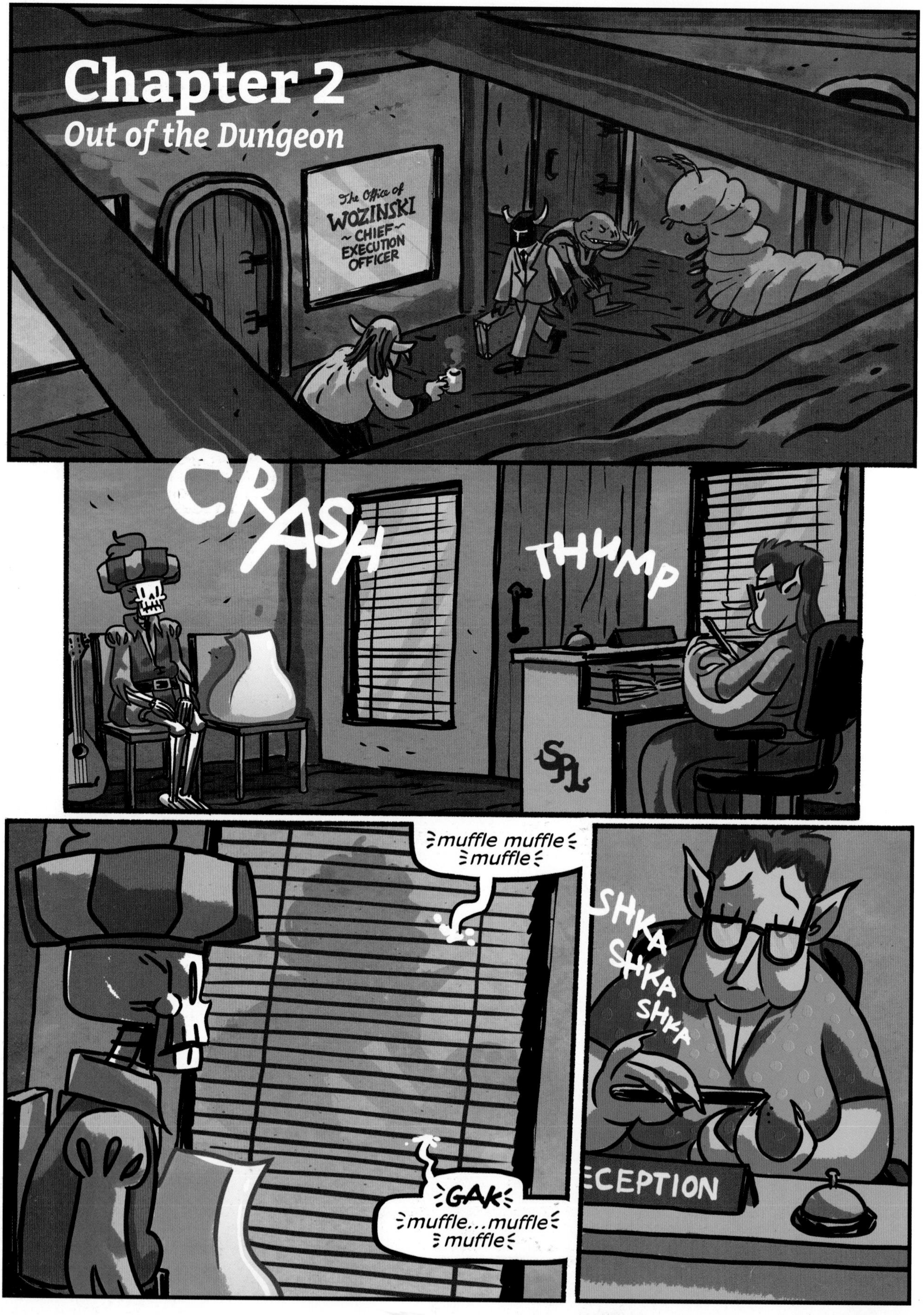
The Office of WOZINSKI ~CHIEF~ EXECUTION OFFICER
CRASH
THUMP
SPL
muffle muffle muffle
GAK muffle...muffle muffle
SHKA SHKA SHKA
ECEPTION

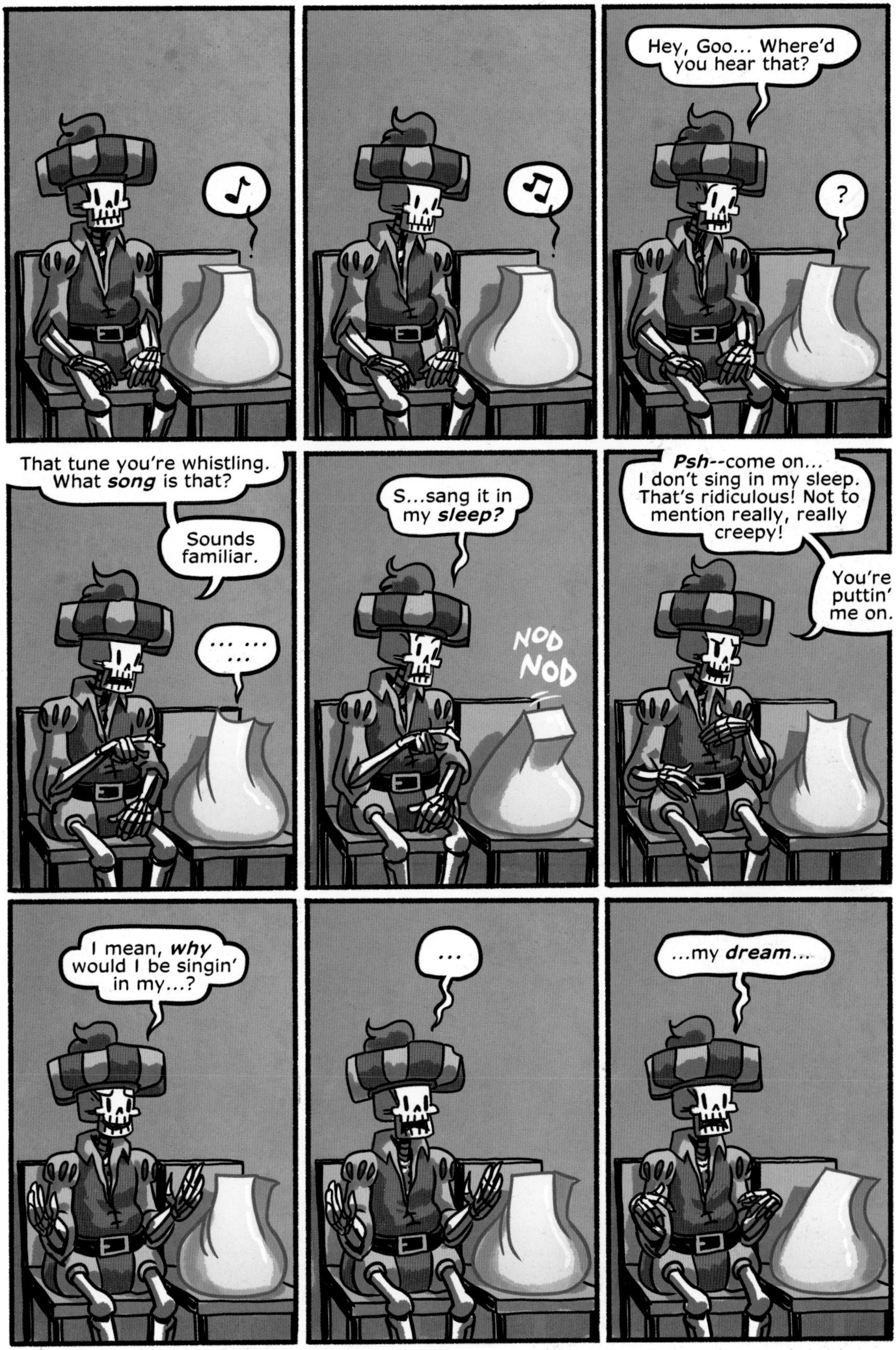
Hey, Goo... Where'd you hear that?
?
That tune you're whistling. What *song* is that?
Sounds familiar.
... ...
S...sang it in my *sleep?*
NOD NOD
Psh--come on... I don't sing in my sleep. That's ridiculous! Not to mention really, really creepy!
You're puttin' me on.
I mean, *why* would I be singin' in my...?
...
...my *dream*...

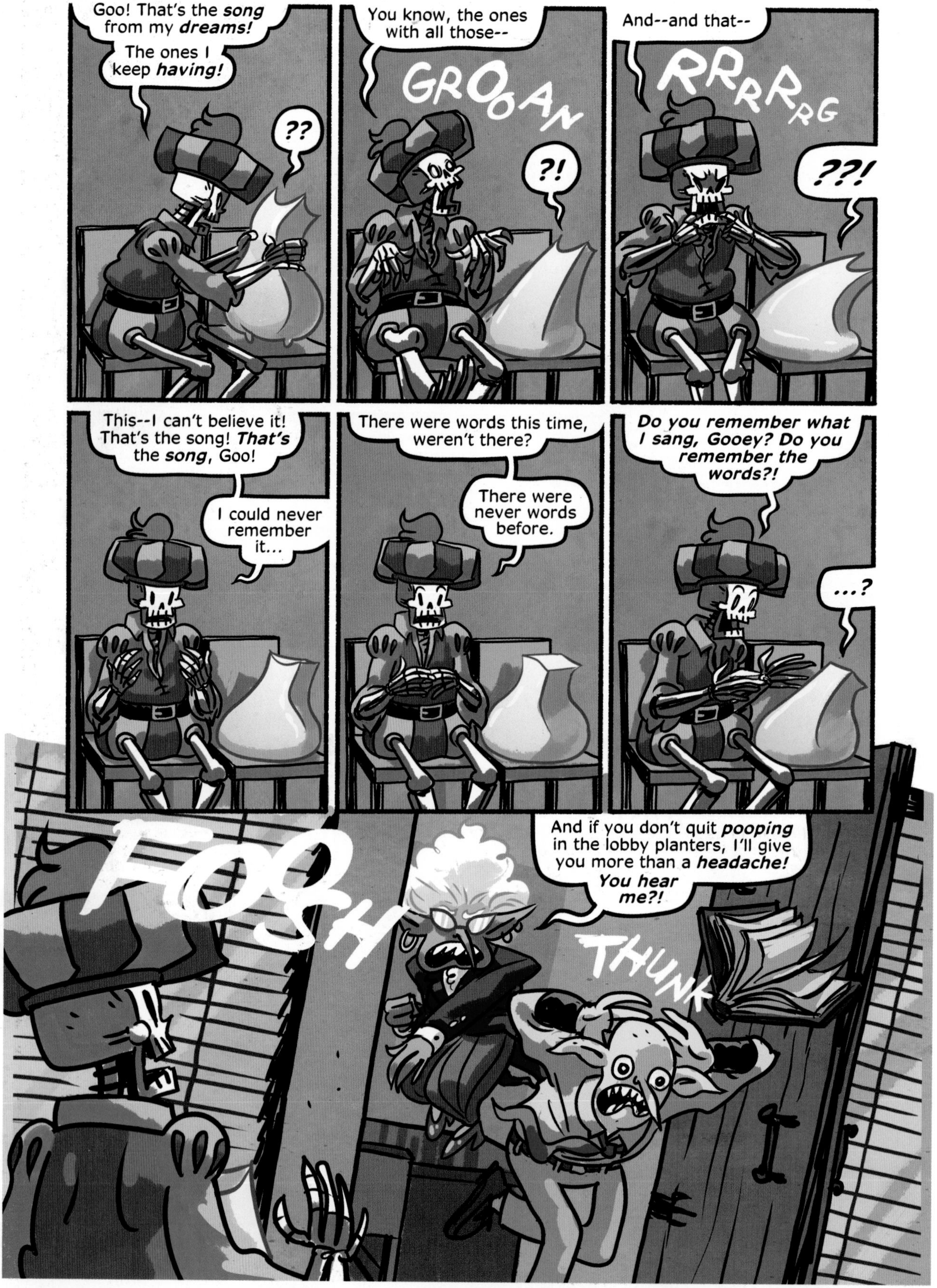
Goo! That's the song from my dreams!
The ones I keep having!
??
You know, the ones with all those--
GROOAN
?!
And--and that--
RRRRRG
??!
This--I can't believe it! That's the song! That's the song, Goo!
I could never remember it...
There were words this time, weren't there?
There were never words before.
Do you remember what I sang, Gooey? Do you remember the words?!
...?
FOSH
And if you don't quit pooping in the lobby planters, I'll give you more than a headache! You hear me?!
THUNK

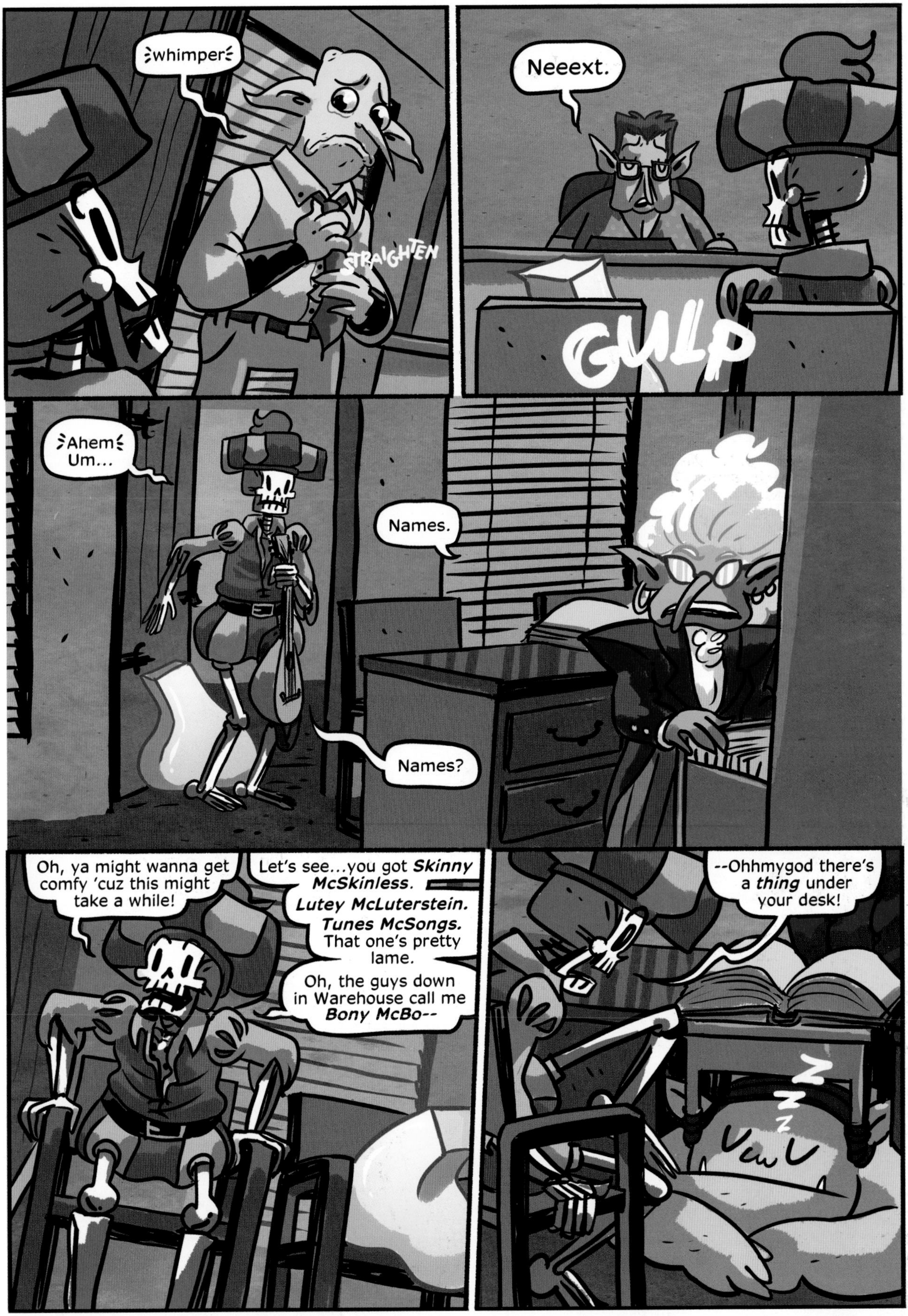
whimper
STRAIGHTEN
Neeext.
GULP
Ahem
Um...
Names.
Names?
Oh, ya might wanna get comfy 'cuz this might take a while!
Let's see...you got *Skinny McSkinless.*
Lutey McLuterstein.
Tunes McSongs. That one's pretty lame.
Oh, the guys down in Warehouse call me *Bony McBo--*
--Ohhmygod there's a *thing* under your desk!
Z Z Z

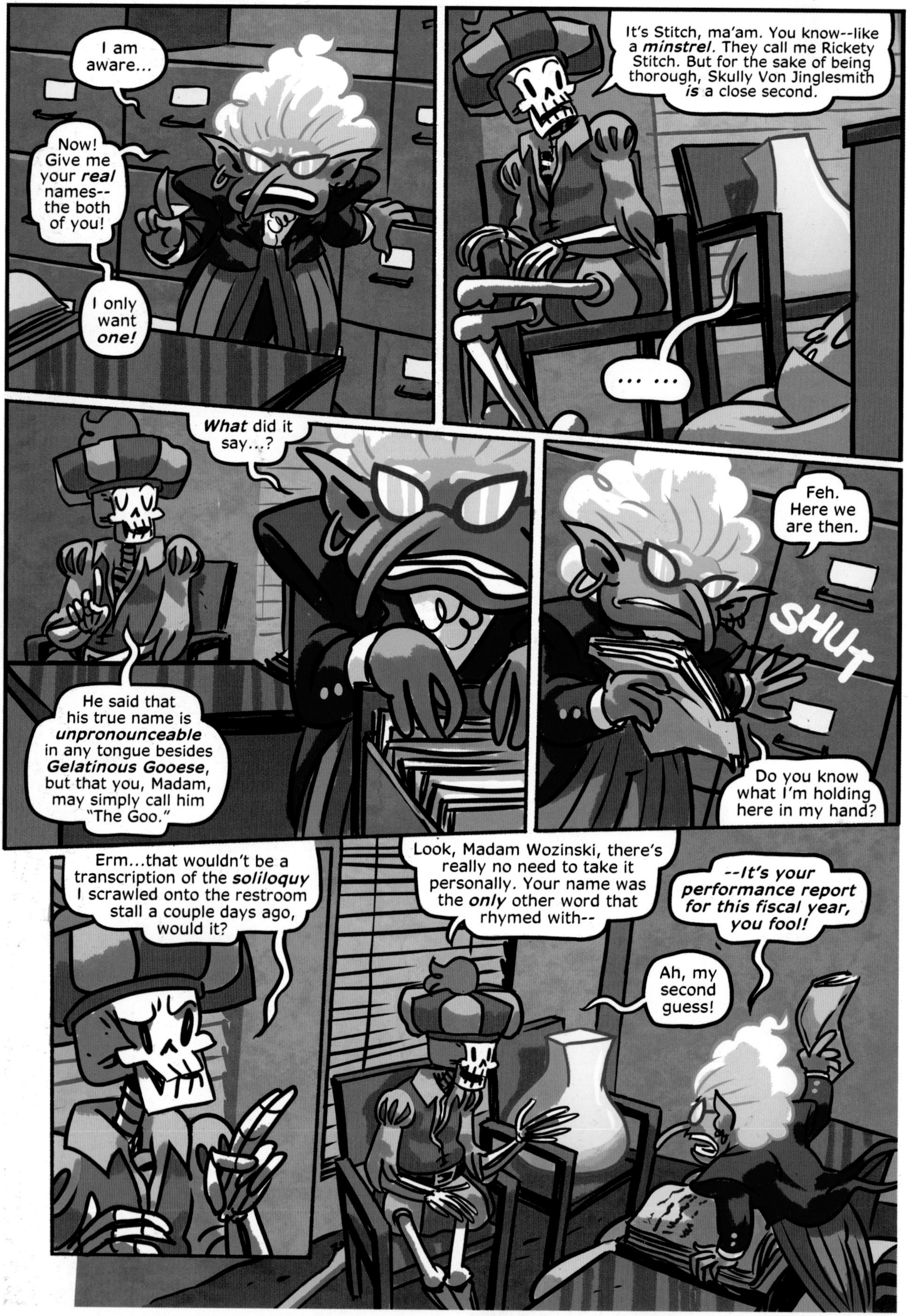
I am aware...
Now! Give me your *real* names-- the both of you!
I only want *one!*
It's Stitch, ma'am. You know--like a *minstrel*. They call me Rickety Stitch. But for the sake of being thorough, Skully Von Jinglesmith *is* a close second.
... ...
What did it say...?
He said that his true name is ***unpronounceable*** in any tongue besides ***Gelatinous Gooese***, but that you, Madam, may simply call him "The Goo."
Feh. Here we are then.
SHUT
Do you know what I'm holding here in my hand?
Erm...that wouldn't be a transcription of the *soliloquy* I scrawled onto the restroom stall a couple days ago, would it?
Look, Madam Wozinski, there's really no need to take it personally. Your name was the *only* other word that rhymed with--
--It's your performance report for this fiscal year, you fool!
Ah, my second guess!

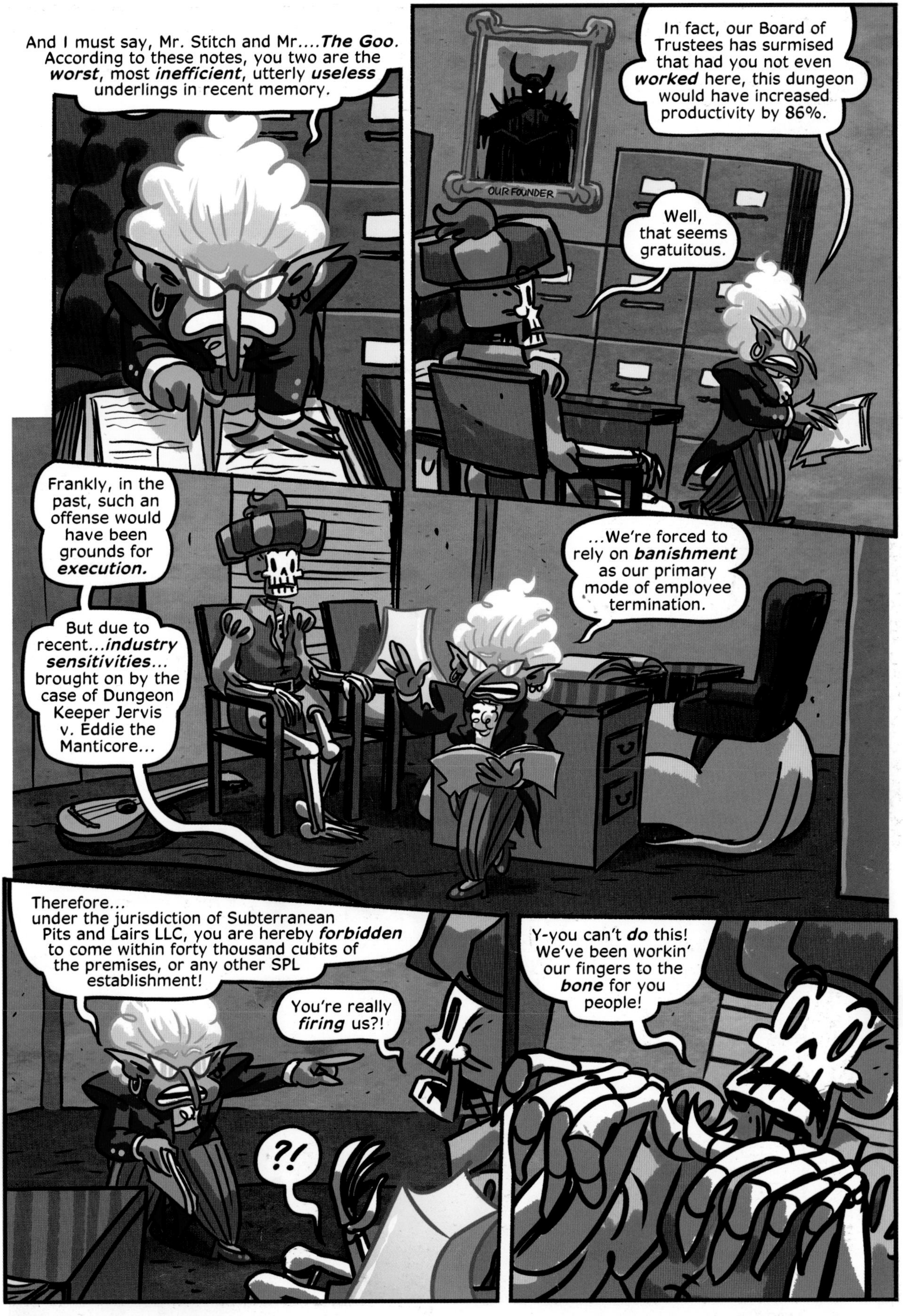

And I must say, Mr. Stitch and Mr....*The Goo*. According to these notes, you two are the ***worst***, most ***inefficient***, utterly ***useless*** underlings in recent memory.
In fact, our Board of Trustees has surmised that had you not even ***worked*** here, this dungeon would have increased productivity by 86%.
OUR FOUNDER
Well, that seems gratuitous.
Frankly, in the past, such an offense would have been grounds for ***execution.***
But due to recent...***industry sensitivities***... brought on by the case of Dungeon Keeper Jervis v. Eddie the Manticore...
...We're forced to rely on ***banishment*** as our primary mode of employee termination.
Therefore... under the jurisdiction of Subterranean Pits and Lairs LLC, you are hereby ***forbidden*** to come within forty thousand cubits of the premises, or any other SPL establishment!
You're really ***firing*** us?!
?!
Y-you can't ***do*** this! We've been workin' our fingers to the ***bone*** for you people!

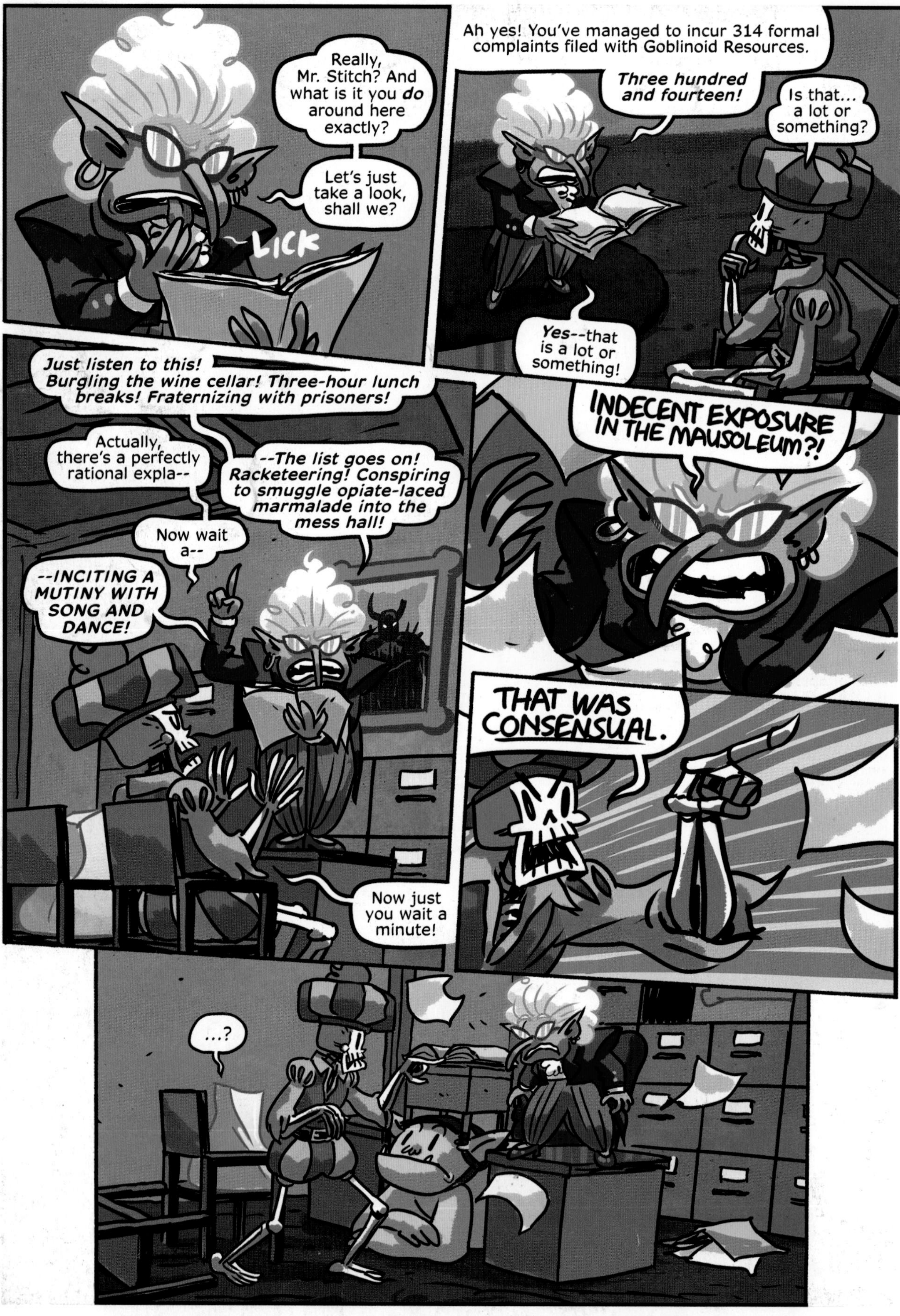
Really, Mr. Stitch? And what is it you *do* around here exactly?
Let's just take a look, shall we?
LICK
Ah yes! You've managed to incur 314 formal complaints filed with Goblinoid Resources.
Three hundred and fourteen!
Is that... a lot or something?
Yes--that is a lot or something!
Just listen to this! Burgling the wine cellar! Three-hour lunch breaks! Fraternizing with prisoners!
Actually, there's a perfectly rational expla--
--The list goes on! Racketeering! Conspiring to smuggle opiate-laced marmalade into the mess hall!
Now wait a--
--INCITING A MUTINY WITH SONG AND DANCE!
Now just you wait a minute!
INDECENT EXPOSURE IN THE MAUSOLEUM?!
THAT WAS CONSENSUAL.
...?

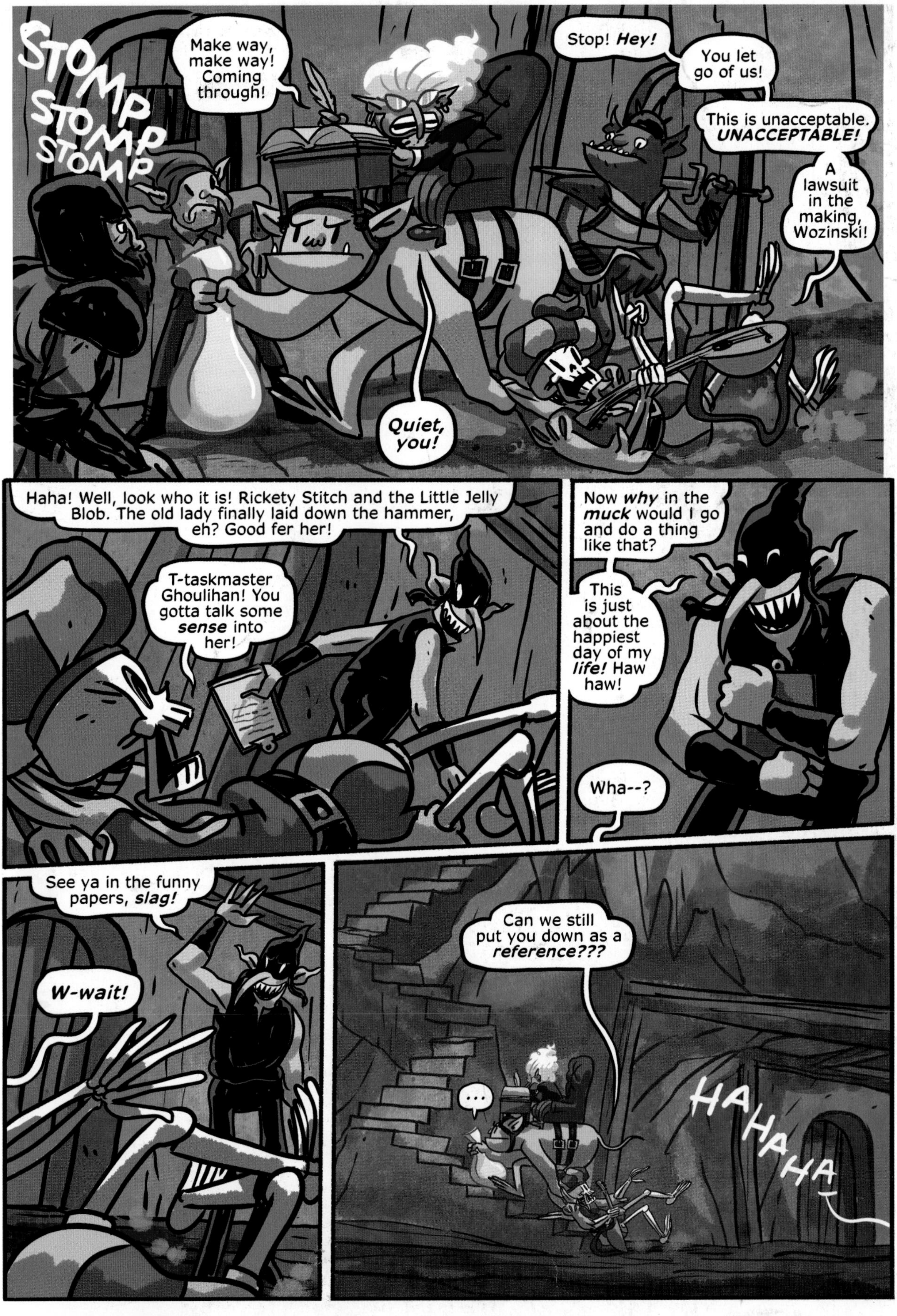
STOMP STOMP STOMP
Make way, make way! Coming through!
Stop! Hey!
You let go of us!
This is unacceptable. UNACCEPTABLE!
A lawsuit in the making, Wozinski!
Quiet, you!
Haha! Well, look who it is! Rickety Stitch and the Little Jelly Blob. The old lady finally laid down the hammer, eh? Good fer her!
T-taskmaster Ghoulihan! You gotta talk some sense into her!
Now why in the muck would I go and do a thing like that?
This is just about the happiest day of my life! Haw haw!
Wha--?
See ya in the funny papers, slag!
W-wait!
Can we still put you down as a reference???
...
HAHAHAHA

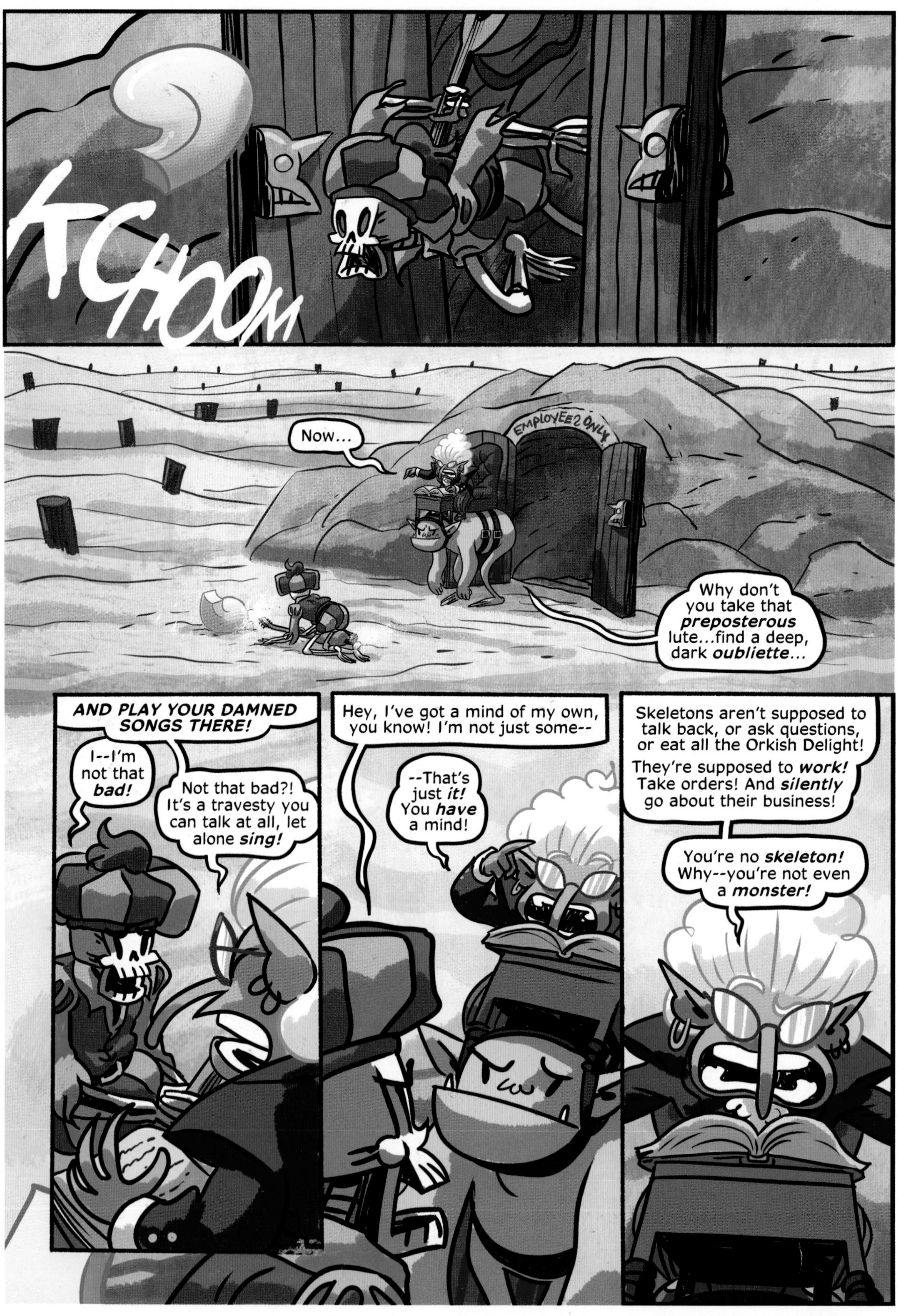
KCHOOM
EMPLOYEES ONLY
Now...
Why don't you take that ***preposterous*** lute...find a deep, dark ***oubliette***...
AND PLAY YOUR DAMNED SONGS THERE!
I--I'm not that ***bad!***
Not that bad?! It's a travesty you can talk at all, let alone ***sing!***
Hey, I've got a mind of my own, you know! I'm not just some--
--That's just ***it!*** You ***have*** a mind!
Skeletons aren't supposed to talk back, or ask questions, or eat all the Orkish Delight!
They're supposed to ***work!*** Take orders! And ***silently*** go about their business!
You're no ***skeleton!*** Why--you're not even a ***monster!***

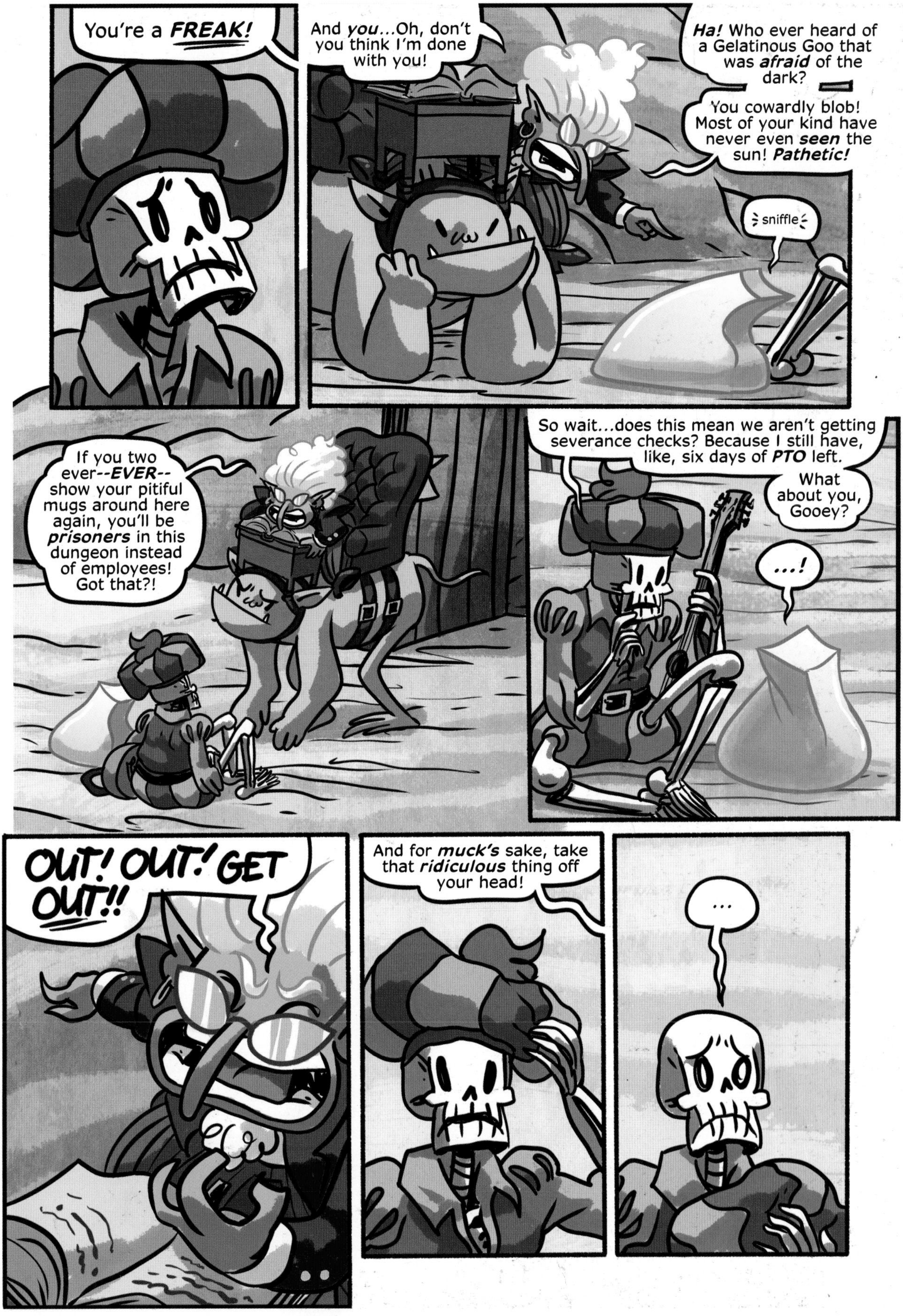

You're a FREAK!
And you...Oh, don't you think I'm done with you!
Ha! Who ever heard of a Gelatinous Goo that was afraid of the dark?
You cowardly blob! Most of your kind have never even seen the sun! Pathetic!
sniffle
If you two ever--EVER--show your pitiful mugs around here again, you'll be prisoners in this dungeon instead of employees! Got that?!
So wait...does this mean we aren't getting severance checks? Because I still have, like, six days of PTO left.
What about you, Gooey?
...!
OUT! OUT! GET OUT!!
And for muck's sake, take that ridiculous thing off your head!
...

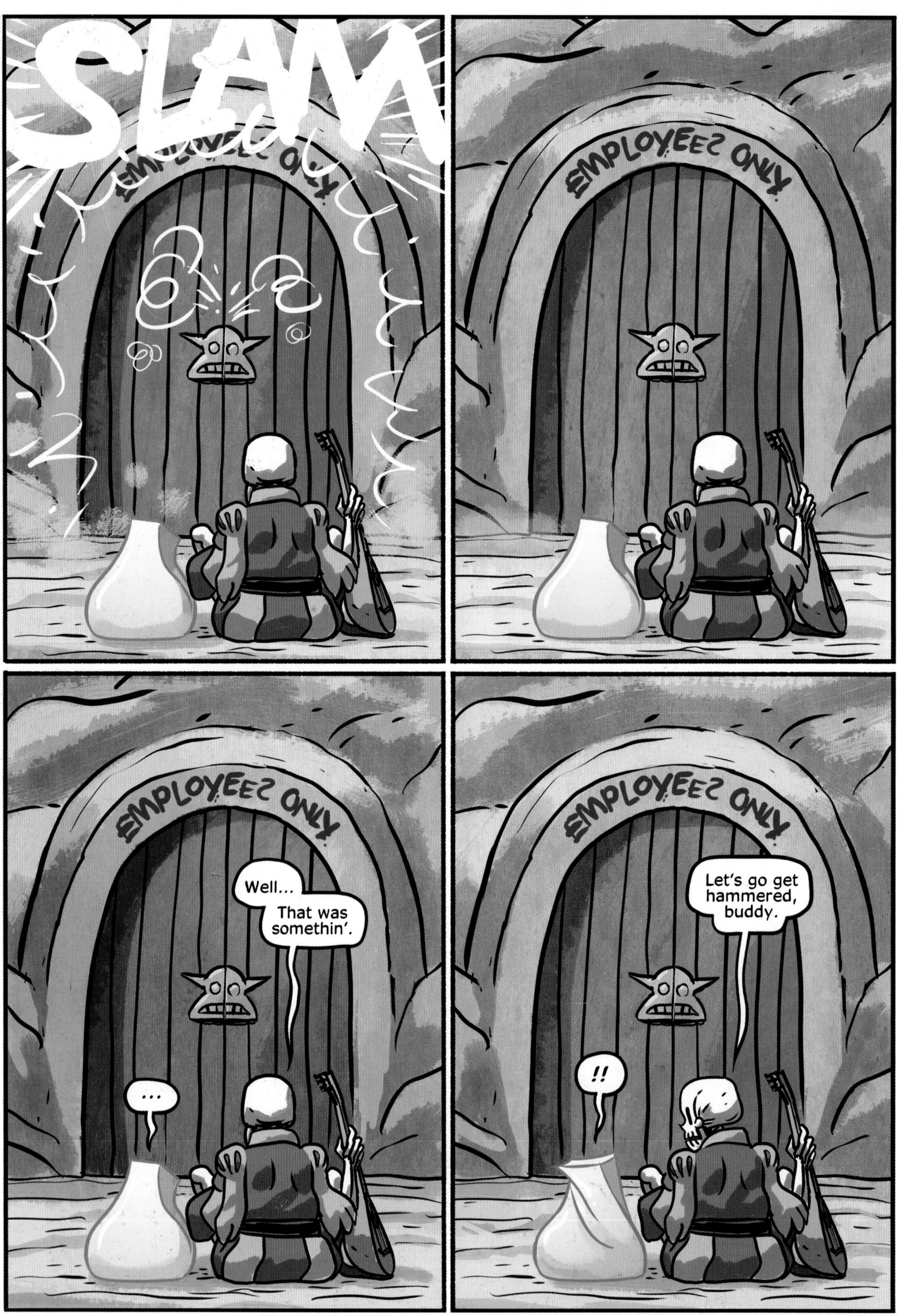
SLAM
EMPLOYEES ONLY
EMPLOYEES ONLY
EMPLOYEES ONLY
Well...
That was somethin'.
...
EMPLOYEES ONLY
Let's go get hammered, buddy.
!!

Chapter 3
Into the Spotlight

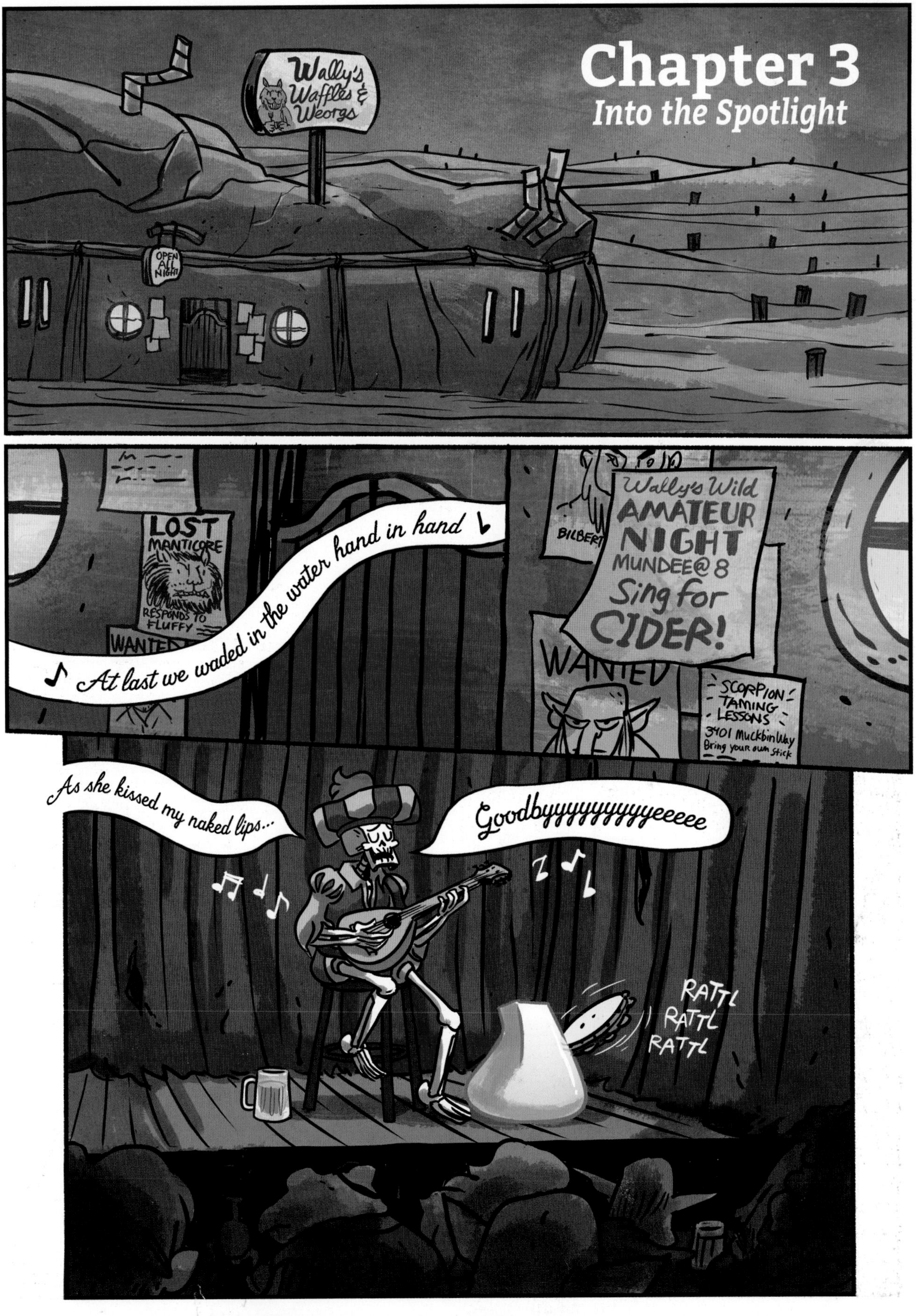

Wally's Waffles & Weorgs
OPEN ALL NIGHT
LOST MANTICORE
RESPONDS TO FLUFFY
WANTED
At last we waded in the water hand in hand
BILBERT
Wally's Wild AMATEUR NIGHT MUNDEE@8 Sing for CIDER!
WANTED
SCORPION TAMING LESSONS
3401 Muckbin Way
Bring your own stick
As she kissed my naked lips...
Goodbyyyyyyyyyeeeee
RATTL
RATTL
RATTL

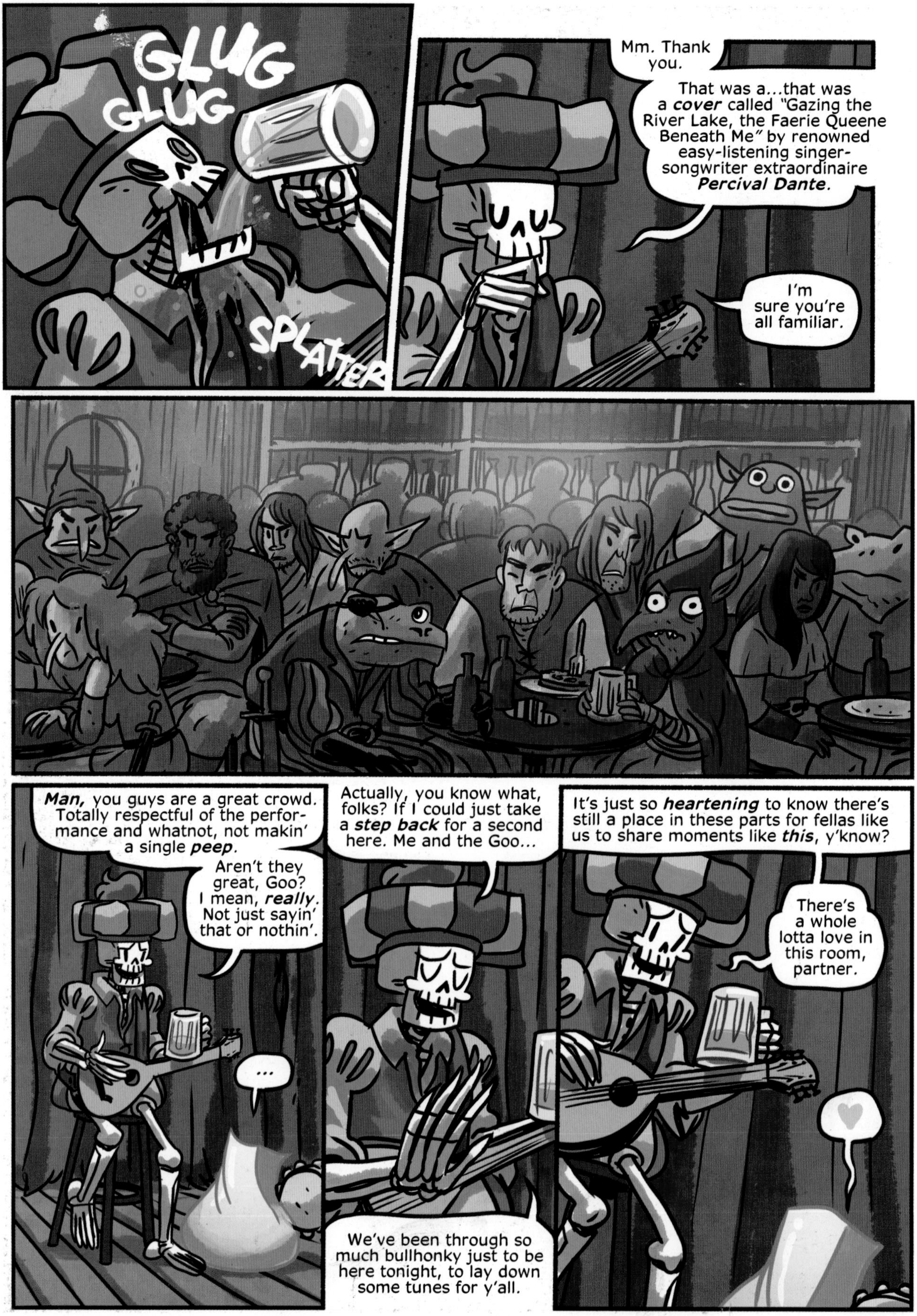
GLUG
GLUG
SPLATTER
Mm. Thank you.
That was a...that was a *cover* called "Gazing the River Lake, the Faerie Queene Beneath Me" by renowned easy-listening singer-songwriter extraordinaire *Percival Dante.*
I'm sure you're all familiar.
Man, you guys are a great crowd. Totally respectful of the performance and whatnot, not makin' a single *peep*.
Aren't they great, Goo? I mean, *really*. Not just sayin' that or nothin'.
...
Actually, you know what, folks? If I could just take a *step back* for a second here. Me and the Goo...
We've been through so much bullhonky just to be here tonight, to lay down some tunes for y'all.
It's just so *heartening* to know there's still a place in these parts for fellas like us to share moments like *this*, y'know?
There's a whole lotta love in this room, partner.

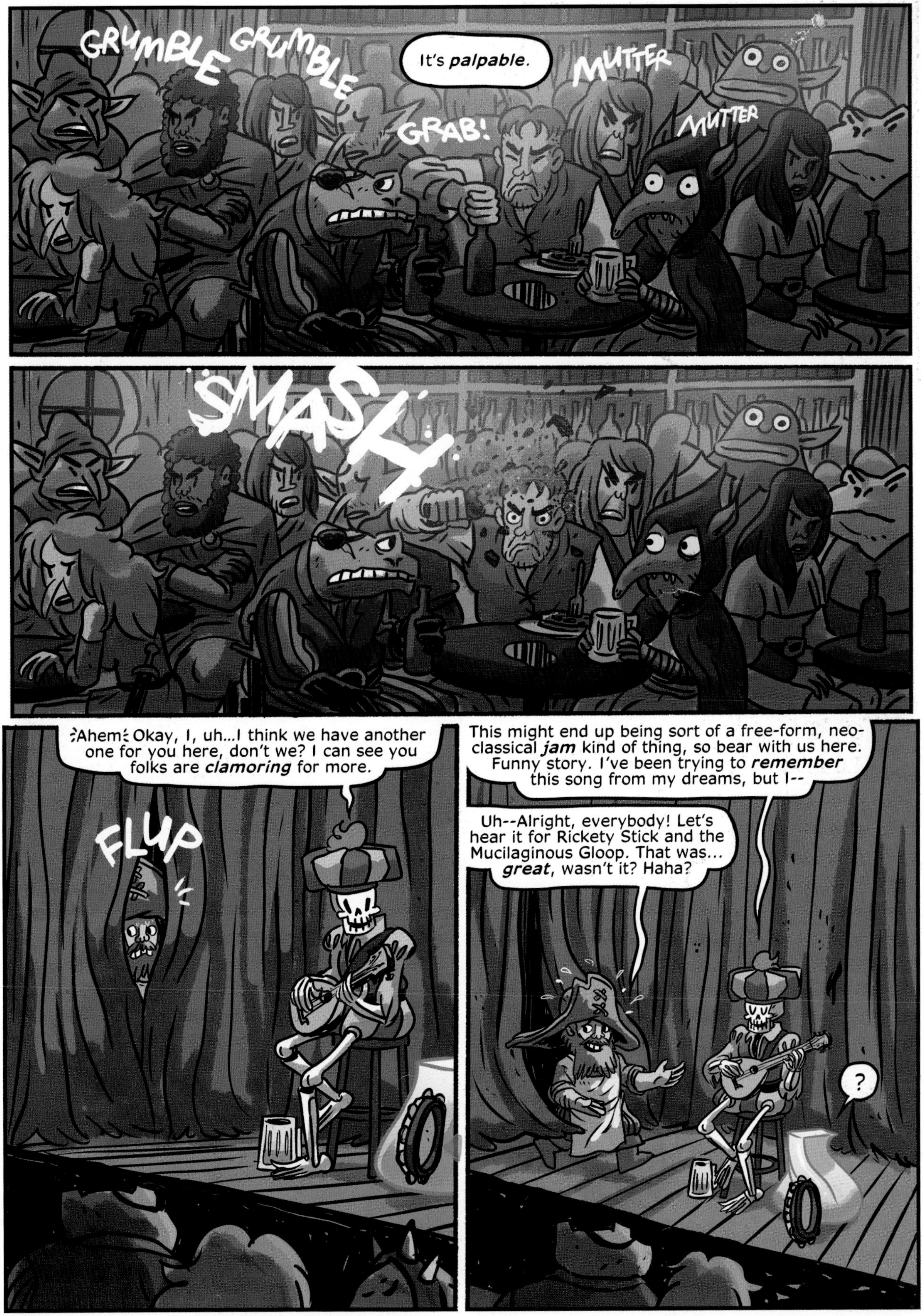
GRUMBLE GRUMBLE
It's *palpable.*
MUTTER
GRAB!
MUTTER
SMASH
Ahem Okay, I, uh...I think we have another one for you here, don't we? I can see you folks are *clamoring* for more.
FLUP
This might end up being sort of a free-form, neo-classical *jam* kind of thing, so bear with us here. Funny story. I've been trying to *remember* this song from my dreams, but I--
Uh--Alright, everybody! Let's hear it for Rickety Stick and the Mucilaginous Gloop. That was... *great*, wasn't it? Haha?
?

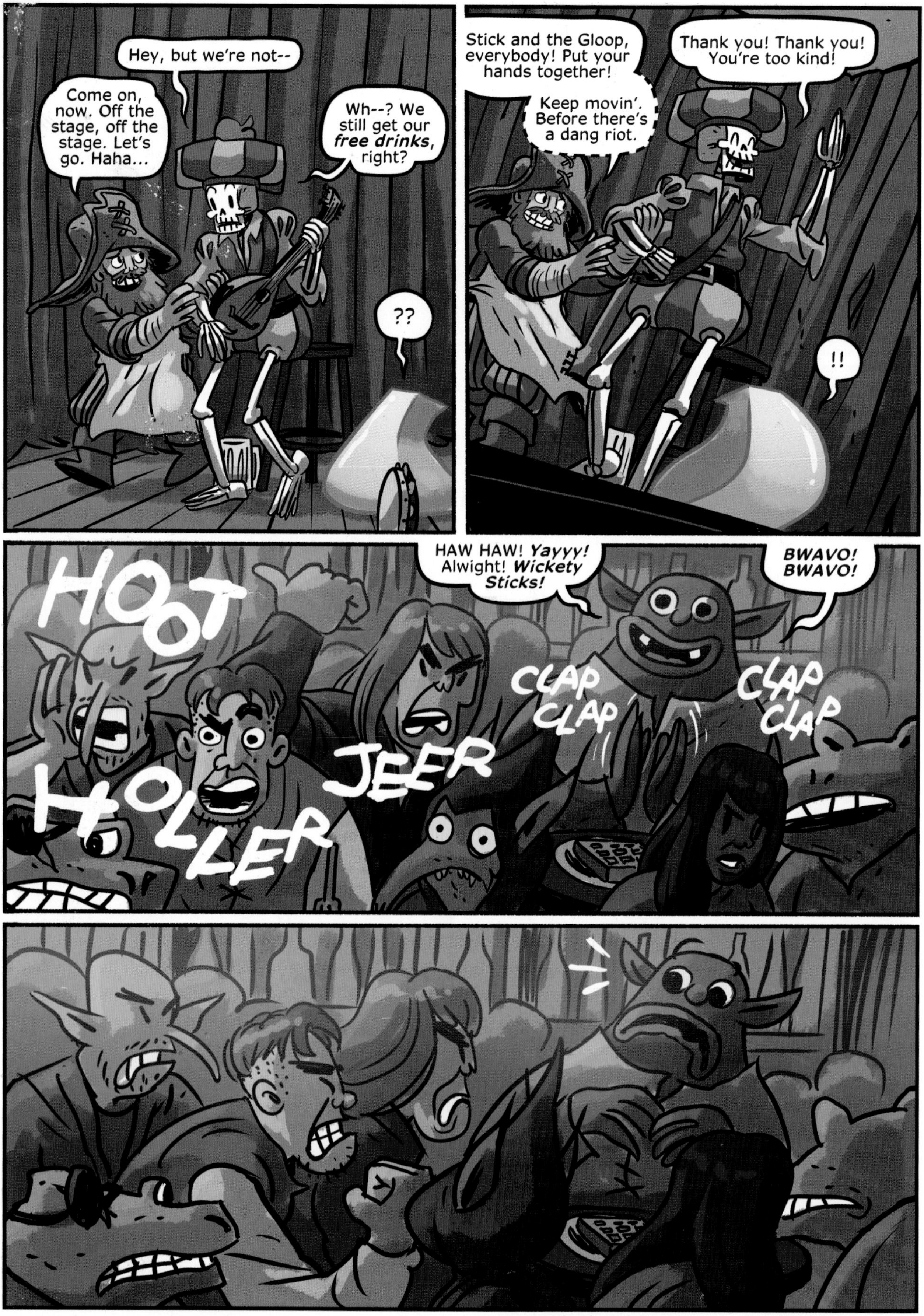
Hey, but we're not--
Come on, now. Off the stage, off the stage. Let's go. Haha...
Wh--? We still get our *free drinks*, right?
??
Stick and the Gloop, everybody! Put your hands together!
Keep movin'. Before there's a dang riot.
Thank you! Thank you! You're too kind!
!!
HOOT
HOLLER
JEER
HAW HAW! *Yayyy!* Alwight! ***Wickety Sticks!***
BWAVO! BWAVO!
CLAP CLAP
CLAP CLAP

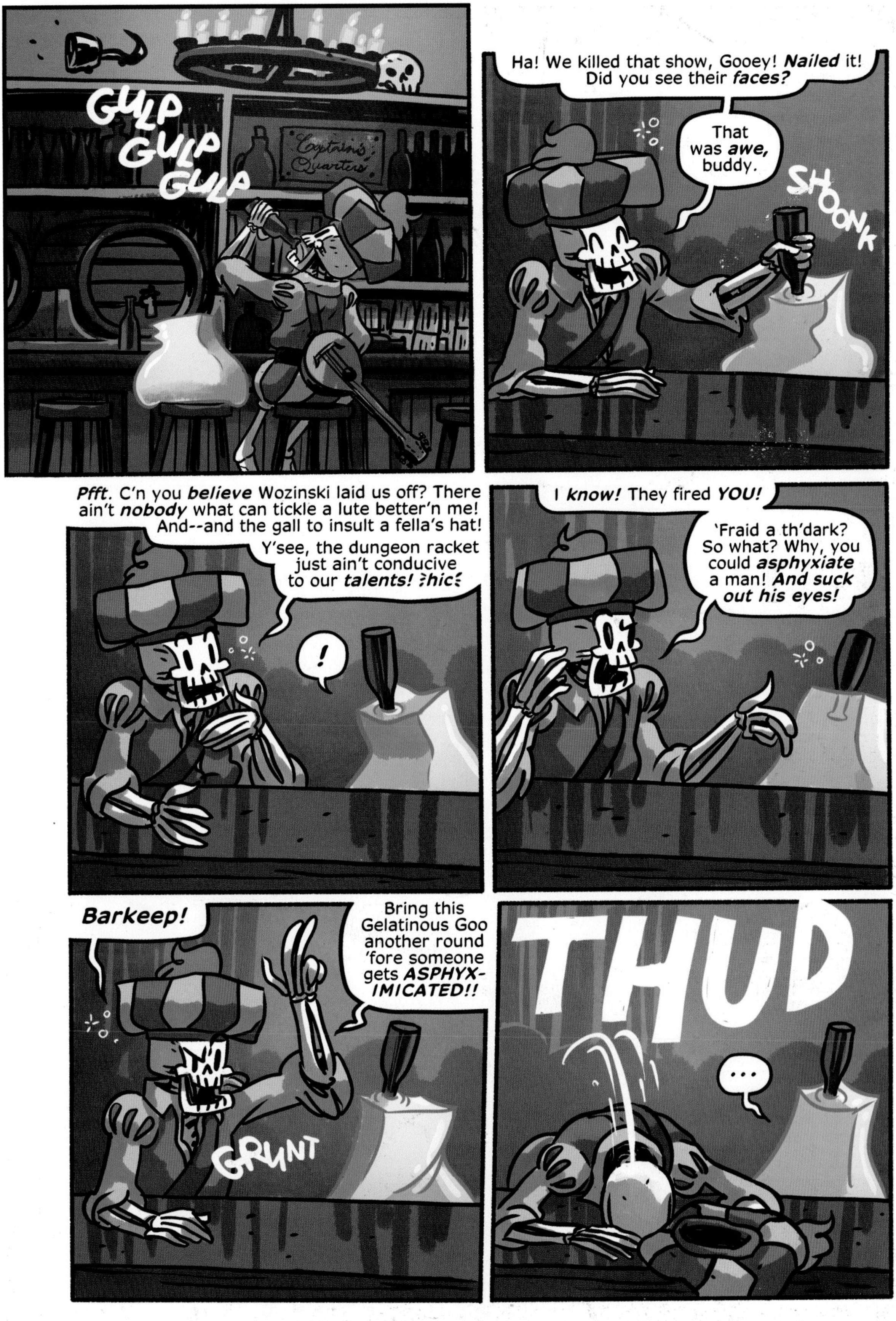
GULP GULP GULP
Captain's Quarters
Ha! We killed that show, Gooey! *Nailed* it! Did you see their *faces?*
That was *awe,* buddy.
SHOONK
Pfft. C'n you *believe* Wozinski laid us off? There ain't *nobody* what can tickle a lute better'n me! And--and the gall to insult a fella's hat!
Y'see, the dungeon racket just ain't conducive to our *talents!* *hic*
!
I *know!* They fired *YOU!*
'Fraid a th'dark? So what? Why, you could *asphyxiate* a man! *And suck out his eyes!*
Barkeep!
Bring this Gelatinous Goo another round 'fore someone gets *ASPHYX-IMICATED!!*
GRUNT
THUD
...

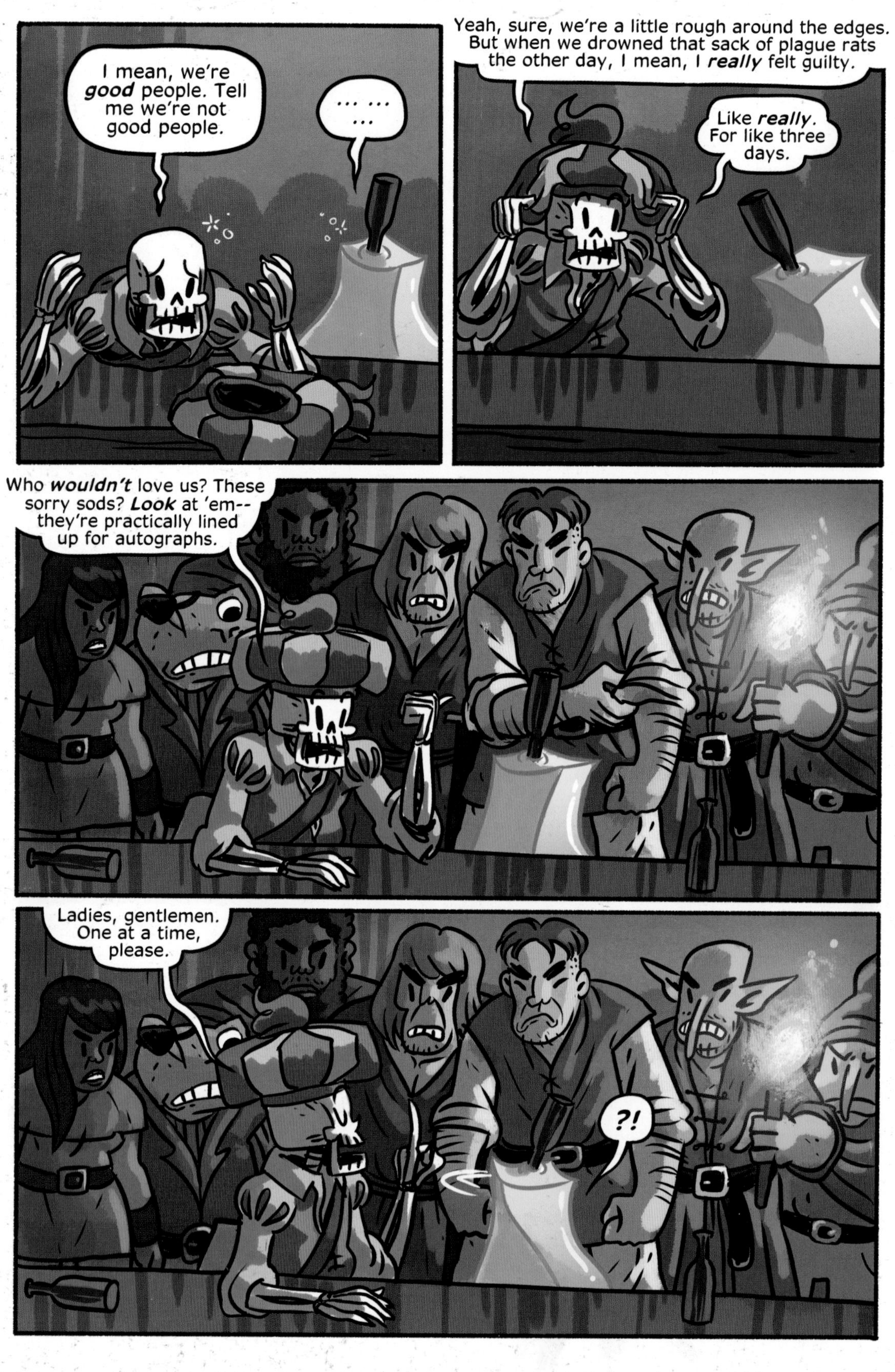
I mean, we're *good* people. Tell me we're not good people.
... ...
Yeah, sure, we're a little rough around the edges. But when we drowned that sack of plague rats the other day, I mean, I *really* felt guilty.
Like *really*. For like three days.
Who *wouldn't* love us? These sorry sods? *Look* at 'em-- they're practically lined up for autographs.
Ladies, gentlemen. One at a time, please.
?!

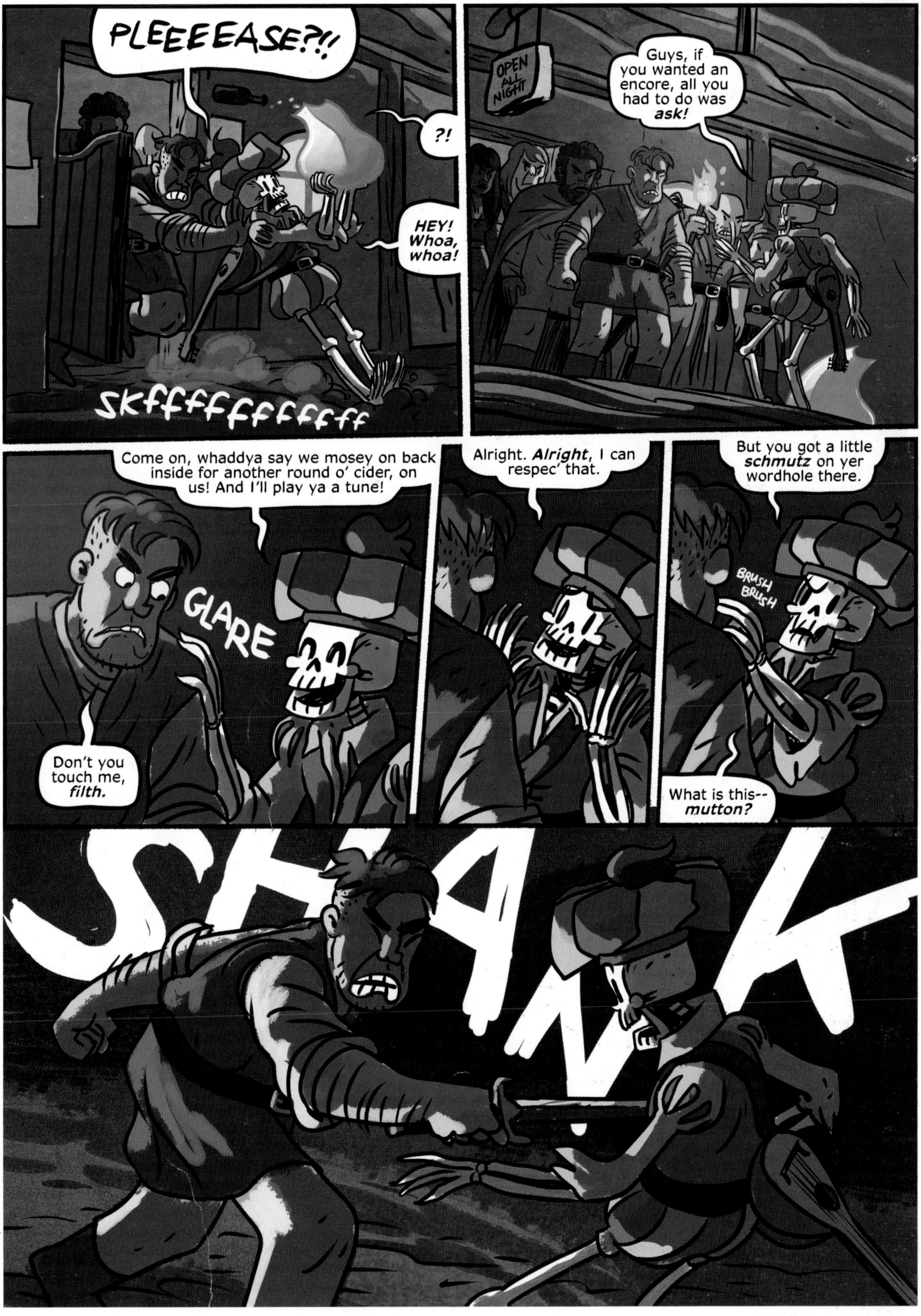
PLEEEEASE?!!
?!
HEY! Whoa, whoa!
SKFFFFFFFFFFF
OPEN ALL NIGHT
Guys, if you wanted an encore, all you had to do was *ask!*
Come on, whaddya say we mosey on back inside for another round o' cider, on us! And I'll play ya a tune!
GLARE
Don't you touch me, *filth.*
Alright. *Alright*, I can respec' that.
But you got a little *schmutz* on yer wordhole there.
BRUSH BRUSH
What is this-- *mutton?*
SHANK

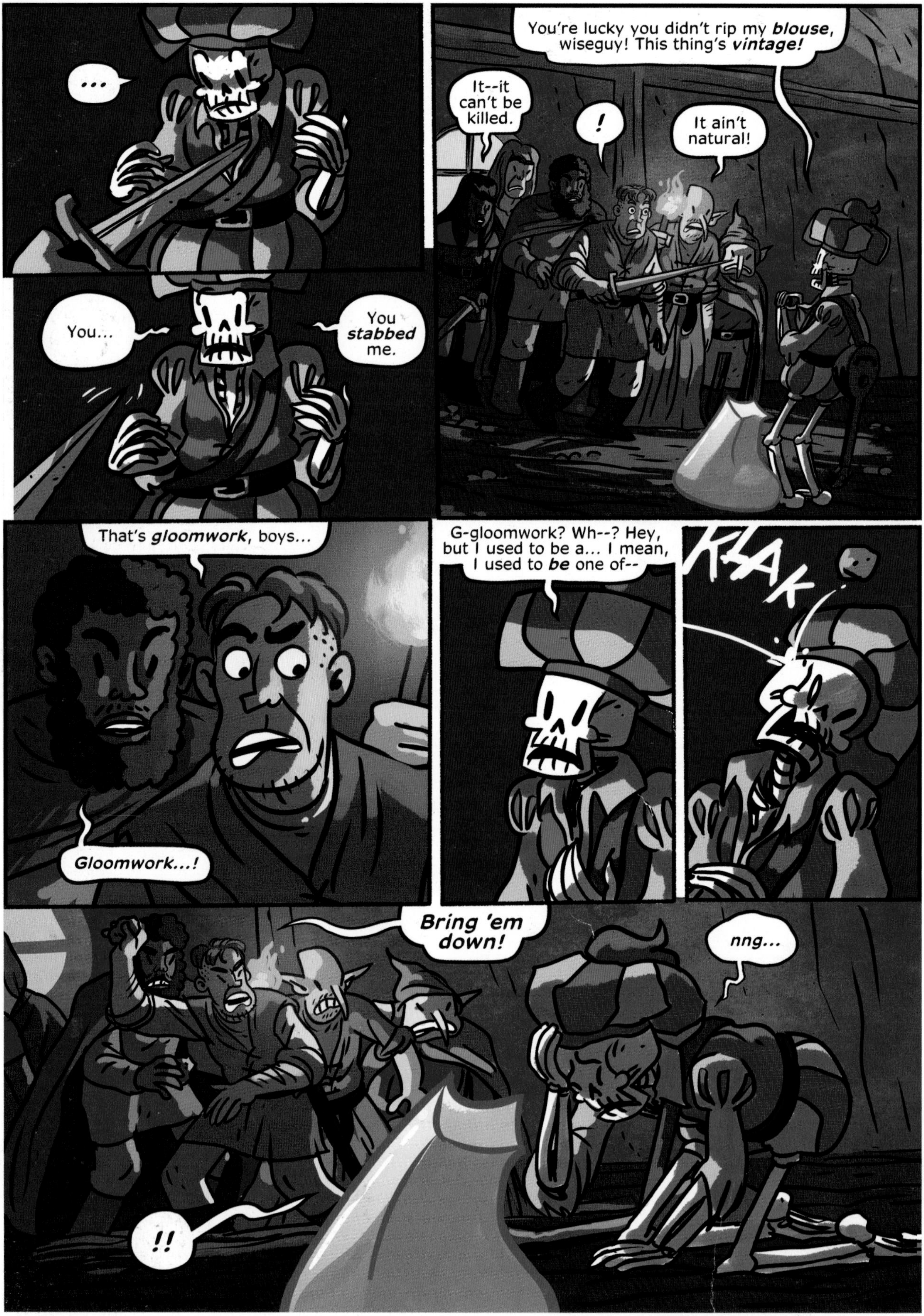
...
You're lucky you didn't rip my *blouse*, wiseguy! This thing's *vintage!*
It--it can't be killed.
!
It ain't natural!
You...
You *stabbed* me.
That's *gloomwork*, boys...
Gloomwork...!
G-gloomwork? Wh--? Hey, but I used to be a... I mean, I used to *be* one of--
KLAK
Bring 'em down!
nng...
!!

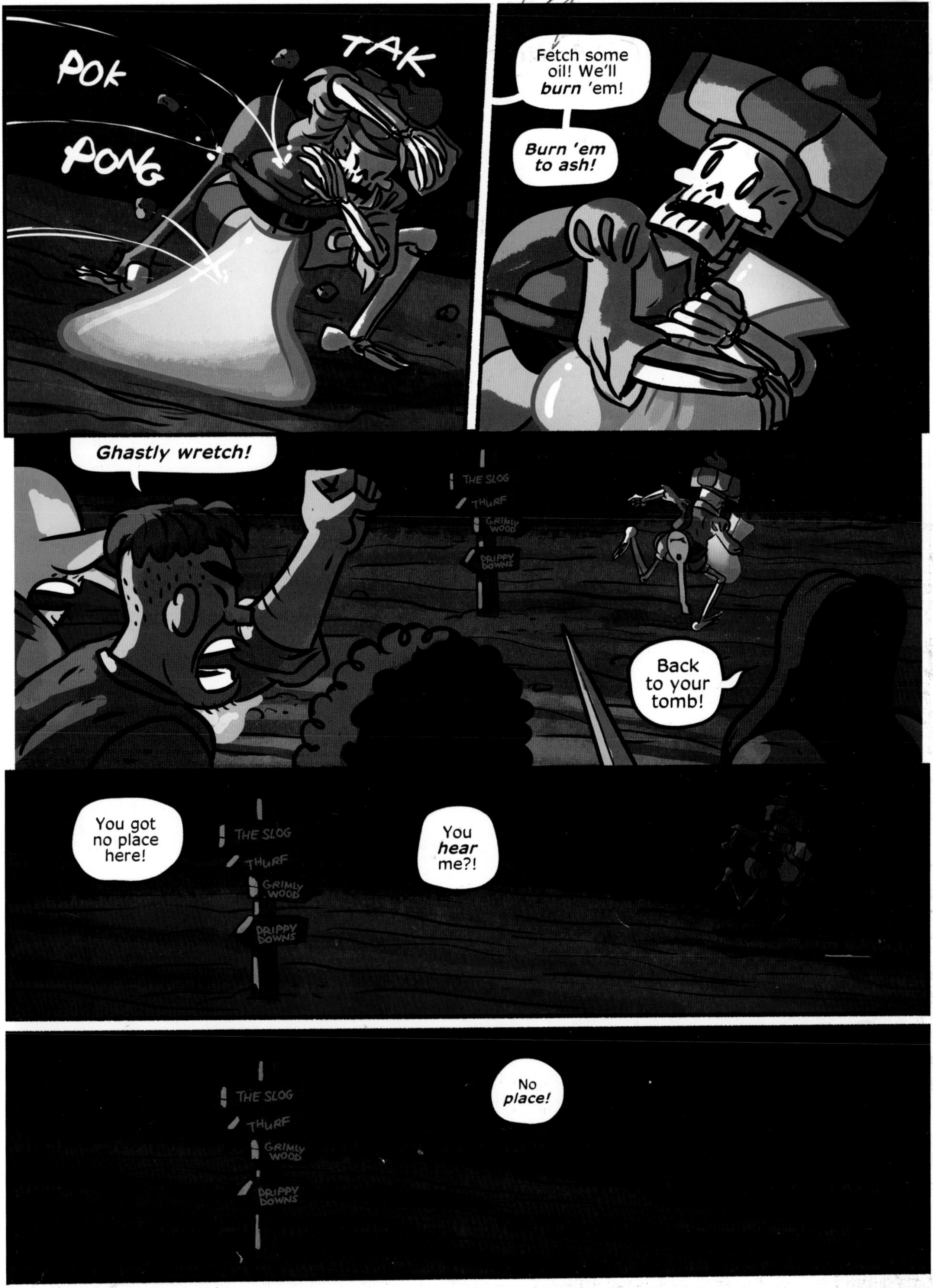
POK
TAK
PONG
Fetch some oil! We'll *burn* 'em!
Burn 'em to ash!
Ghastly wretch!
THE SLOG
THURF
GRIMLY WOOD
DRIPPY DOWNS
Back to your tomb!
You got no place here!
THE SLOG
THURF
GRIMLY WOOD
DRIPPY DOWNS
You *hear* me?!
THE SLOG
THURF
GRIMLY WOOD
DRIPPY DOWNS
No *place!*

Chapter 4
Under the Starlight

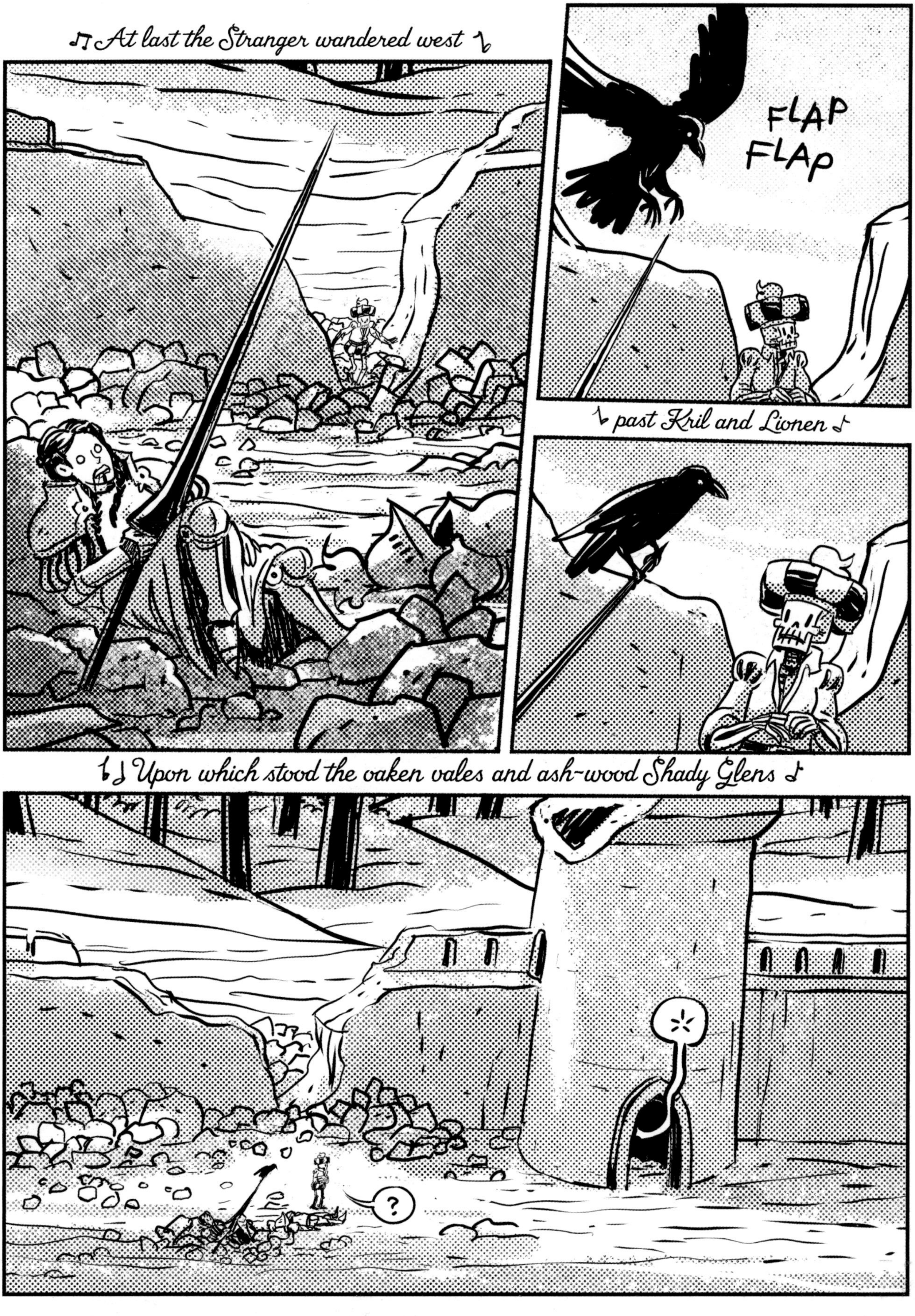
At last the Stranger wandered west
FLAP FLAP
past Kril and Lionen
Upon which stood the oaken vales and ash-wood Shady Glens
?

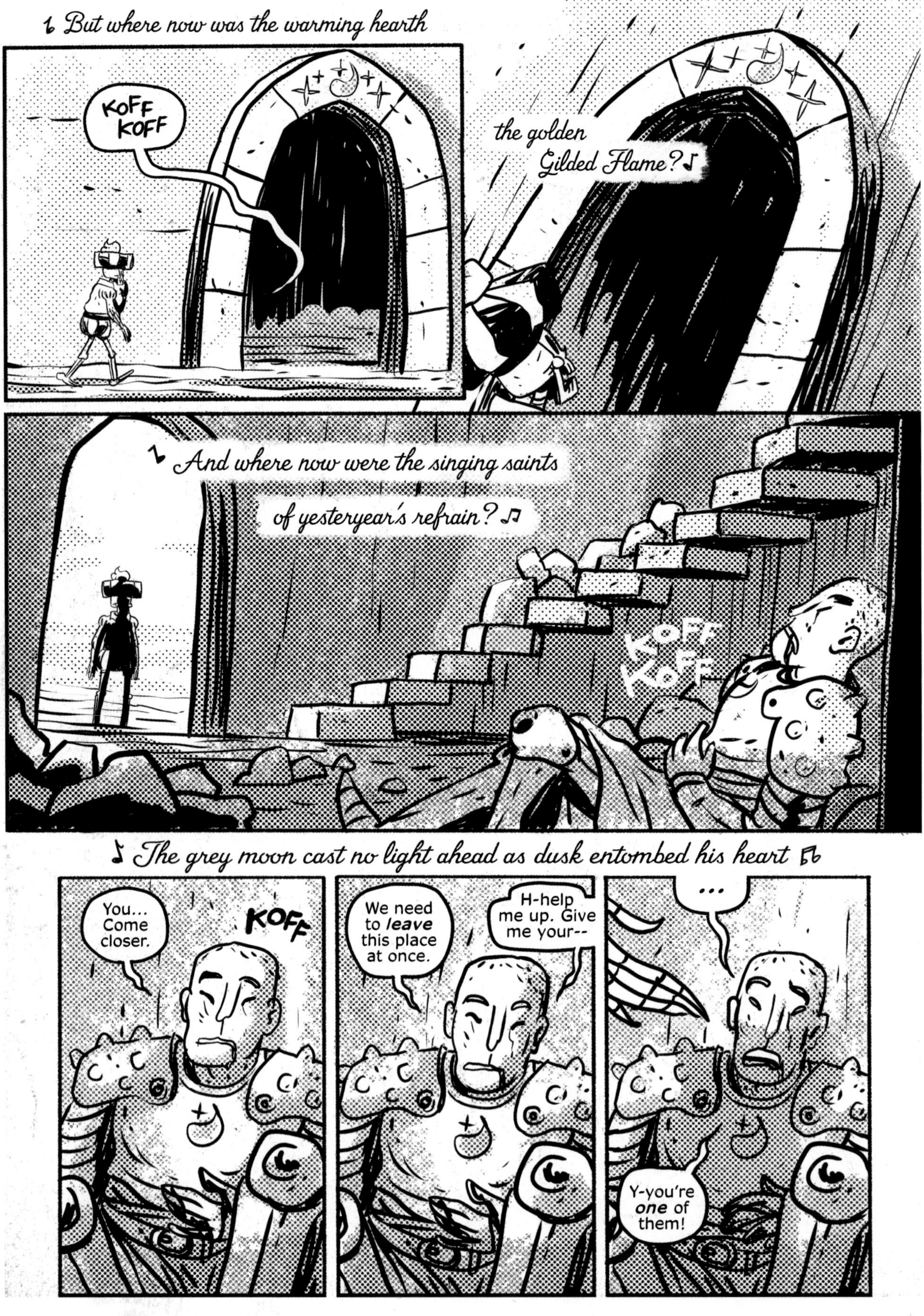
But where now was the warming hearth
KOFF KOFF
the golden Gilded Flame?
And where now were the singing saints
of yesteryear's refrain?
KOFF KOFF
The grey moon cast no light ahead as dusk entombed his heart
You... Come closer.
KOFF
We need to *leave* this place at once.
H-help me up. Give me your--
...
Y-you're *one* of them!

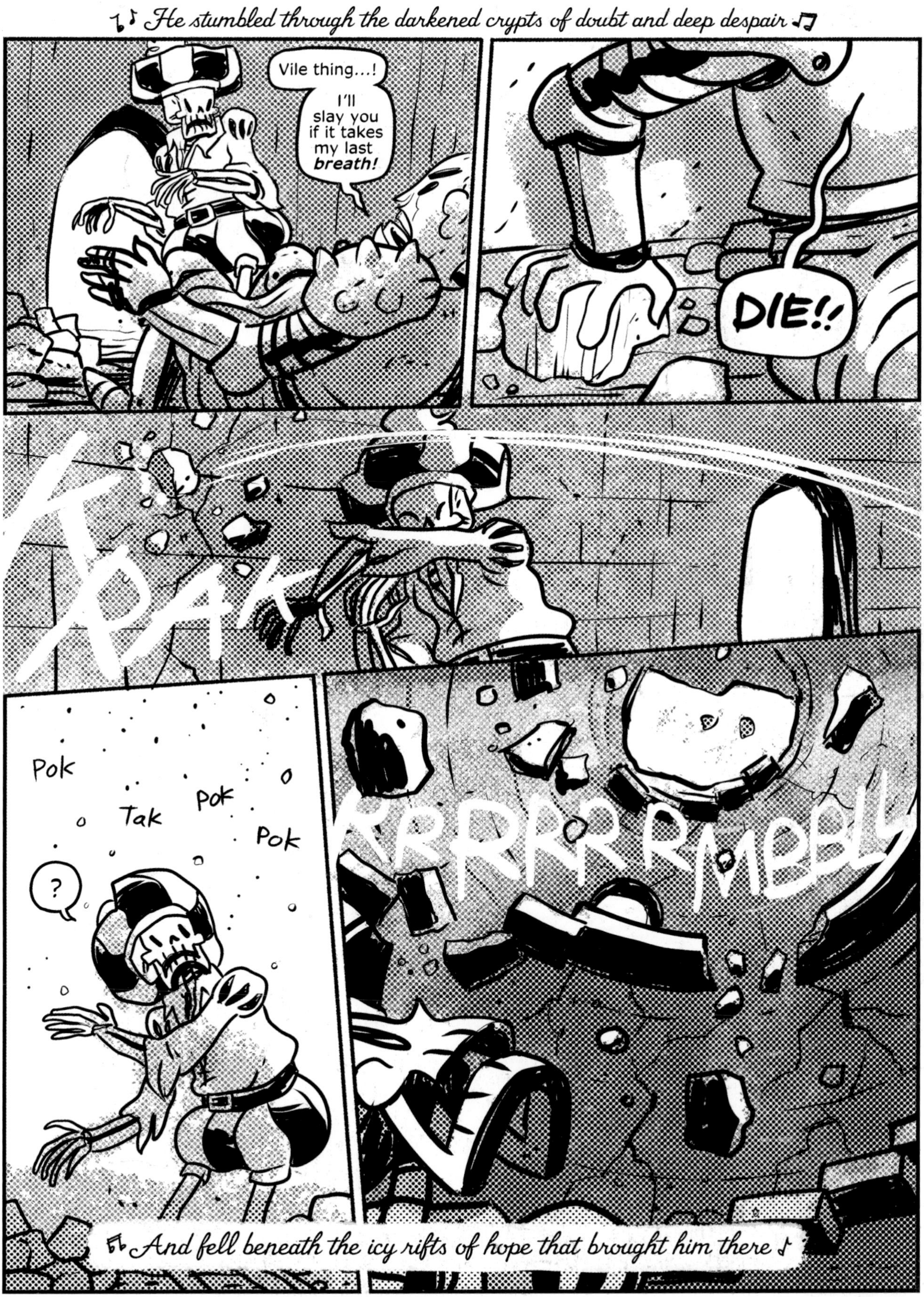
He stumbled through the darkened crypts of doubt and deep despair
Vile thing...!
I'll slay you if it takes my last *breath!*
DIE!!
KRAK
Pok
Tak
Pok
Pok
?
RRRRRRRMBBLL
And fell beneath the icy rifts of hope that brought him there

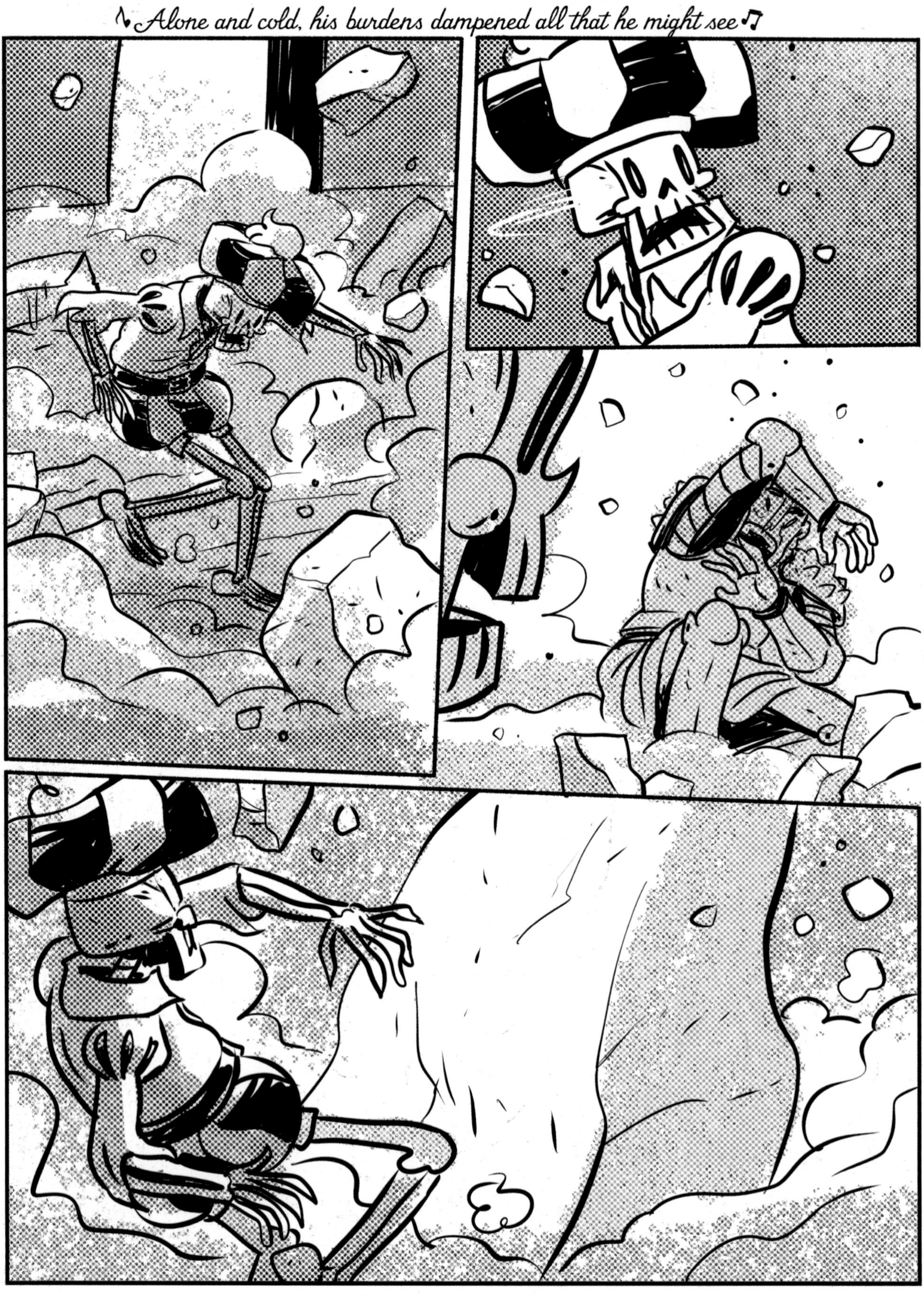
♪ Alone and cold, his burdens dampened all that he might see ♫

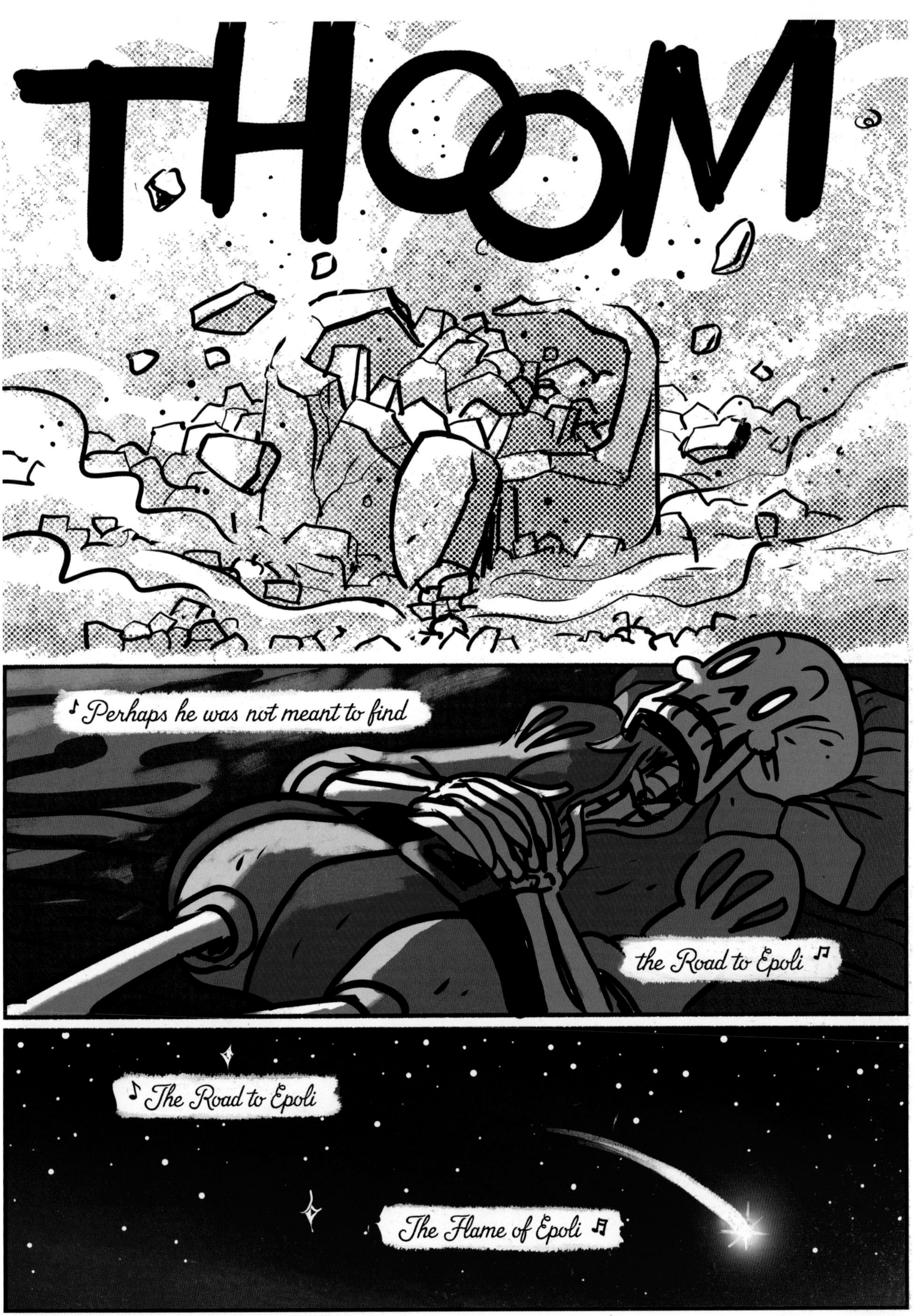
THOOM
♪ Perhaps he was not meant to find
the Road to Epoli ♫
♪ The Road to Epoli
The Flame of Epoli ♫

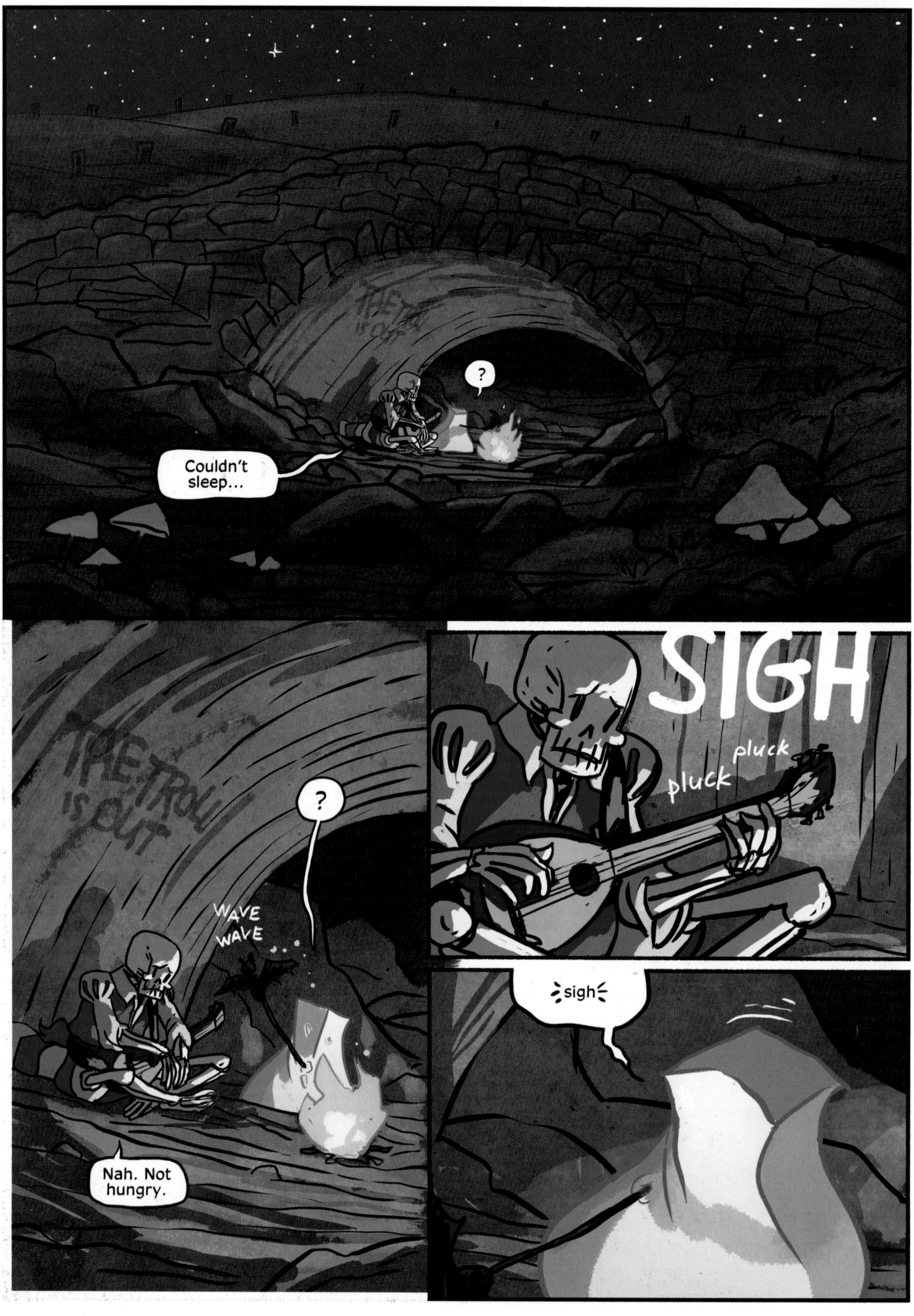
?
Couldn't sleep...
THE TROLL IS OUT
?
WAVE WAVE
Nah. Not hungry.
SIGH
pluck pluck
sigh

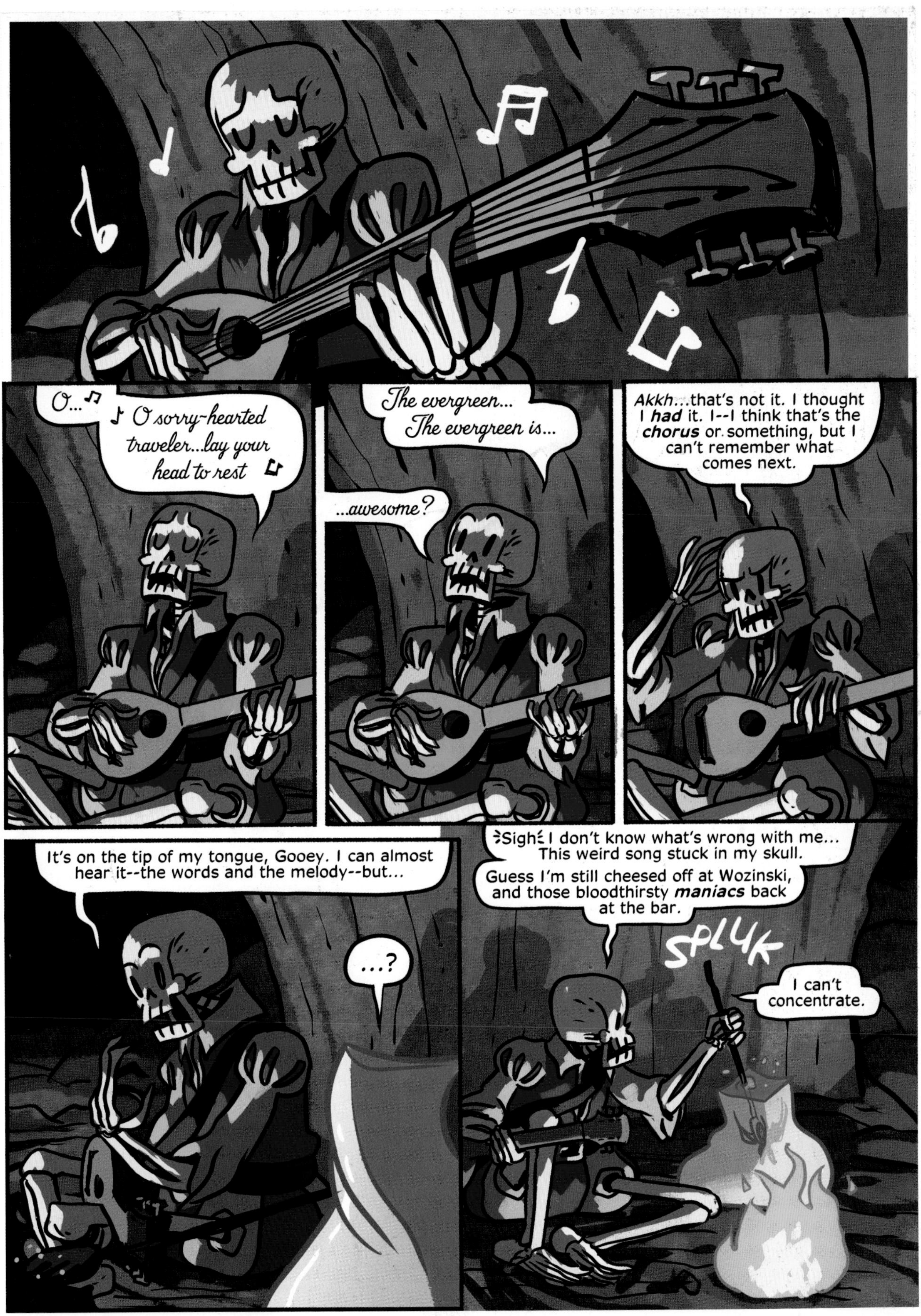
O...
O sorry-hearted traveler...lay your head to rest
The evergreen... The evergreen is...
...awesome?
Akkh...that's not it. I thought I *had* it. I--I think that's the *chorus* or something, but I can't remember what comes next.
It's on the tip of my tongue, Gooey. I can almost hear it--the words and the melody--but...
...?
Sigh I don't know what's wrong with me... This weird song stuck in my skull.
Guess I'm still cheesed off at Wozinski, and those bloodthirsty *maniacs* back at the bar.
SPLUK
I can't concentrate.

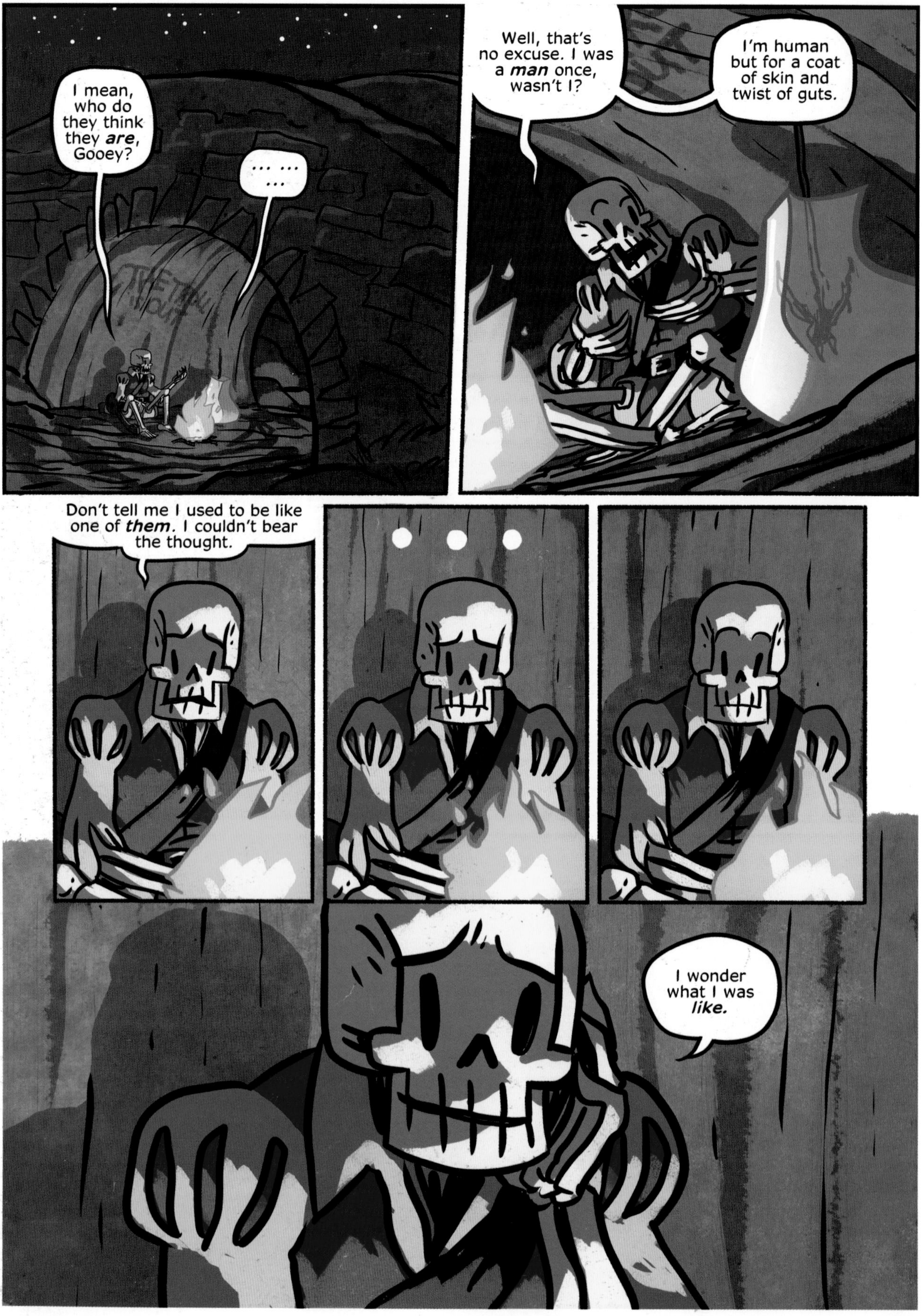

I mean, who do they think they *are*, Gooey?
... ...
Well, that's no excuse. I was a *man* once, wasn't I?
I'm human but for a coat of skin and twist of guts.
Don't tell me I used to be like one of *them*. I couldn't bear the thought.
I wonder what I was *like.*

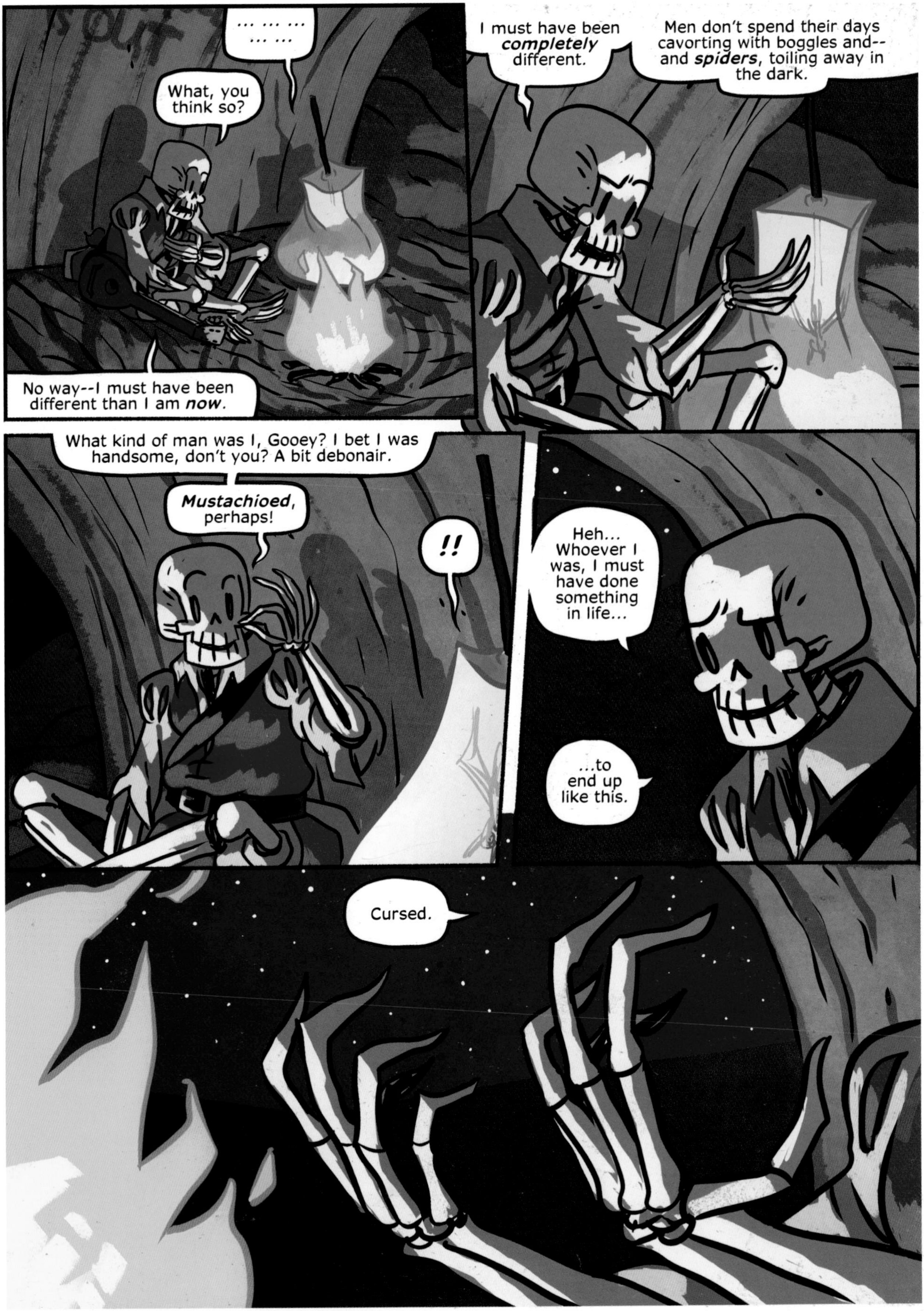
... ...
... ...
What, you think so?
No way--I must have been different than I am *now*.
I must have been *completely* different.
Men don't spend their days cavorting with boggles and-- and *spiders*, toiling away in the dark.
What kind of man was I, Gooey? I bet I was handsome, don't you? A bit debonair.
Mustachioed, perhaps!
!!
Heh... Whoever I was, I must have done something in life...
...to end up like this.
Cursed.

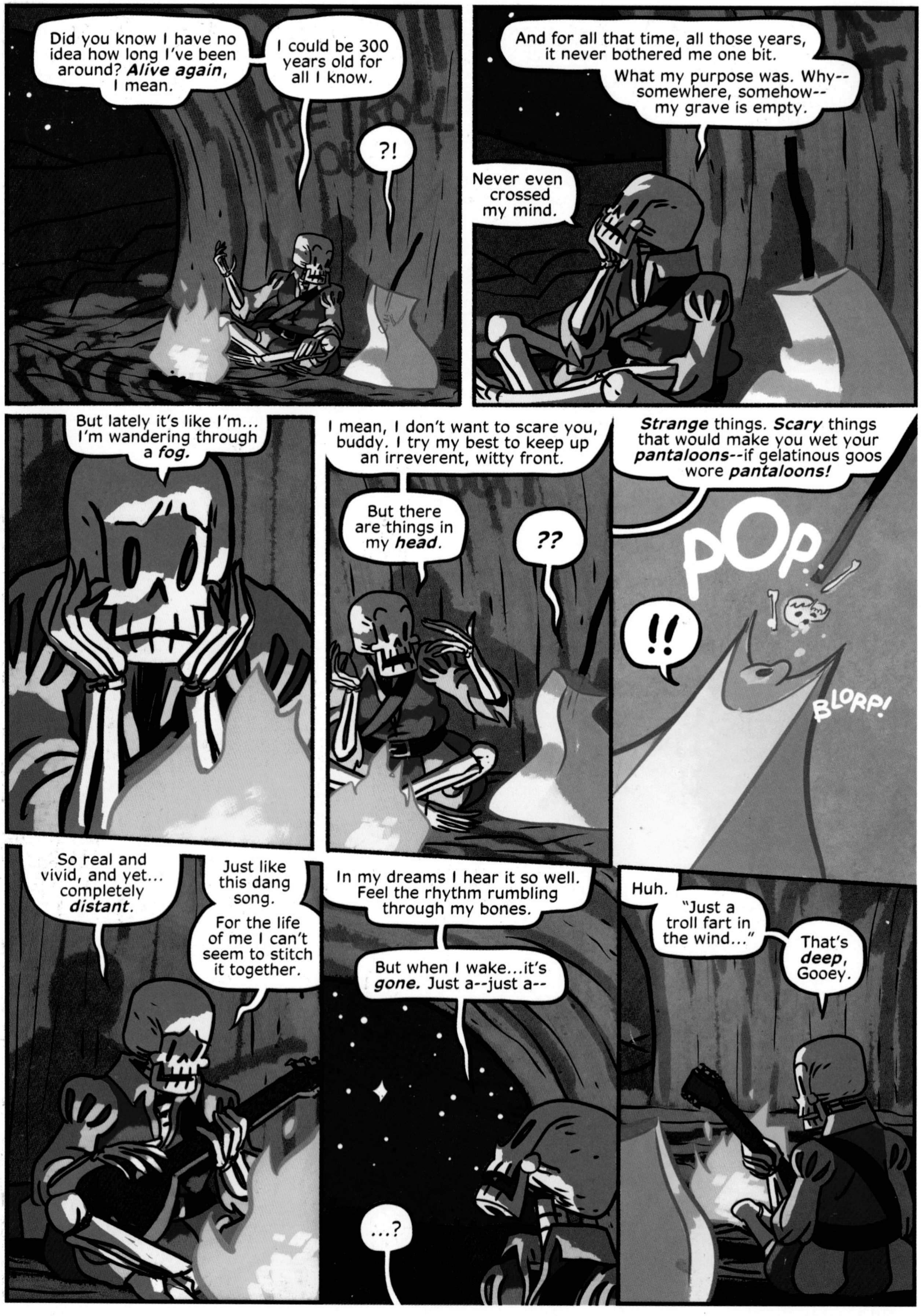

Did you know I have no idea how long I've been around? *Alive again*, I mean.
I could be 300 years old for all I know.
?!
And for all that time, all those years, it never bothered me one bit.
What my purpose was. Why--somewhere, somehow--my grave is empty.
Never even crossed my mind.
But lately it's like I'm... I'm wandering through a *fog.*
I mean, I don't want to scare you, buddy. I try my best to keep up an irreverent, witty front.
But there are things in my *head*.
??
Strange things. *Scary* things that would make you wet your *pantaloons*--if gelatinous goos wore *pantaloons!*
POP
!!
BLORP!
So real and vivid, and yet... completely *distant*.
Just like this dang song.
For the life of me I can't seem to stitch it together.
In my dreams I hear it so well. Feel the rhythm rumbling through my bones.
But when I wake...it's *gone.* Just a--just a--
...?
Huh.
"Just a troll fart in the wind..."
That's *deep*, Gooey.

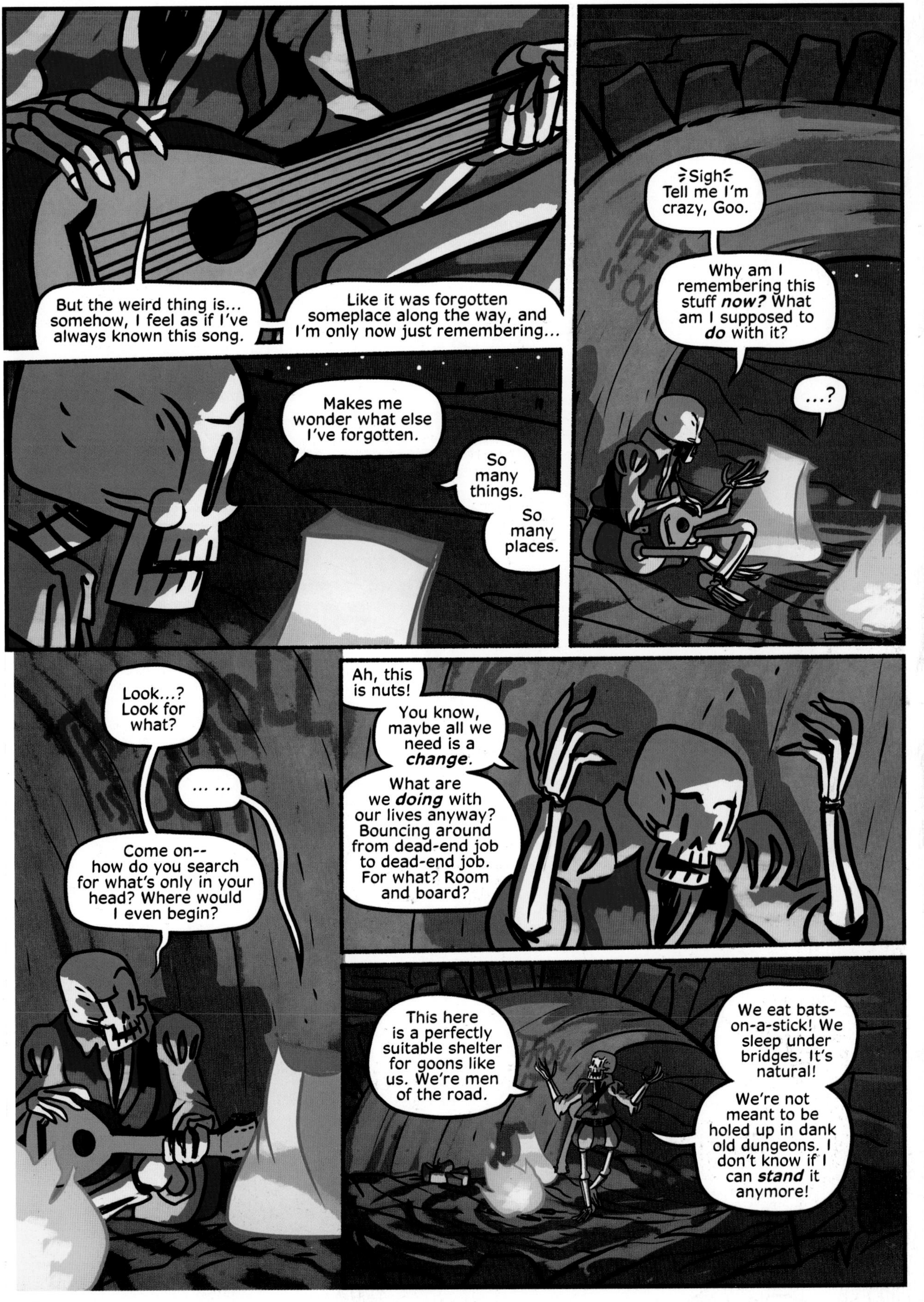

But the weird thing is... somehow, I feel as if I've always known this song.
Like it was forgotten someplace along the way, and I'm only now just remembering...
Makes me wonder what else I've forgotten.
So many things.
So many places.
⚞Sigh⚟ Tell me I'm crazy, Goo.
Why am I remembering this stuff *now?* What am I supposed to *do* with it?
...?
Look...? Look for what?
... ...
Come on-- how do you search for what's only in your head? Where would I even begin?
Ah, this is nuts!
You know, maybe all we need is a *change*.
What are we *doing* with our lives anyway? Bouncing around from dead-end job to dead-end job. For what? Room and board?
This here is a perfectly suitable shelter for goons like us. We're men of the road.
We eat bats-on-a-stick! We sleep under bridges. It's natural!
We're not meant to be holed up in dank old dungeons. I don't know if I can *stand* it anymore!

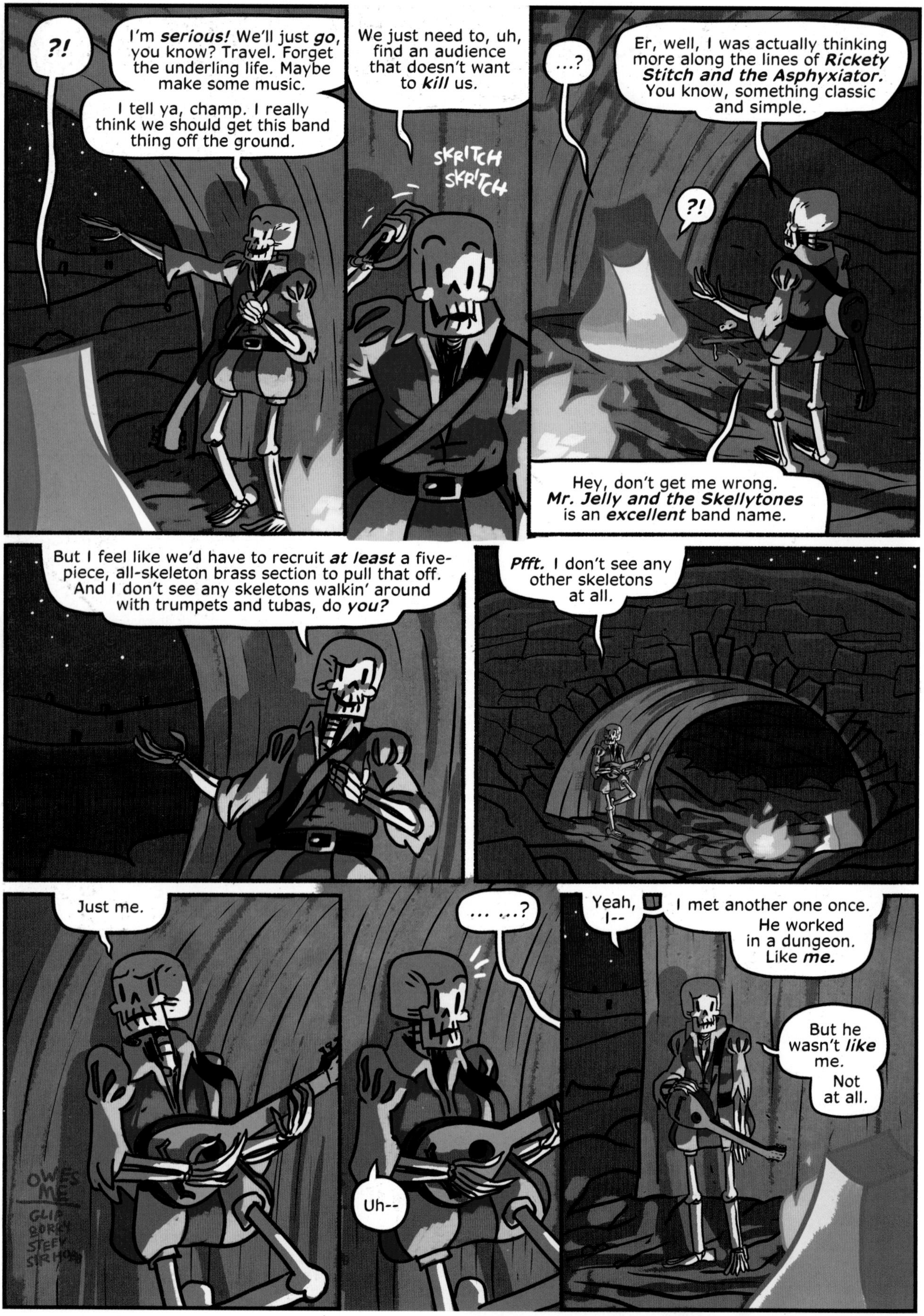

?!
I'm *serious!* We'll just *go*, you know? Travel. Forget the underling life. Maybe make some music.
I tell ya, champ. I really think we should get this band thing off the ground.
We just need to, uh, find an audience that doesn't want to *kill* us.
SKRITCH SKRITCH
...?
Er, well, I was actually thinking more along the lines of ***Rickety Stitch and the Asphyxiator.*** You know, something classic and simple.
?!
Hey, don't get me wrong. ***Mr. Jelly and the Skellytones*** is an *excellent* band name.
But I feel like we'd have to recruit ***at least*** a five-piece, all-skeleton brass section to pull that off. And I don't see any skeletons walkin' around with trumpets and tubas, do ***you?***
Pfft. I don't see any other skeletons at all.
Just me.
OWES ME
... ...?
Uh--
Yeah, I--
I met another one once.
He worked in a dungeon. Like ***me.***
But he wasn't ***like*** me.
Not at all.

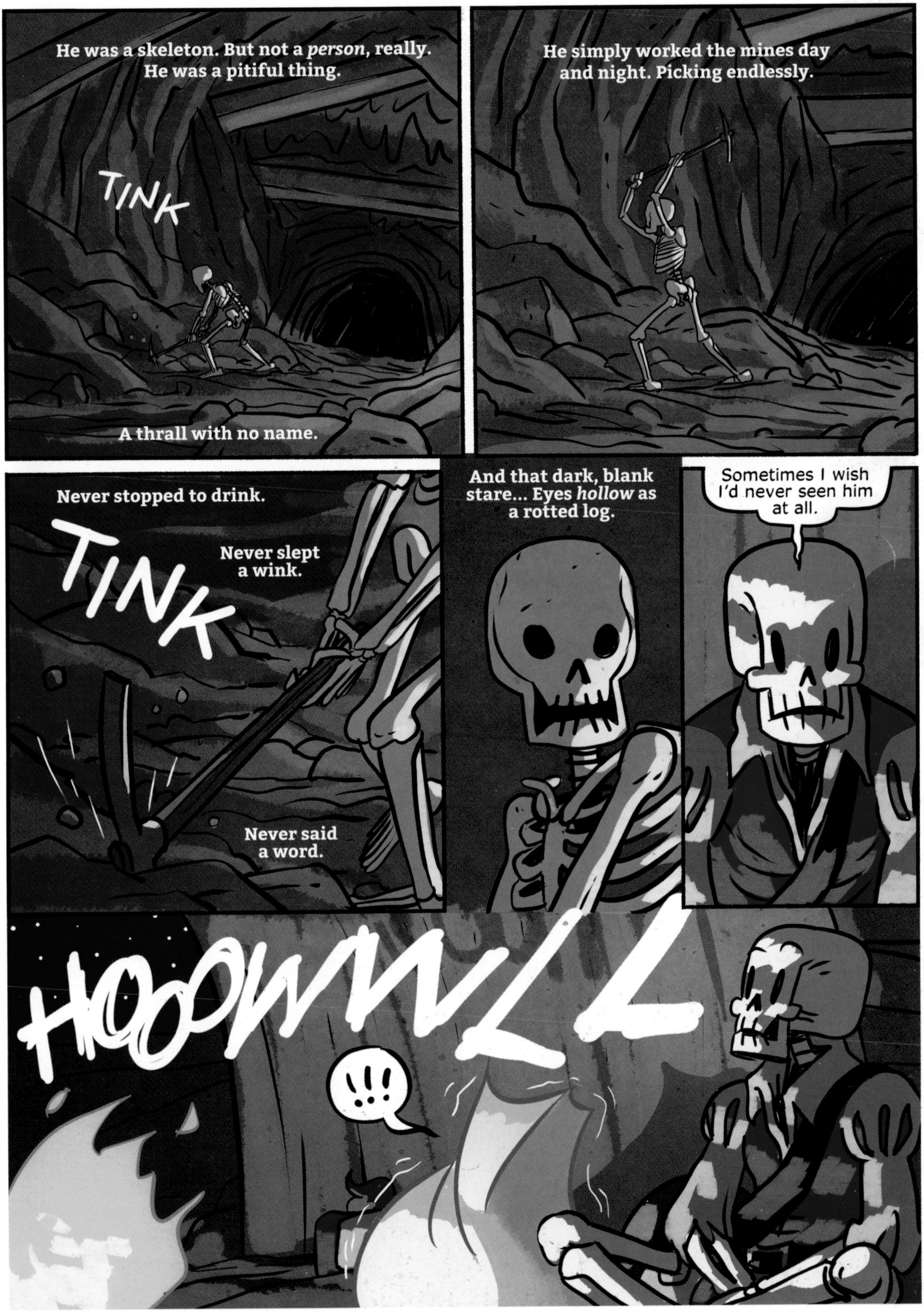
He was a skeleton. But not a *person*, really. He was a pitiful thing.
TINK
A thrall with no name.
He simply worked the mines day and night. Picking endlessly.
Never stopped to drink.
TINK
Never slept a wink.
Never said a word.
And that dark, blank stare... Eyes *hollow* as a rotted log.
Sometimes I wish I'd never seen him at all.
HOOOWWLL
!!!

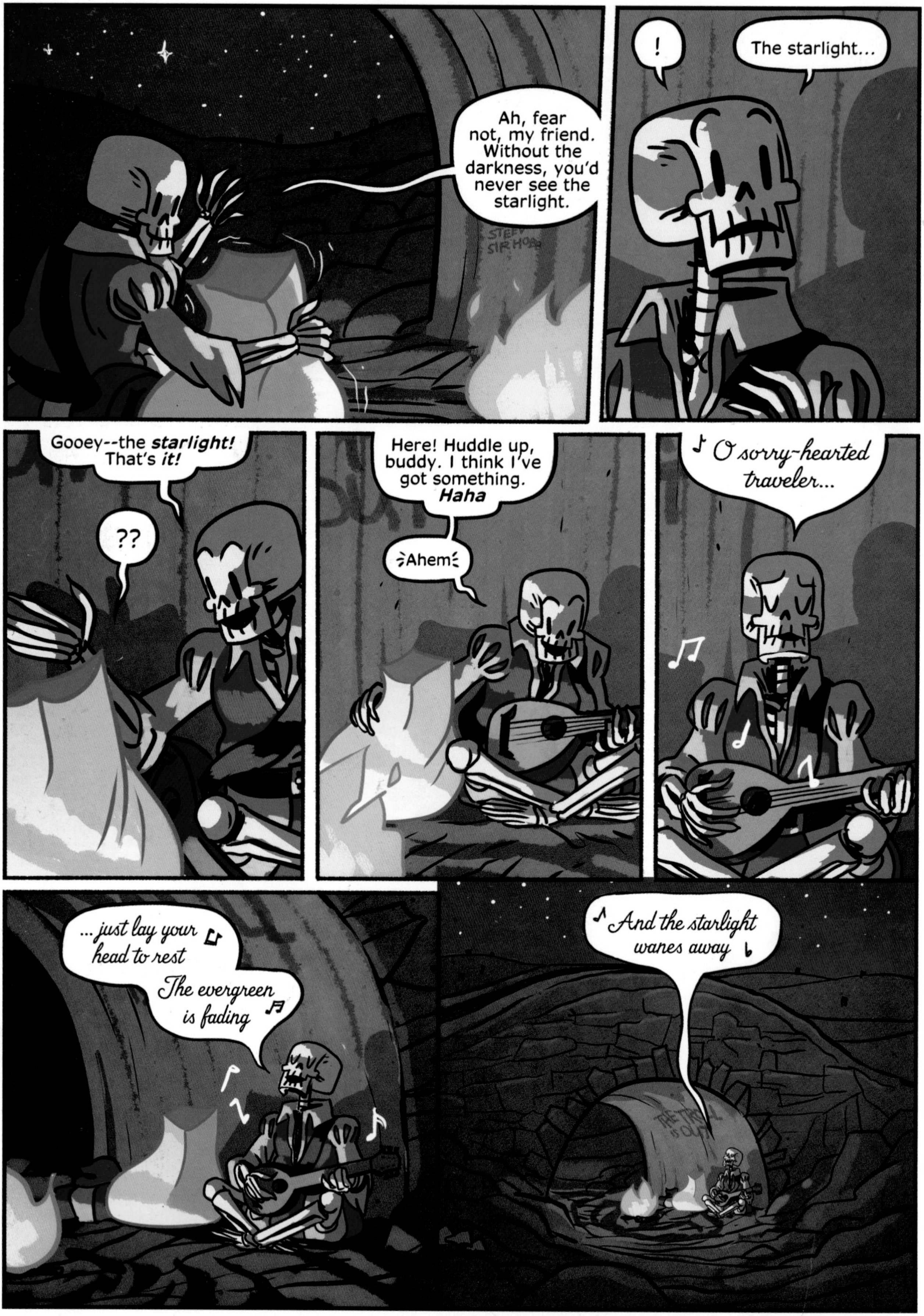
Ah, fear not, my friend. Without the darkness, you'd never see the starlight.
!
The starlight...
Gooey--the **starlight!** That's *it!*
??
Here! Huddle up, buddy. I think I've got something. ***Haha***
Ahem
O sorry-hearted traveler...
...just lay your head to rest
The evergreen is fading
And the starlight wanes away

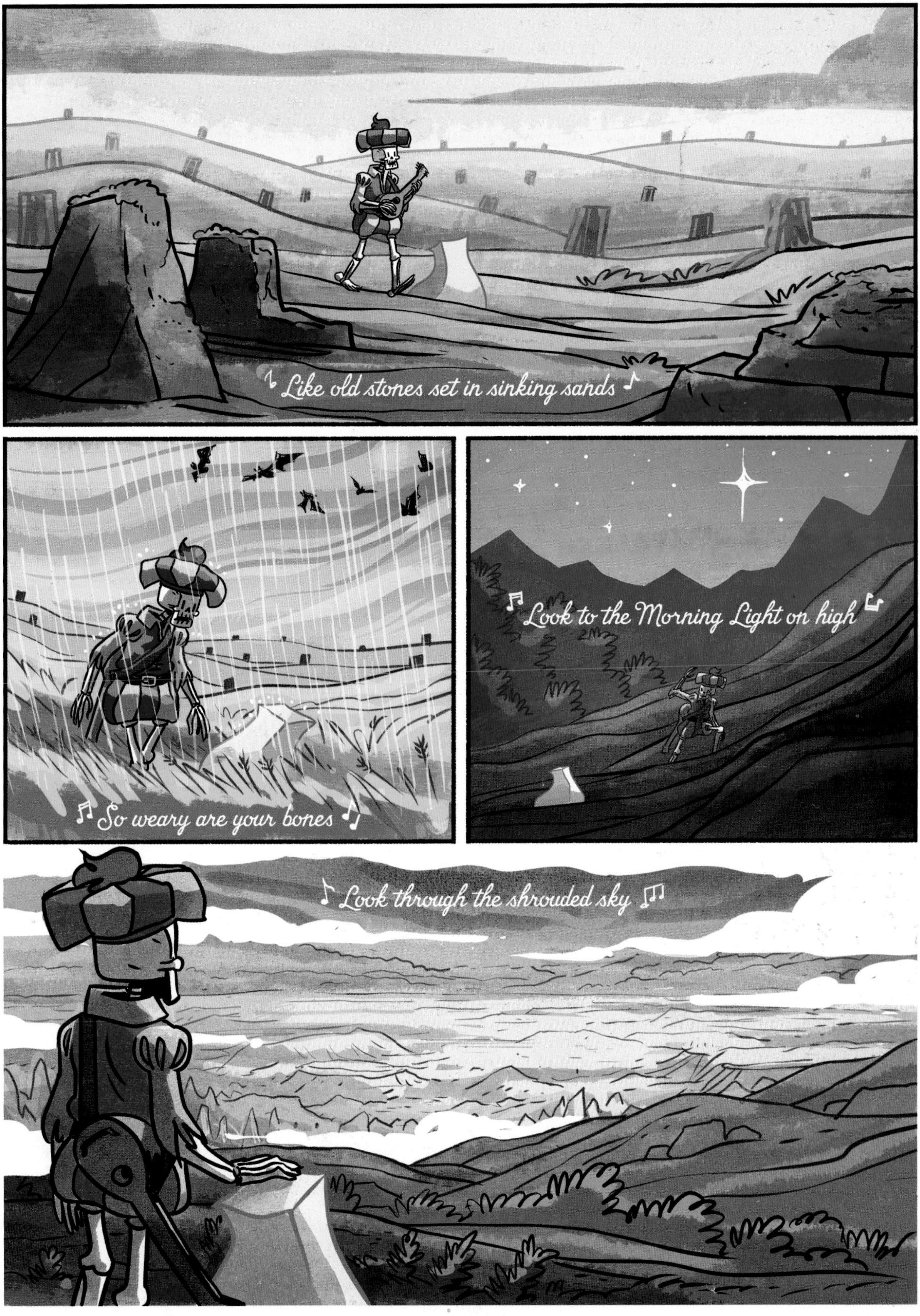
Like old stones set in sinking sands
So weary are your bones
Look to the Morning Light on high
Look through the shrouded sky

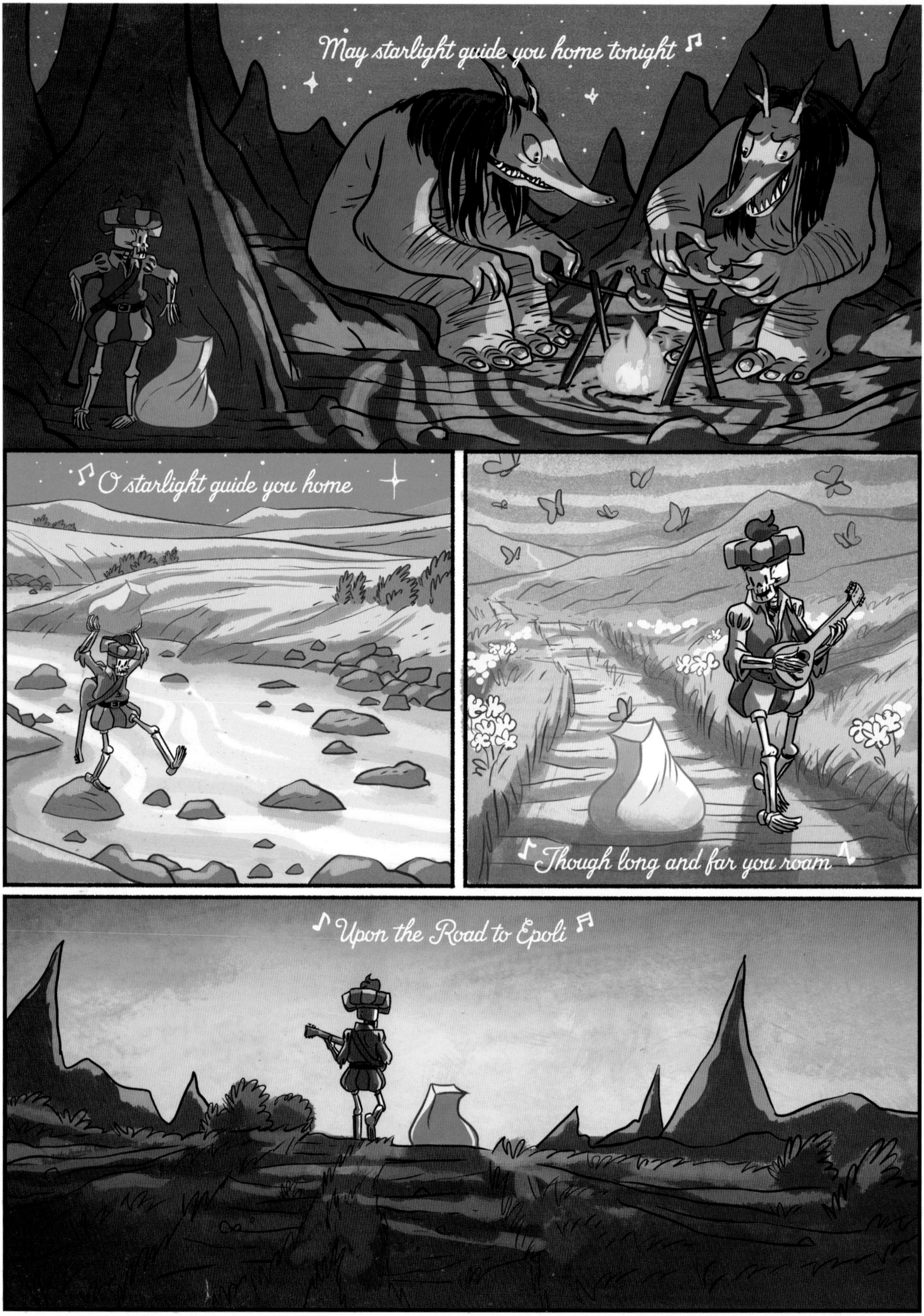
May starlight guide you home tonight
O starlight guide you home
Though long and far you roam
Upon the Road to Epoli

Chapter 5
Something to Look For

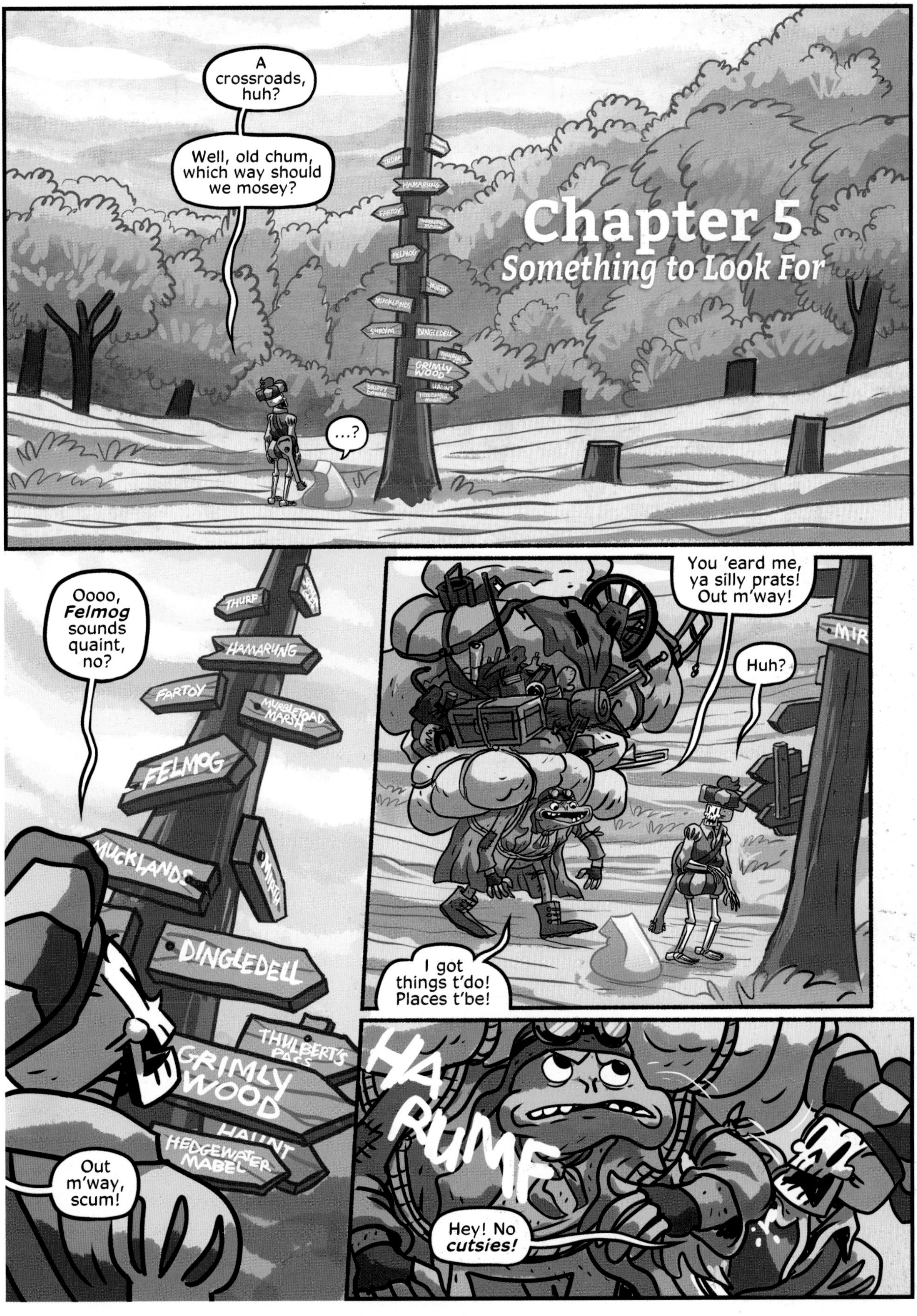

A crossroads, huh?
Well, old chum, which way should we mosey?
...?
Oooo, ***Felmog*** sounds quaint, no?
THURF
HAMARUNG
FARTOY
MURBLETOAD MARSH
FELMOG
MUCKLANDS
DINGLEDELL
THULBERT'S PASS
GRIMLY WOOD
HAINT
HEDGEWATER MABEL
Out m'way, scum!
You 'eard me, ya silly prats! Out m'way!
Huh?
I got things t'do! Places t'be!
HA RUMF
Hey! No ***cutsies!***

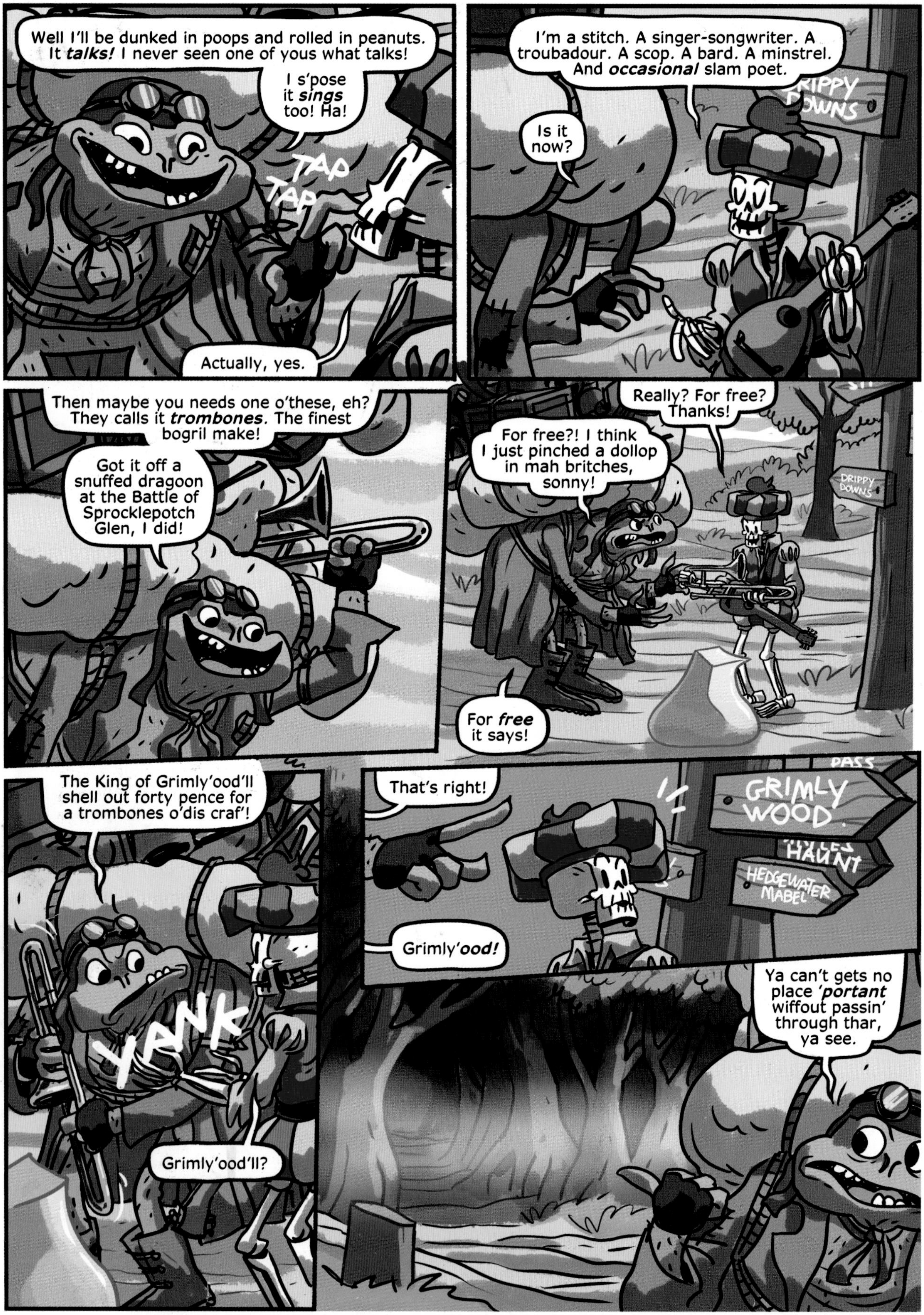

Well I'll be dunked in poops and rolled in peanuts. It *talks!* I never seen one of yous what talks!
I s'pose it *sings* too! Ha!
TAP TAP
Actually, yes.
I'm a stitch. A singer-songwriter. A troubadour. A scop. A bard. A minstrel. And *occasional* slam poet.
Is it now?
DRIPPY DOWNS
Then maybe you needs one o'these, eh? They calls it *trombones*. The finest bogril make!
Got it off a snuffed dragoon at the Battle of Sprocklepotch Glen, I did!
Really? For free? Thanks!
For free?! I think I just pinched a dollop in mah britches, sonny!
DRIPPY DOWNS
For *free* it says!
The King of Grimly'ood'll shell out forty pence for a trombones o'dis craf'!
YANK
Grimly'ood'll?
That's right!
GRIMLY WOOD
HAUNT
HEDGEWATER MABEL
Grimly'*ood!*
Ya can't gets no place *'portant* wiffout passin' through thar, ya see.

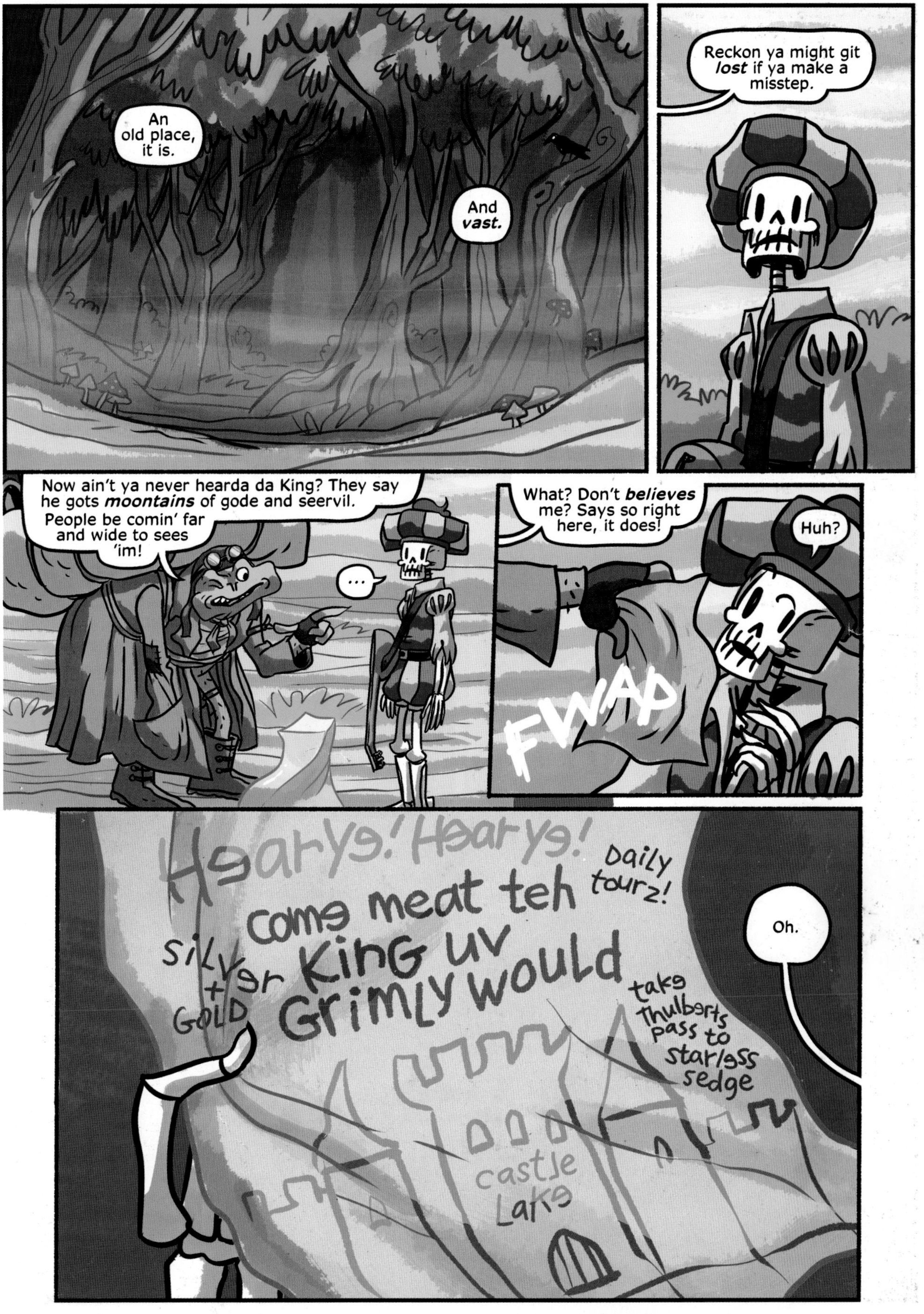

An old place, it is.
And *vast.*
Reckon ya might git *lost* if ya make a misstep.
Now ain't ya never hearda da King? They say he gots *moontains* of gode and seervil. People be comin' far and wide to sees 'im!
...
What? Don't *believes* me? Says so right here, it does!
Huh?
FWAP
Hear ye! Hear ye!
Daily tourz!
Come meat teh King uv Grimlywould
silver + GOLD
take Thulberts pass to starless sedge
castle Lake
Oh.

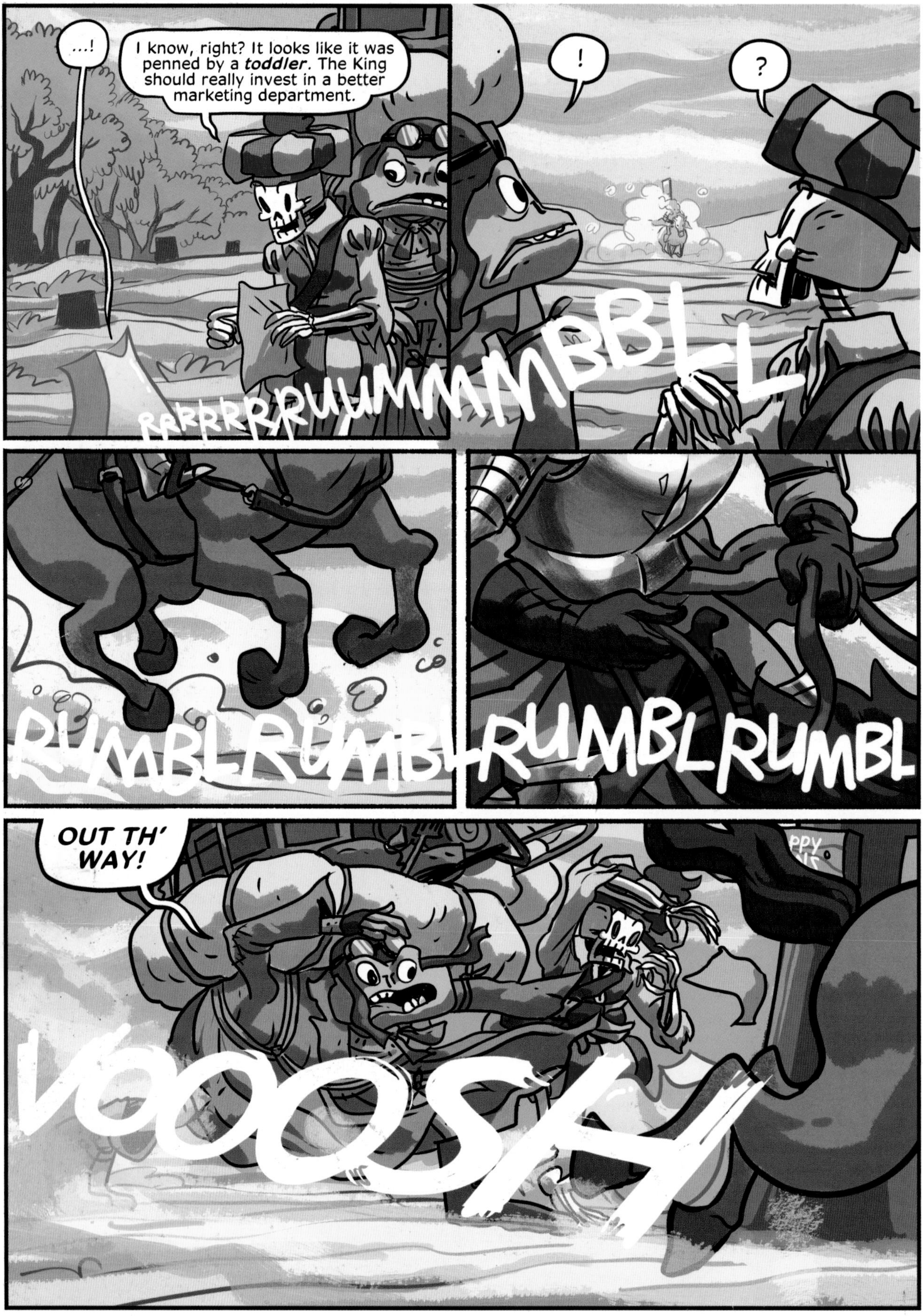
...!
I know, right? It looks like it was penned by a *toddler*. The King should really invest in a better marketing department.
!
?
RRRRRRRUUMMMMBBLLL
RUMBLRUMBLRUMBLRUMBL
OUT TH' WAY!
VOOOSH

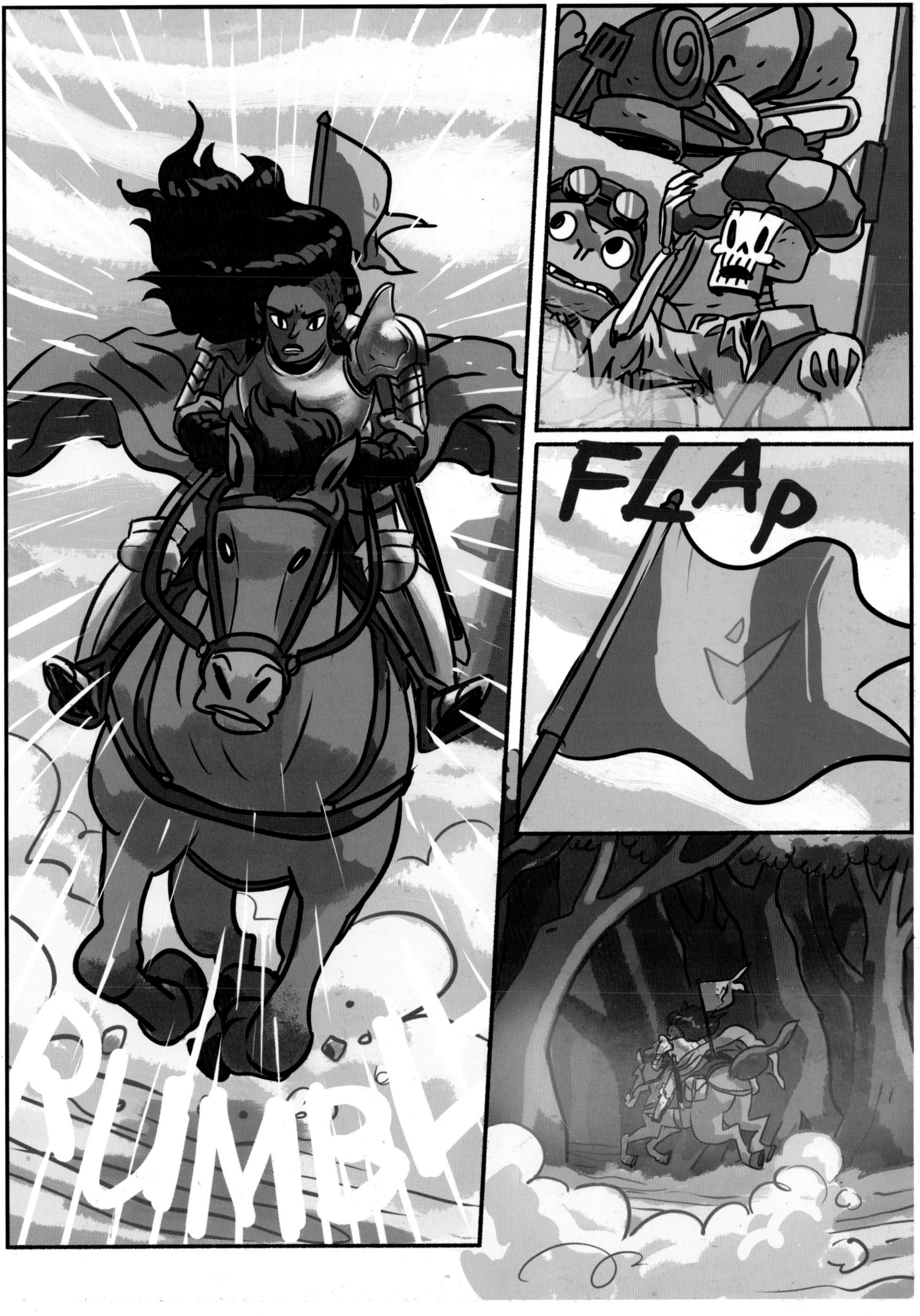
RUMBL
FLAp

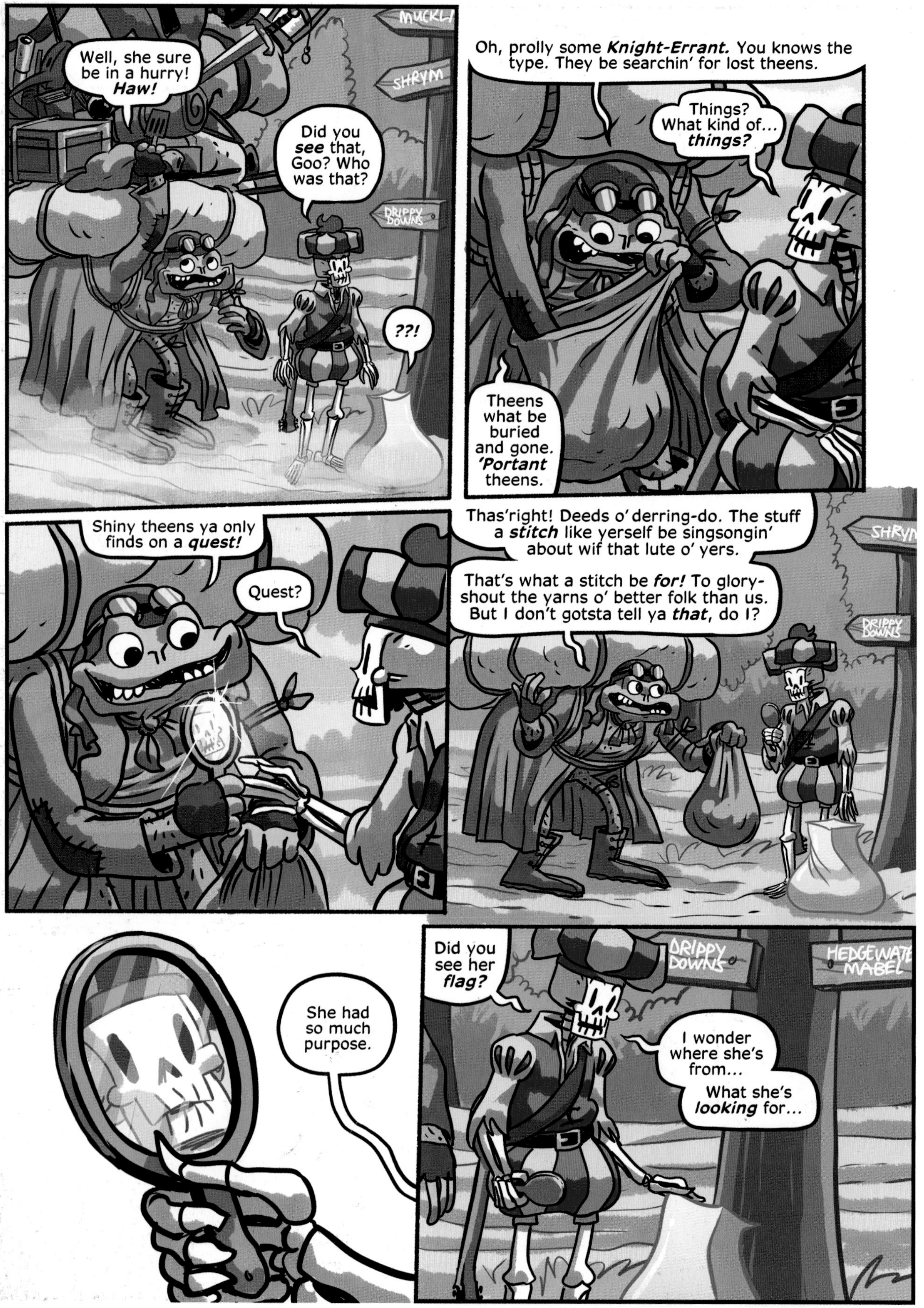
MUCKL
SHRYM
Well, she sure be in a hurry! *Haw!*
Did you *see* that, Goo? Who was that?
DRIPPY DOWNS
??!
Oh, prolly some *Knight-Errant.* You knows the type. They be searchin' for lost theens.
Things? What kind of... *things?*
Theens what be buried and gone. *'Portant* theens.
Shiny theens ya only finds on a *quest!*
Quest?
Thas'right! Deeds o' derring-do. The stuff a *stitch* like yerself be singsongin' about wif that lute o' yers.
That's what a stitch be *for!* To glory-shout the yarns o' better folk than us. But I don't gotsta tell ya *that*, do I?
SHRYM
DRIPPY DOWNS
She had so much purpose.
Did you see her *flag?*
DRIPPY DOWNS
HEDGEWATE MABEL
I wonder where she's from...
What she's *looking* for...

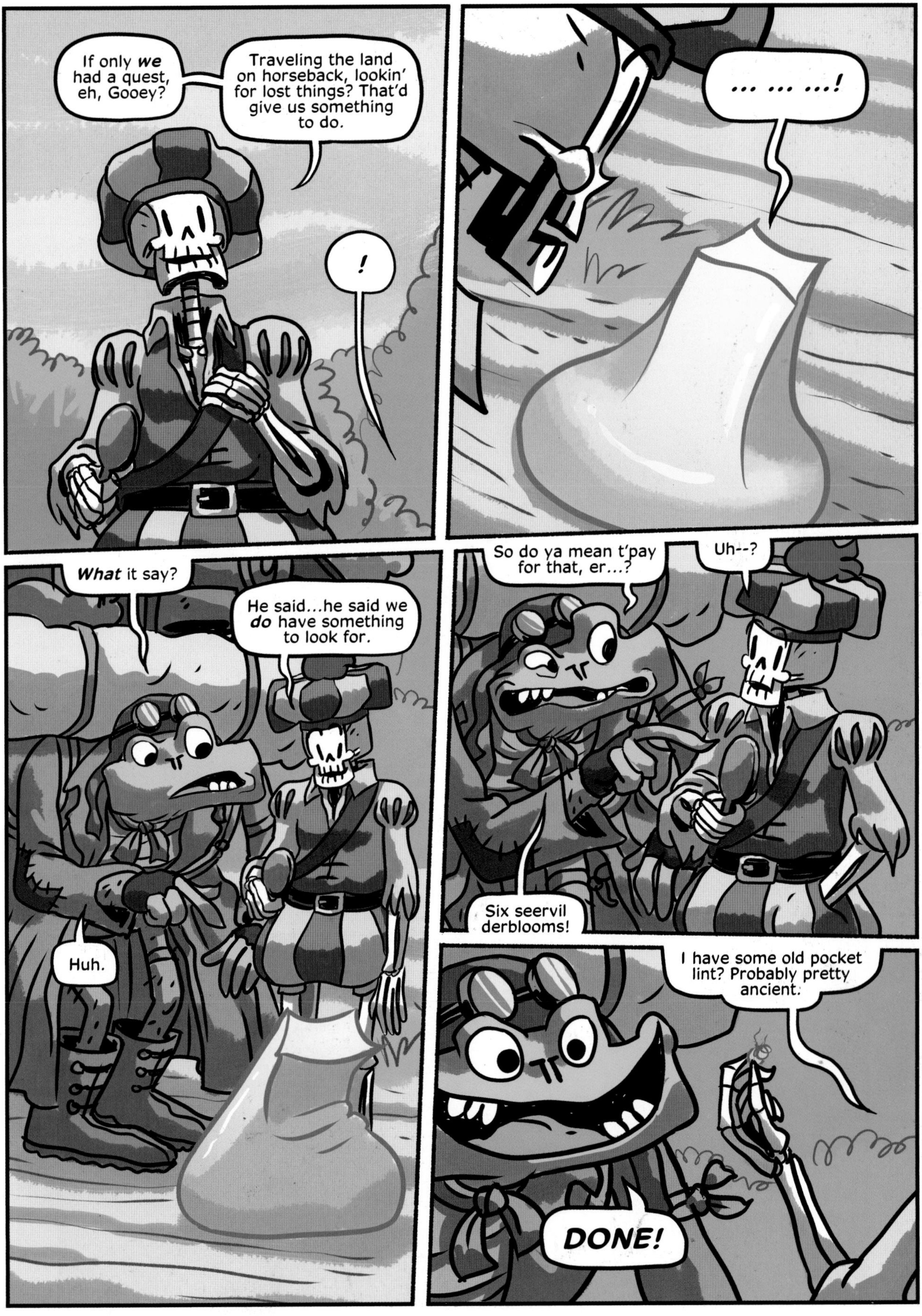

If only *we* had a quest, eh, Gooey?
Traveling the land on horseback, lookin' for lost things? That'd give us something to do.
!
... ...!
What it say?
He said...he said we *do* have something to look for.
Huh.
So do ya mean t'pay for that, er...?
Uh--?
Six seervil derblooms!
I have some old pocket lint? Probably pretty ancient.
DONE!

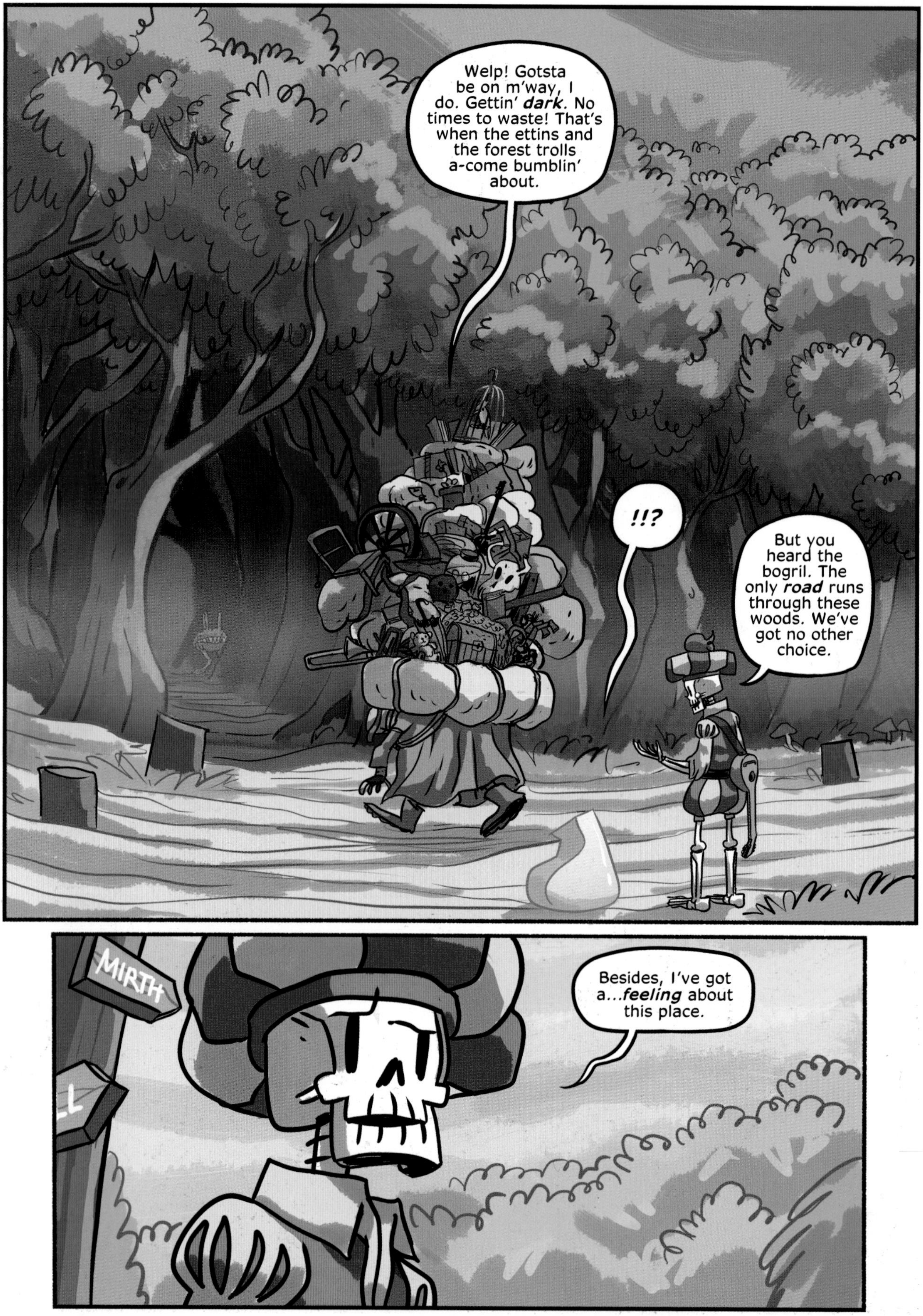
Welp! Gotsta be on m'way, I do. Gettin' *dark*. No times to waste! That's when the ettins and the forest trolls a-come bumblin' about.
!!?
But you heard the bogril. The only *road* runs through these woods. We've got no other choice.
MIRTH
Besides, I've got a...*feeling* about this place.

Chapter 6
Enter Grimly Wood

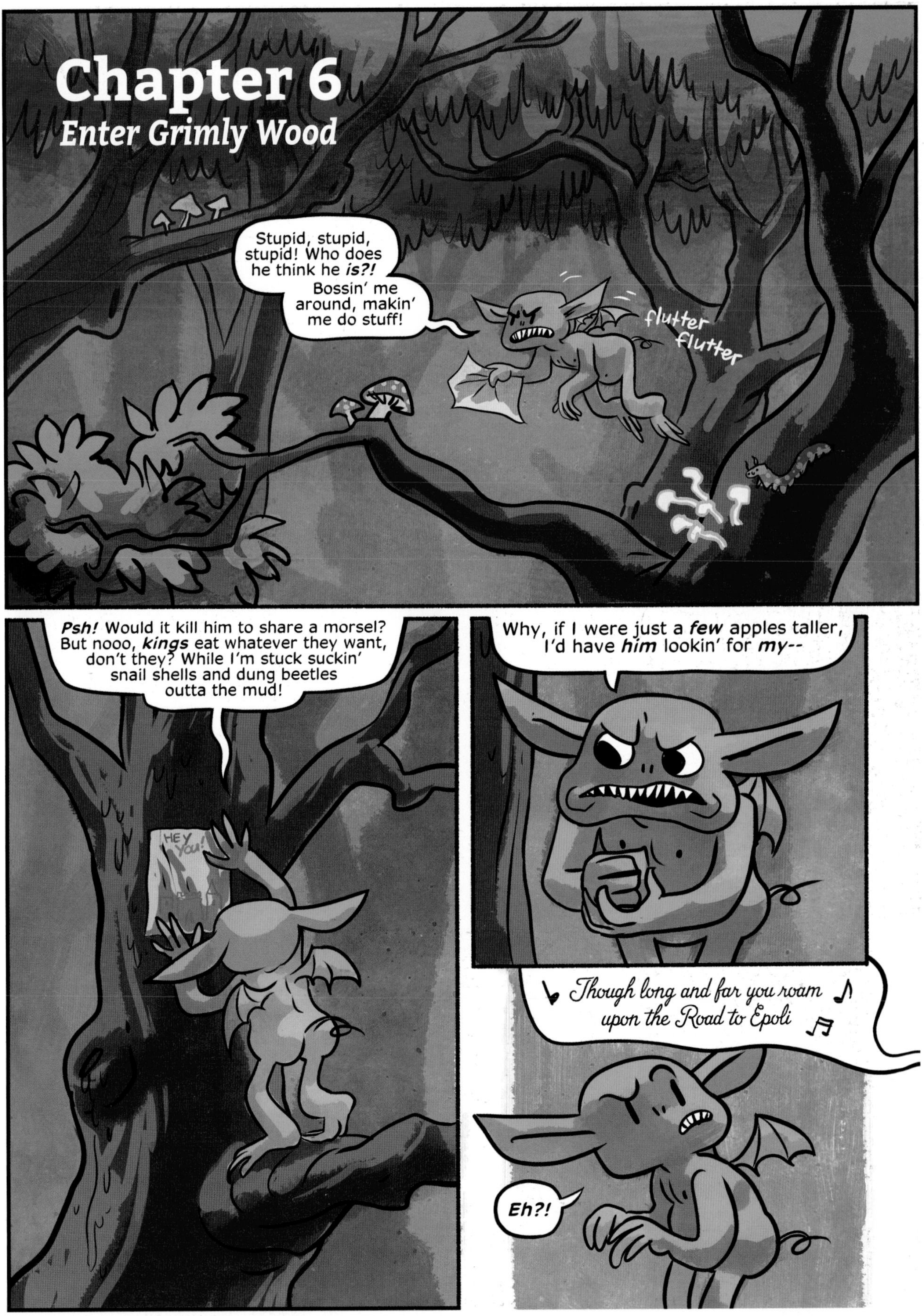

Stupid, stupid, stupid! Who does he think he *is?!*
Bossin' me around, makin' me do stuff!
flutter flutter
Psh! Would it kill him to share a morsel? But nooo, ***kings*** eat whatever they want, don't they? While I'm stuck suckin' snail shells and dung beetles outta the mud!
HEY YOU!
Why, if I were just a ***few*** apples taller, I'd have ***him*** lookin' for ***my***--
♪ Though long and far you roam upon the Road to Epoli ♪
Eh?!

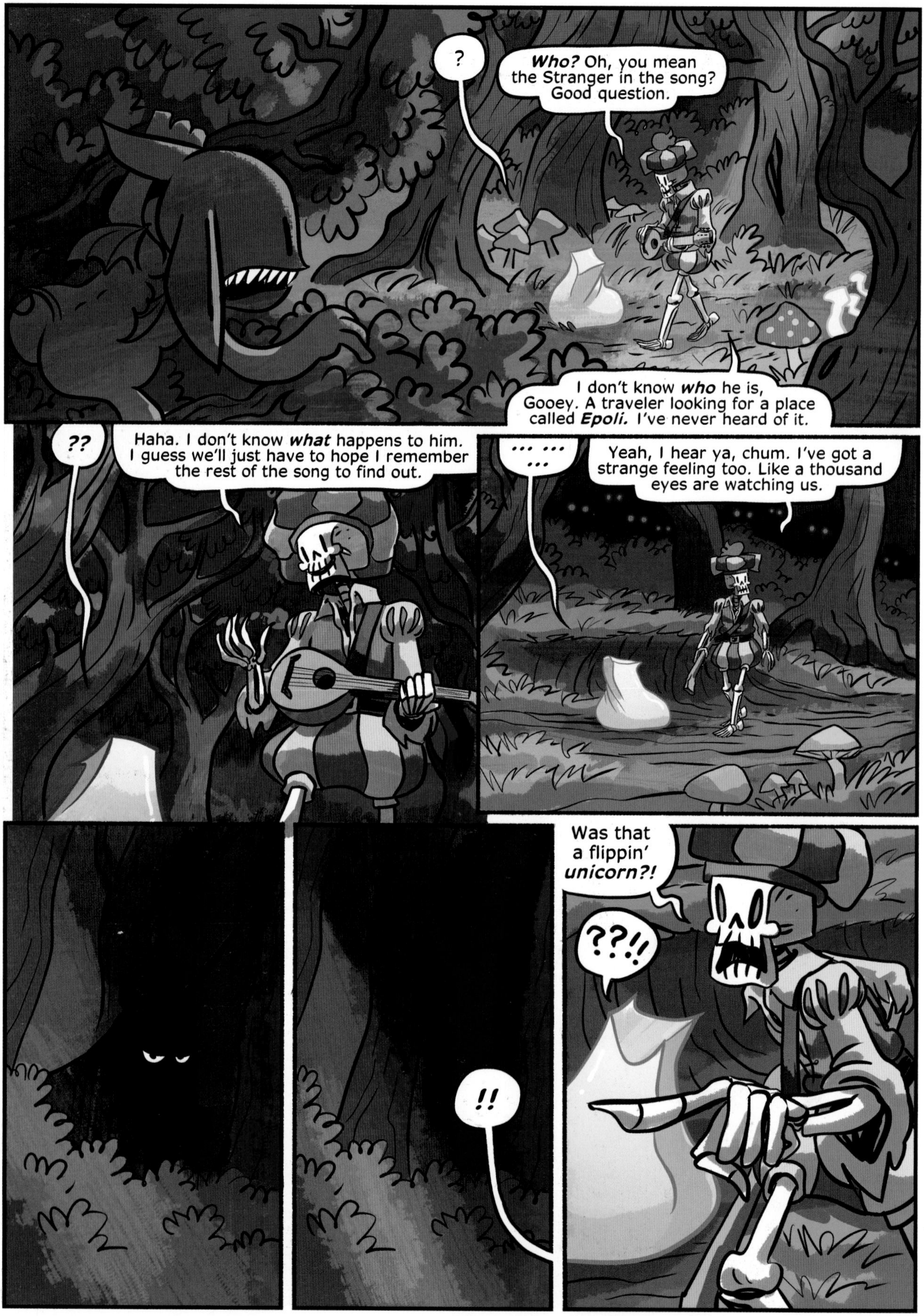
?
Who? Oh, you mean the Stranger in the song? Good question.
I don't know who he is, Gooey. A traveler looking for a place called Epoli. I've never heard of it.
??
Haha. I don't know what happens to him. I guess we'll just have to hope I remember the rest of the song to find out.
... ...
Yeah, I hear ya, chum. I've got a strange feeling too. Like a thousand eyes are watching us.
!!
Was that a flippin' unicorn?!
??!!

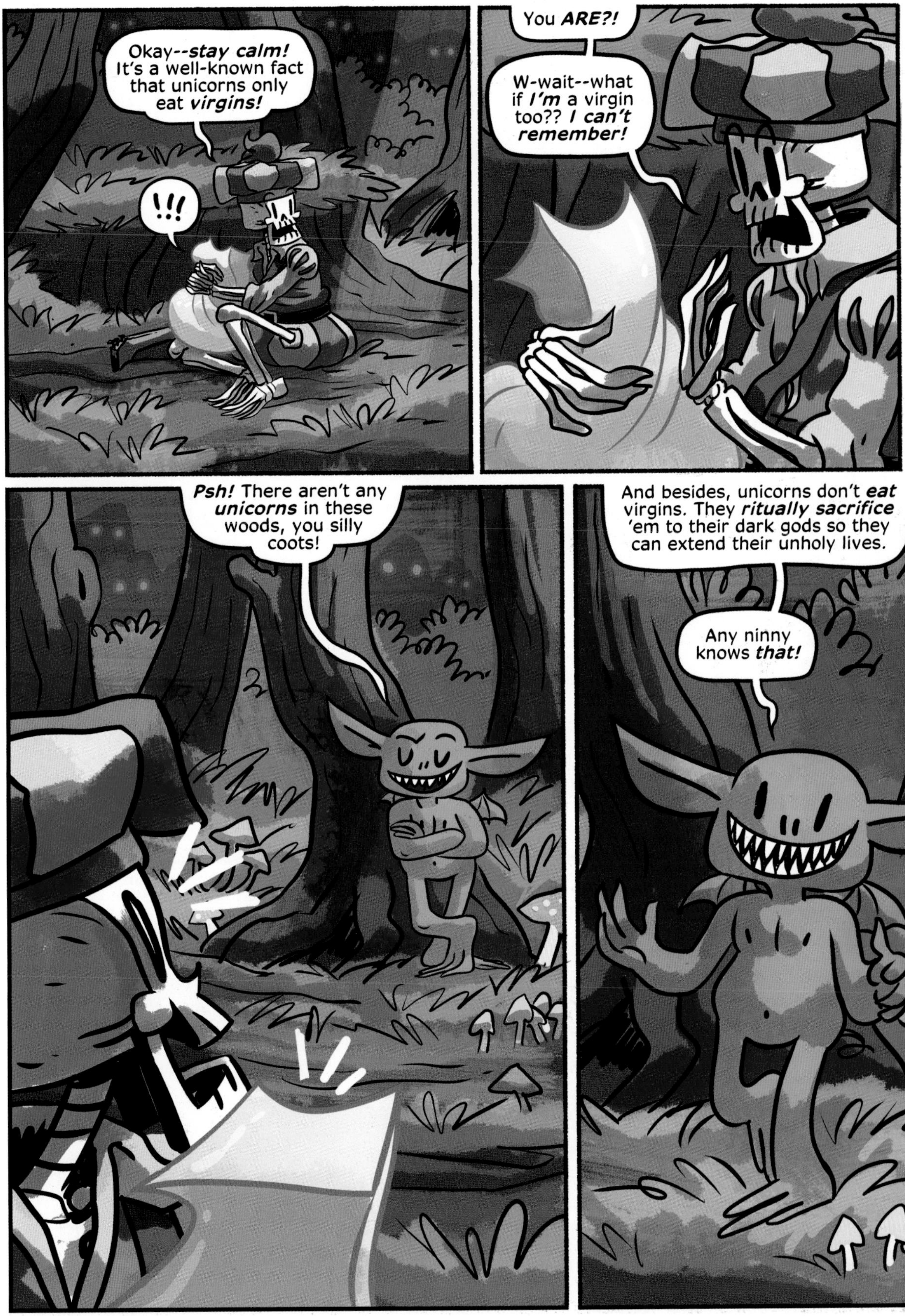

Okay--*stay calm!* It's a well-known fact that unicorns only eat *virgins!*
!!!
You *ARE?!*
W-wait--what if *I'm* a virgin too?? *I can't remember!*
Psh! There aren't any *unicorns* in these woods, you silly coots!
And besides, unicorns don't *eat* virgins. They *ritually sacrifice* 'em to their dark gods so they can extend their unholy lives.
Any ninny knows *that!*

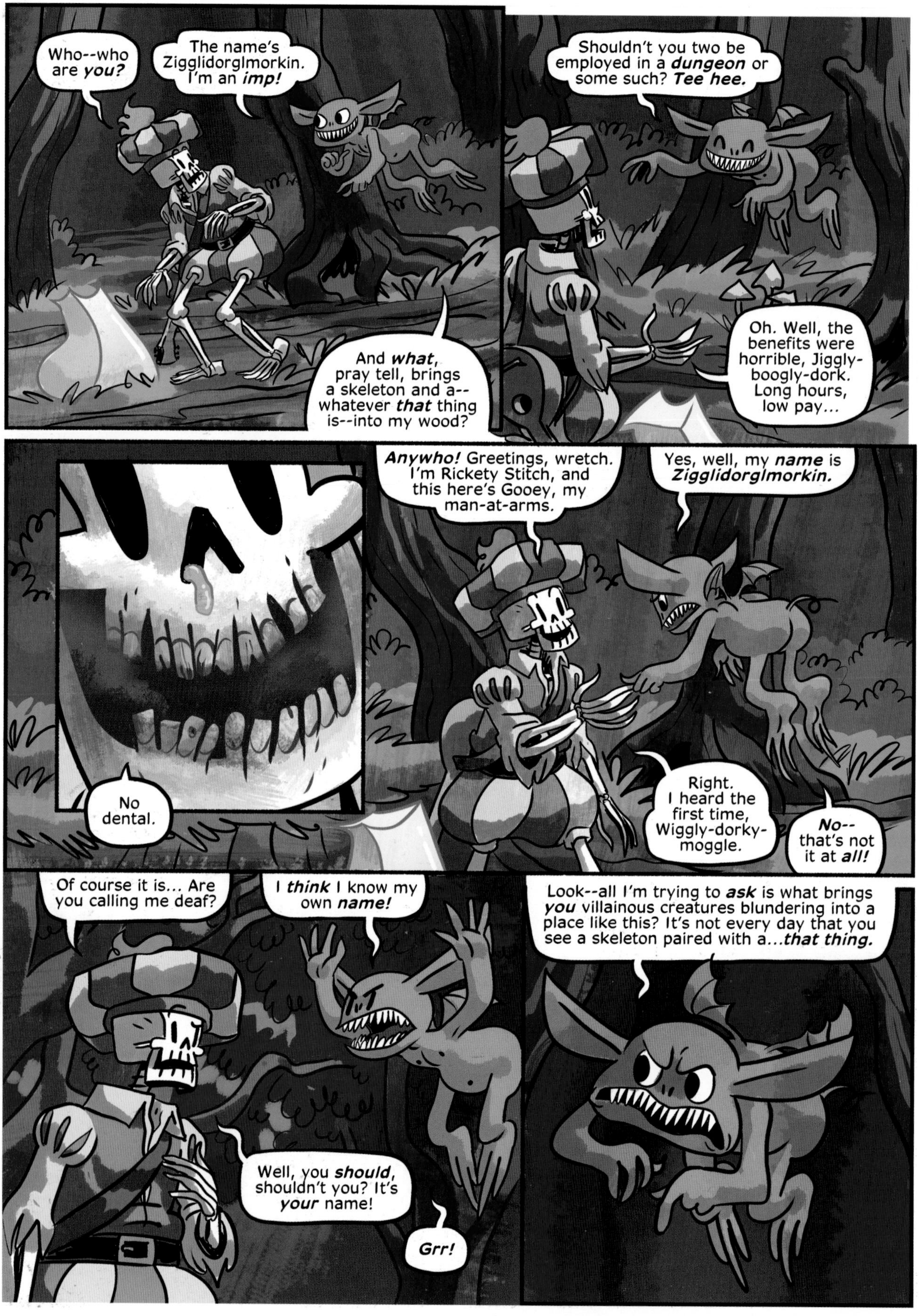
Who--who are *you?*
The name's Zigglidorglmorkin. I'm an *imp!*
And *what,* pray tell, brings a skeleton and a--whatever *that* thing is--into my wood?
Shouldn't you two be employed in a *dungeon* or some such? *Tee hee.*
Oh. Well, the benefits were horrible, Jiggly-boogly-dork. Long hours, low pay...
No dental.
Anywho! Greetings, wretch. I'm Rickety Stitch, and this here's Gooey, my man-at-arms.
Yes, well, my *name* is *Zigglidorglmorkin.*
Right. I heard the first time, Wiggly-dorky-moggle.
No--that's not it at *all!*
Of course it is... Are you calling me deaf?
I *think* I know my own *name!*
Well, you *should*, shouldn't you? It's *your* name!
Grr!
Look--all I'm trying to *ask* is what brings *you* villainous creatures blundering into a place like this? It's not every day that you see a skeleton paired with a...*that thing.*

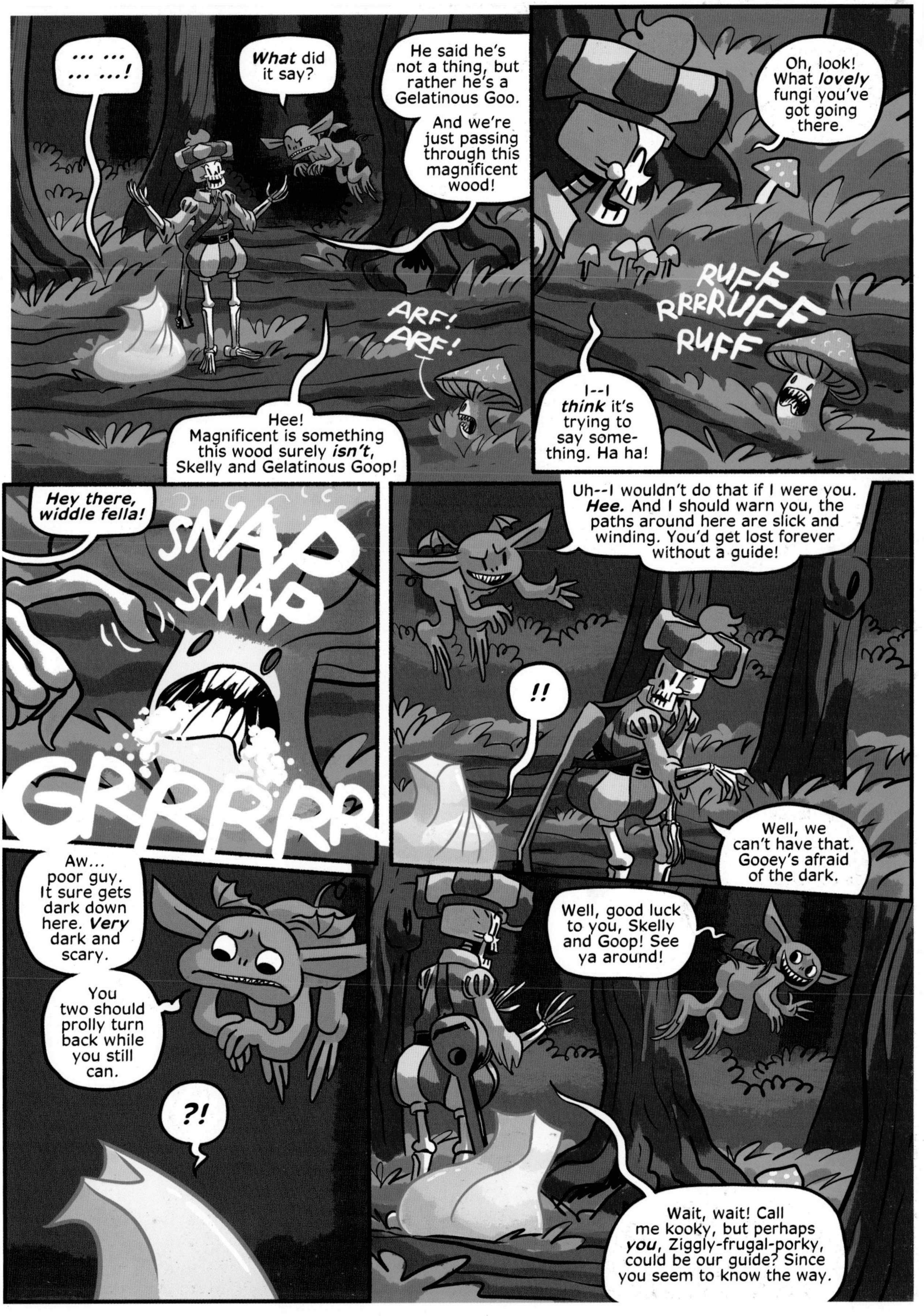
... ...!
What did it say?
He said he's not a thing, but rather he's a Gelatinous Goo.
And we're just passing through this magnificent wood!
ARF! ARF!
Hee! Magnificent is something this wood surely isn't, Skelly and Gelatinous Goop!
Oh, look! What lovely fungi you've got going there.
RUFF RRRRUFF RUFF
I--I think it's trying to say some-thing. Ha ha!
Hey there, widdle fella!
SNAP SNAP
GRRRRR
Uh--I wouldn't do that if I were you. Hee. And I should warn you, the paths around here are slick and winding. You'd get lost forever without a guide!
!!
Well, we can't have that. Gooey's afraid of the dark.
Aw... poor guy. It sure gets dark down here. Very dark and scary.
You two should prolly turn back while you still can.
?!
Well, good luck to you, Skelly and Goop! See ya around!
Wait, wait! Call me kooky, but perhaps you, Ziggly-frugal-porky, could be our guide? Since you seem to know the way.

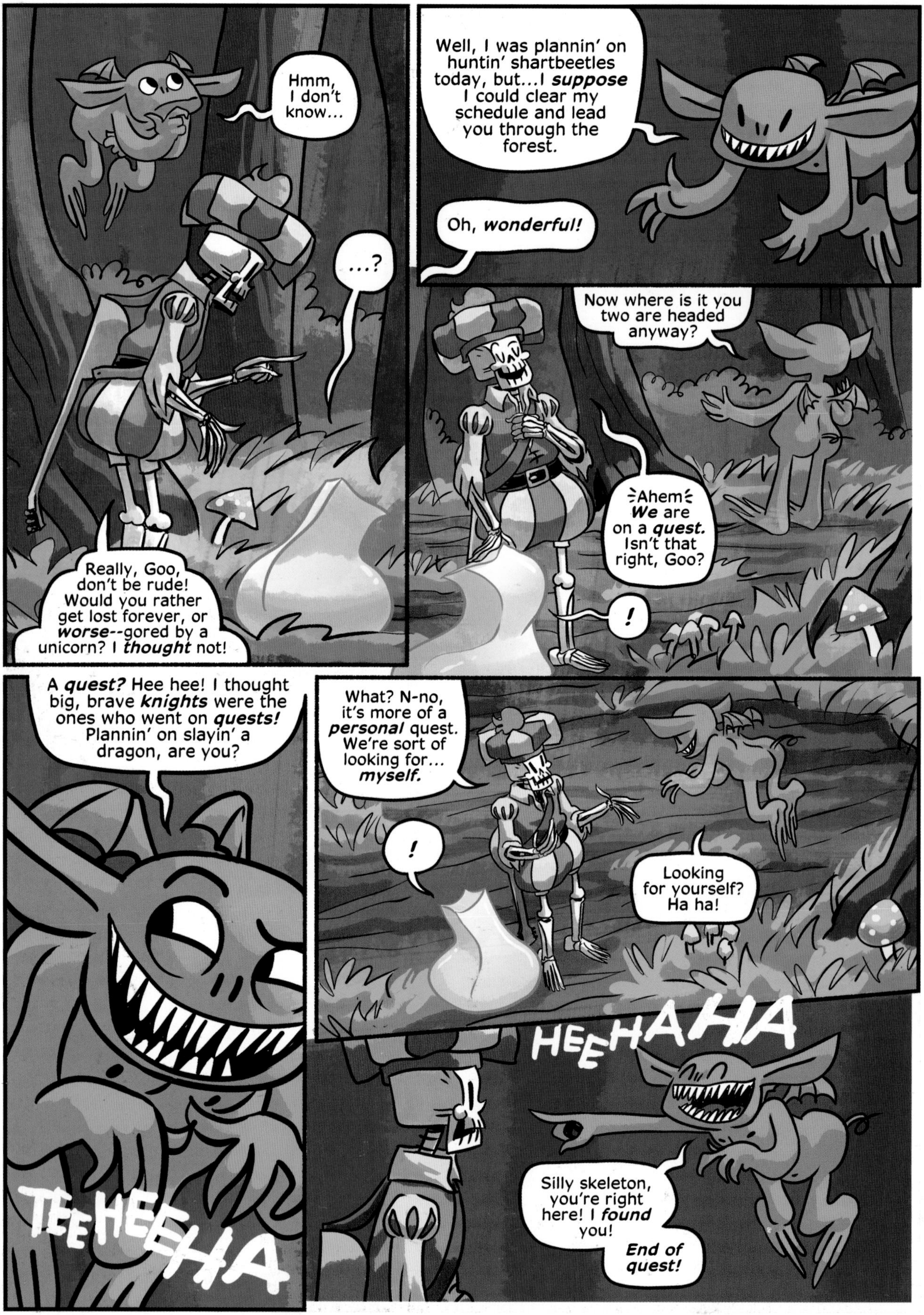
Hmm, I don't know...
...?
Really, Goo, don't be rude! Would you rather get lost forever, or *worse*--gored by a unicorn? I *thought* not!
Well, I was plannin' on huntin' shartbeetles today, but...I *suppose* I could clear my schedule and lead you through the forest.
Oh, *wonderful!*
Now where is it you two are headed anyway?
Ahem *We* are on a *quest.* Isn't that right, Goo?
!
A *quest?* Hee hee! I thought big, brave *knights* were the ones who went on *quests!* Plannin' on slayin' a dragon, are you?
TEEHEEHA
What? N-no, it's more of a *personal* quest. We're sort of looking for... *myself.*
!
Looking for yourself? Ha ha!
HEEHAHA
Silly skeleton, you're right here! I *found* you!
End of quest!

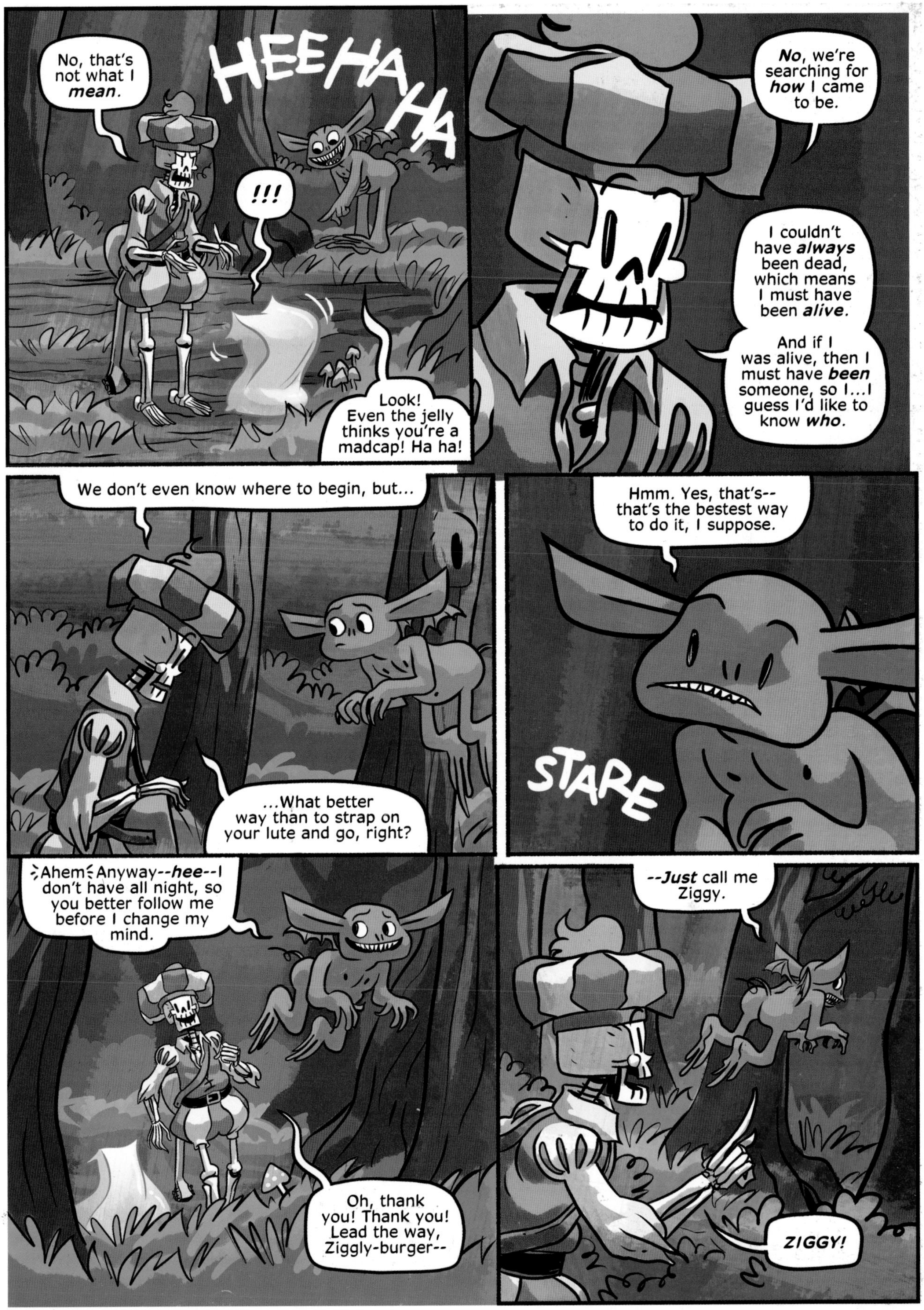
No, that's not what I *mean*.
HEE HA HA HA
!!!
Look! Even the jelly thinks you're a madcap! Ha ha!
No, we're searching for *how* I came to be.
I couldn't have *always* been dead, which means I must have been *alive*.
And if I was alive, then I must have *been* someone, so I...I guess I'd like to know *who*.
We don't even know where to begin, but...
...What better way than to strap on your lute and go, right?
Hmm. Yes, that's--that's the bestest way to do it, I suppose.
STARE
Ahem Anyway--*hee*--I don't have all night, so you better follow me before I change my mind.
Oh, thank you! Thank you! Lead the way, Ziggly-burger--
--*Just* call me Ziggy.
ZIGGY!

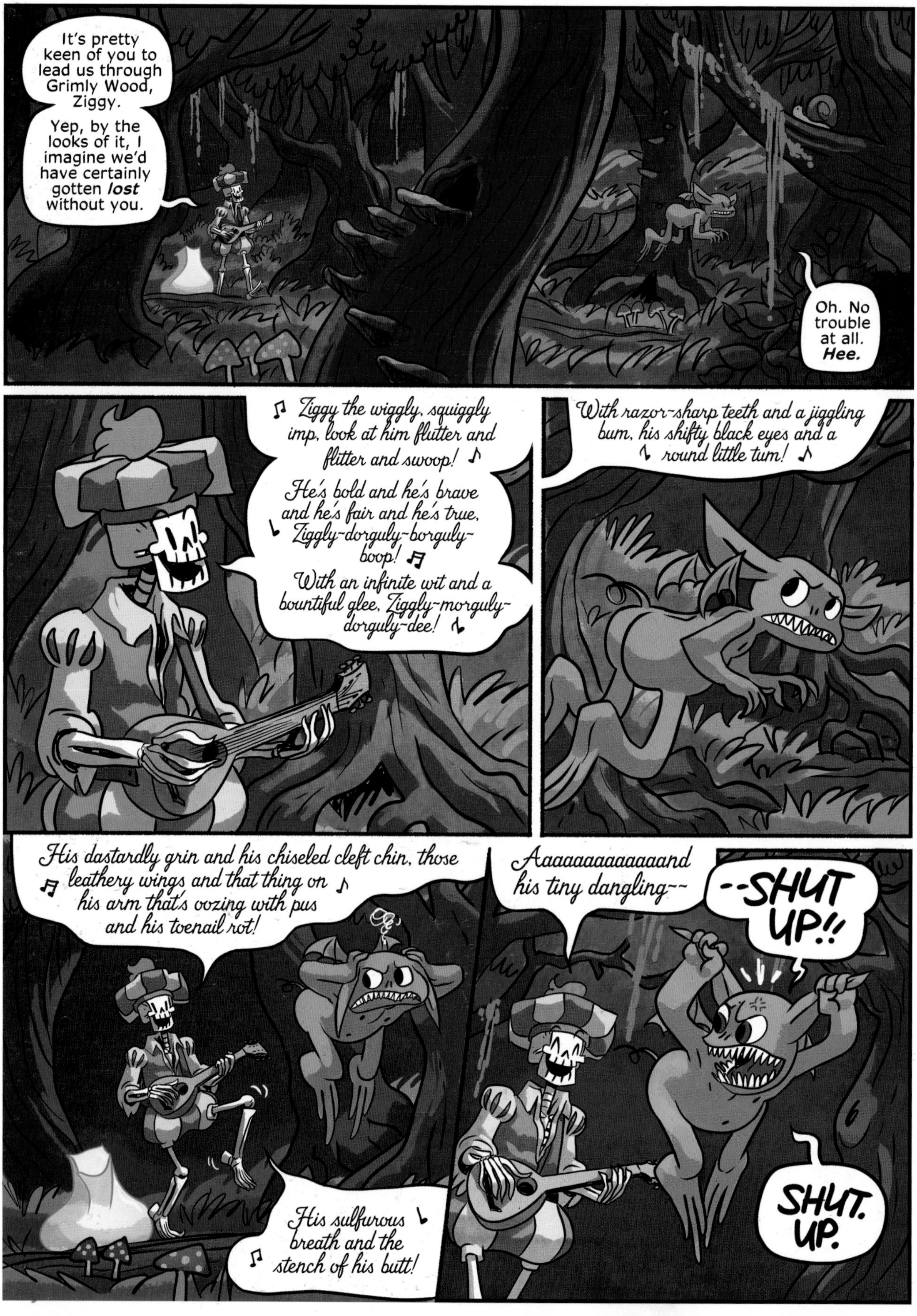
It's pretty keen of you to lead us through Grimly Wood, Ziggy.
Yep, by the looks of it, I imagine we'd have certainly gotten ***lost*** without you.
Oh. No trouble at all. ***Hee.***
♫ Ziggy the wiggly, squiggly imp, look at him flutter and flitter and swoop! ♪
He's bold and he's brave and he's fair and he's true, Ziggly-dorguly-borguly-boop! ♫
With an infinite wit and a bountiful glee, Ziggly-morguly-dorguly-dee! ♪
With razor-sharp teeth and a jiggling bum, his shifty black eyes and a round little tum! ♪
♫ His dastardly grin and his chiseled cleft chin, those leathery wings and that thing on his arm that's oozing with pus and his toenail rot! ♪
♫ His sulfurous breath and the stench of his butt! ♪
Aaaaaaaaaaaaand his tiny dangling--
--SHUT UP!!
SHUT. UP.

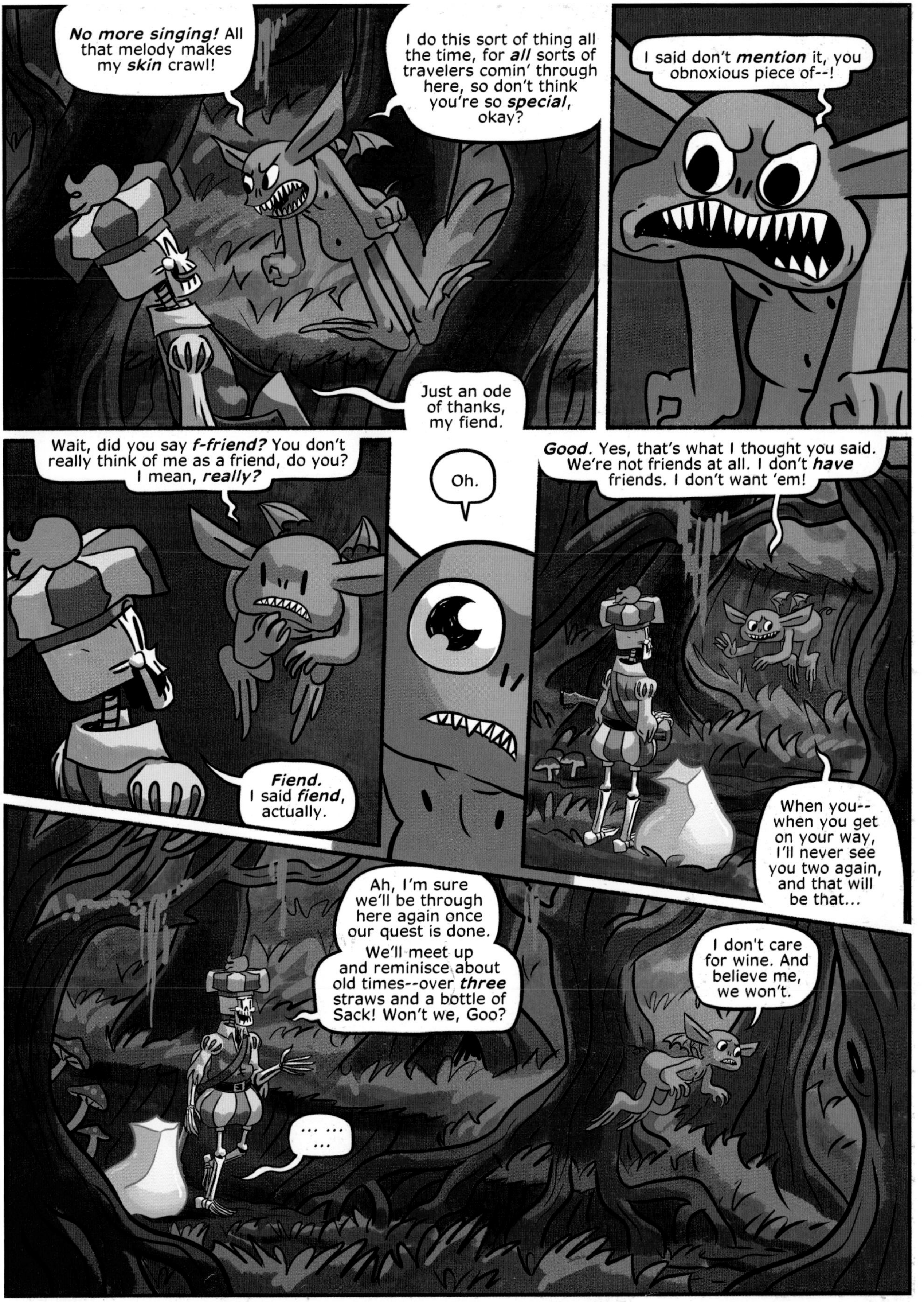
No more singing! All that melody makes my skin crawl!
I do this sort of thing all the time, for all sorts of travelers comin' through here, so don't think you're so special, okay?
Just an ode of thanks, my fiend.
I said don't mention it, you obnoxious piece of--!
Wait, did you say f-friend? You don't really think of me as a friend, do you? I mean, really?
Fiend. I said fiend, actually.
Oh.
Good. Yes, that's what I thought you said. We're not friends at all. I don't have friends. I don't want 'em!
When you-- when you get on your way, I'll never see you two again, and that will be that...
Ah, I'm sure we'll be through here again once our quest is done.
We'll meet up and reminisce about old times--over three straws and a bottle of Sack! Won't we, Goo?
... ...
I don't care for wine. And believe me, we won't.

Chapter 7

Castle Lake

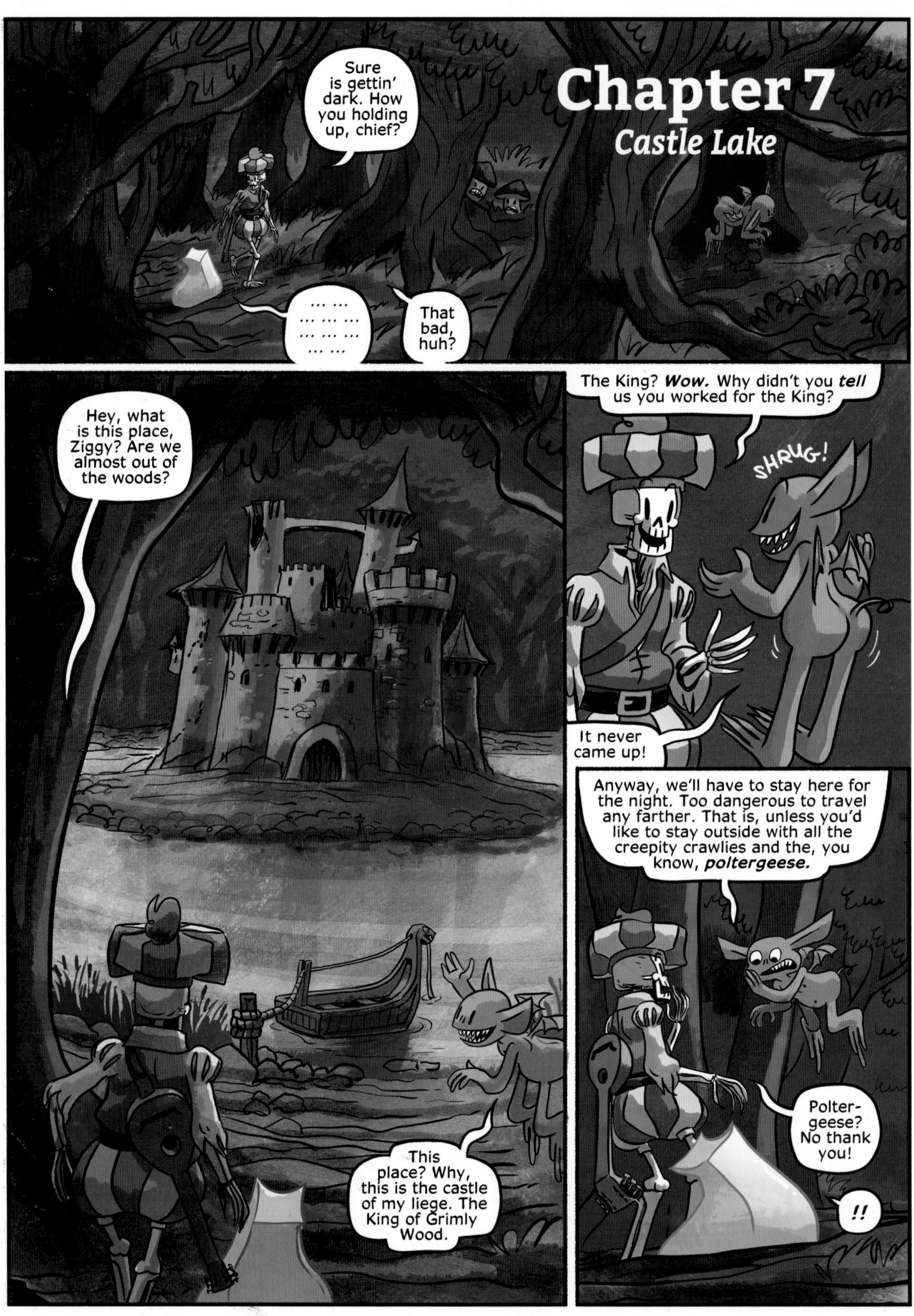

Sure is gettin' dark. How you holding up, chief?
... ...
That bad, huh?
Hey, what is this place, Ziggy? Are we almost out of the woods?
This place? Why, this is the castle of my liege. The King of Grimly Wood.
The King? ***Wow.*** Why didn't you ***tell*** us you worked for the King?
SHRUG!
It never came up!
Anyway, we'll have to stay here for the night. Too dangerous to travel any farther. That is, unless you'd like to stay outside with all the creepity crawlies and the, you know, ***poltergeese.***
Polter-geese? No thank you!
!!

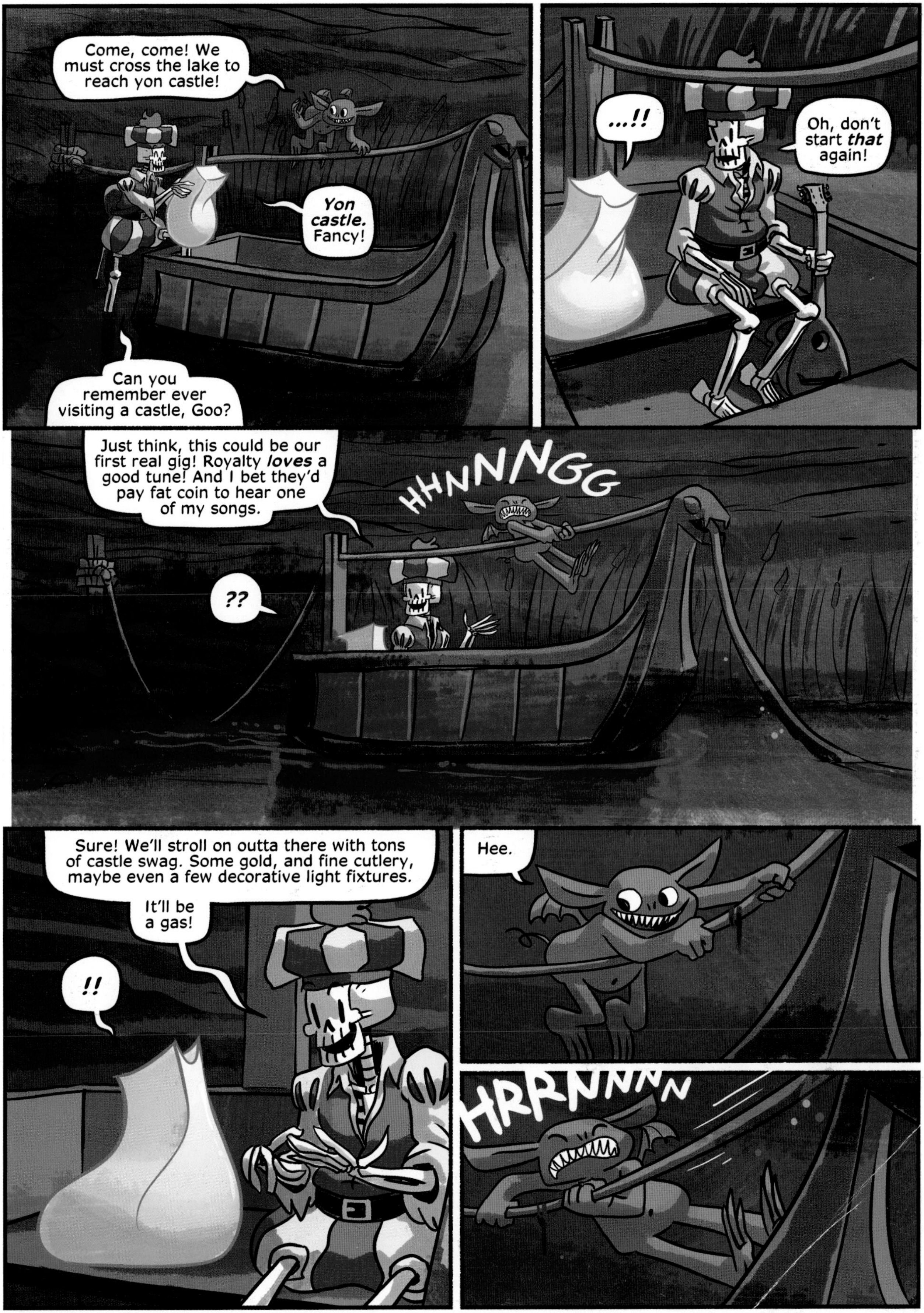
Come, come! We must cross the lake to reach yon castle!
Yon castle. Fancy!
Can you remember ever visiting a castle, Goo?
...!!
Oh, don't start that again!
Just think, this could be our first real gig! Royalty loves a good tune! And I bet they'd pay fat coin to hear one of my songs.
HHNNNGG
??
Sure! We'll stroll on outta there with tons of castle swag. Some gold, and fine cutlery, maybe even a few decorative light fixtures.
It'll be a gas!
!!
Hee.
HRRNNNN

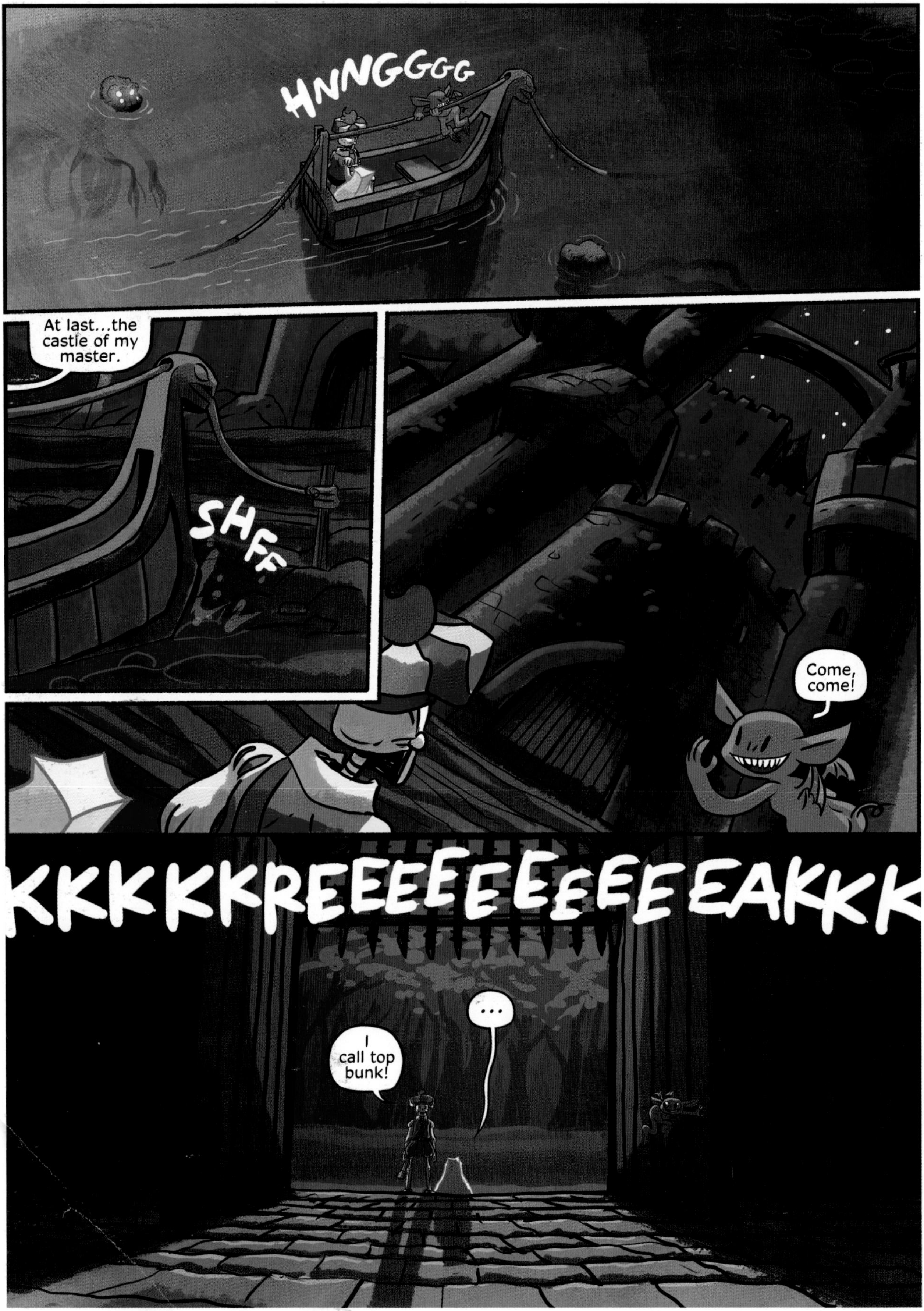
HNNGGGG
At last...the castle of my master.
SHFF
Come, come!
KKKKKREEEEEEEEEEEAKKK
I call top bunk!
...

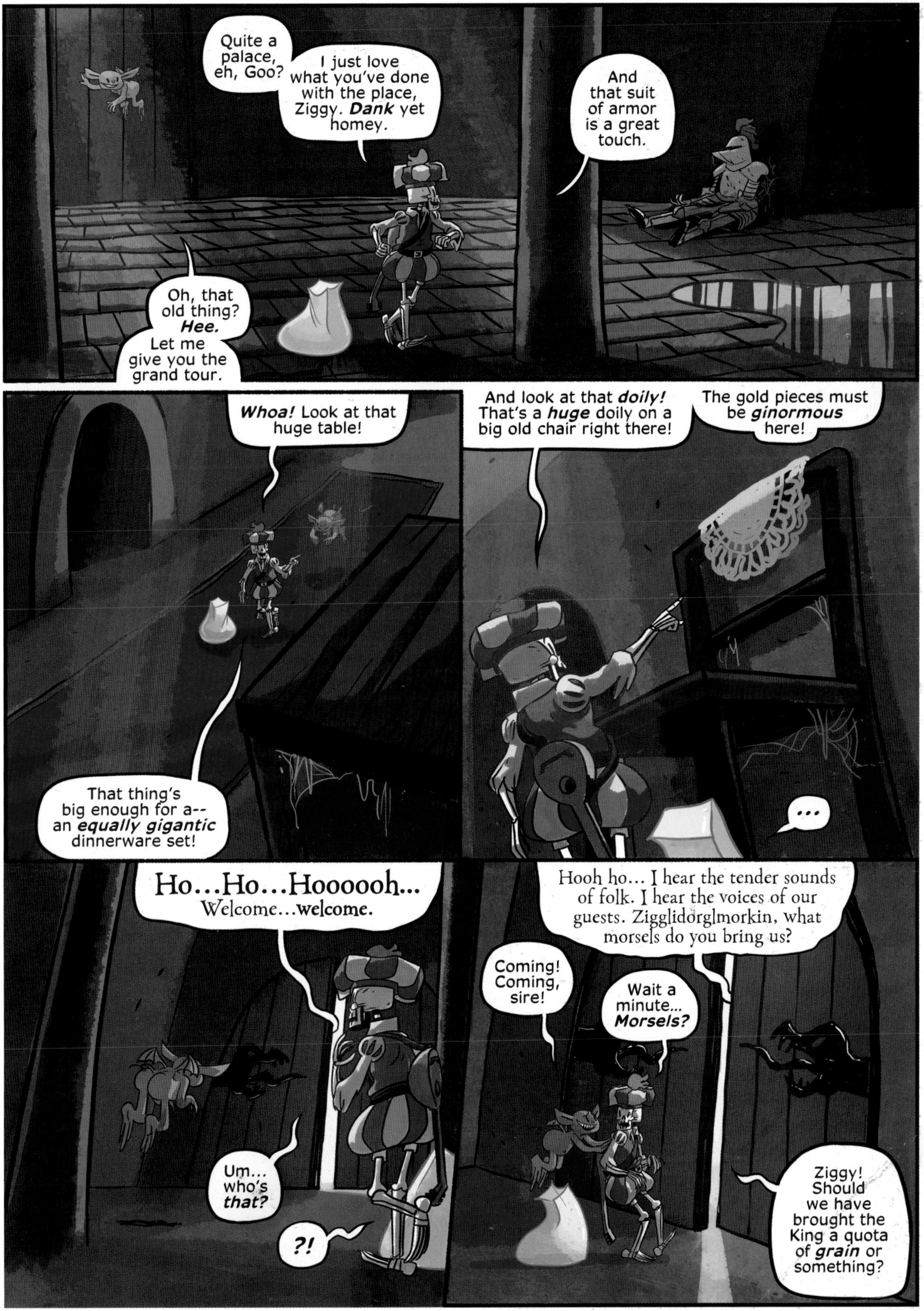
Quite a palace, eh, Goo?
I just love what you've done with the place, Ziggy. **Dank** yet homey.
Oh, that old thing? **Hee.**
Let me give you the grand tour.
And that suit of armor is a great touch.
Whoa! Look at that huge table!
That thing's big enough for a-- an **equally gigantic** dinnerware set!
And look at that **doily!** That's a **huge** doily on a big old chair right there!
The gold pieces must be **ginormous** here!
...
Ho...Ho...Hoooooh...
Welcome...**welcome.**
Um... who's **that?**
?!
Hooh ho... I hear the tender sounds of folk. I hear the voices of our guests. Zigglidorglmorkin, what morsels do you bring us?
Coming! Coming, sire!
Wait a minute... **Morsels?**
Ziggy! Should we have brought the King a quota of **grain** or something?

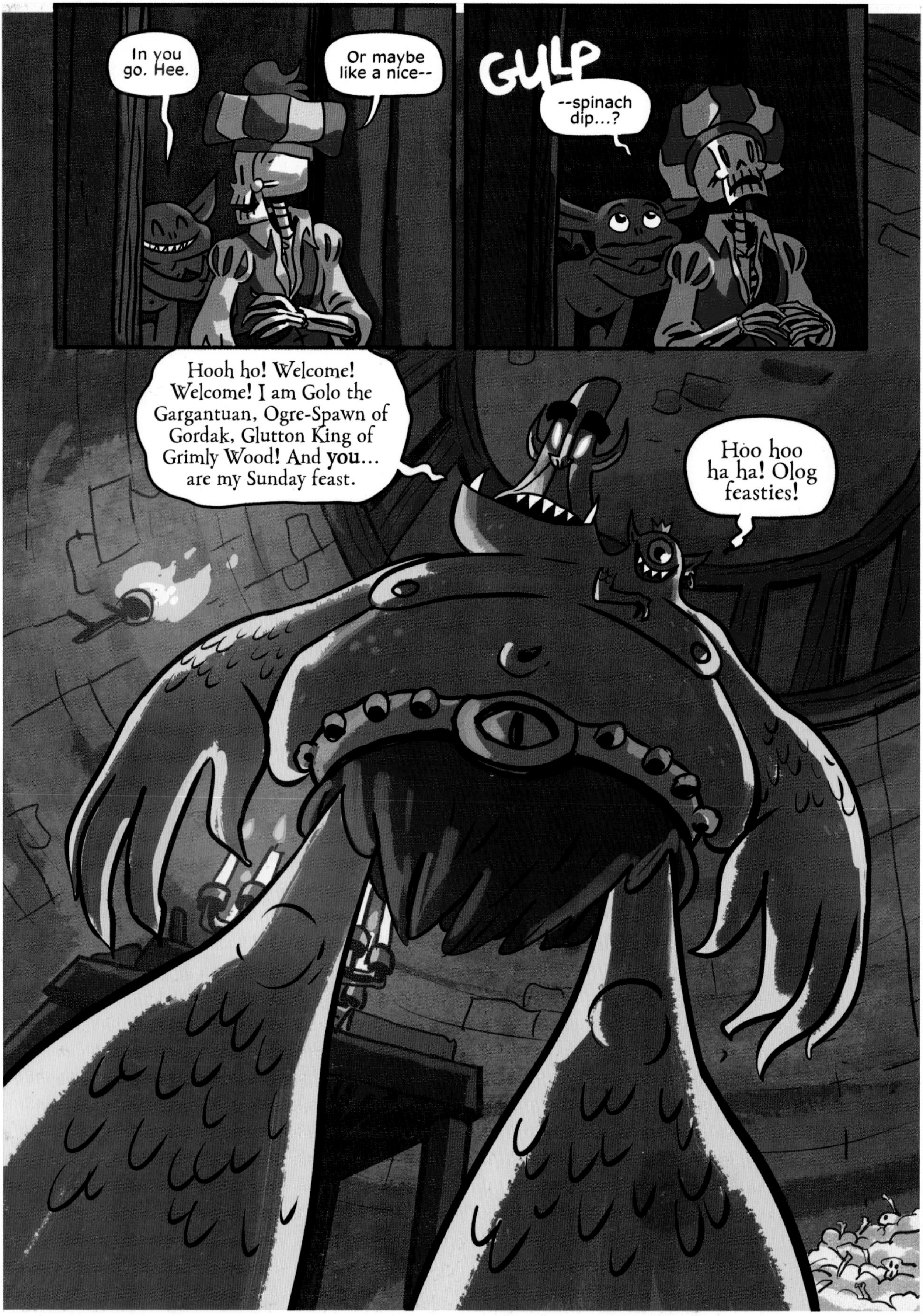
In you go. Hee.
Or maybe like a nice--
GULP
--spinach dip...?
Hooh ho! Welcome! Welcome! I am Golo the Gargantuan, Ogre-Spawn of Gordak, Glutton King of Grimly Wood! And you... are my Sunday feast.
Hoo hoo ha ha! Olog feasties!

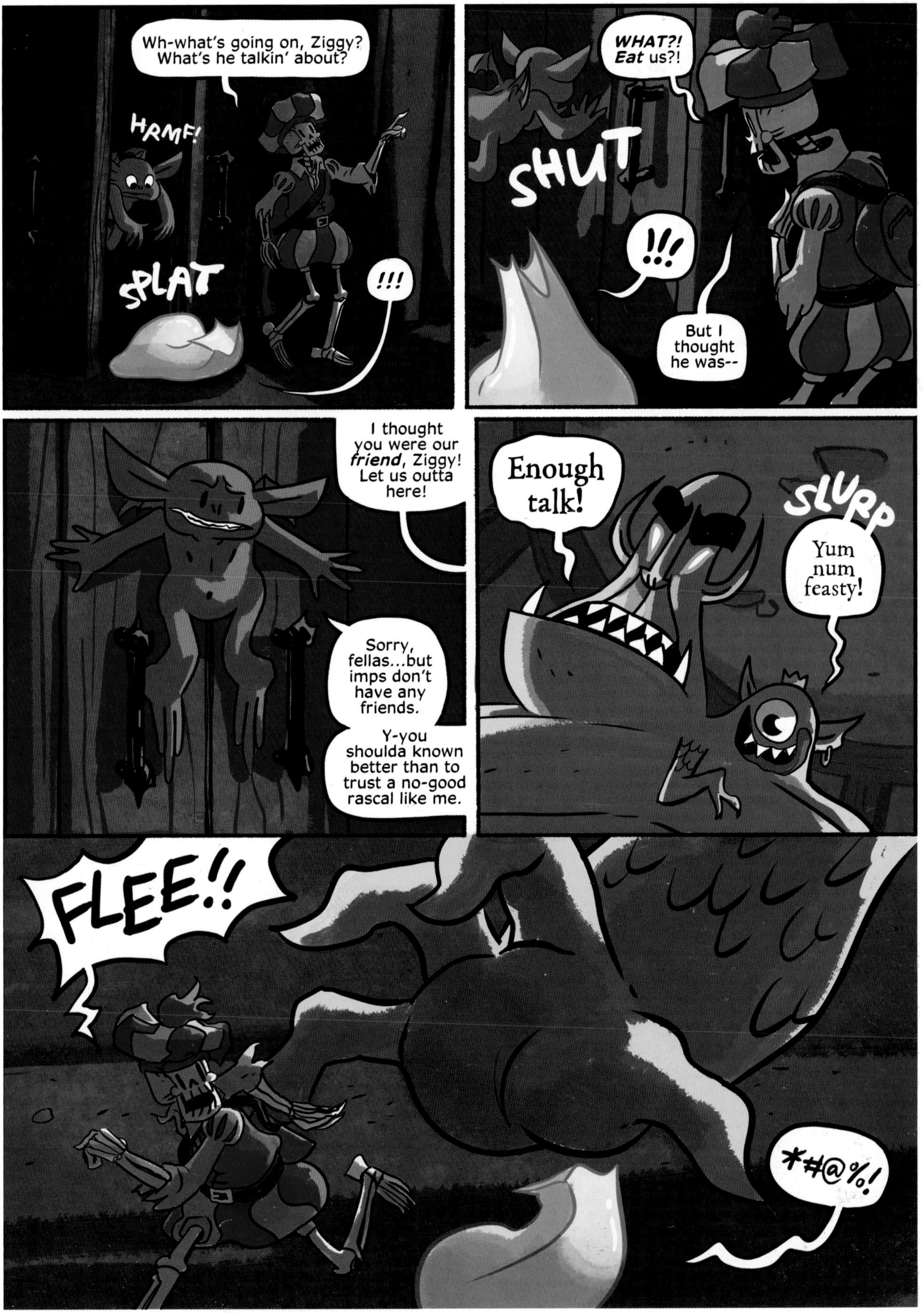

Wh-what's going on, Ziggy? What's he talkin' about?
HRMF!
SPLAT
!!!
WHAT?! Eat us?!
SHUT
!!!
But I thought he was--
I thought you were our *friend*, Ziggy! Let us outta here!
Sorry, fellas...but imps don't have any friends.
Y-you shoulda known better than to trust a no-good rascal like me.
Enough talk!
SLURP
Yum num feasty!
FLEE!!
*#@%!

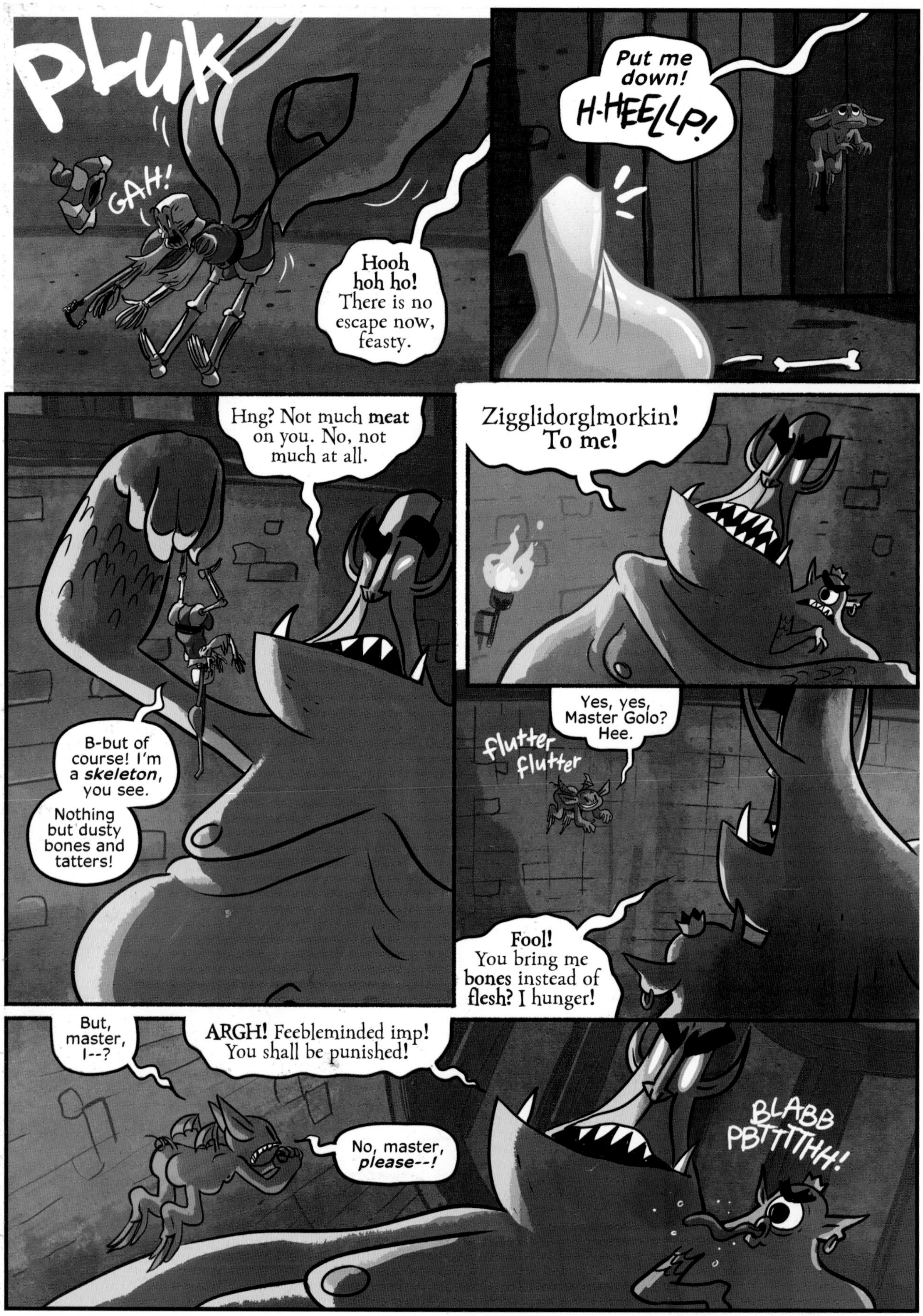
PLUK
GAH!
Hooh hoh ho! There is no escape now, feasty.
Put me down! H-HEELLP!
Hng? Not much meat on you. No, not much at all.
B-but of course! I'm a *skeleton*, you see.
Nothing but dusty bones and tatters!
Zigglidorglmorkin! To me!
flutter flutter
Yes, yes, Master Golo? Hee.
Fool! You bring me bones instead of flesh? I hunger!
But, master, I--?
ARGH! Feebleminded imp! You shall be punished!
No, master, *please--!*
BLABB PBTTTTHH!

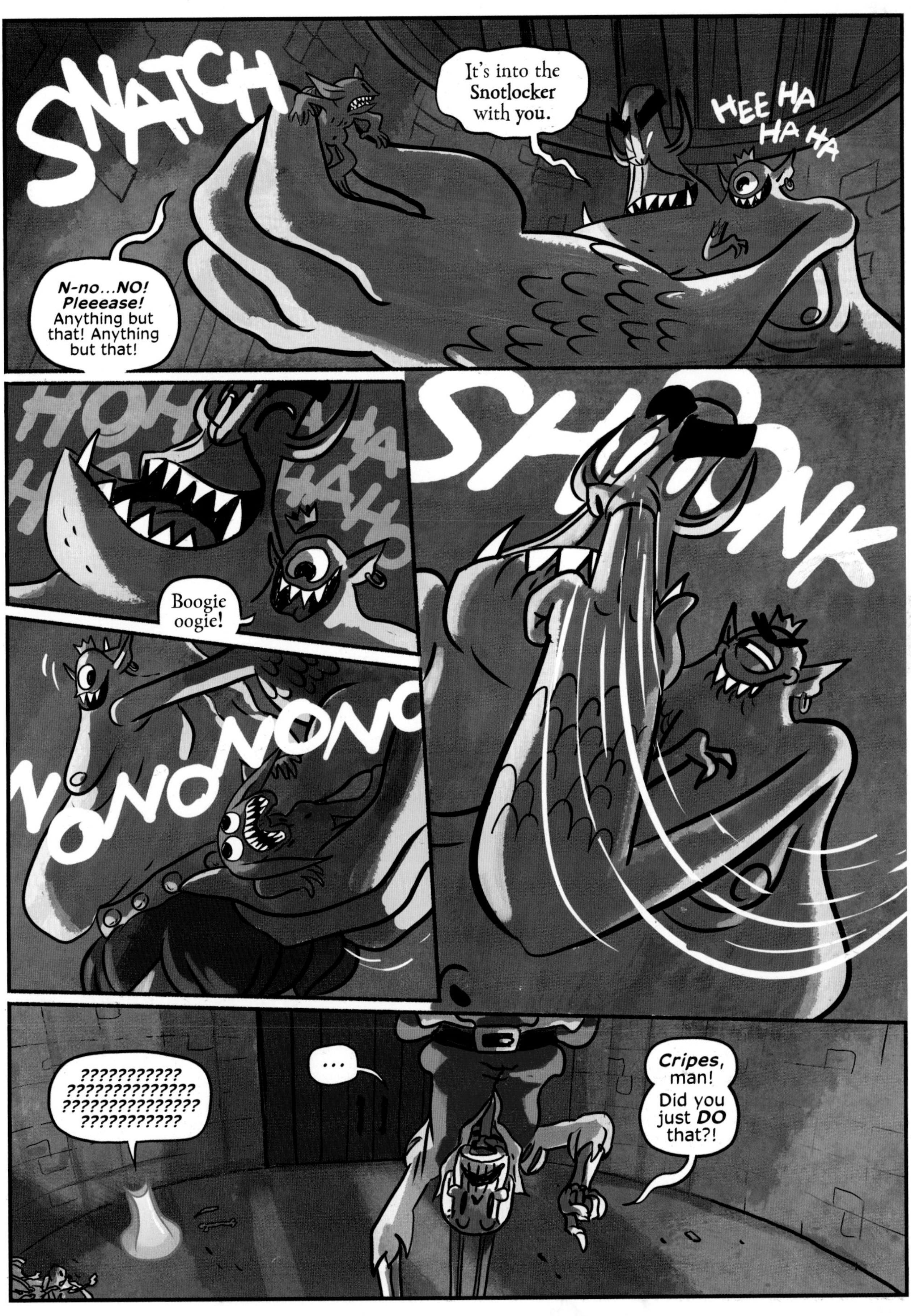
SNATCH
It's into the Snotlocker with you.
HEE HA HA HA HA
N-no...NO! Pleeease! Anything but that! Anything but that!
HOHOHAHAHAHO
Boogie oogie!
SHLONK
NONONONONO
???????????
??????????????
???????????????
???????????
...
Cripes, man! Did you just DO that?!

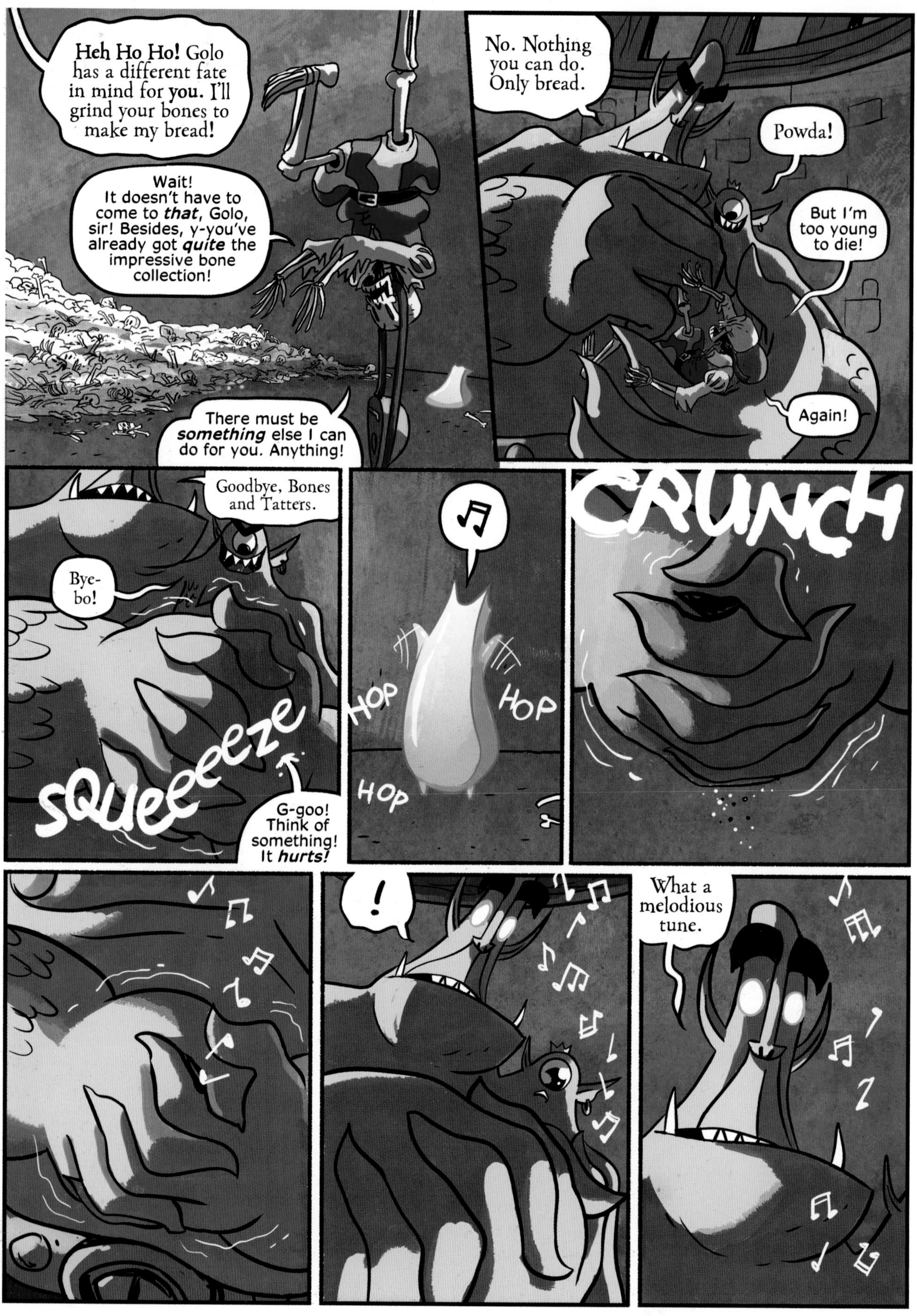

Heh Ho Ho! Golo has a different fate in mind for you. I'll grind your bones to make my bread!
Wait! It doesn't have to come to *that*, Golo, sir! Besides, y-you've already got *quite* the impressive bone collection!
There must be *something* else I can do for you. Anything!
No. Nothing you can do. Only bread.
Powda!
But I'm too young to die!
Again!
Goodbye, Bones and Tatters.
Bye-bo!
SQUEEEEZE
G-goo! Think of something! It *hurts!*
♫
HOP
HOP
HOP
CRUNCH
!
What a melodious tune.

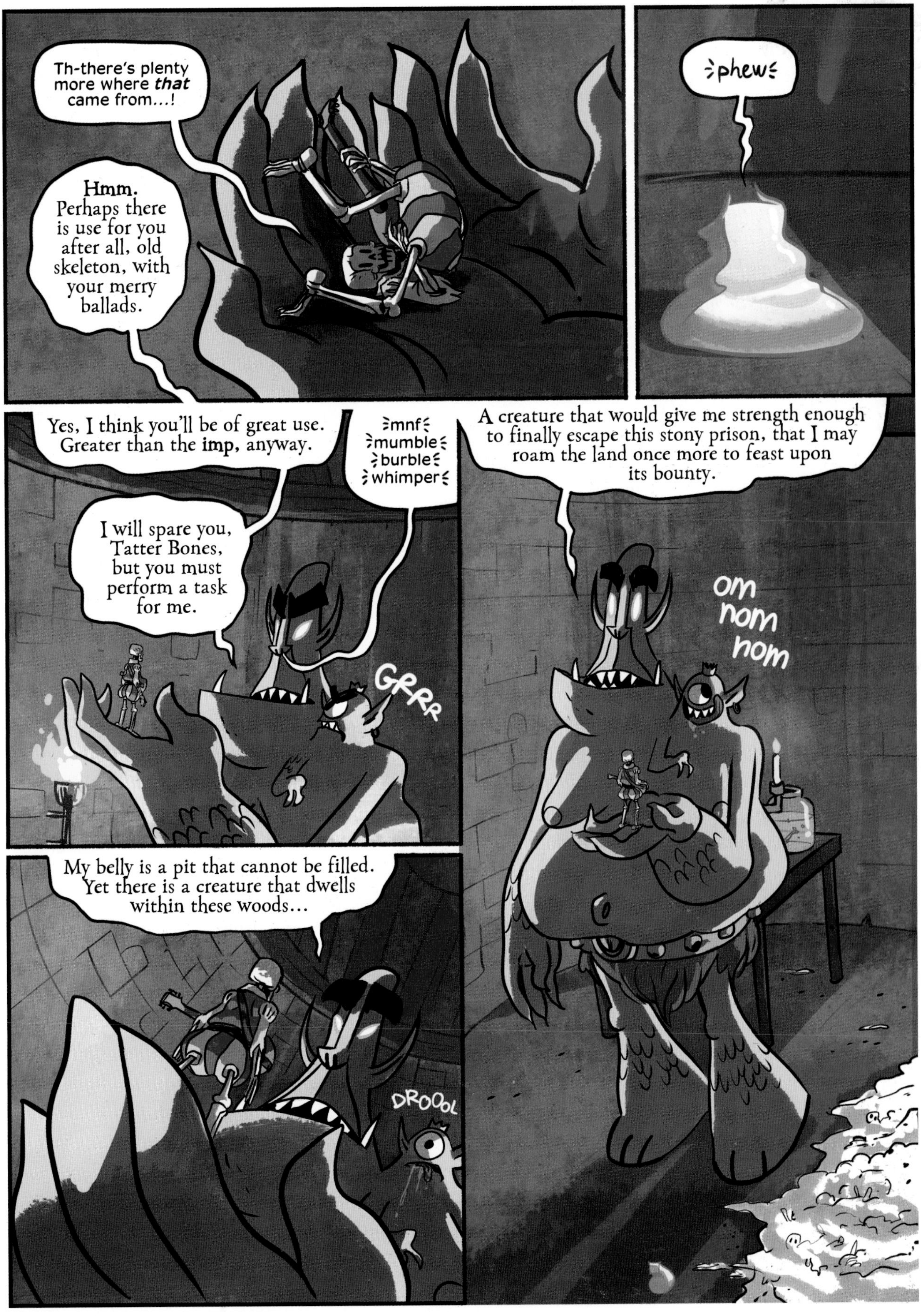
Th-there's plenty more where *that* came from...!
Hmm. Perhaps there is use for you after all, old skeleton, with your merry ballads.
phew
Yes, I think you'll be of great use. Greater than the **imp**, anyway.
mnf mumble burble whimper
I will spare you, Tatter Bones, but you must perform a task for me.
GRRR
My belly is a pit that cannot be filled. Yet there is a creature that dwells within these woods...
DROOOL
A creature that would give me strength enough to finally escape this stony prison, that I may roam the land once more to feast upon its bounty.
om nom nom

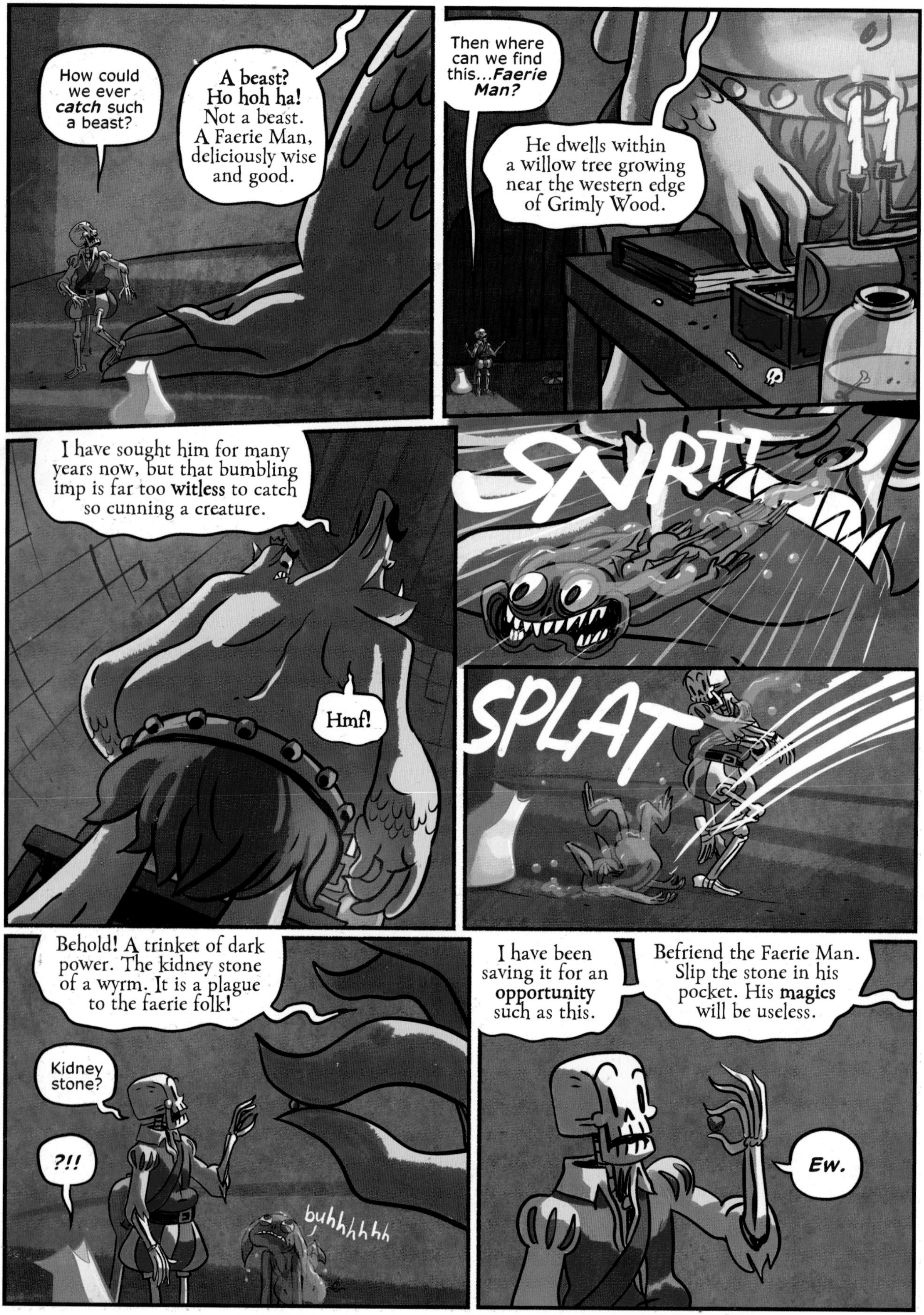
How could we ever *catch* such a beast?
A beast? Ho hoh ha! Not a beast. A Faerie Man, deliciously wise and good.
Then where can we find this...*Faerie Man?*
He dwells within a willow tree growing near the western edge of Grimly Wood.
I have sought him for many years now, but that bumbling imp is far too **witless** to catch so cunning a creature.
Hmf!
SNRTT
SPLAT
Behold! A trinket of dark power. The kidney stone of a wyrm. It is a plague to the faerie folk!
Kidney stone?
?!!
buhhhhhh
I have been saving it for an **opportunity** such as this.
Befriend the Faerie Man. Slip the stone in his pocket. His **magics** will be useless.
Ew.

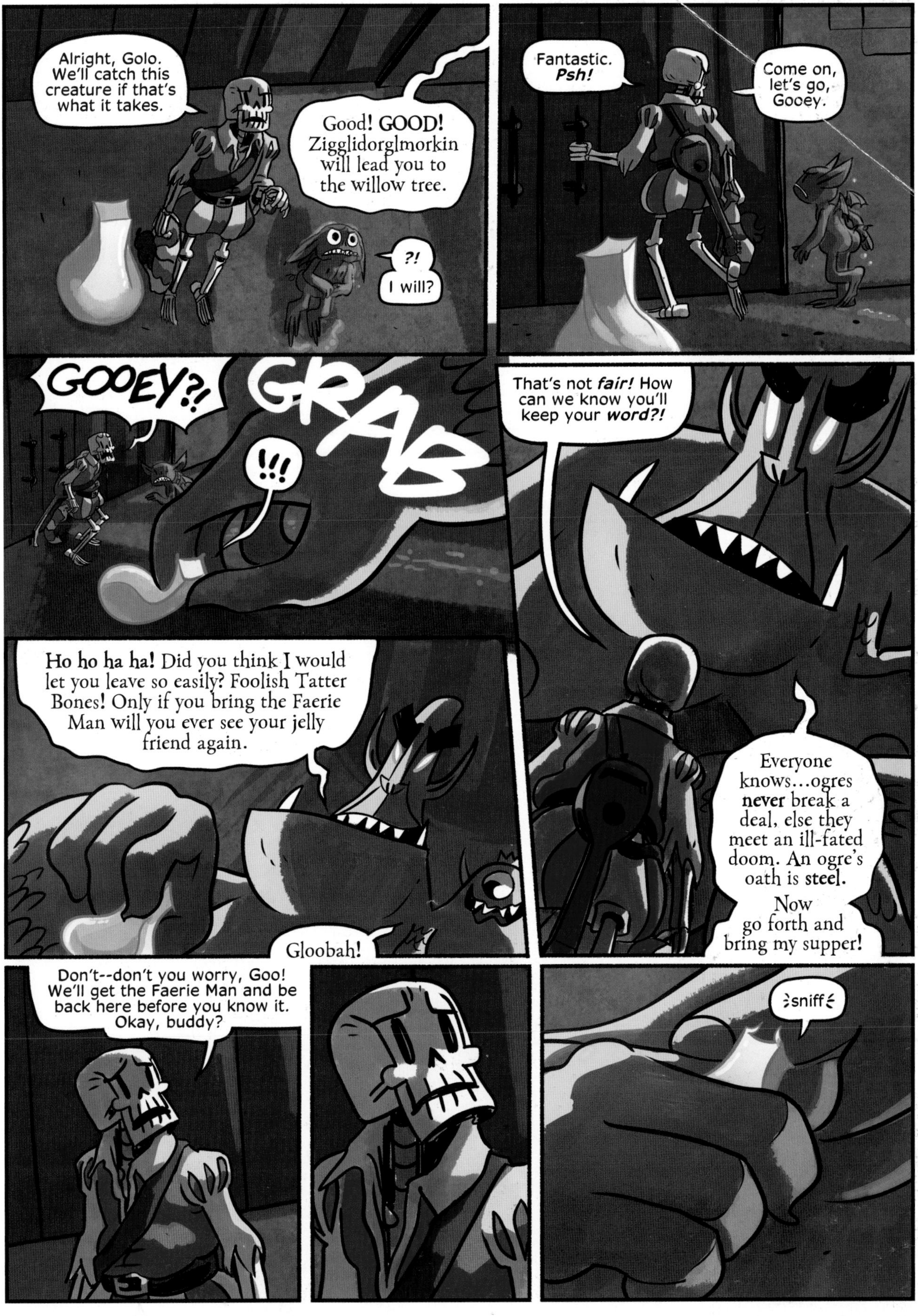

Alright, Golo. We'll catch this creature if that's what it takes.
Good! GOOD! Zigglidorglmorkin will lead you to the willow tree.
?! I will?
Fantastic. *Psh!*
Come on, let's go, Gooey.
GOOEY?!
GRAB
!!!
That's not *fair!* How can we know you'll keep your *word?!*
Ho ho ha ha! Did you think I would let you leave so easily? Foolish Tatter Bones! Only if you bring the Faerie Man will you ever see your jelly friend again.
Gloobah!
Everyone knows...ogres **never** break a deal, else they meet an ill-fated doom. An ogre's oath is **steel.**
Now go forth and bring my supper!
Don't--don't you worry, Goo! We'll get the Faerie Man and be back here before you know it. Okay, buddy?
sniff

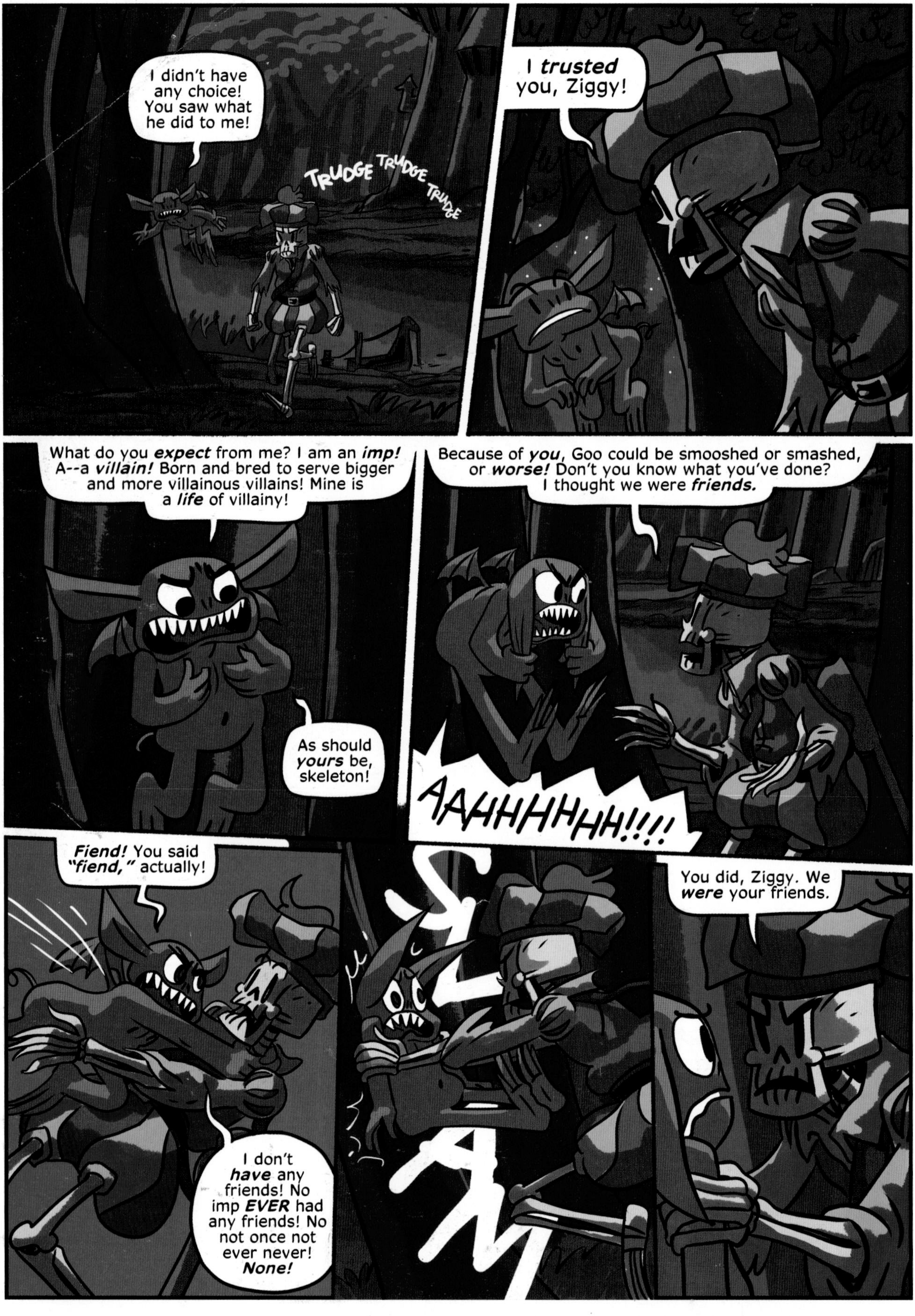
I didn't have any choice! You saw what he did to me!
TRUDGE TRUDGE TRUDGE
I *trusted* you, Ziggy!
What do you *expect* from me? I am an *imp!* A--a *villain!* Born and bred to serve bigger and more villainous villains! Mine is a *life* of villainy!
As should *yours* be, skeleton!
Because of *you*, Goo could be smooshed or smashed, or *worse!* Don't you know what you've done? I thought we were *friends.*
AAHHHHHH!!!!
Fiend! You said *"fiend,"* actually!
I don't *have* any friends! No imp *EVER* had any friends! No not once not ever never! *None!*
SLAM
You did, Ziggy. We *were* your friends.

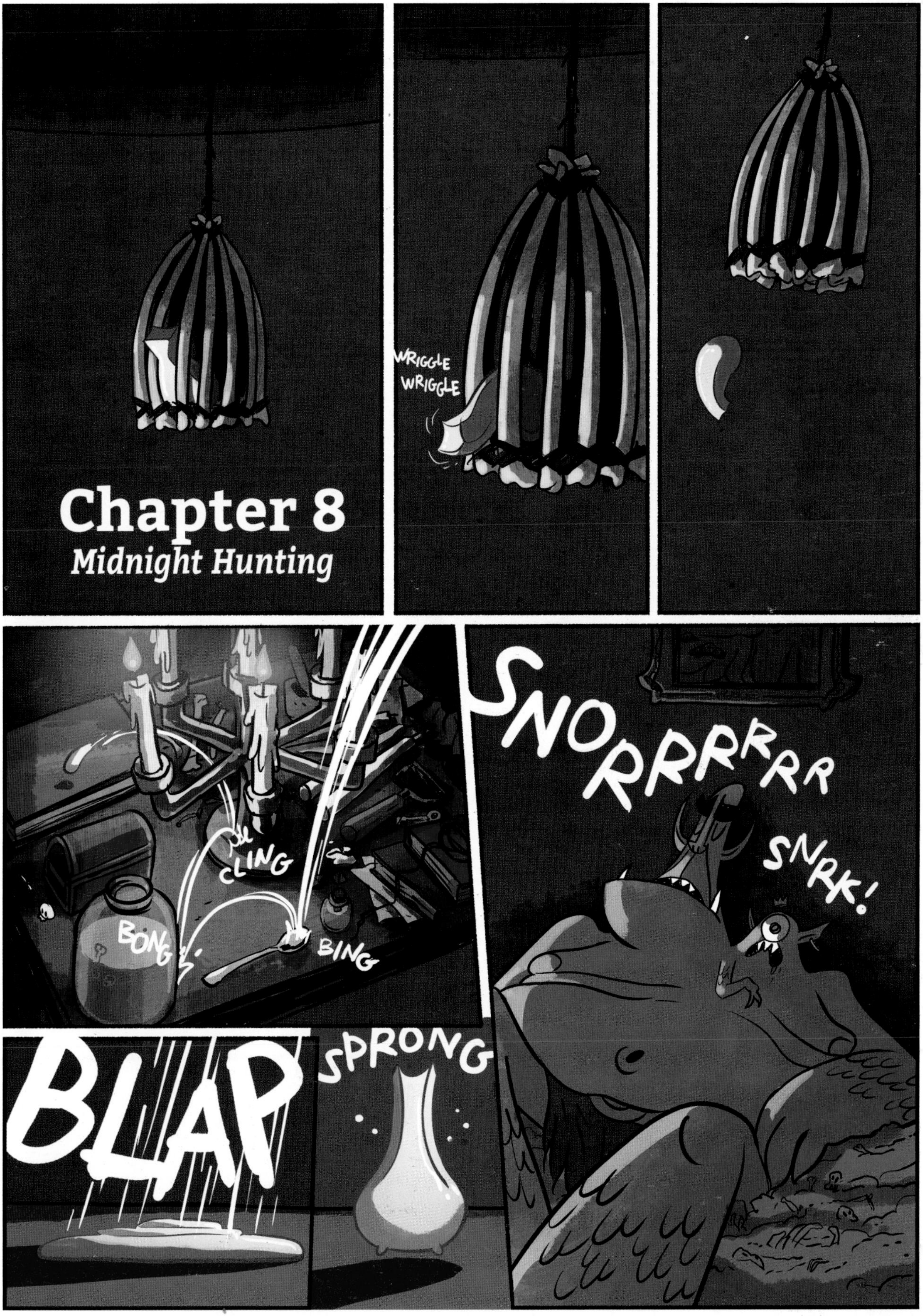

Chapter 8
Midnight Hunting
WRIGGLE
WRIGGLE
CLING
BONG
BING
SNORRRRRR
SNRK!
BLAP
SPRONG

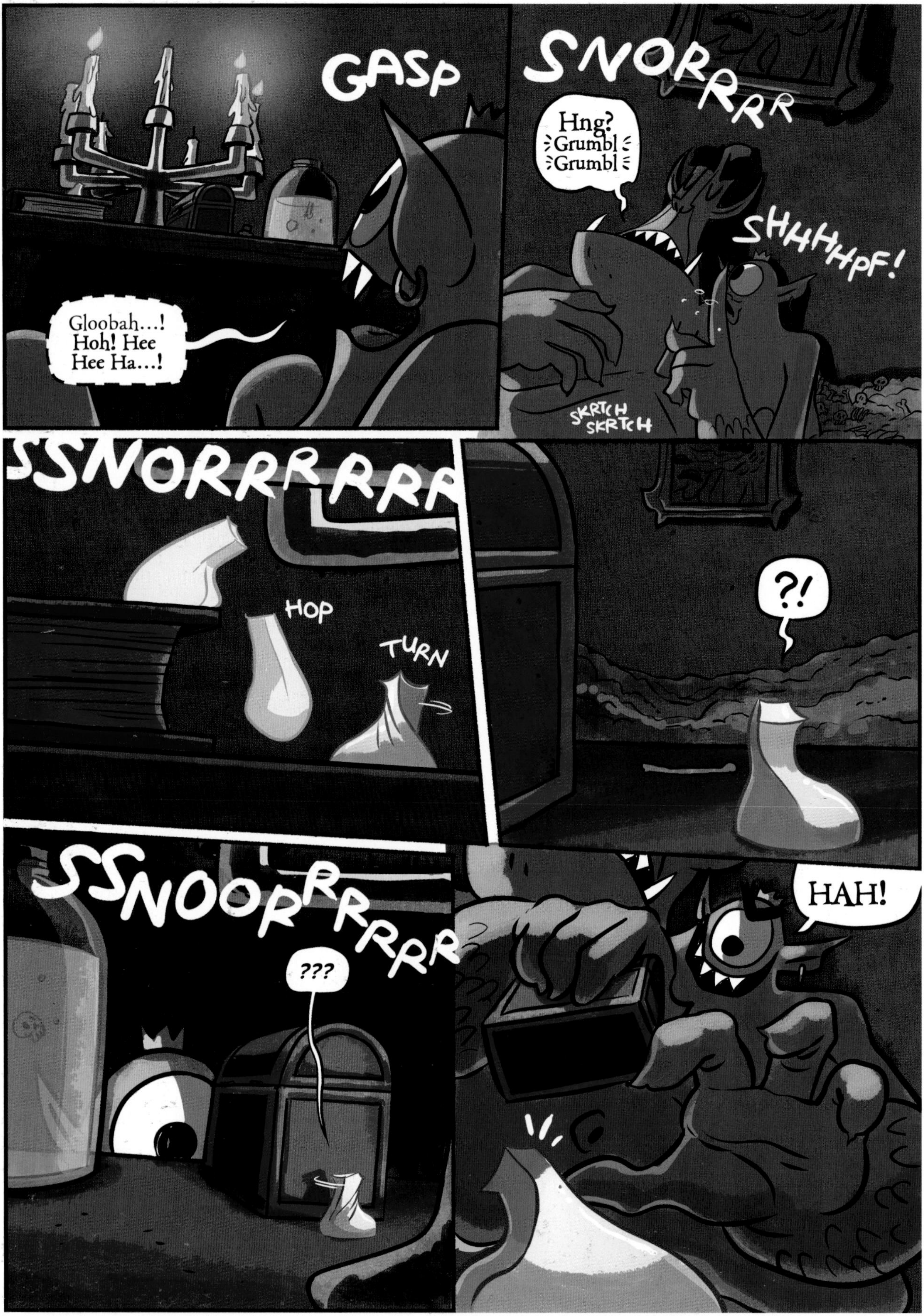
GASP
Gloobah...! Hoh! Hee Hee Ha...!
SNORRRR
Hng? Grumbl Grumbl
SHHHHPF!
SKRTCH SKRTCH
SSNORRRRRR
HOP
TURN
?!
SSNOORRRRRR
???
HAH!

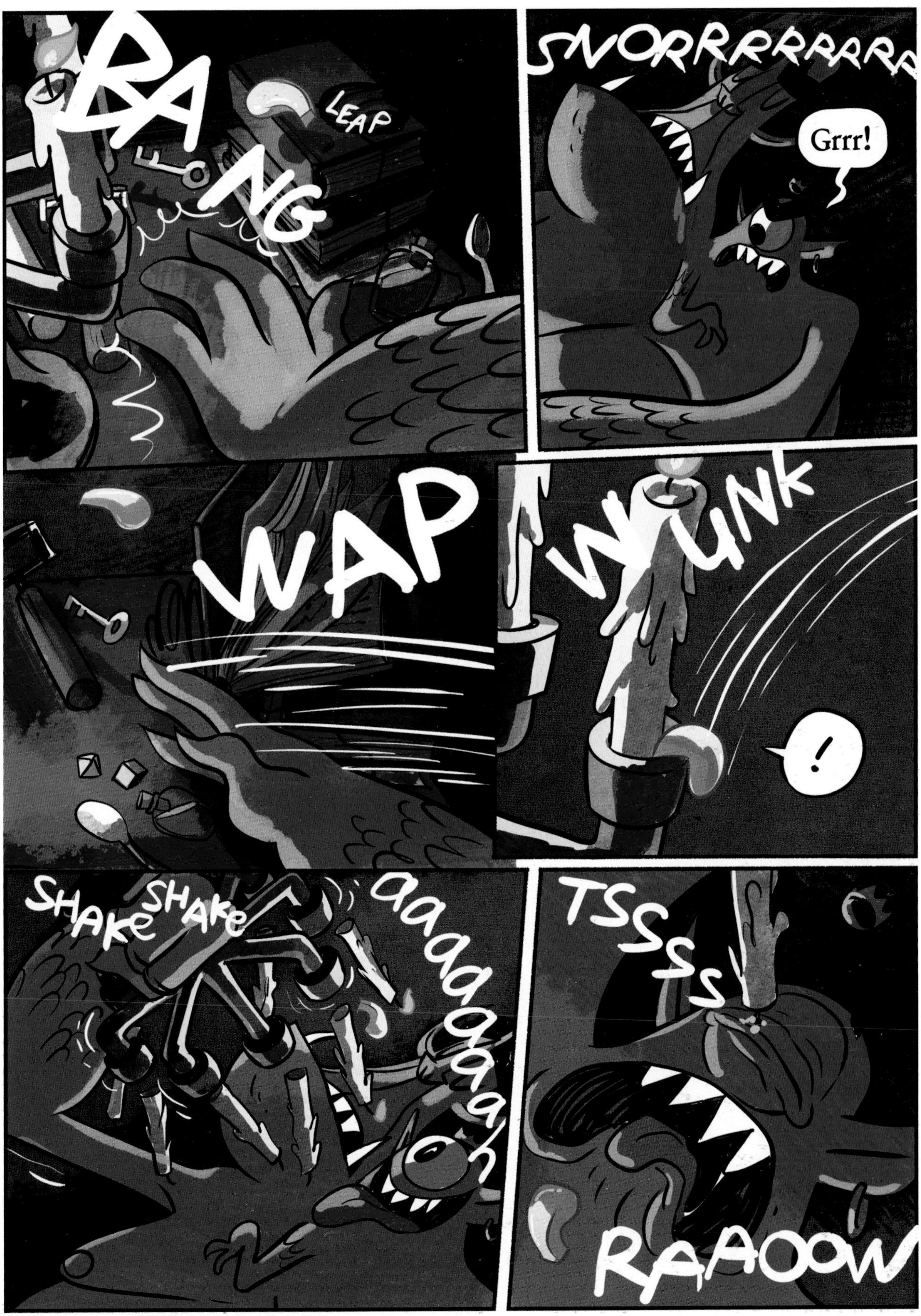
BANG
LEAP
SNORRRRRRRR
Grrr!
WAP
WUNK
!
SHAKE SHAKE
aaaaaaaah
TSSSSS
RAAOOW

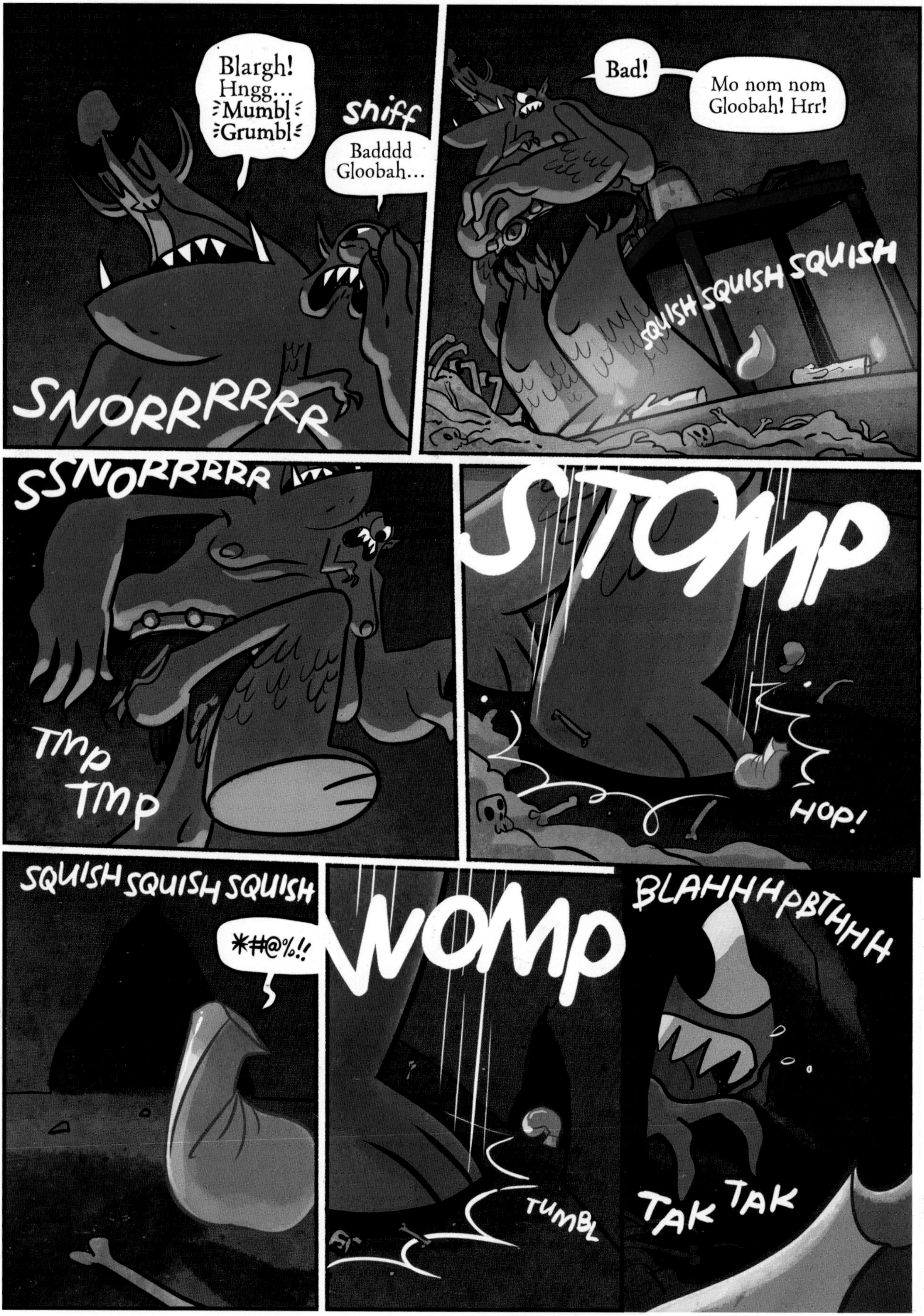
Blargh! Hngg… Mumbl Grumbl
sniff
Badddd Gloobah…
SNORRRRRR
Bad!
Mo nom nom Gloobah! Hrr!
SQUISH SQUISH SQUISH
SSNORRRRRR
TMP TMP
STOMP
HOP!
SQUISH SQUISH SQUISH
*#@%!!
WOMP
TUMBL
BLAHHHPBTHHH
TAK TAK

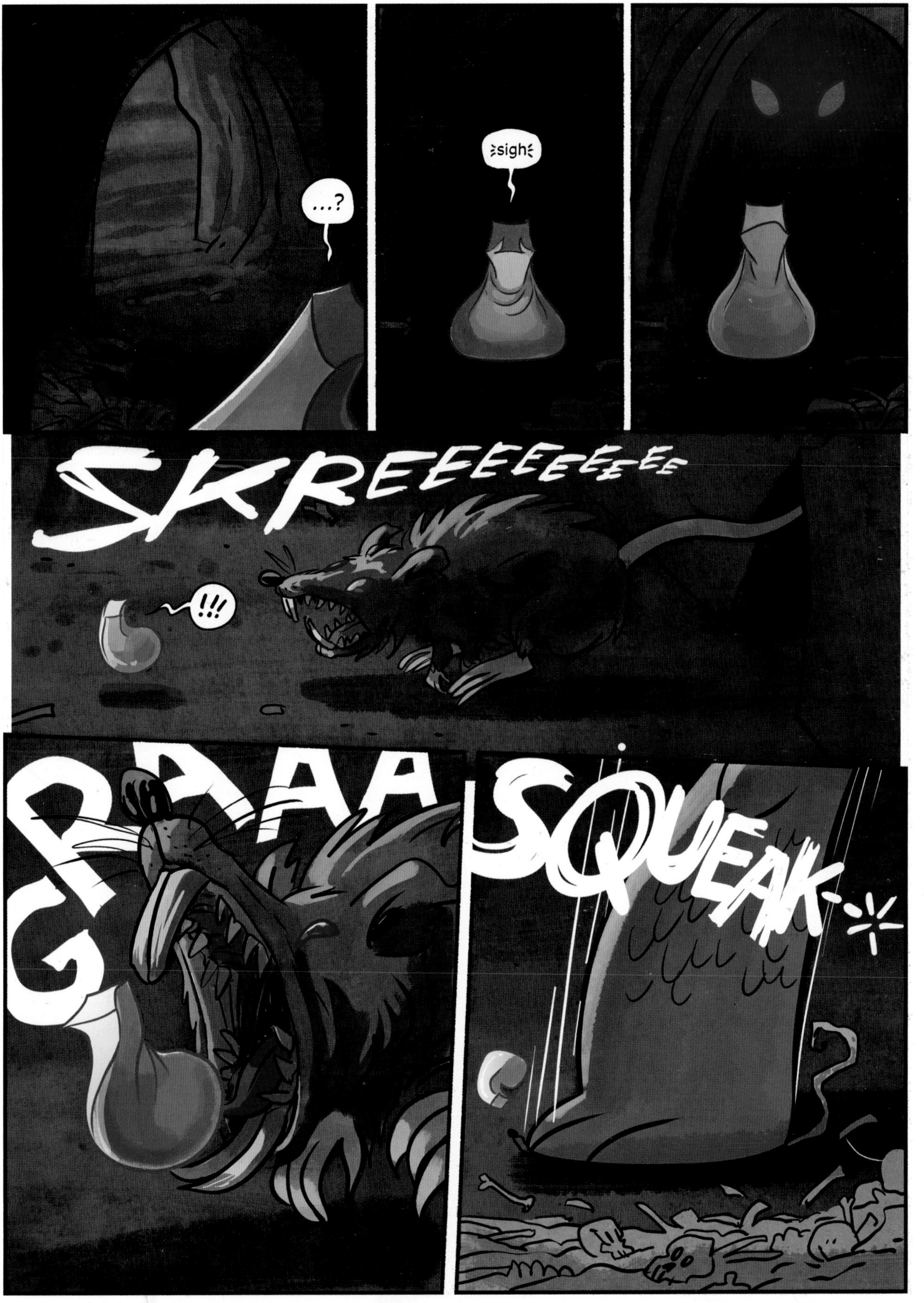
...?
sigh
SKREEEEEEEEEE
!!!
GRAAA
SQUEAK

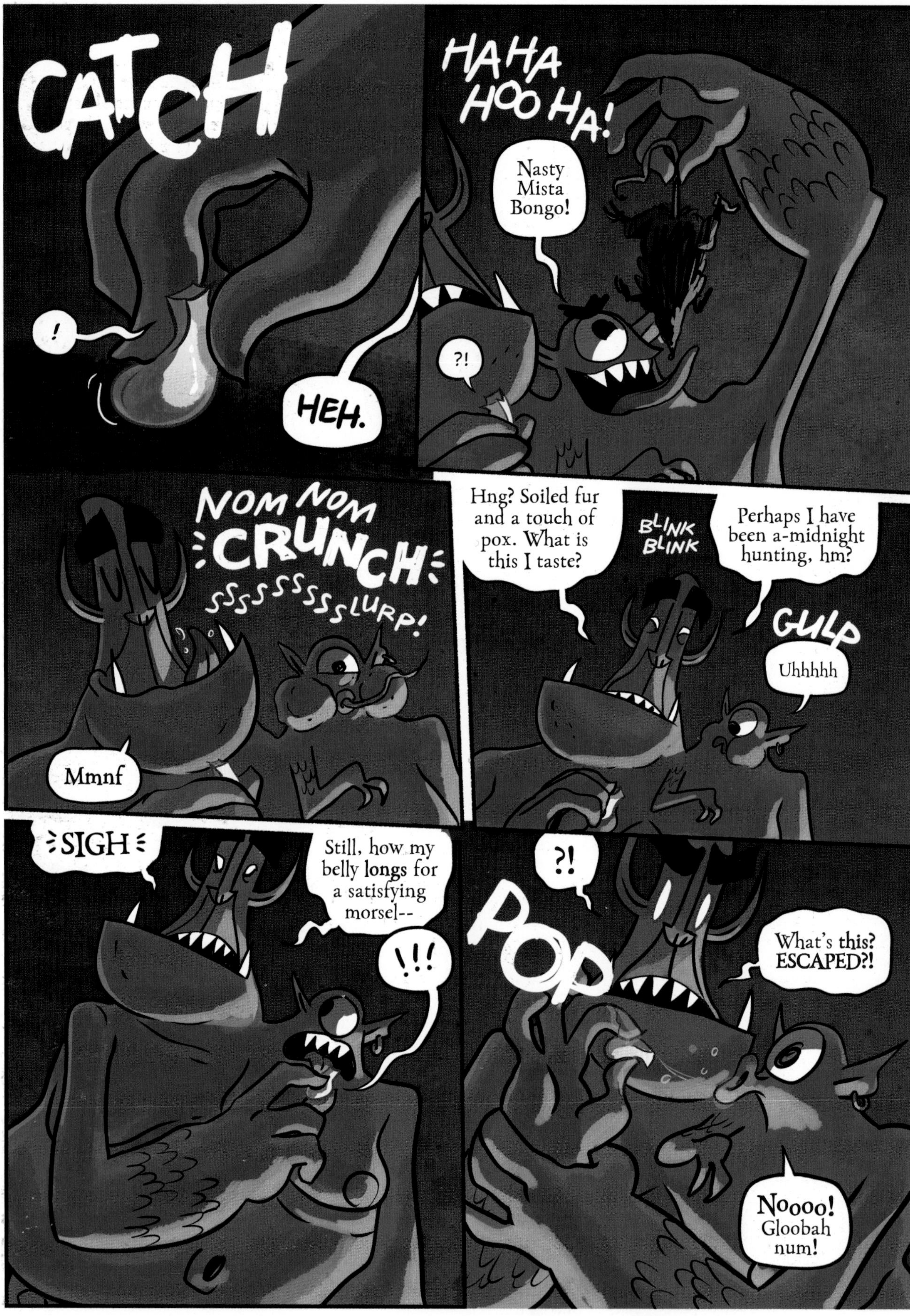
CATCH
!
HEH.
HAHA HOOHA!
Nasty Mista Bongo!
?!
NOM NOM
CRUNCH
SSSSSSSSSLURP!
Mmnf
Hng? Soiled fur and a touch of pox. What is this I taste?
BLINK BLINK
Perhaps I have been a-midnight hunting, hm?
GULP
Uhhhhh
SIGH
Still, how my belly longs for a satisfying morsel--
!!!
?!
POP
What's this? ESCAPED?!
Noooo! Gloobah num!

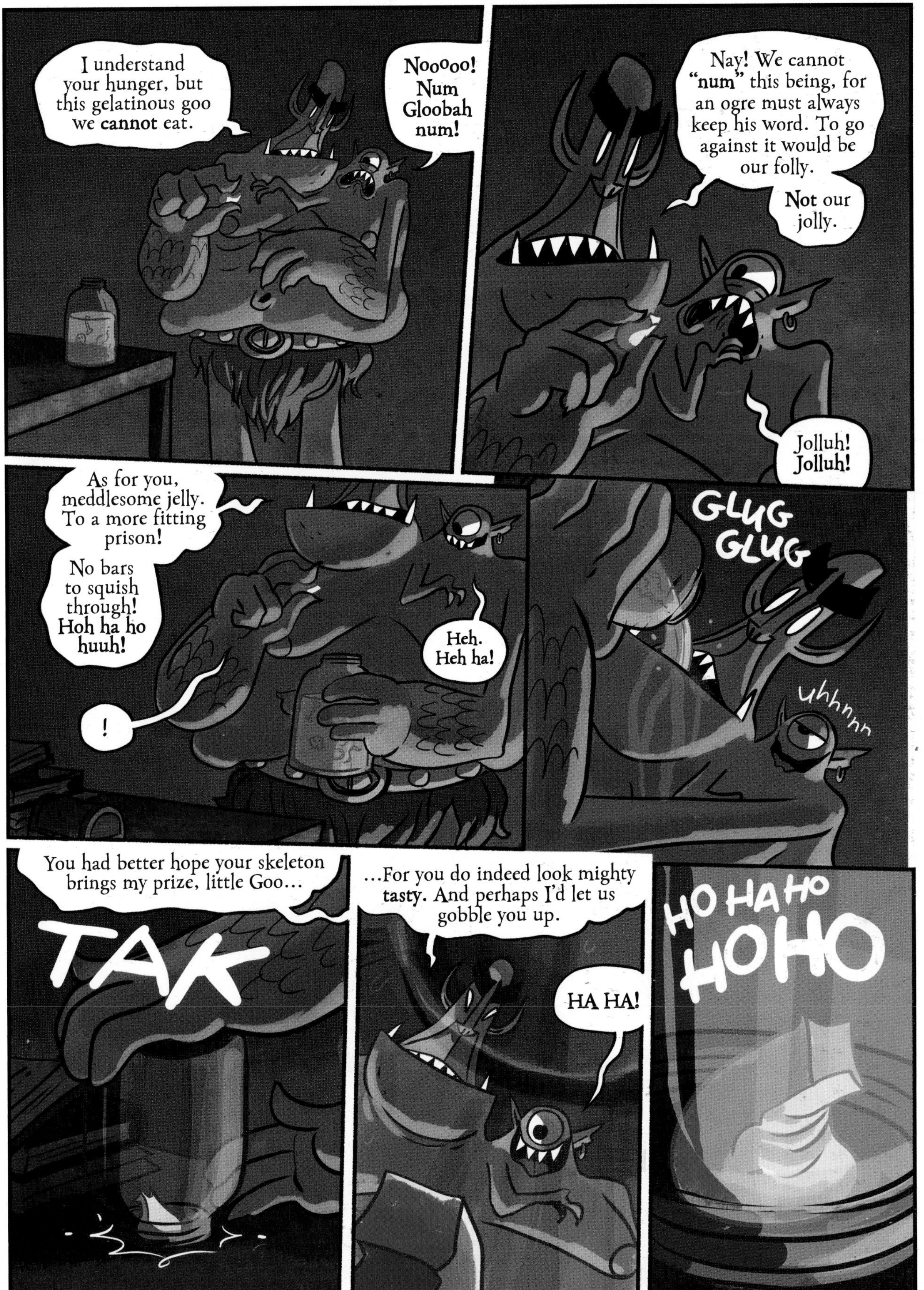

I understand your hunger, but this gelatinous goo we **cannot** eat.
Noooooo! Num Gloobah num!
Nay! We cannot **"num"** this being, for an ogre must always keep his word. To go against it would be our folly.
Not our jolly.
Jolluh! Jolluh!
As for you, meddlesome jelly. To a more fitting prison!
No bars to squish through! **Hoh ha ho huuh!**
Heh. Heh ha!
!
GLUG GLUG
uhhnnn
You had better hope your skeleton brings my prize, little Goo...
TAK
...For you do indeed look mighty **tasty.** And perhaps I'd let us gobble you up.
HA HA!
HO HA HO
HOHO

Chapter 9
Songweaver

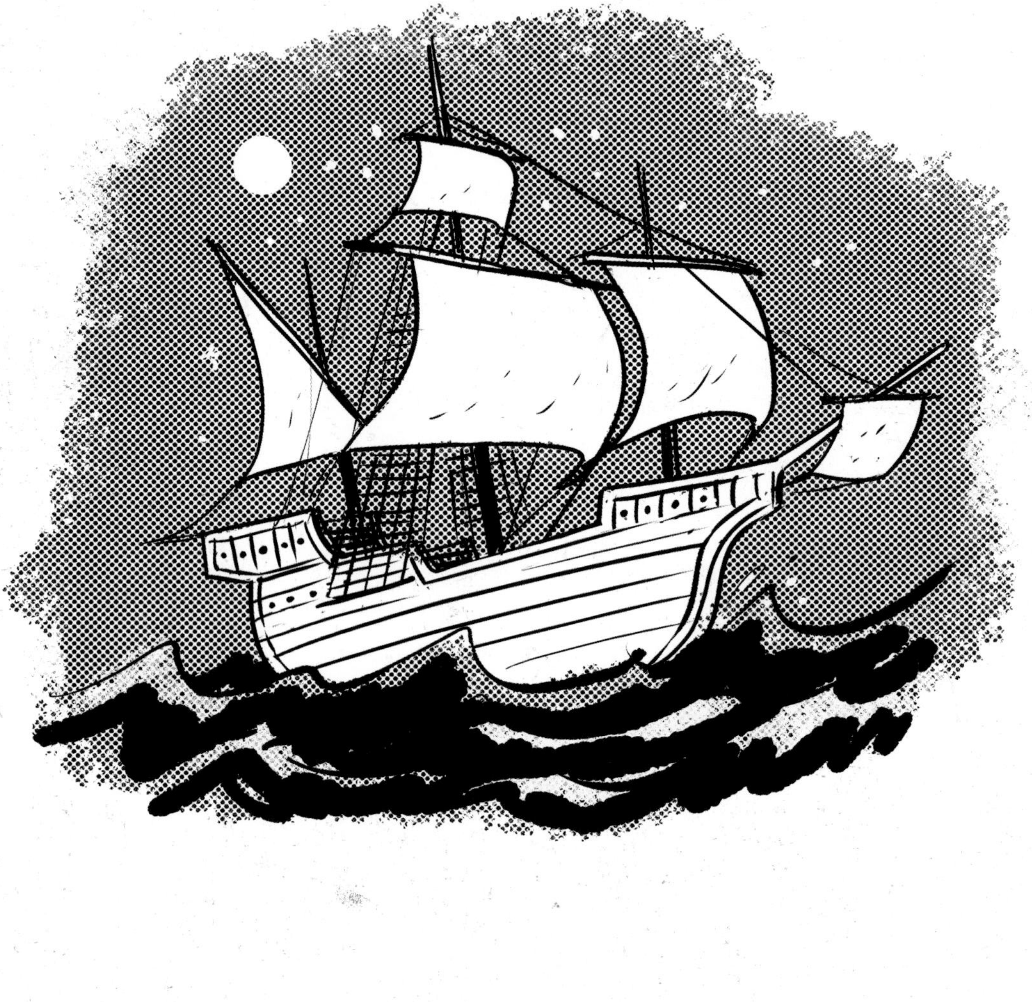

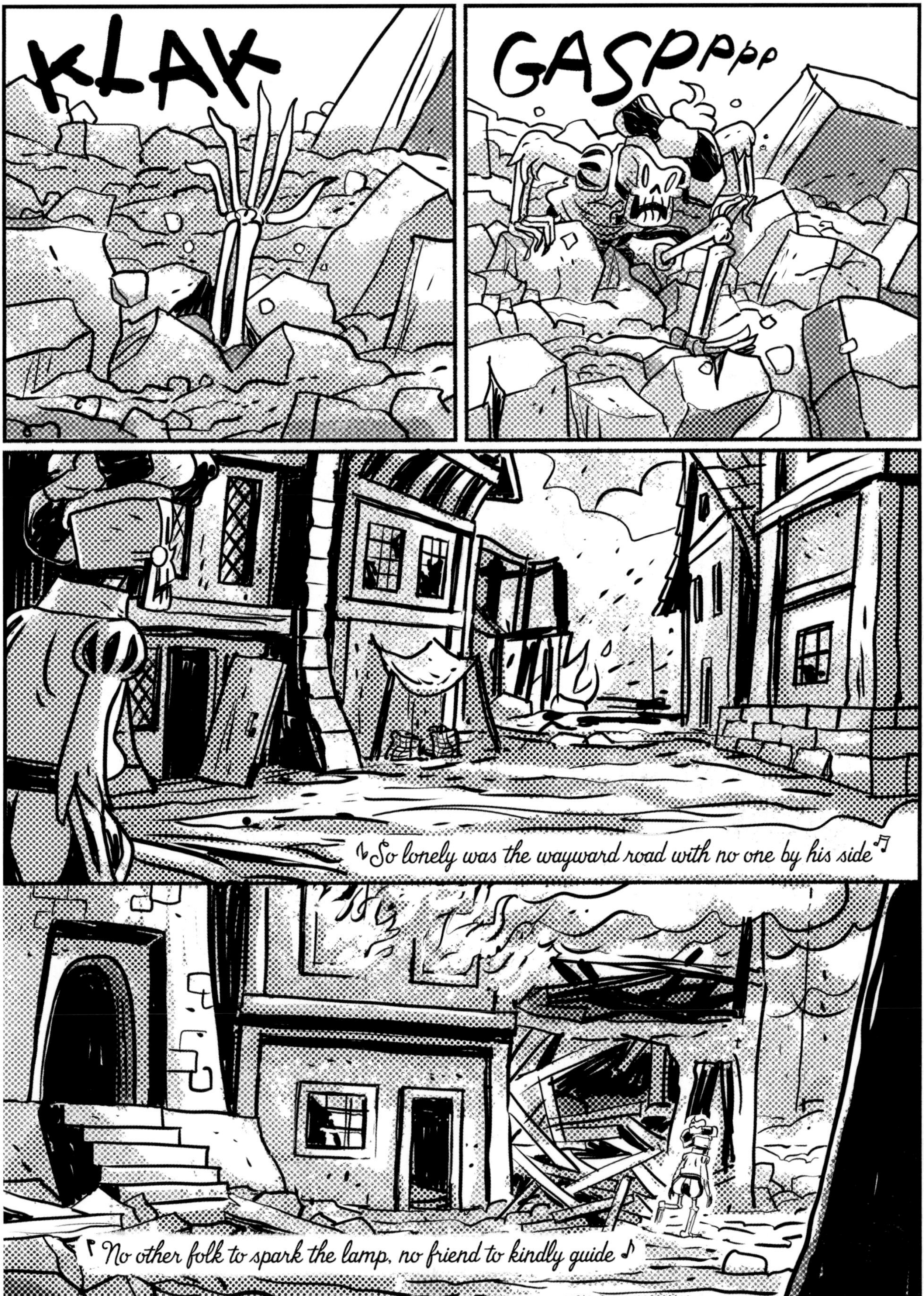
KLAK
GASPppp
So lonely was the wayward road with no one by his side
No other folk to spark the lamp, no friend to kindly guide

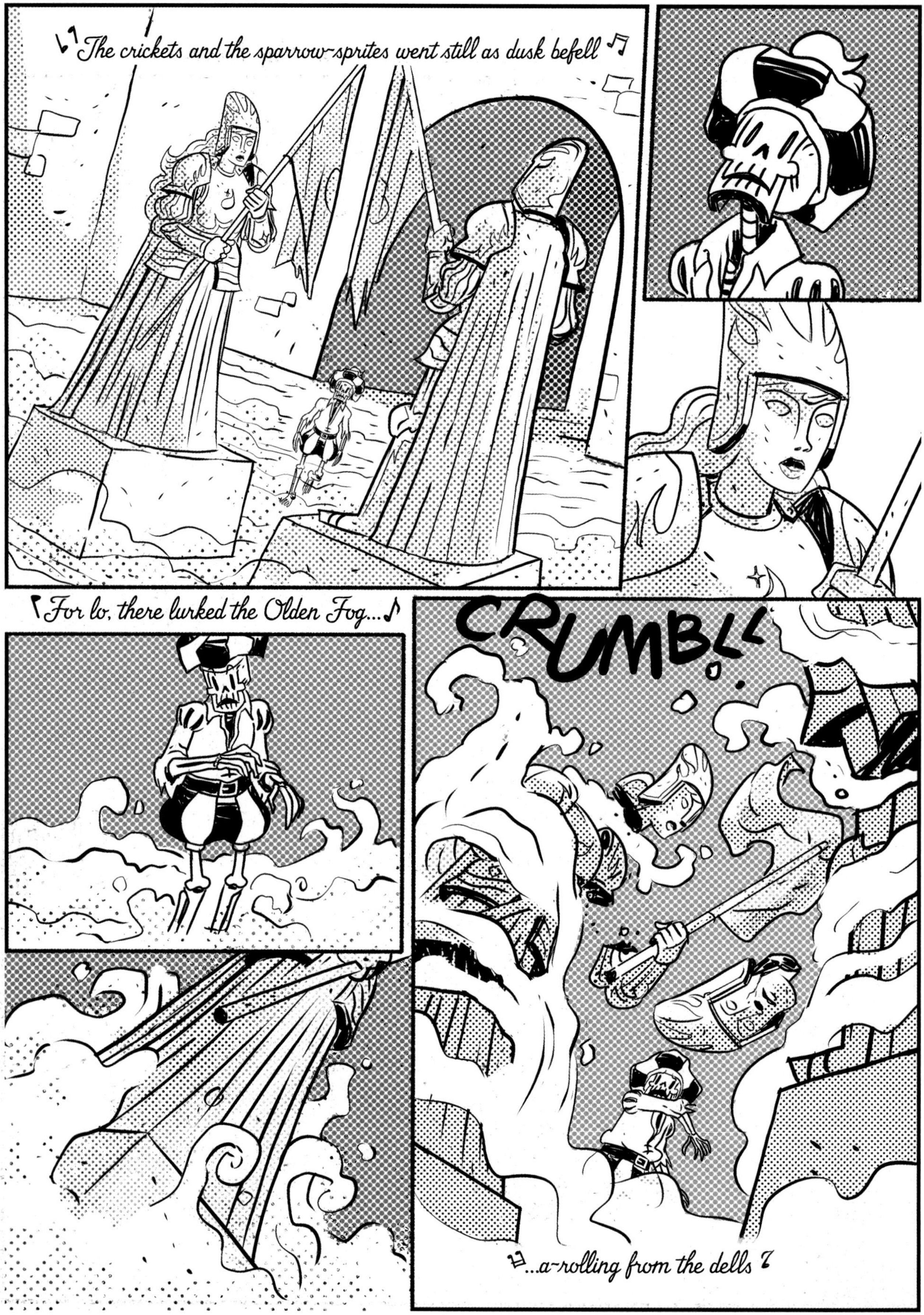
The crickets and the sparrow-sprites went still as dusk befell
For lo, there lurked the Olden Fog...
CRUMBLL
...a-rolling from the dells

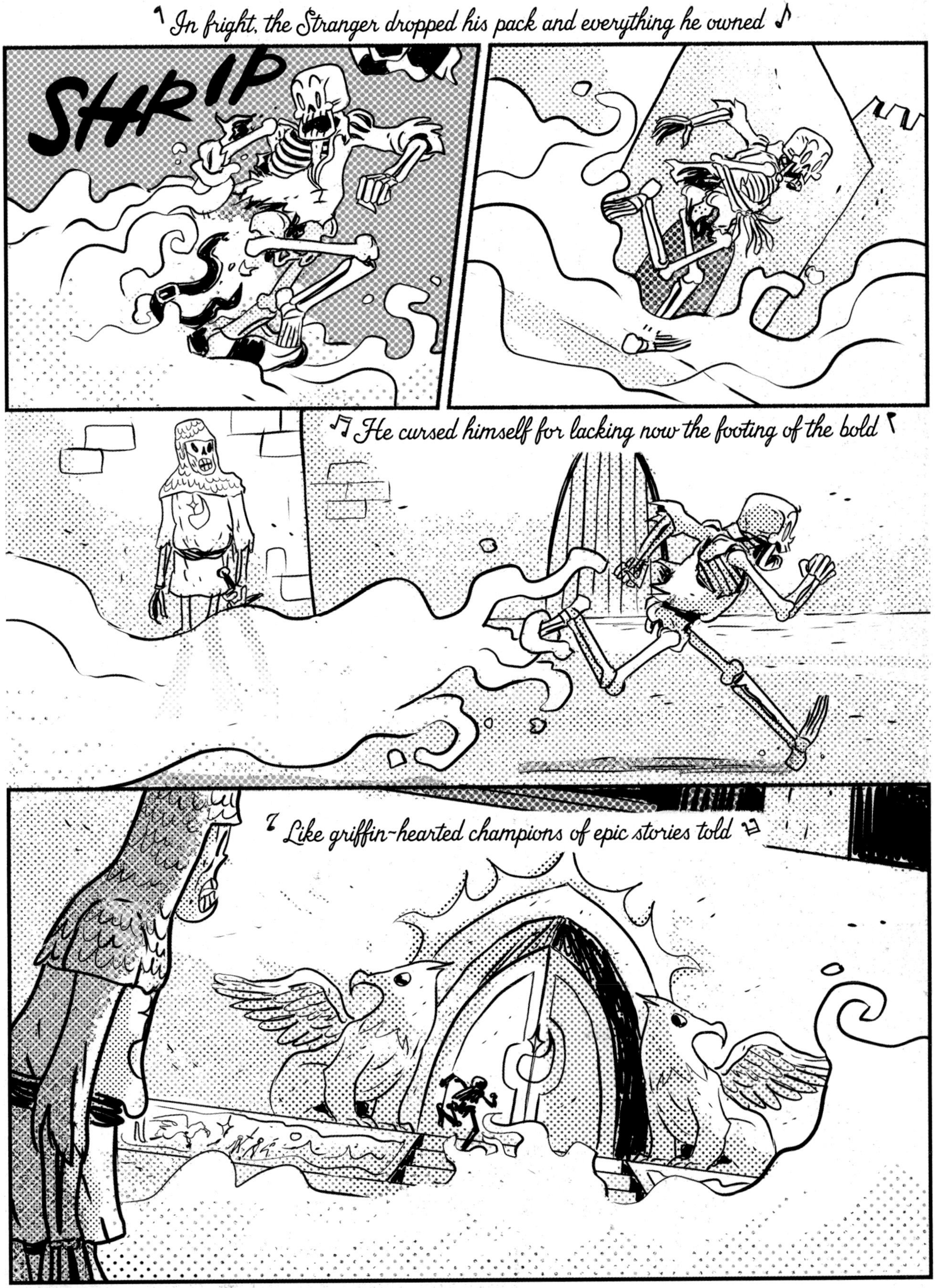
In fright, the Stranger dropped his pack and everything he owned
SHRIP
He cursed himself for lacking now the footing of the bold
Like griffin-hearted champions of epic stories told

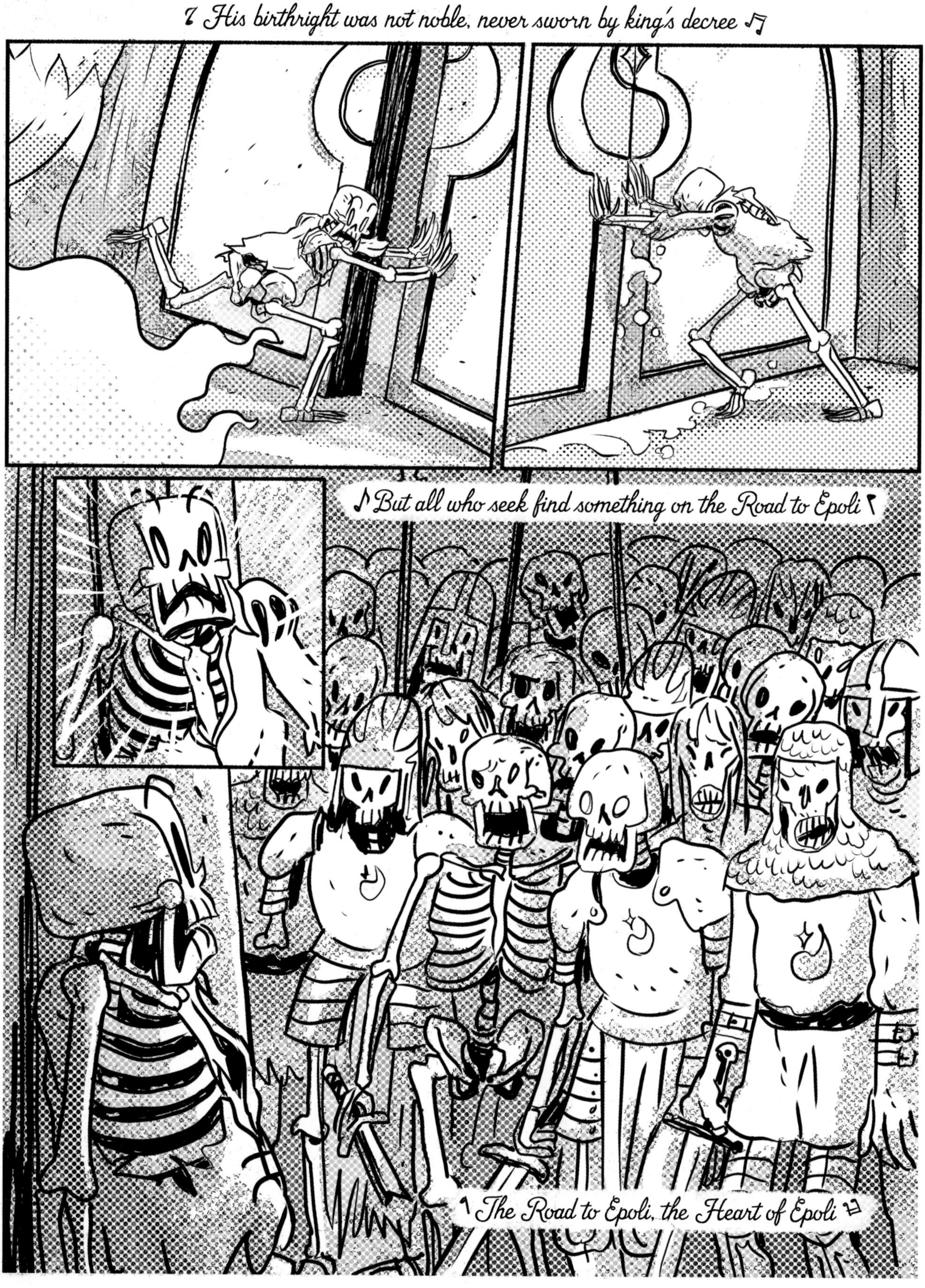
His birthright was not noble, never sworn by king's decree
But all who seek find something on the Road to Epoli
The Road to Epoli, the Heart of Epoli

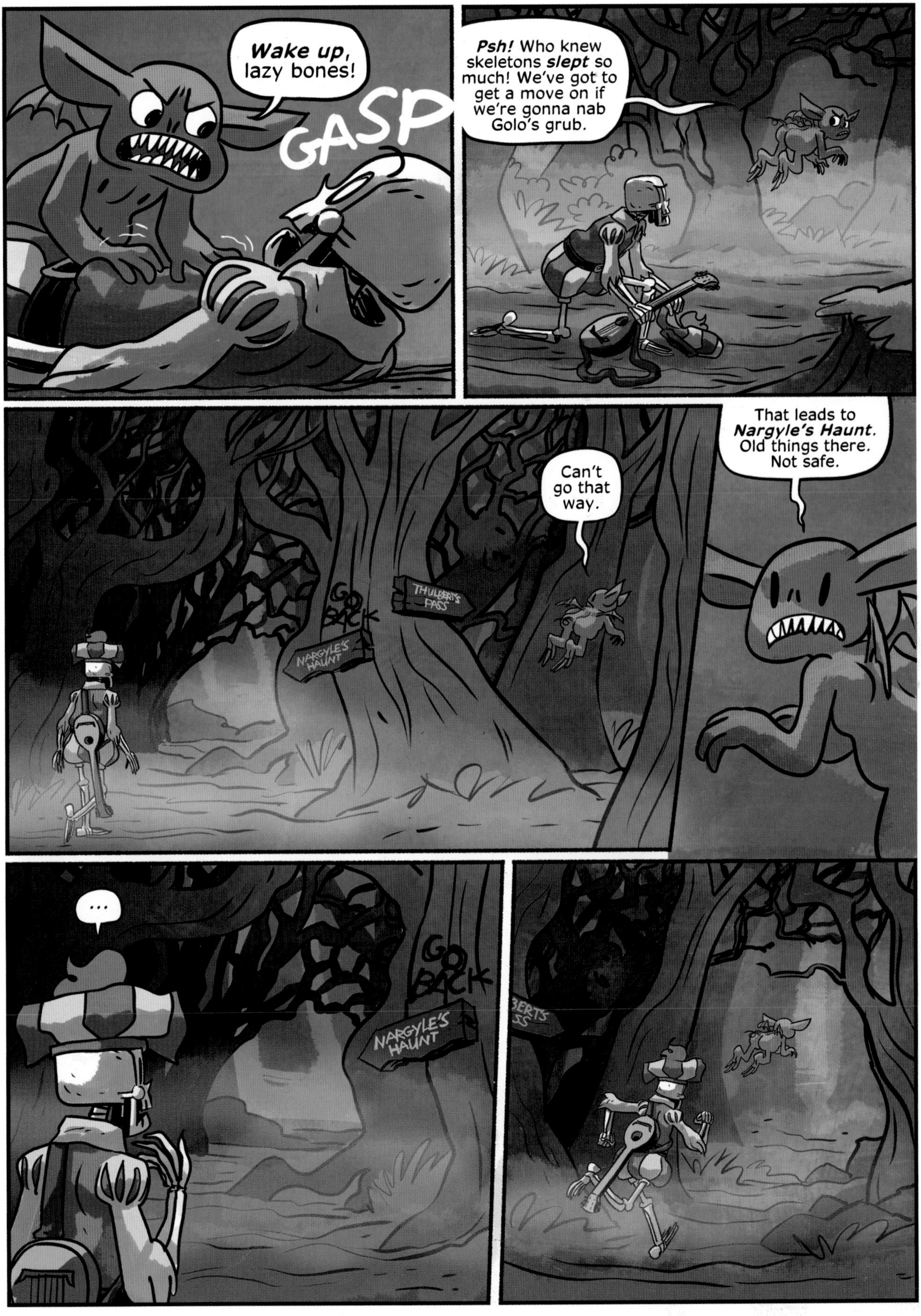
Wake up, lazy bones!
GASP
Psh! Who knew skeletons slept so much! We've got to get a move on if we're gonna nab Golo's grub.
GO BACK
THULBERT'S PASS
NARGYLE'S HAUNT
Can't go that way.
That leads to Nargyle's Haunt. Old things there. Not safe.
...
GO BACK
NARGYLE'S HAUNT

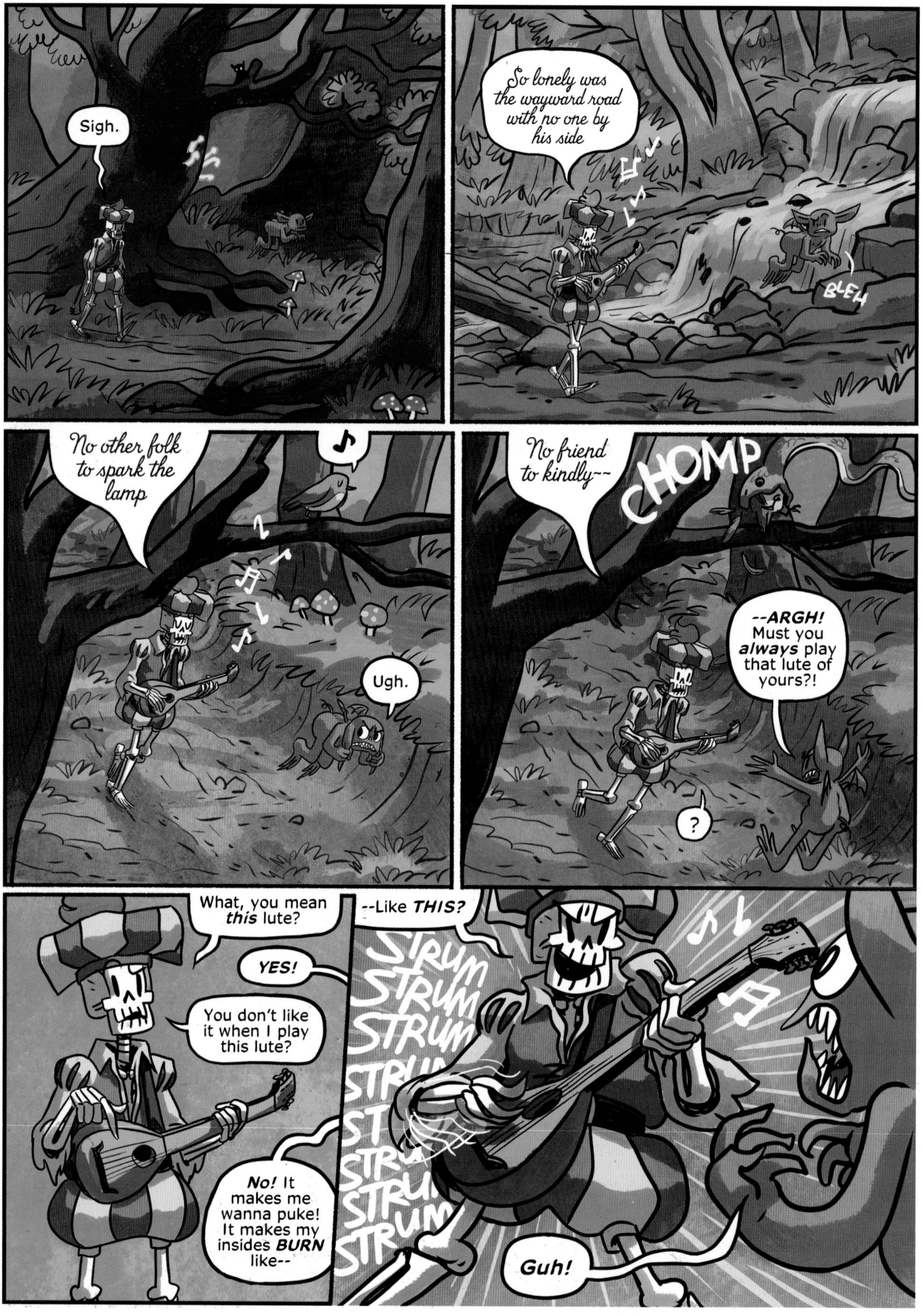
Sigh.
So lonely was the wayward road with no one by his side
BLEH
No other folk to spark the lamp
Ugh.
No friend to kindly--
CHOMP
--*ARGH!* Must you *always* play that lute of yours?!
?
What, you mean *this* lute?
YES!
You don't like it when I play this lute?
No! It makes me wanna puke! It makes my insides *BURN* like--
--Like *THIS?*
STRUM STRUM STRUM STRUM STRUM
Guh!

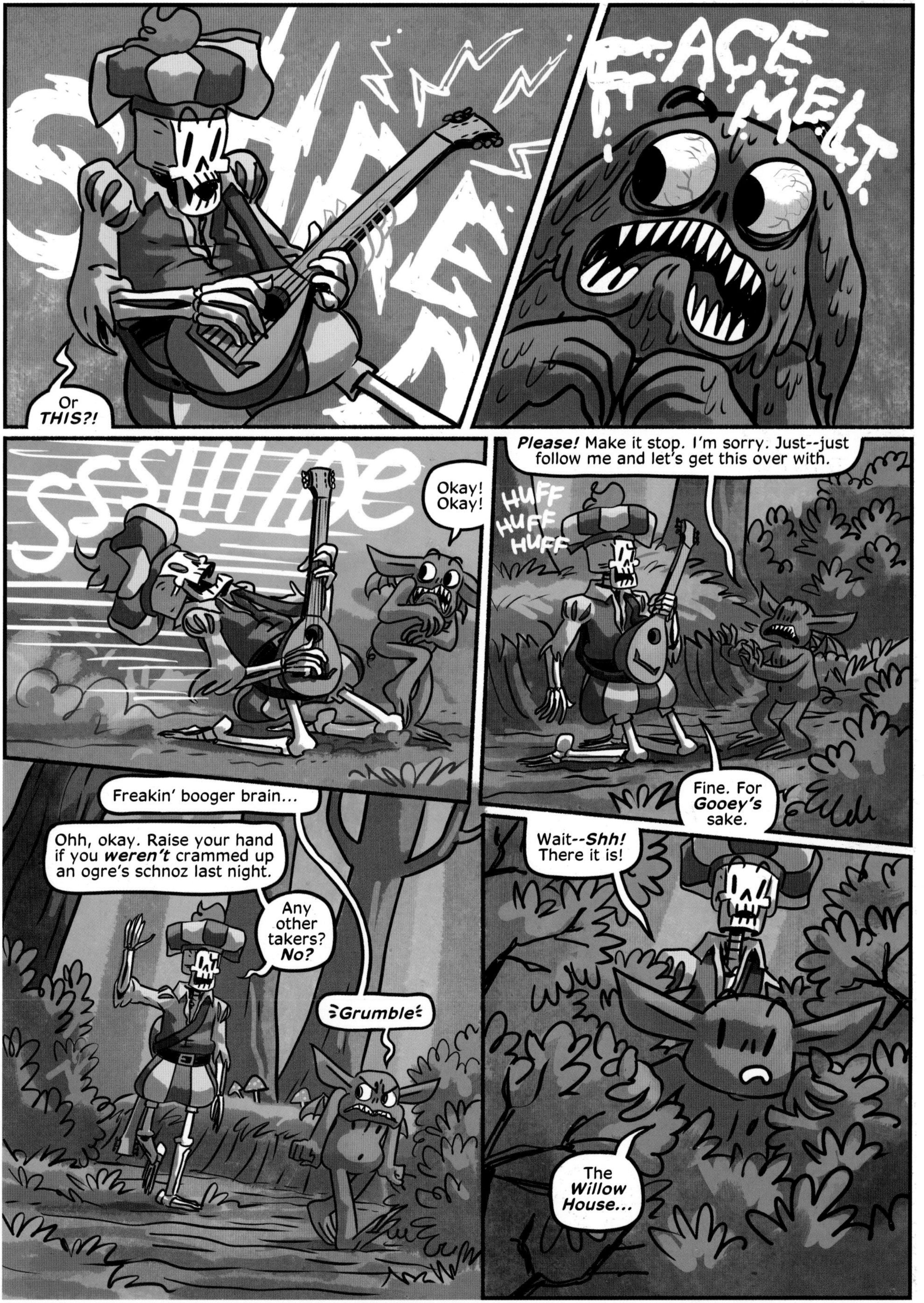
SHRED
Or THIS?!
FACE MELT
SSSLIDE
Okay! Okay!
Please! Make it stop. I'm sorry. Just--just follow me and let's get this over with.
HUFF HUFF HUFF
Fine. For Gooey's sake.
Freakin' booger brain...
Ohh, okay. Raise your hand if you weren't crammed up an ogre's schnoz last night.
Any other takers? No?
Grumble
Wait--Shh! There it is!
The Willow House...

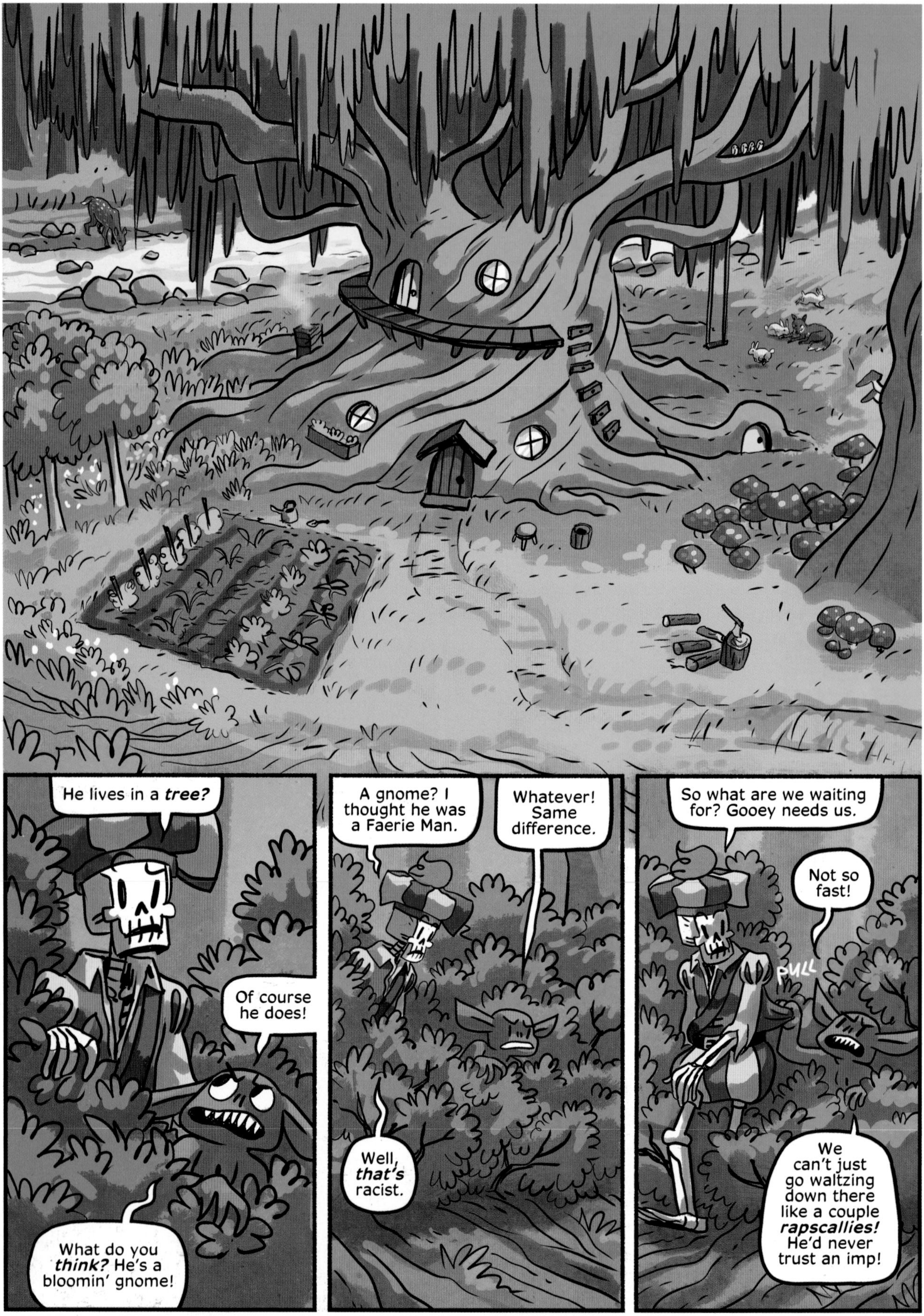

He lives in a *tree?*
Of course he does!
What do you *think?* He's a bloomin' gnome!
A gnome? I thought he was a Faerie Man.
Well, *that's* racist.
Whatever! Same difference.
So what are we waiting for? Gooey needs us.
Not so fast!
PULL
We can't just go waltzing down there like a couple *rapscallies!* He'd never trust an imp!

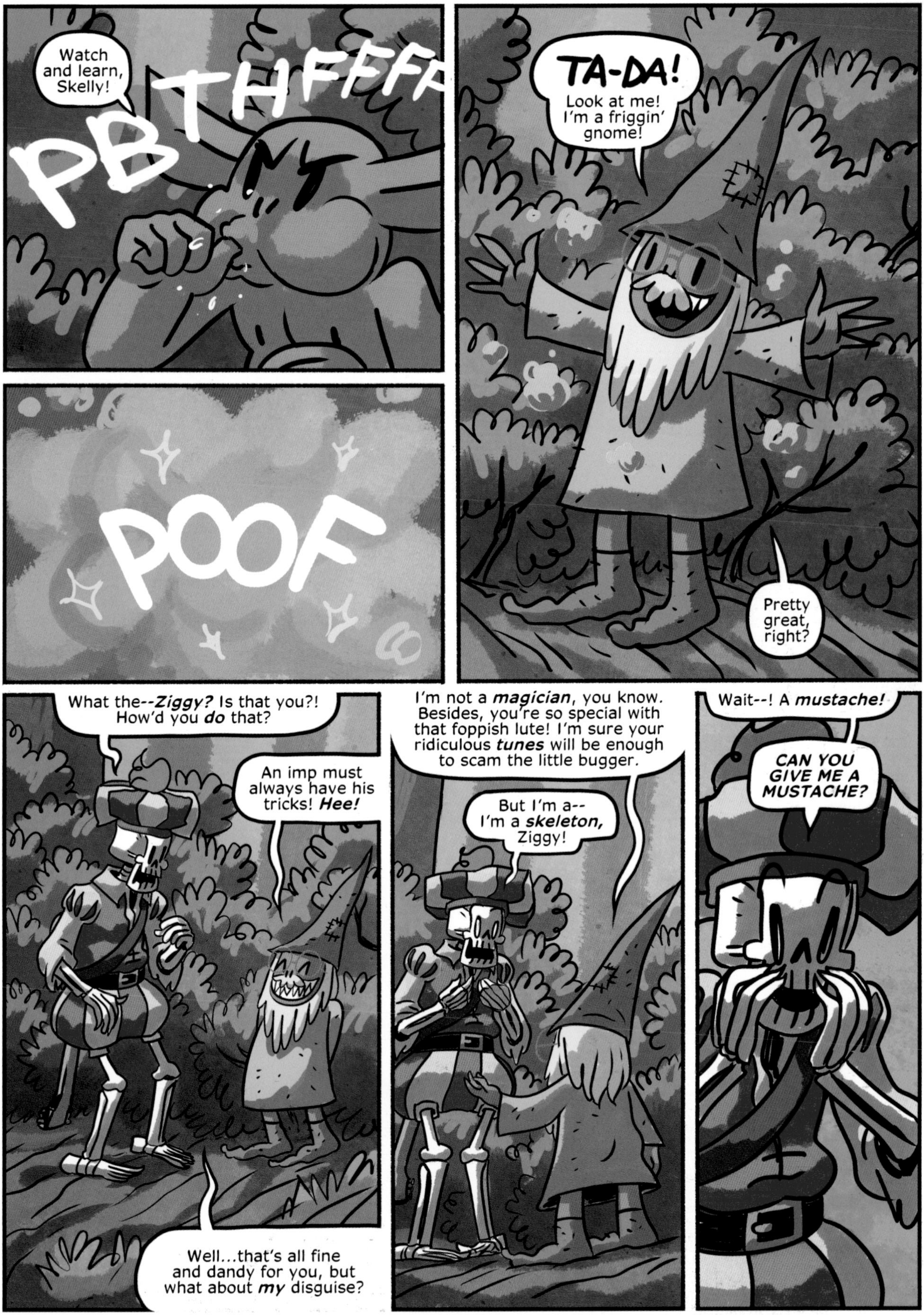
Watch and learn, Skelly!
PBTHFFFF
POOF
TA-DA!
Look at me! I'm a friggin' gnome!
Pretty great, right?
What the--*Ziggy?* Is that you?! How'd you *do* that?
An imp must always have his tricks! *Hee!*
Well...that's all fine and dandy for you, but what about *my* disguise?
I'm not a *magician*, you know. Besides, you're so special with that foppish lute! I'm sure your ridiculous *tunes* will be enough to scam the little bugger.
But I'm a-- I'm a *skeleton,* Ziggy!
Wait--! A *mustache!*
CAN YOU GIVE ME A MUSTACHE?

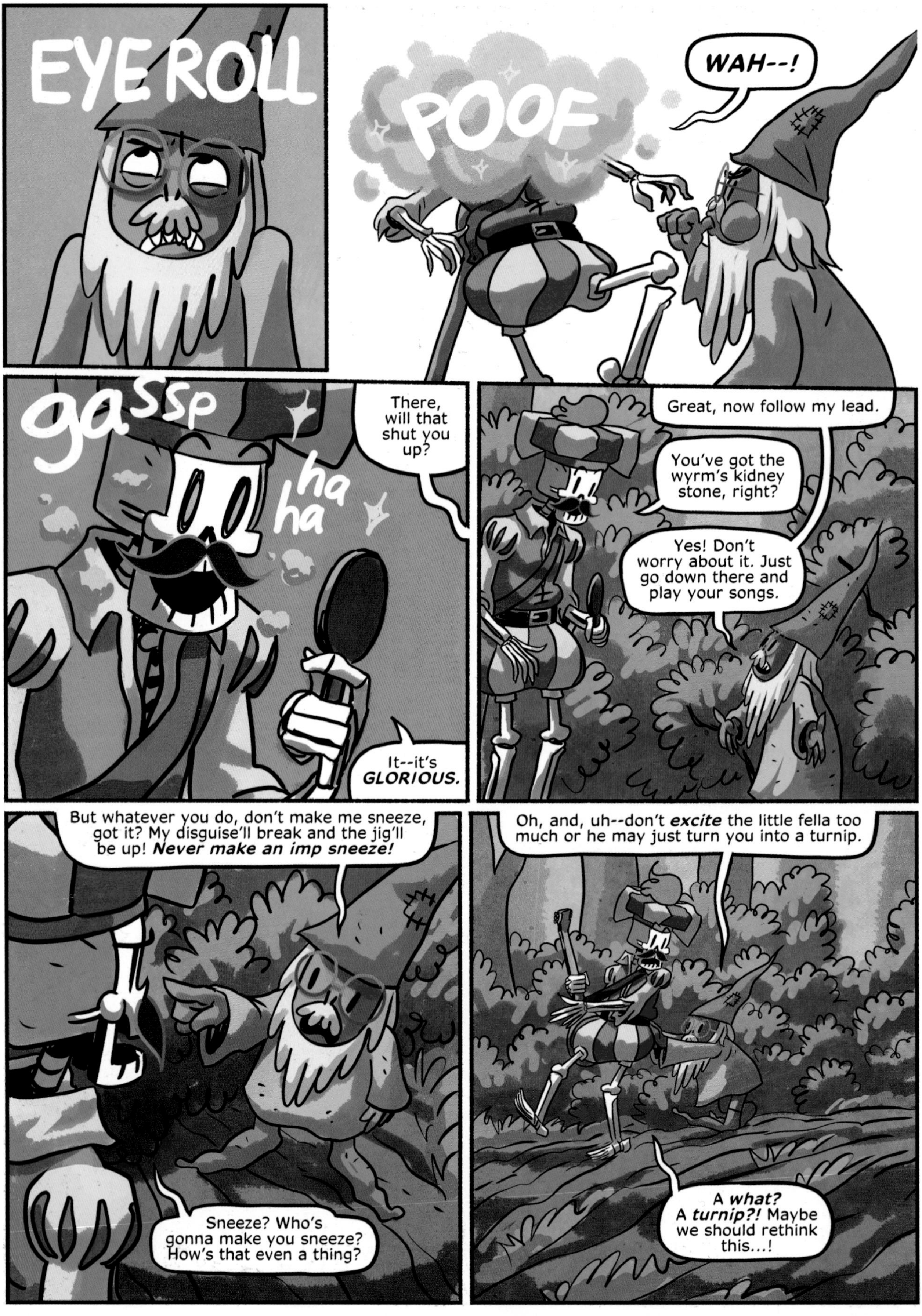
EYE ROLL
POOF
WAH--!
gaSSp
haha
There, will that shut you up?
It--it's GLORIOUS.
Great, now follow my lead.
You've got the wyrm's kidney stone, right?
Yes! Don't worry about it. Just go down there and play your songs.
But whatever you do, don't make me sneeze, got it? My disguise'll break and the jig'll be up! ***Never make an imp sneeze!***
Sneeze? Who's gonna make you sneeze? How's that even a thing?
Oh, and, uh--don't ***excite*** the little fella too much or he may just turn you into a turnip.
A ***what?*** A ***turnip?!*** Maybe we should rethink this...!

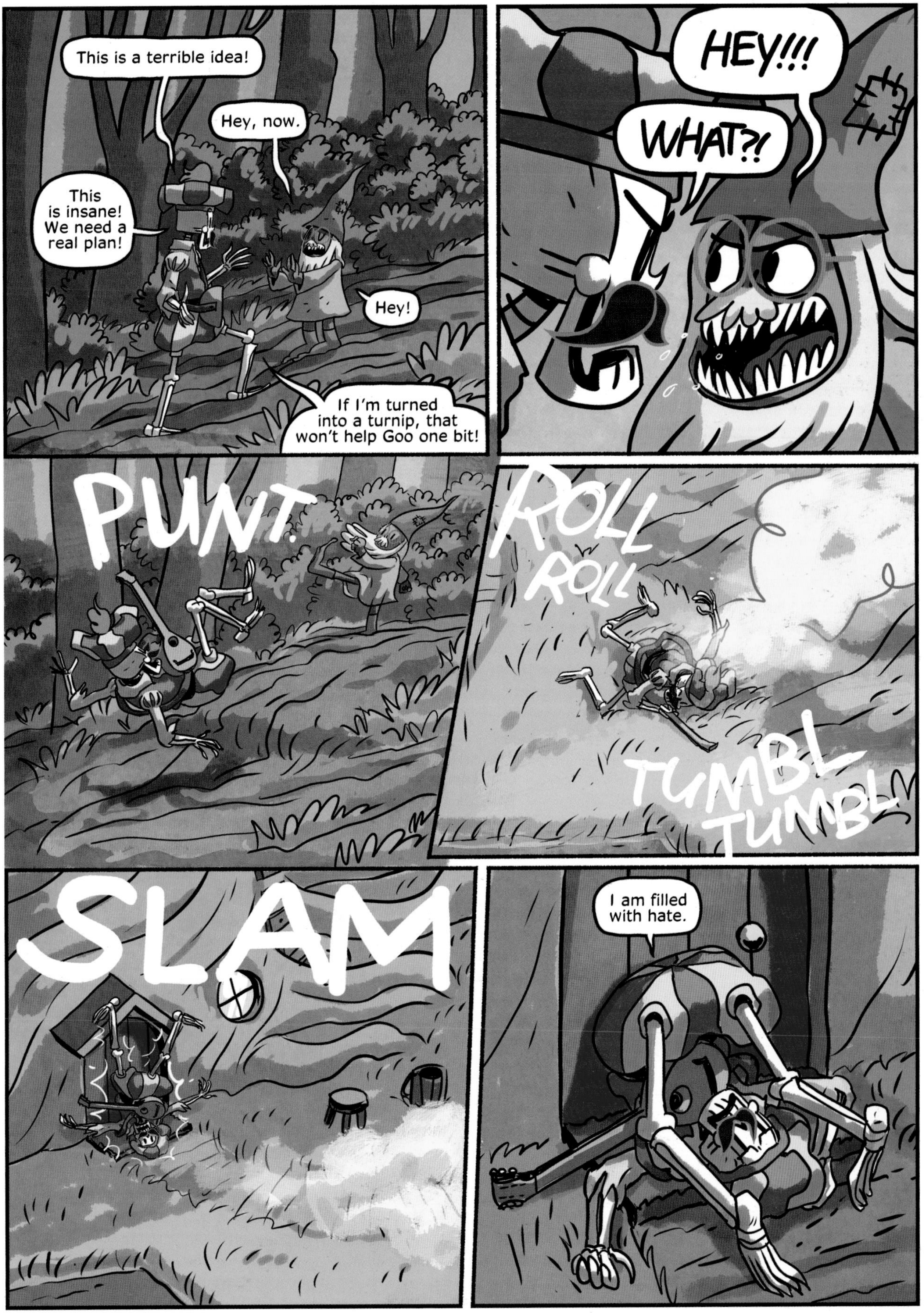
This is a terrible idea!
Hey, now.
This is insane! We need a real plan!
Hey!
If I'm turned into a turnip, that won't help Goo one bit!
HEY!!!
WHAT?!
PUNT.
ROLL
ROLL
TUMBL
TUMBL
SLAM
I am filled with hate.

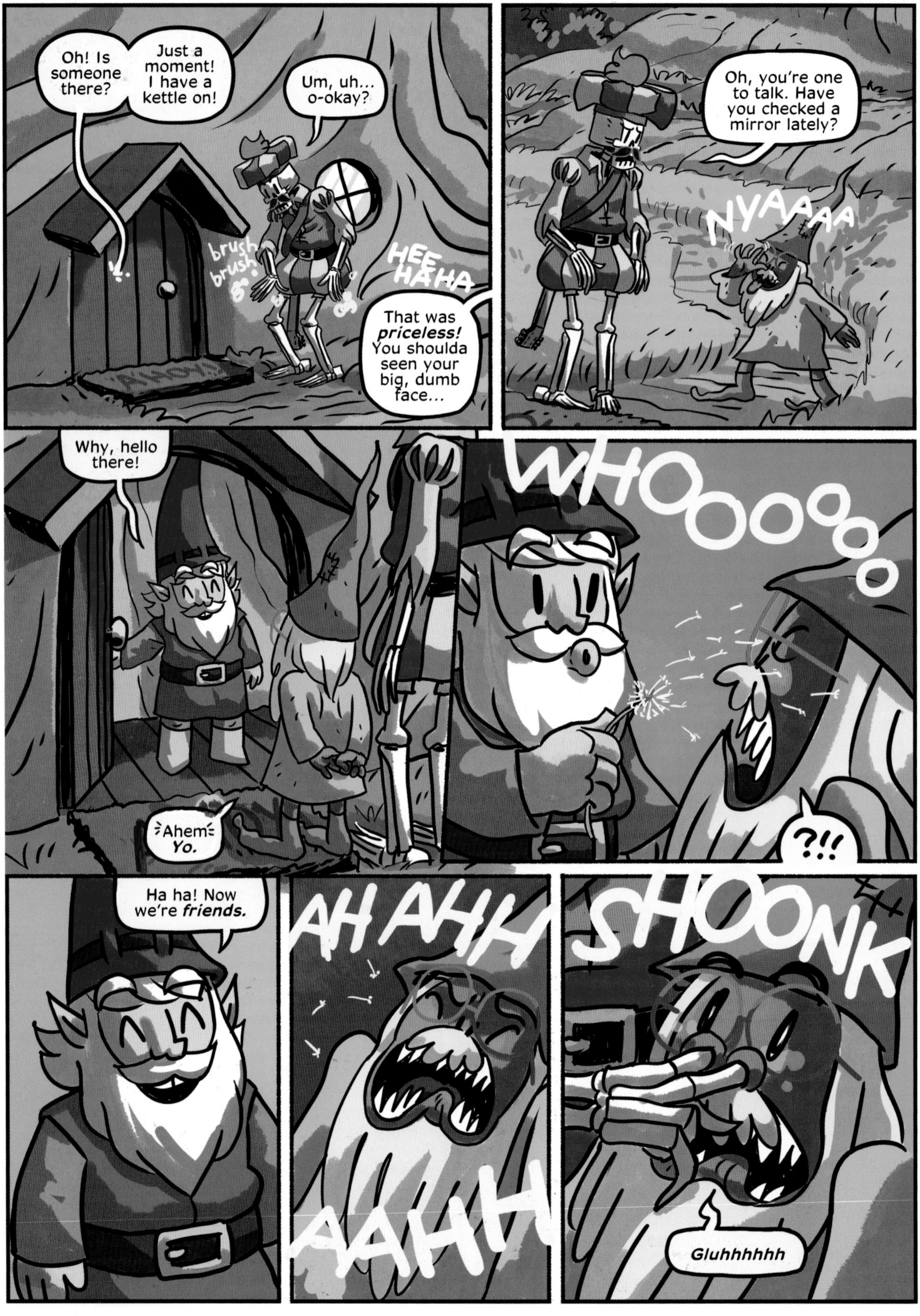

Oh! Is someone there?
Just a moment! I have a kettle on!
Um, uh... o-okay?
brush brush
HEE HAHA
That was *priceless!* You shoulda seen your big, dumb face...
Oh, you're one to talk. Have you checked a mirror lately?
NYAAAAA
Why, hello there!
Ahem
Yo.
WHOOOooooo
?!!
Ha ha! Now we're *friends.*
AH AHH AAHH
SHOONK
Gluhhhhhh

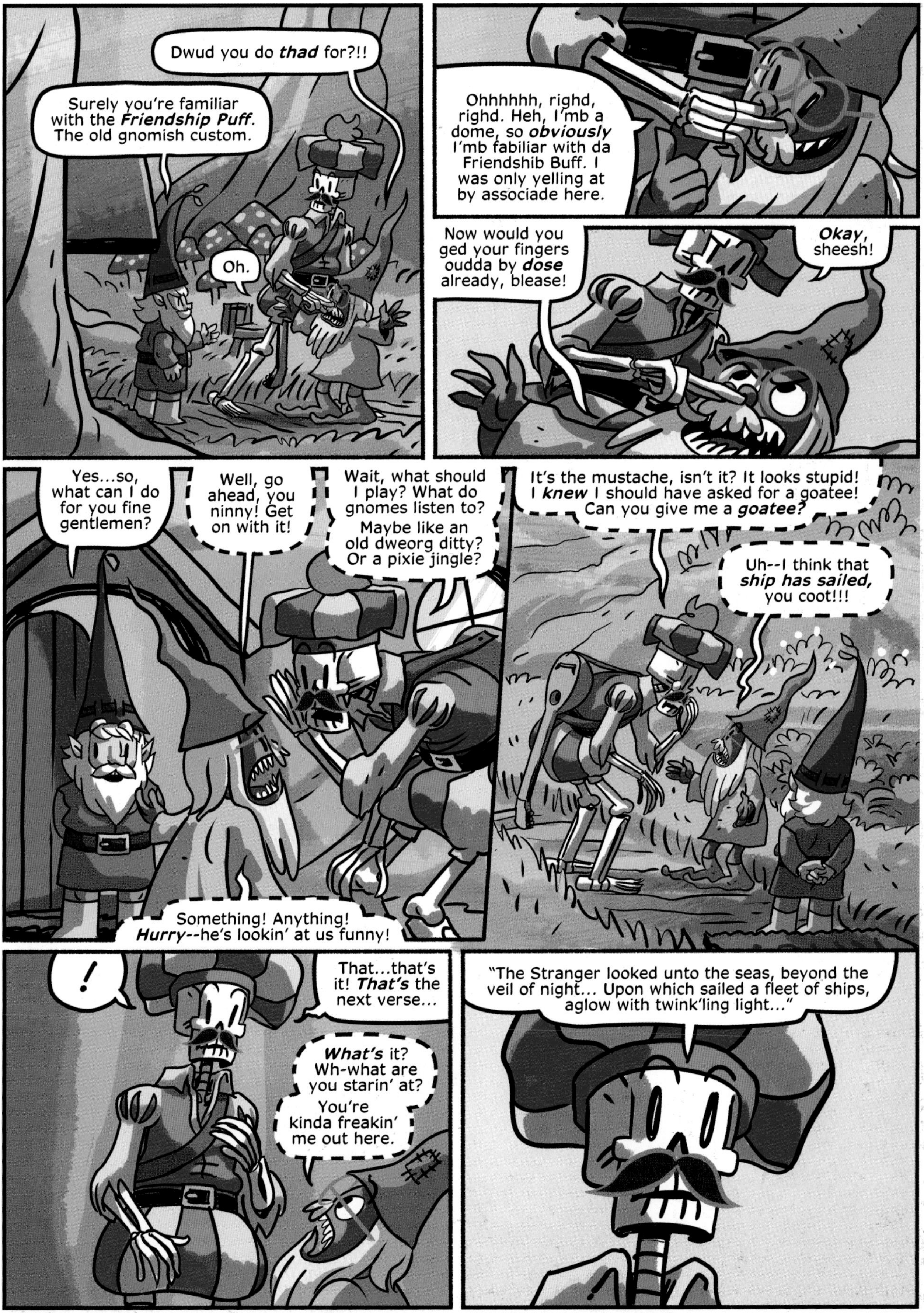

Dwud you do ***thad*** for?!!
Surely you're familiar with the ***Friendship Puff***. The old gnomish custom.
Oh.
Ohhhhhh, righd, righd. Heh, I'mb a dome, so ***obviously*** I'mb fabiliar with da Friendshib Buff. I was only yelling at by associade here.
Now would you ged your fingers oudda by ***dose*** already, blease!
Okay, sheesh!
Yes...so, what can I do for you fine gentlemen?
Well, go ahead, you ninny! Get on with it!
Wait, what should I play? What do gnomes listen to? Maybe like an old dweorg ditty? Or a pixie jingle?
Something! Anything! ***Hurry***--he's lookin' at us funny!
It's the mustache, isn't it? It looks stupid! I ***knew*** I should have asked for a goatee! Can you give me a ***goatee?***
Uh--I think that ***ship has sailed,*** you coot!!!
!
That...that's it! ***That's*** the next verse...
What's it? Wh-what are you starin' at? You're kinda freakin' me out here.
"The Stranger looked unto the seas, beyond the veil of night... Upon which sailed a fleet of ships, aglow with twink'ling light..."

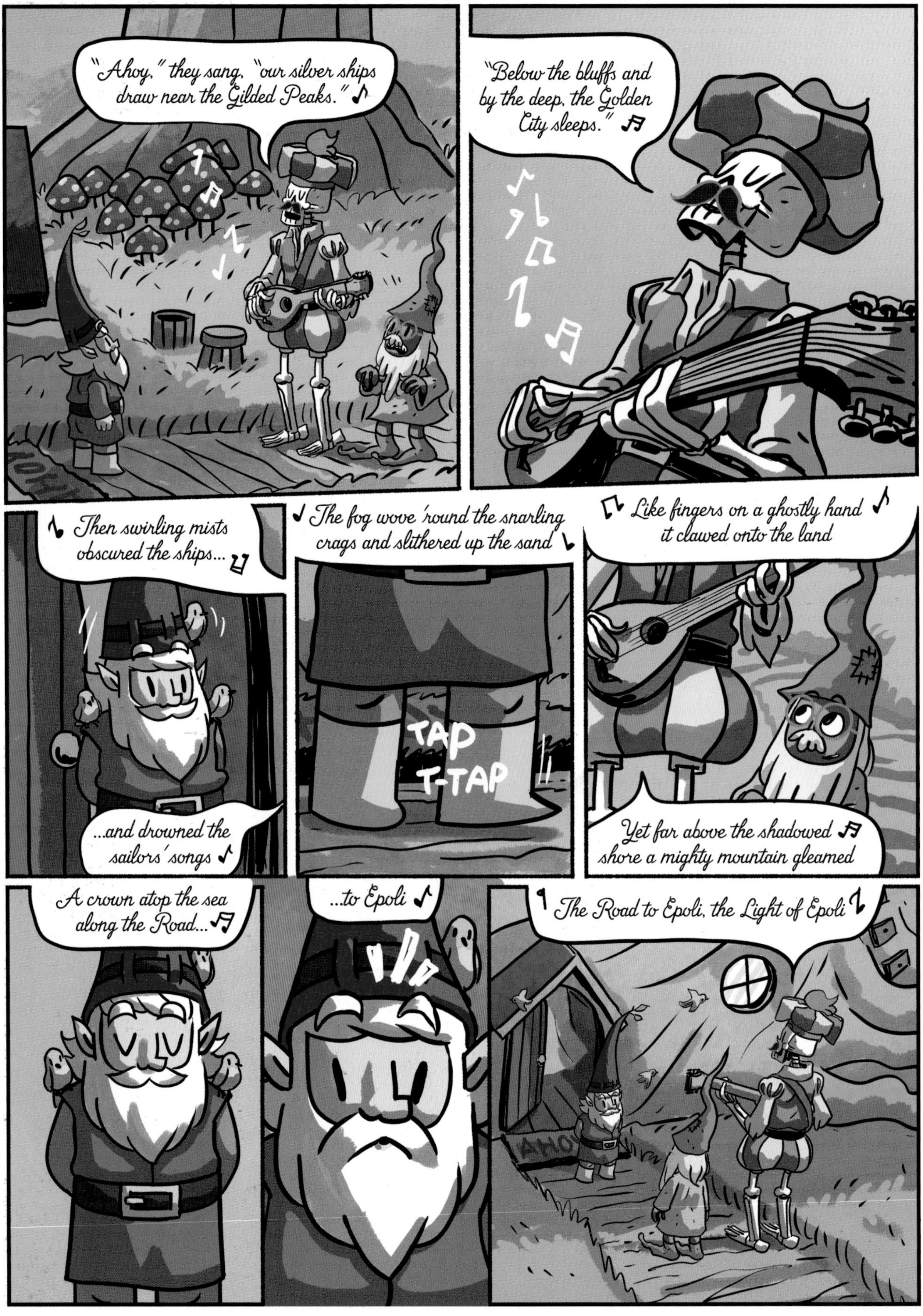
"Ahoy," they sang, "our silver ships draw near the Gilded Peaks."
"Below the bluffs and by the deep, the Golden City sleeps."
Then swirling mists obscured the ships...
...and drowned the sailors' songs
The fog wove 'round the snarling crags and slithered up the sand
TAP T-TAP
Like fingers on a ghostly hand it clawed onto the land
Yet far above the shadowed shore a mighty mountain gleamed
A crown atop the sea along the Road...
...to Epoli
The Road to Epoli, the Light of Epoli
AHOY

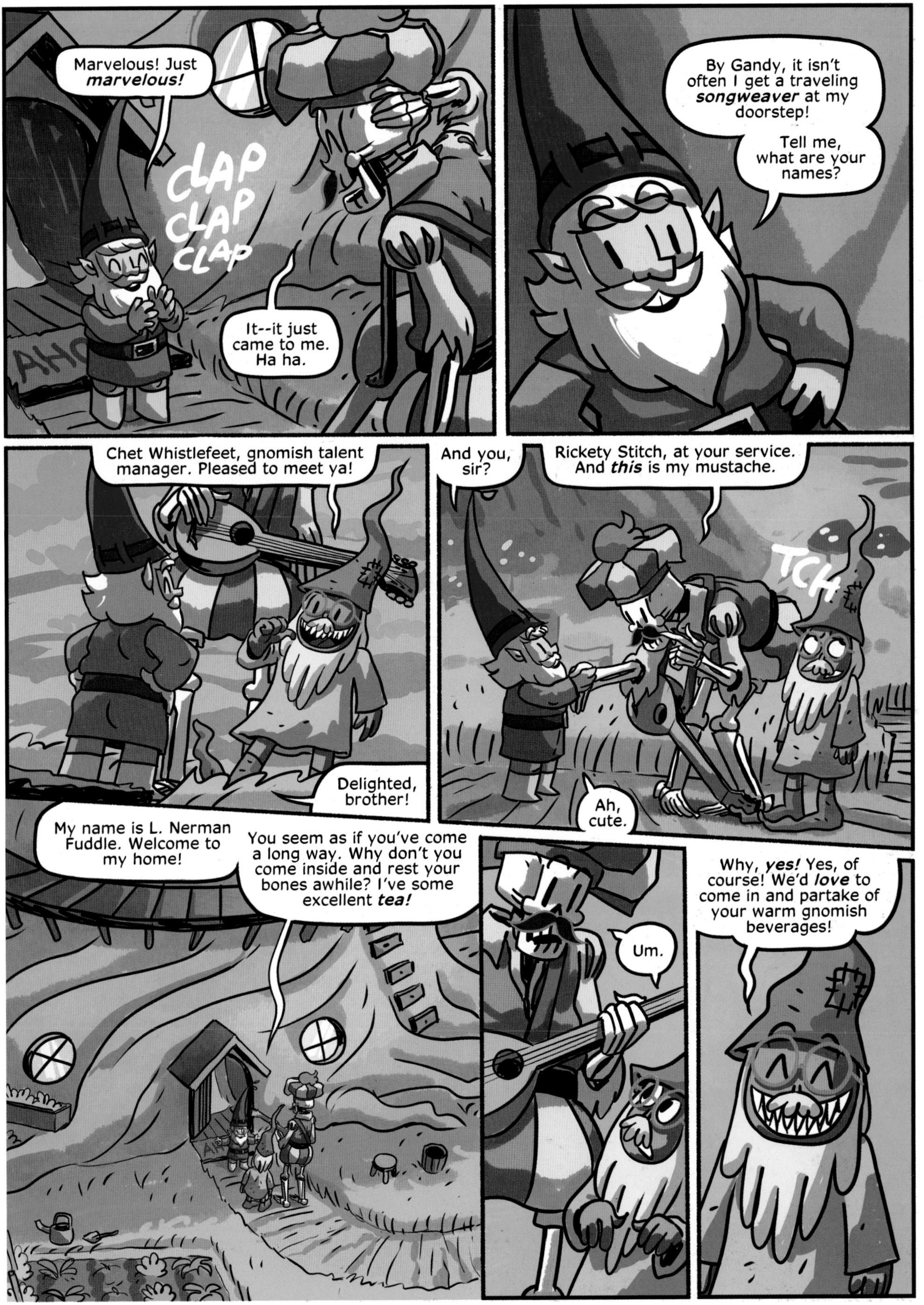

Marvelous! Just *marvelous!*
CLAP CLAP CLAP
It--it just came to me. Ha ha.
By Gandy, it isn't often I get a traveling *songweaver* at my doorstep!
Tell me, what are your names?
Chet Whistlefeet, gnomish talent manager. Pleased to meet ya!
Delighted, brother!
And you, sir?
Rickety Stitch, at your service. And *this* is my mustache.
TCH
Ah, cute.
My name is L. Nerman Fuddle. Welcome to my home!
You seem as if you've come a long way. Why don't you come inside and rest your bones awhile? I've some excellent *tea!*
Um.
Why, *yes!* Yes, of course! We'd *love* to come in and partake of your warm gnomish beverages!

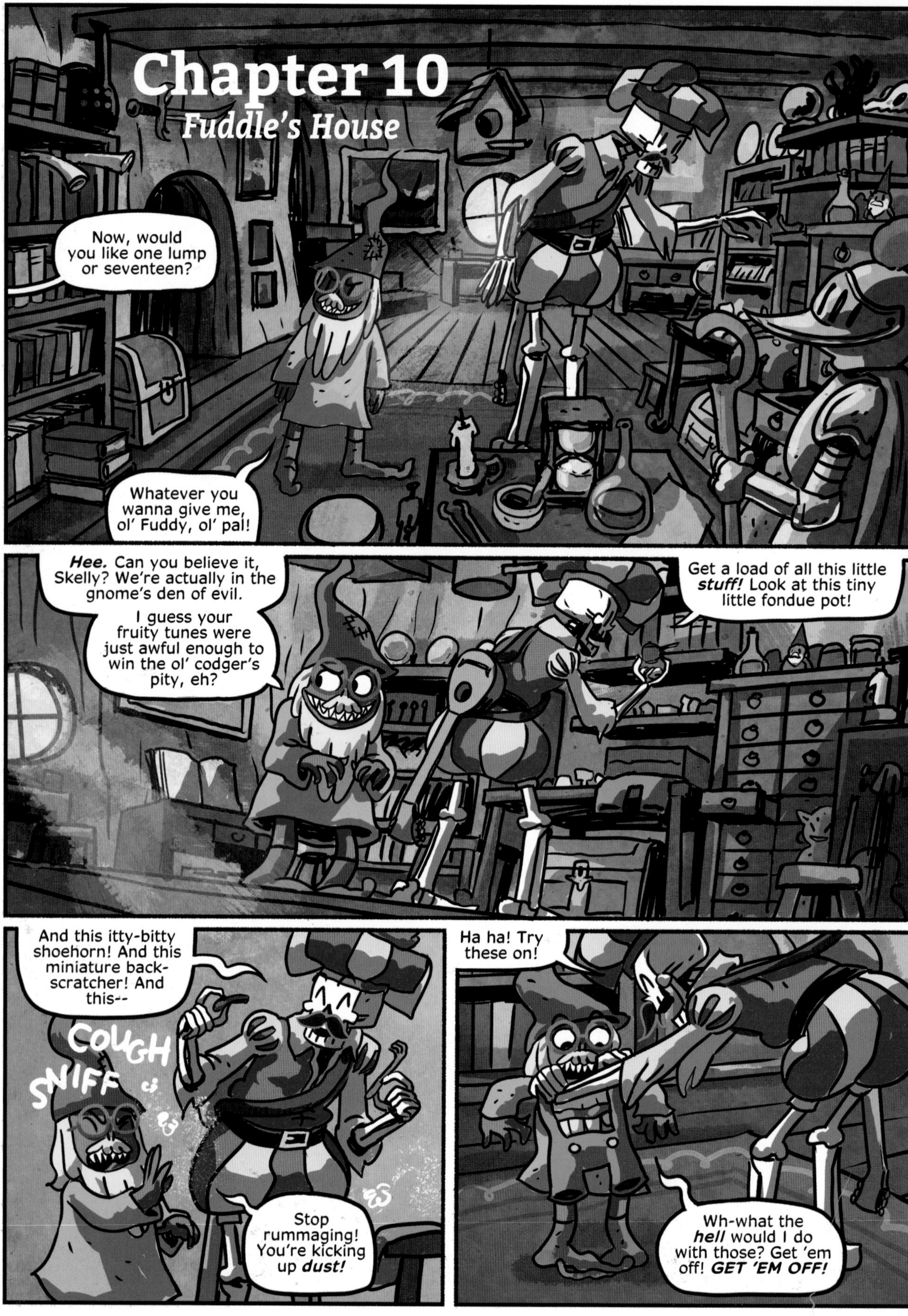
Chapter 10
Fuddle's House
Now, would you like one lump or seventeen?
Whatever you wanna give me, ol' Fuddy, ol' pal!
Hee. Can you believe it, Skelly? We're actually in the gnome's den of evil.
I guess your fruity tunes were just awful enough to win the ol' codger's pity, eh?
Get a load of all this little ***stuff!*** Look at this tiny little fondue pot!
And this itty-bitty shoehorn! And this miniature back-scratcher! And this--
COUGH
SNIFF
Stop rummaging! You're kicking up ***dust!***
Ha ha! Try these on!
Wh-what the ***hell*** would I do with those? Get 'em off! ***GET 'EM OFF!***

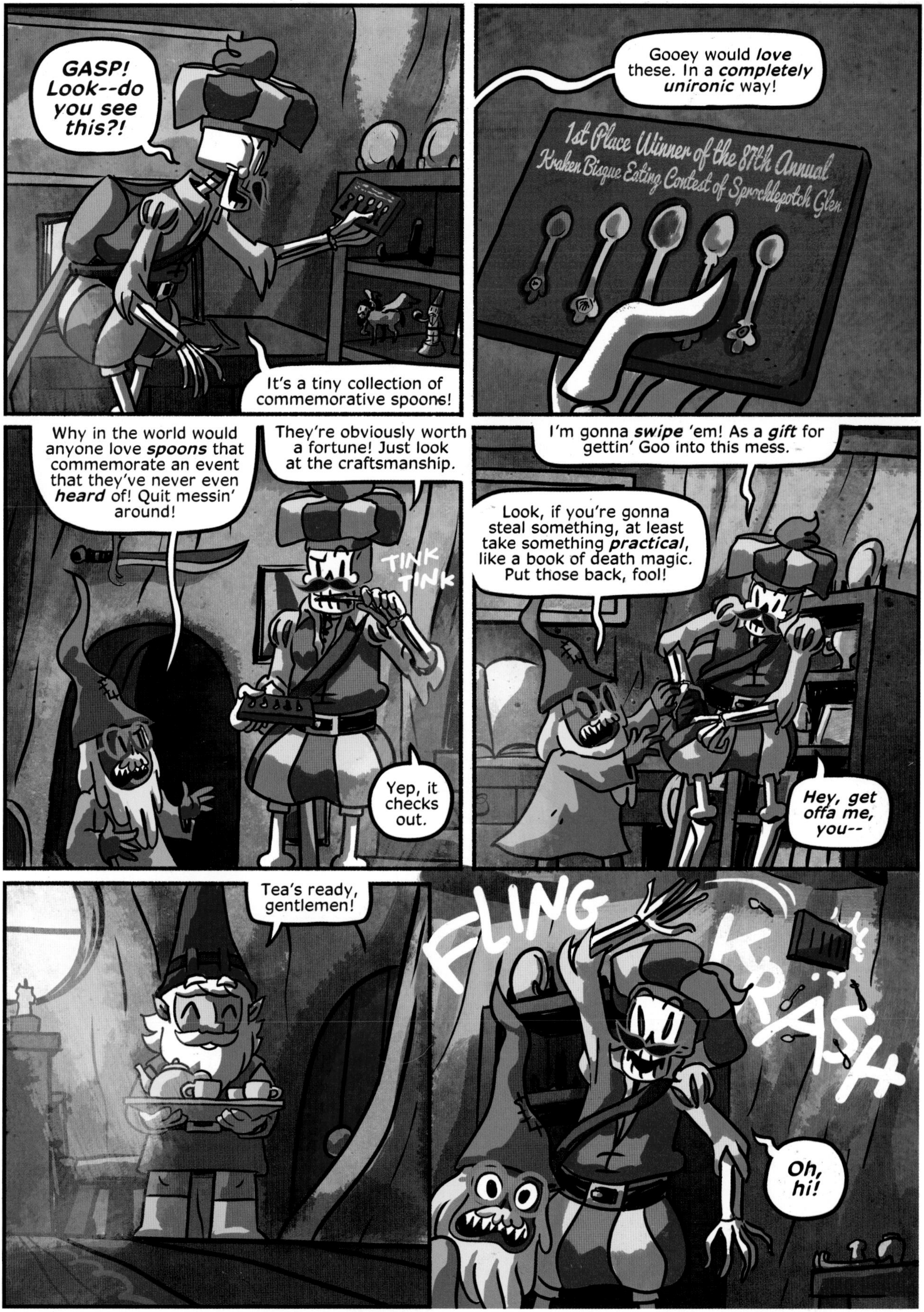
GASP! Look--do you see this?!
It's a tiny collection of commemorative spoons!
Gooey would love these. In a completely unironic way!
1st Place Winner of the 87th Annual Kraken Bisque Eating Contest of Sprocklepotch Glen
Why in the world would anyone love spoons that commemorate an event that they've never even heard of! Quit messin' around!
They're obviously worth a fortune! Just look at the craftsmanship.
TINK TINK
Yep, it checks out.
I'm gonna swipe 'em! As a gift for gettin' Goo into this mess.
Look, if you're gonna steal something, at least take something practical, like a book of death magic. Put those back, fool!
Hey, get offa me, you--
Tea's ready, gentlemen!
FLING
KRASH
Oh, hi!

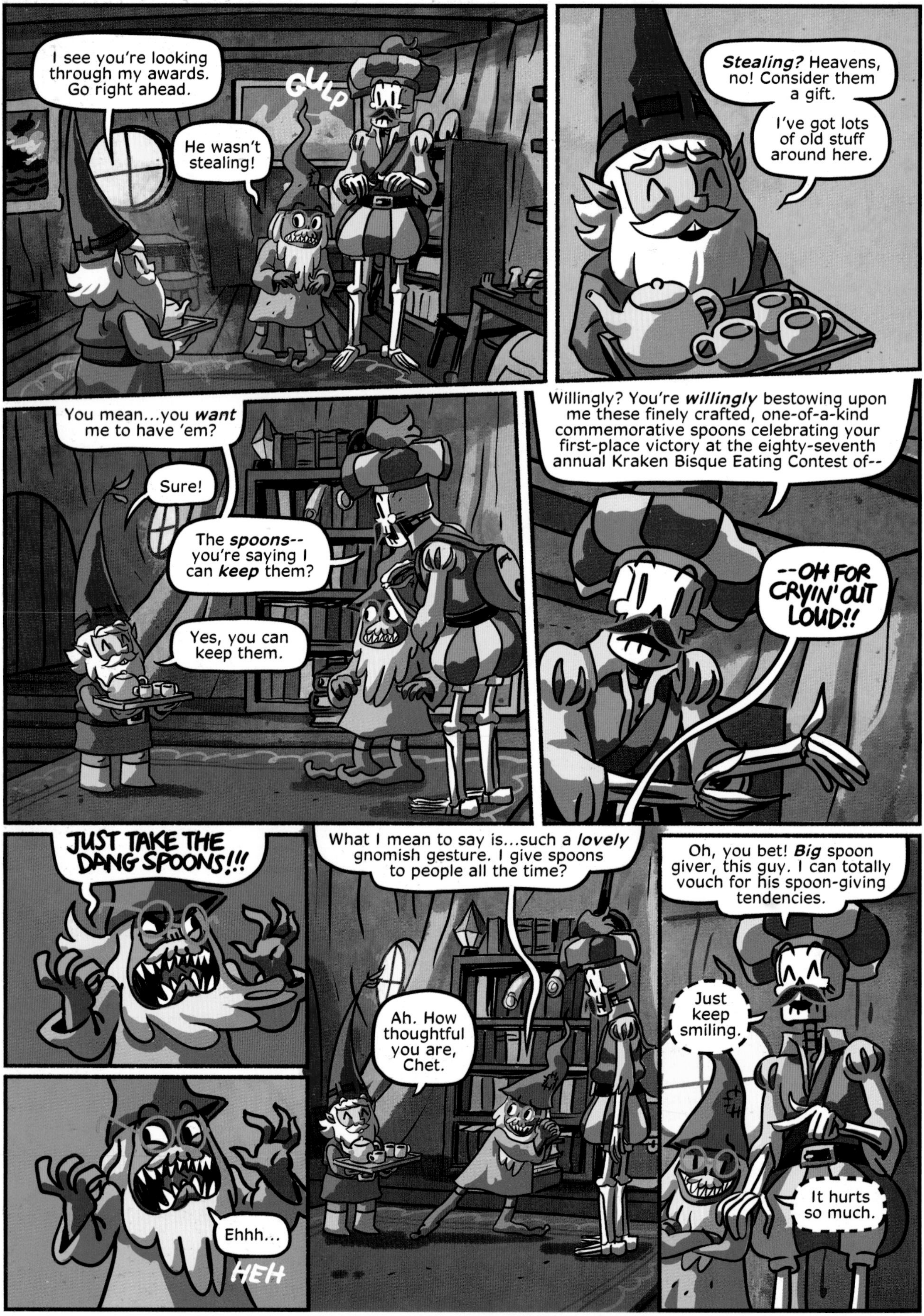
I see you're looking through my awards. Go right ahead.
GULP
He wasn't stealing!
Stealing? Heavens, no! Consider them a gift.
I've got lots of old stuff around here.
You mean...you *want* me to have 'em?
Sure!
The *spoons*-- you're saying I can *keep* them?
Yes, you can keep them.
Willingly? You're *willingly* bestowing upon me these finely crafted, one-of-a-kind commemorative spoons celebrating your first-place victory at the eighty-seventh annual Kraken Bisque Eating Contest of--
--OH FOR CRYIN' OUT LOUD!!
JUST TAKE THE DANG SPOONS!!!
Ehhh...
HEH
What I mean to say is...such a *lovely* gnomish gesture. I give spoons to people all the time?
Ah. How thoughtful you are, Chet.
Oh, you bet! *Big* spoon giver, this guy. I can totally vouch for his spoon-giving tendencies.
Just keep smiling.
It hurts so much.

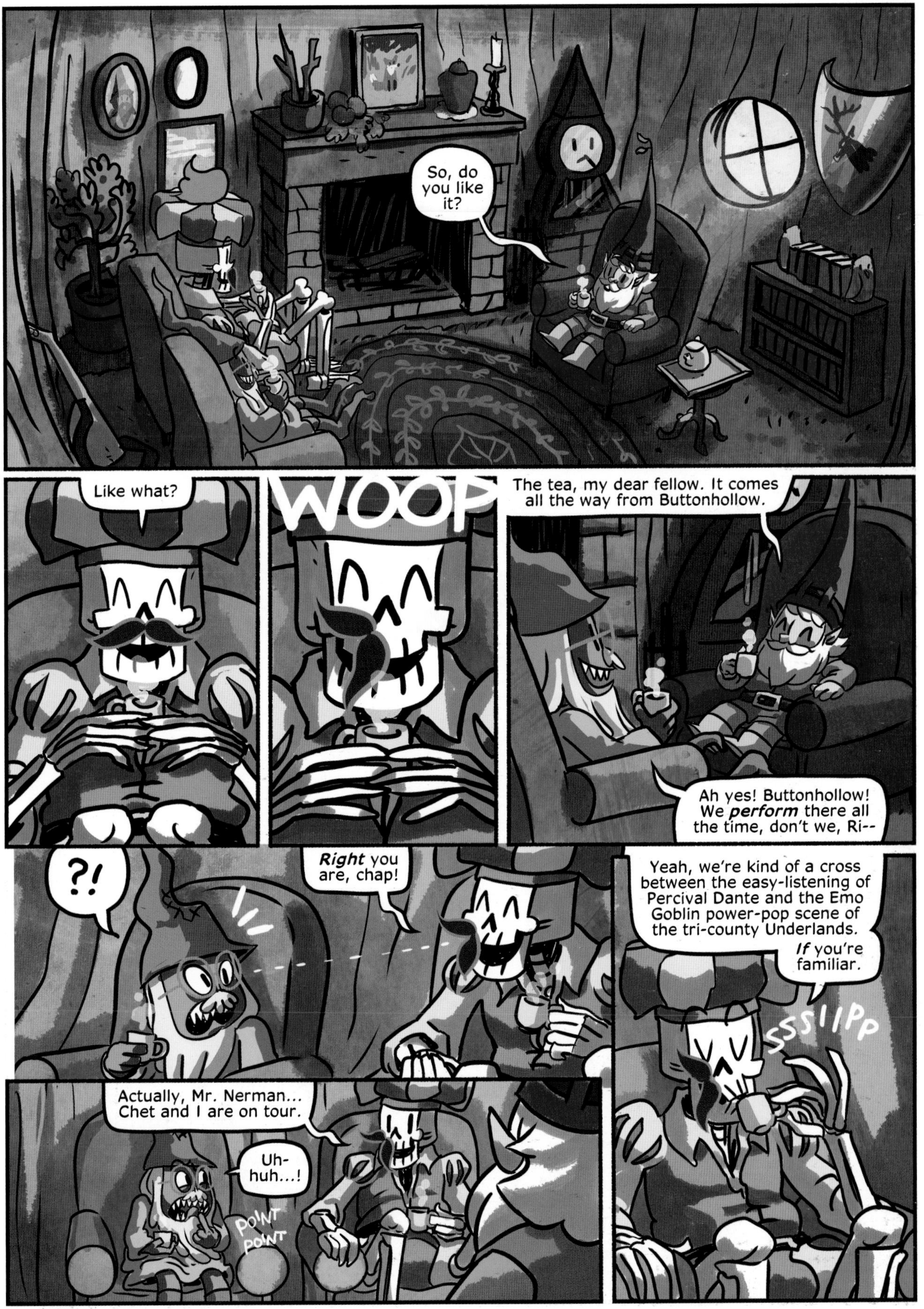

So, do you like it?
Like what?
WOOP
The tea, my dear fellow. It comes all the way from Buttonhollow.
Ah yes! Buttonhollow! We *perform* there all the time, don't we, Ri--
?!
Right you are, chap!
Yeah, we're kind of a cross between the easy-listening of Percival Dante and the Emo Goblin power-pop scene of the tri-county Underlands.
If you're familiar.
SSSIIPP
Actually, Mr. Nerman... Chet and I are on tour.
Uh-huh...!
POINT POINT

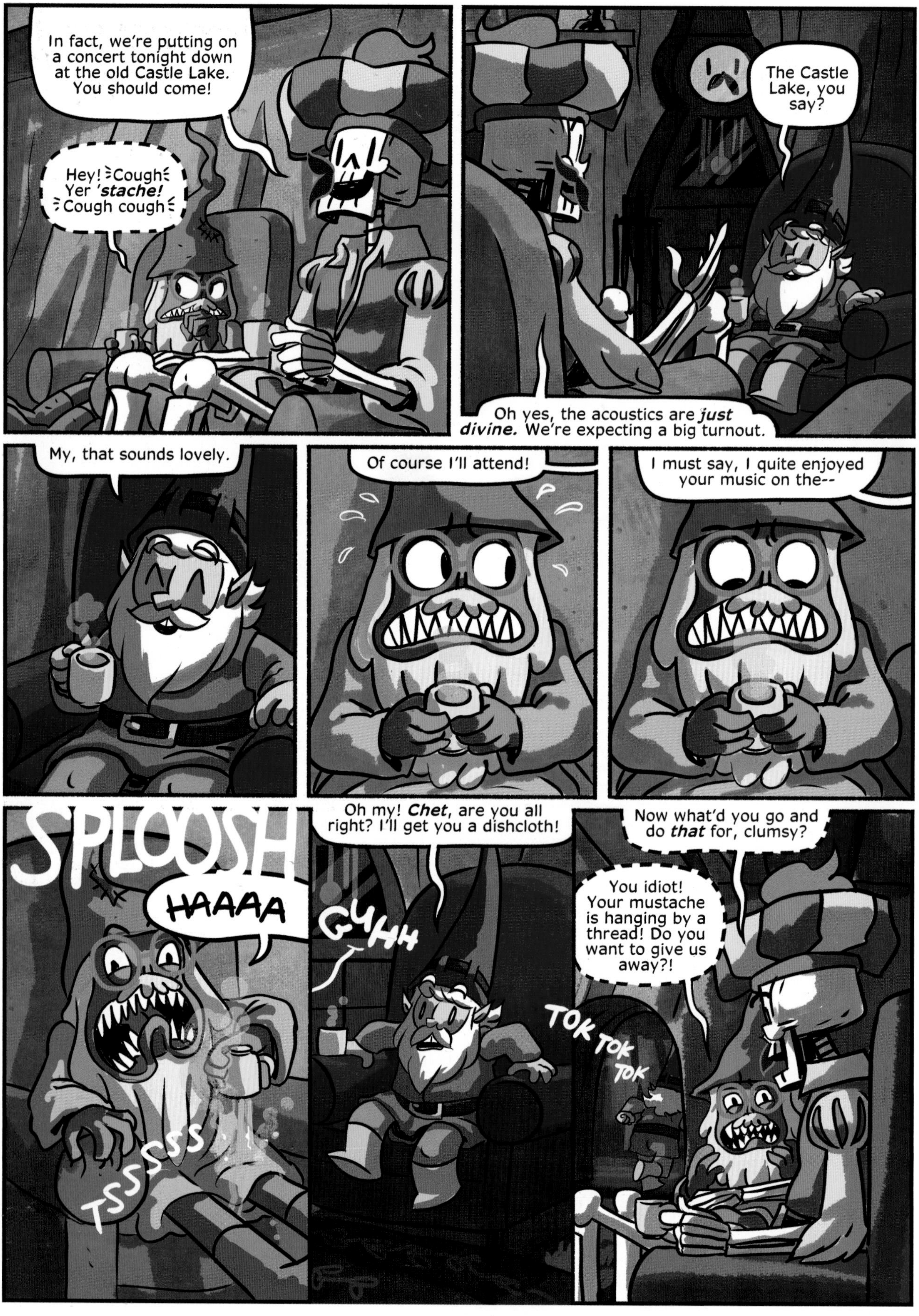

In fact, we're putting on a concert tonight down at the old Castle Lake. You should come!
Hey! Cough! Yer 'stache! Cough cough
The Castle Lake, you say?
Oh yes, the acoustics are just divine. We're expecting a big turnout.
My, that sounds lovely.
Of course I'll attend!
I must say, I quite enjoyed your music on the--
SPLOOSH
HAAAA
TSSSSS
Oh my! Chet, are you all right? I'll get you a dishcloth!
GYHH
Now what'd you go and do that for, clumsy?
You idiot! Your mustache is hanging by a thread! Do you want to give us away?!
TOK TOK TOK

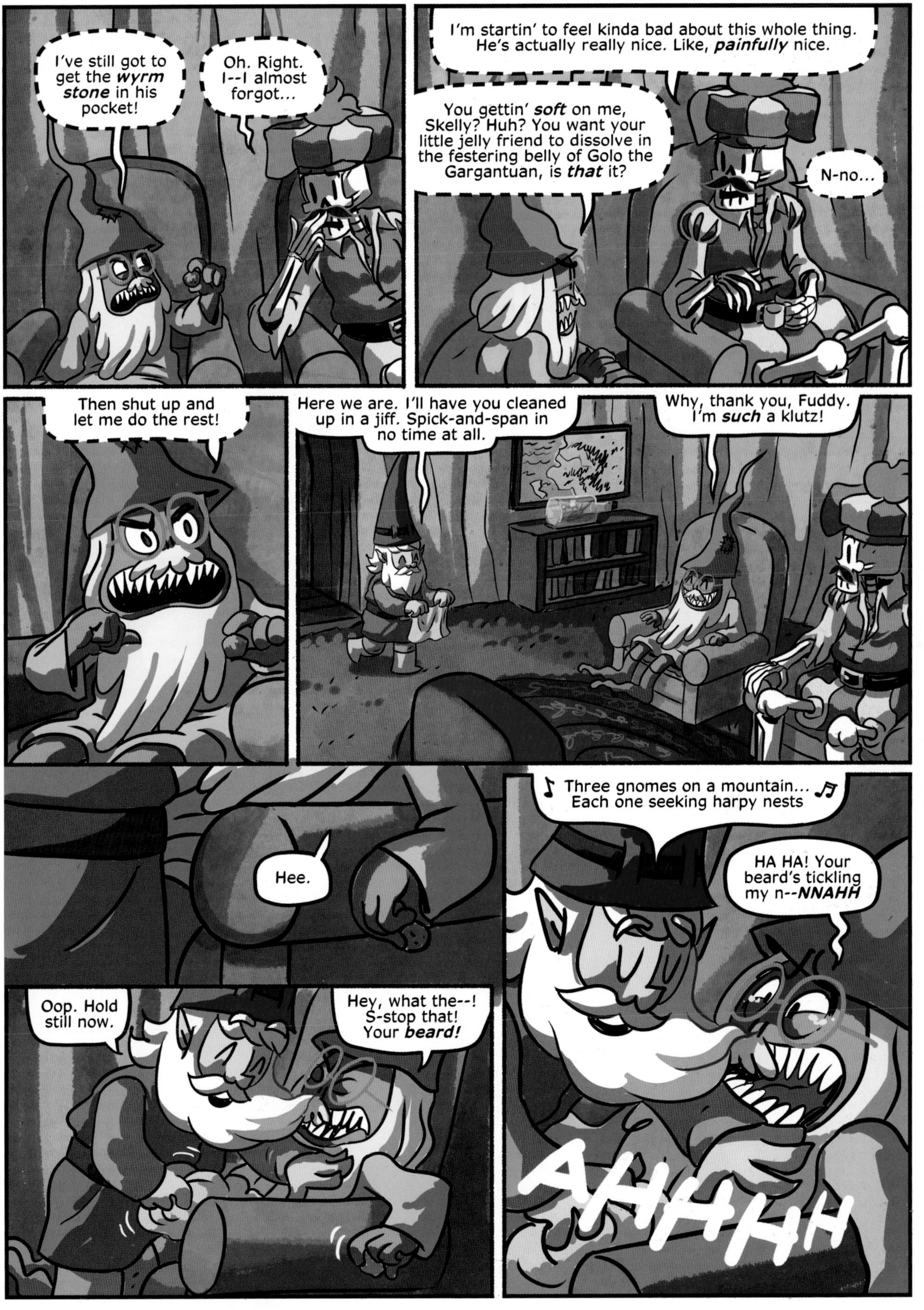
I've still got to get the *wyrm stone* in his pocket!
Oh. Right. I--I almost forgot...
I'm startin' to feel kinda bad about this whole thing. He's actually really nice. Like, *painfully* nice.
You gettin' *soft* on me, Skelly? Huh? You want your little jelly friend to dissolve in the festering belly of Golo the Gargantuan, is *that* it?
N-no...
Then shut up and let me do the rest!
Here we are. I'll have you cleaned up in a jiff. Spick-and-span in no time at all.
Why, thank you, Fuddy. I'm *such* a klutz!
Hee.
♪ Three gnomes on a mountain... Each one seeking harpy nests ♫
HA HA! Your beard's tickling my n--*NNAHH*
Oop. Hold still now.
Hey, what the--! S-stop that! Your *beard!*
AHHHHH

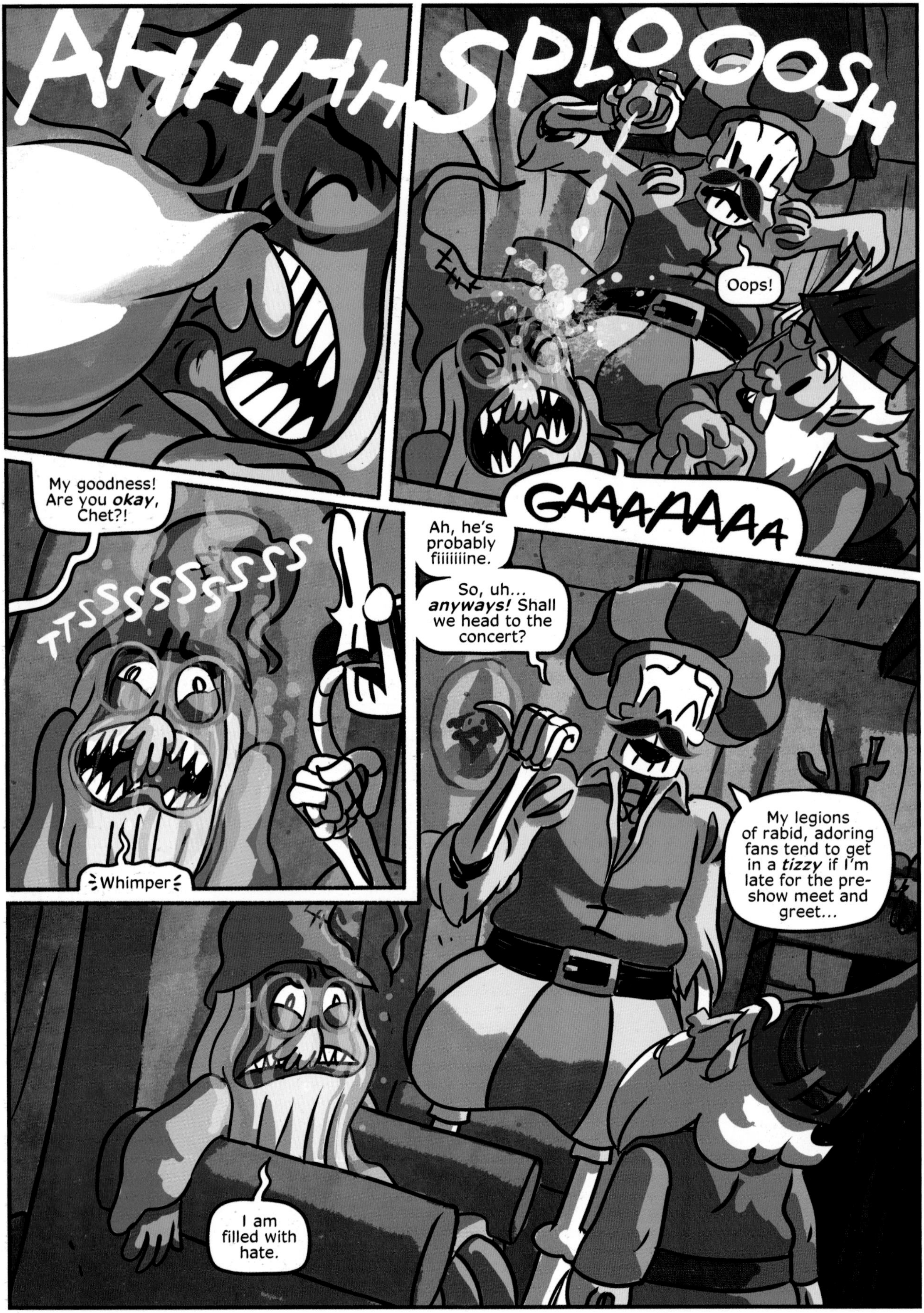
AHHHHH
SPLOOOOSH
Oops!
GAAAAAAA
My goodness! Are you *okay*, Chet?!
TTSSSSSSSSSS
Whimper
Ah, he's probably fiiiiiiine.
So, uh... ***anyways!*** Shall we head to the concert?
My legions of rabid, adoring fans tend to get in a *tizzy* if I'm late for the pre-show meet and greet...
I am filled with hate.

Chapter 11
Prison of Stone

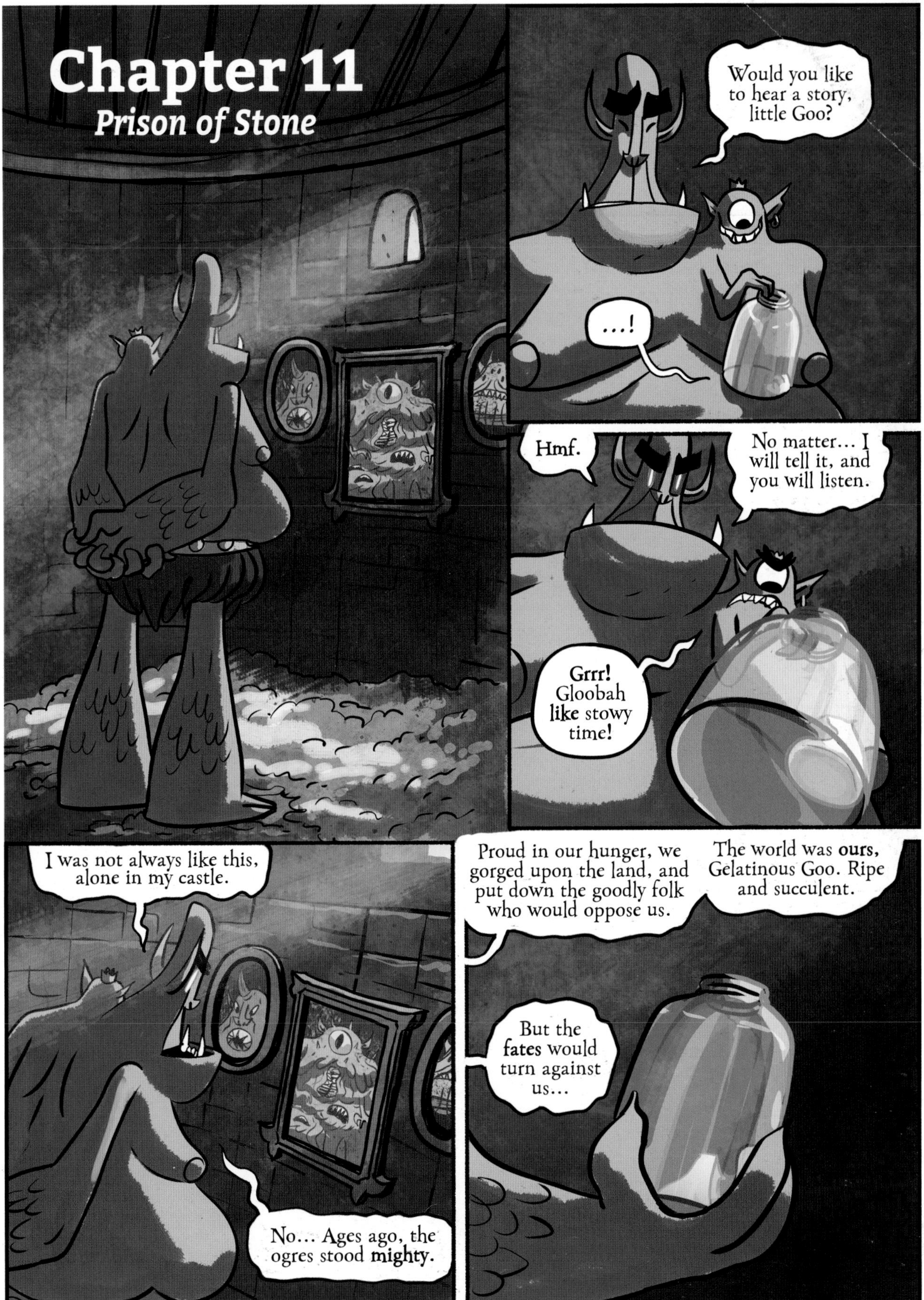

Would you like to hear a story, little Goo?
...!
Hmf.
No matter... I will tell it, and you will listen.
Grrr! Gloobah **like** stowy time!
I was not always like this, alone in my castle.
No... Ages ago, the ogres stood **mighty**.
Proud in our hunger, we gorged upon the land, and put down the goodly folk who would oppose us.
The world was **ours,** Gelatinous Goo. Ripe and succulent.
But the **fates** would turn against us...

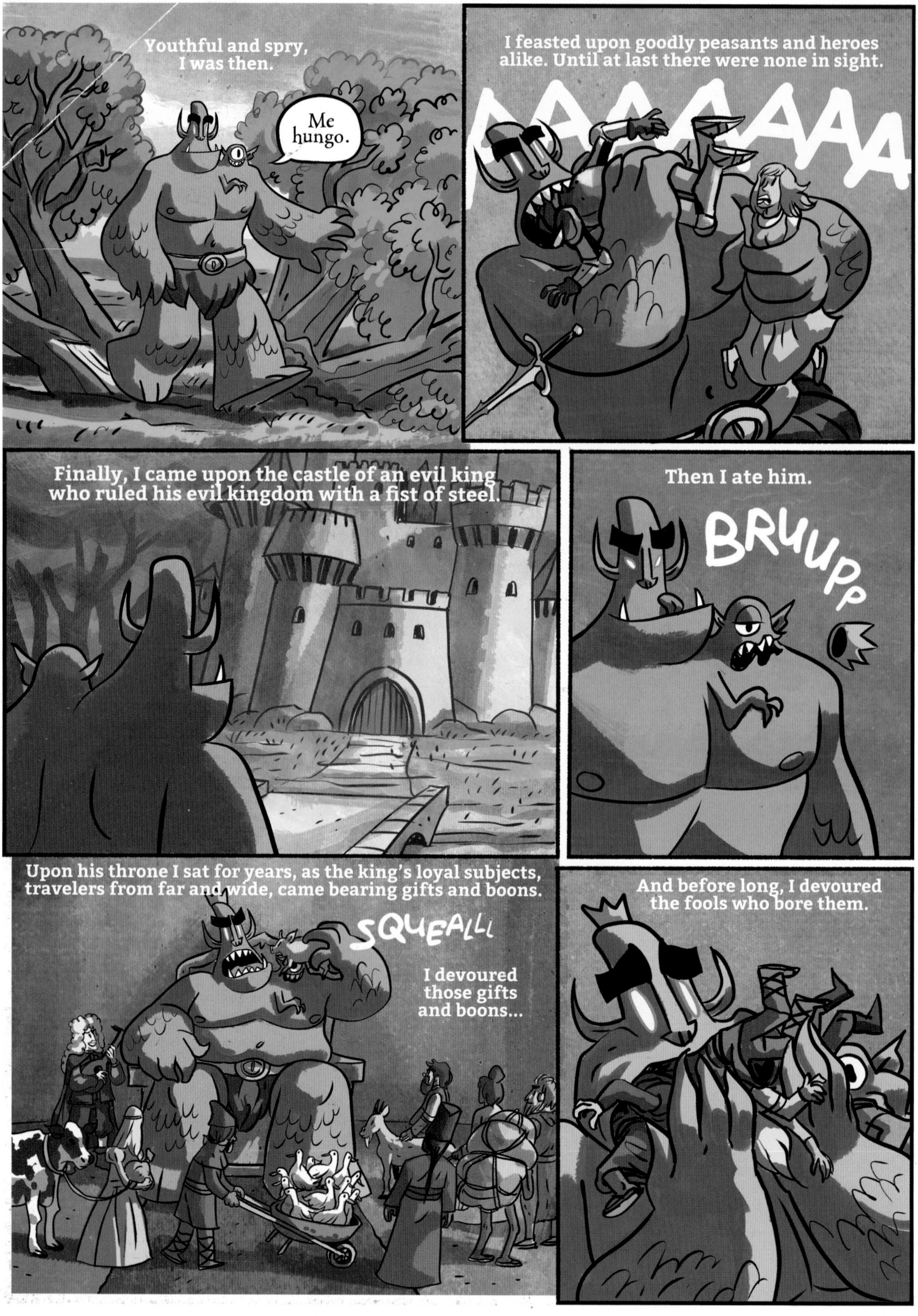
Youthful and spry, I was then.
Me hungo.
I feasted upon goodly peasants and heroes alike. Until at last there were none in sight.
AAAAAAA
Finally, I came upon the castle of an evil king who ruled his evil kingdom with a fist of steel.
Then I ate him.
BRUUPP
Upon his throne I sat for years, as the king's loyal subjects, travelers from far and wide, came bearing gifts and boons.
SQUEALL
I devoured those gifts and boons...
And before long, I devoured the fools who bore them.

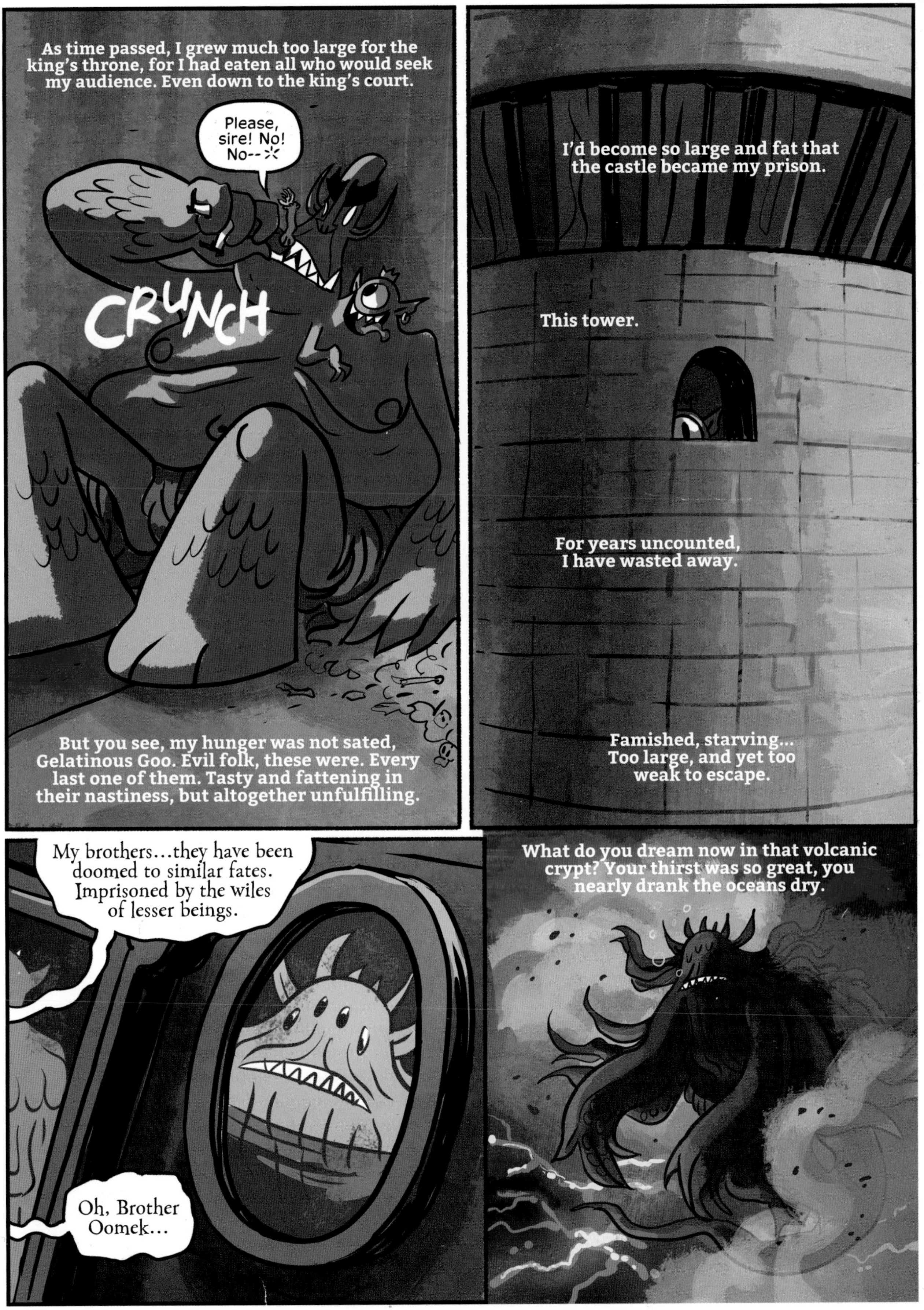
As time passed, I grew much too large for the king's throne, for I had eaten all who would seek my audience. Even down to the king's court.
Please, sire! No! No--
CRUNCH
But you see, my hunger was not sated, Gelatinous Goo. Evil folk, these were. Every last one of them. Tasty and fattening in their nastiness, but altogether unfulfilling.
I'd become so large and fat that the castle became my prison.
This tower.
For years uncounted, I have wasted away.
Famished, starving... Too large, and yet too weak to escape.
My brothers...they have been doomed to similar fates. Imprisoned by the wiles of lesser beings.
Oh, Brother Oomek...
What do you dream now in that volcanic crypt? Your thirst was so great, you nearly drank the oceans dry.

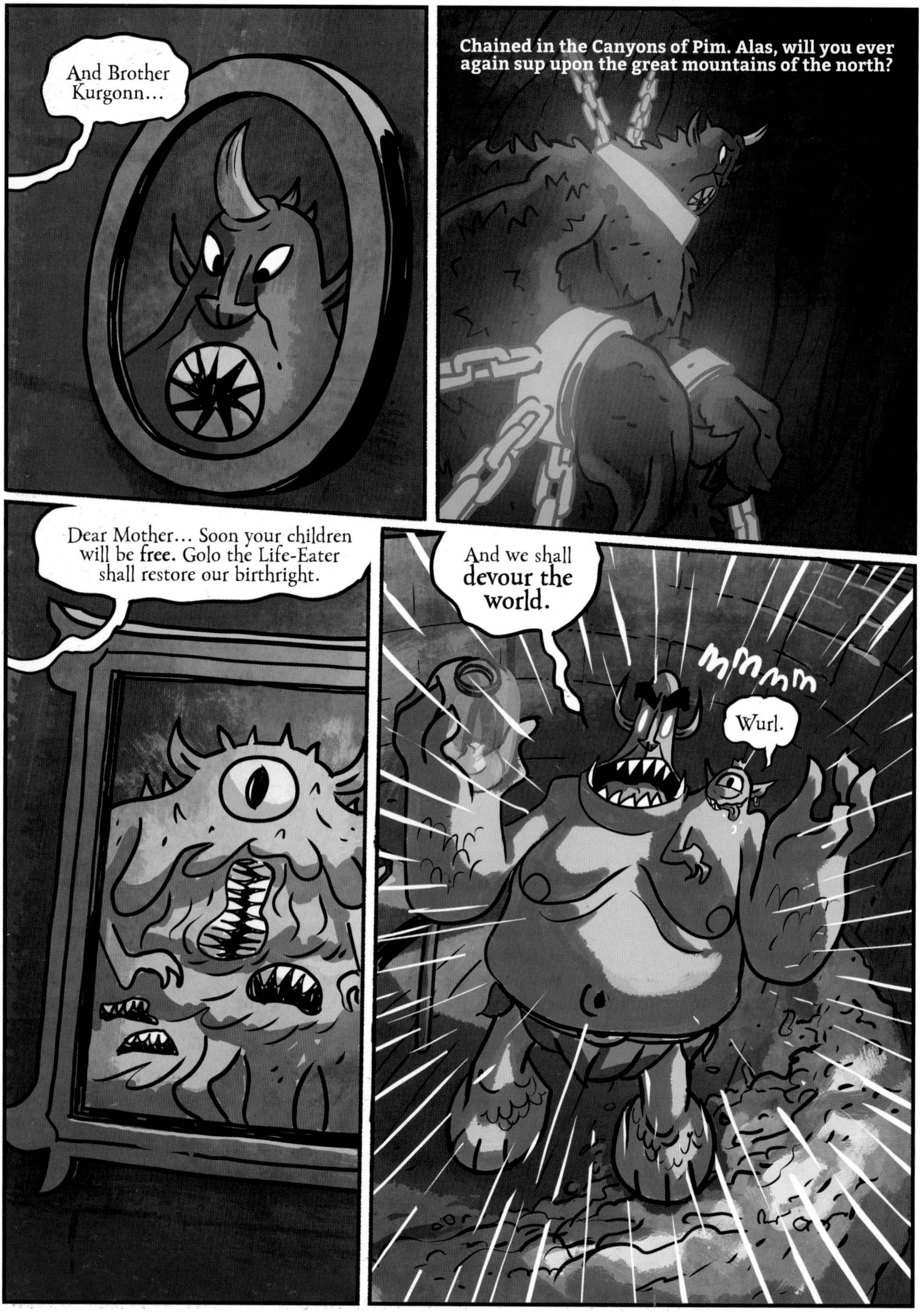

And Brother Kurgonn...
Chained in the Canyons of Pim. Alas, will you ever again sup upon the great mountains of the north?
Dear Mother... Soon your children will be **free.** Golo the Life-Eater shall restore our birthright.
And we shall **devour the world.**
MMMM
Wurl.

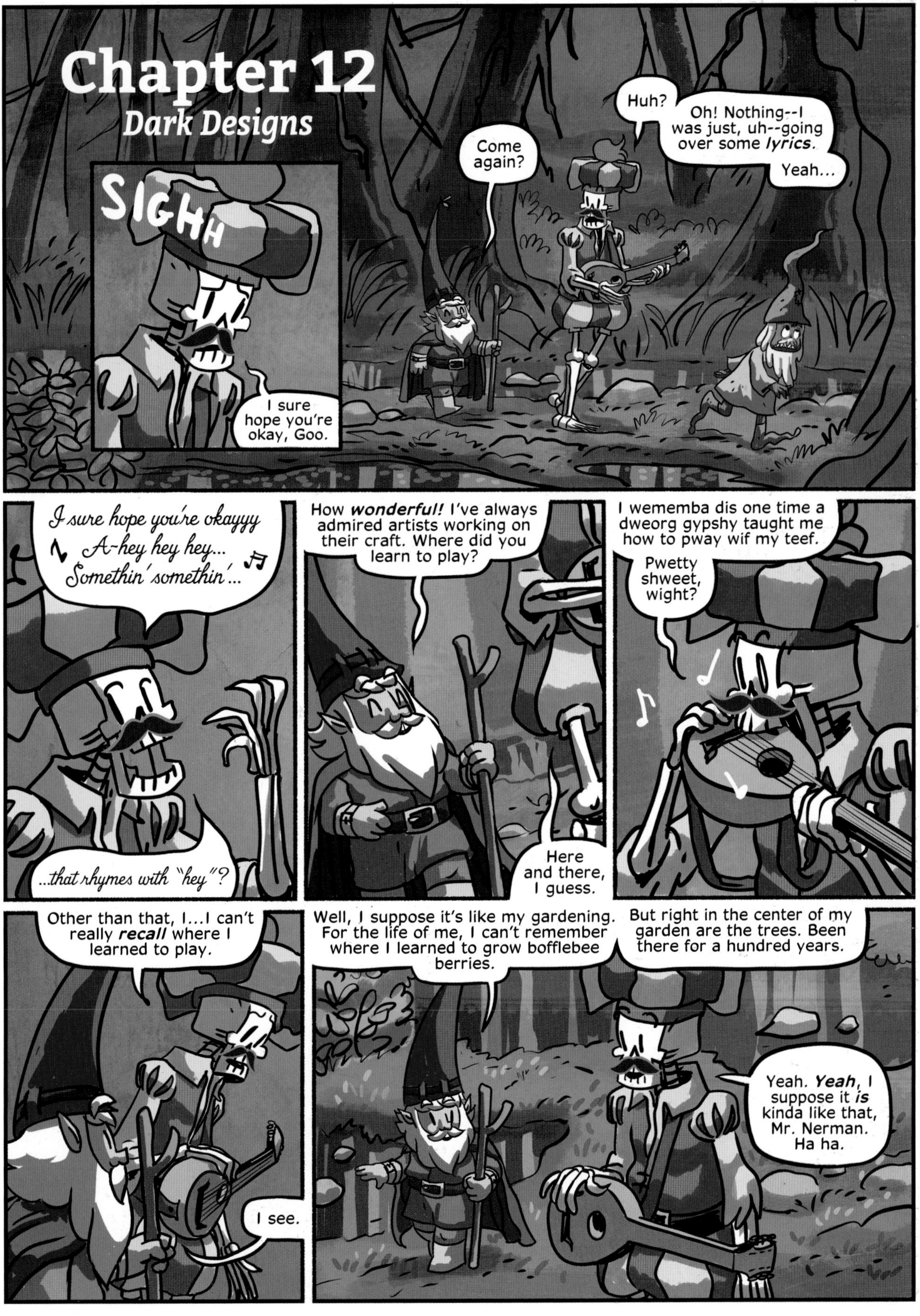

Chapter 12
Dark Designs
SIGHH
I sure hope you're okay, Goo.
Come again?
Huh?
Oh! Nothing--I was just, uh--going over some *lyrics*.
Yeah...
I sure hope you're okayyy A-hey hey hey... Somethin' somethin'...
...that rhymes with "hey"?
How ***wonderful!*** I've always admired artists working on their craft. Where did you learn to play?
Here and there, I guess.
I wememba dis one time a dweorg gypshy taught me how to pway wif my teef.
Pwetty shweet, wight?
Other than that, I...I can't really ***recall*** where I learned to play.
I see.
Well, I suppose it's like my gardening. For the life of me, I can't remember where I learned to grow bofflebee berries.
But right in the center of my garden are the trees. Been there for a hundred years.
Yeah. ***Yeah***, I suppose it *is* kinda like that, Mr. Nerman. Ha ha.

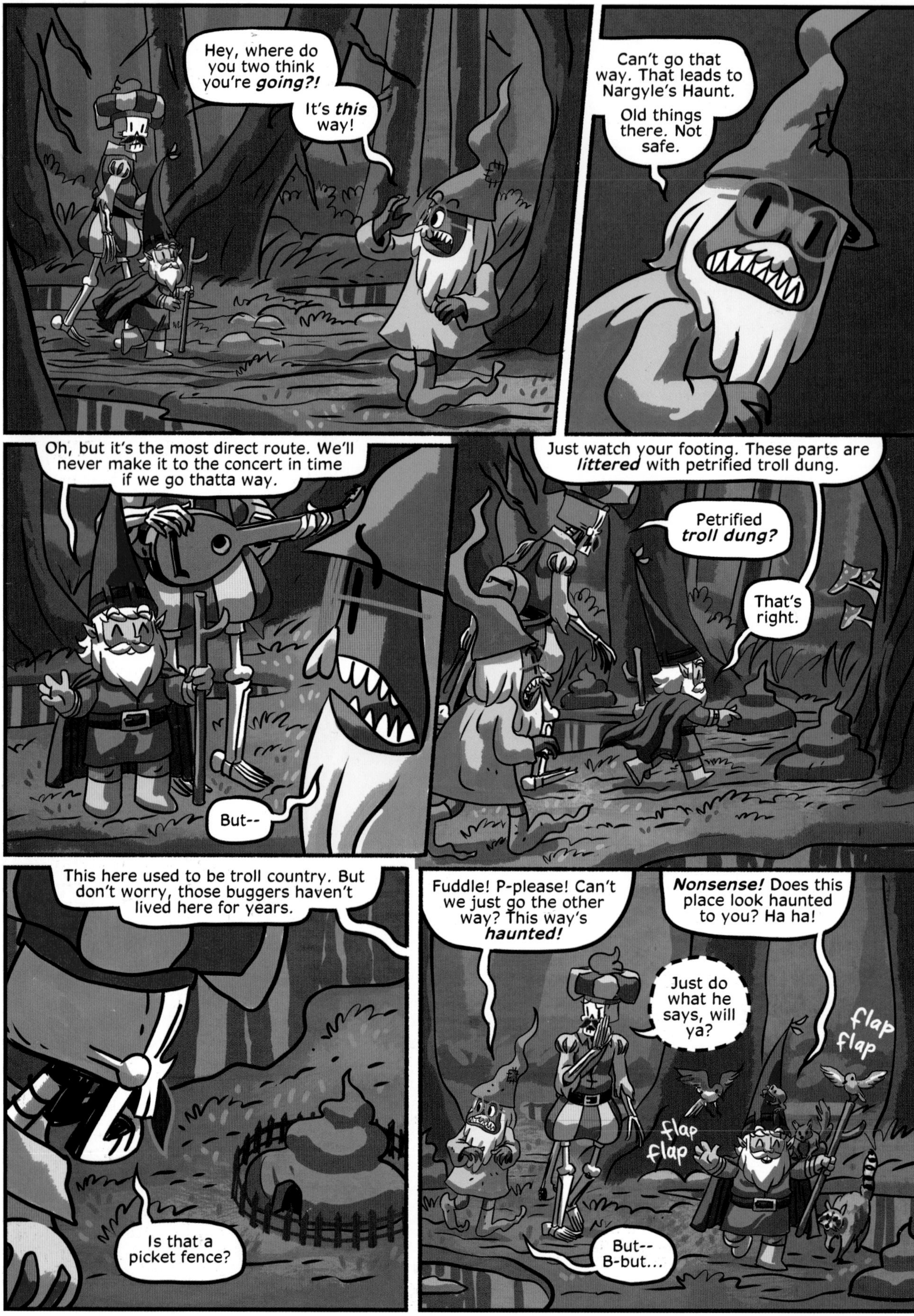
Hey, where do you two think you're ***going?!***
It's ***this*** way!
Can't go that way. That leads to Nargyle's Haunt.
Old things there. Not safe.
Oh, but it's the most direct route. We'll never make it to the concert in time if we go thatta way.
But--
Just watch your footing. These parts are ***littered*** with petrified troll dung.
Petrified ***troll dung?***
That's right.
This here used to be troll country. But don't worry, those buggers haven't lived here for years.
Is that a picket fence?
Fuddle! P-please! Can't we just go the other way? This way's ***haunted!***
Nonsense! Does this place look haunted to you? Ha ha!
Just do what he says, will ya?
flap flap
flap flap
But-- B-but...

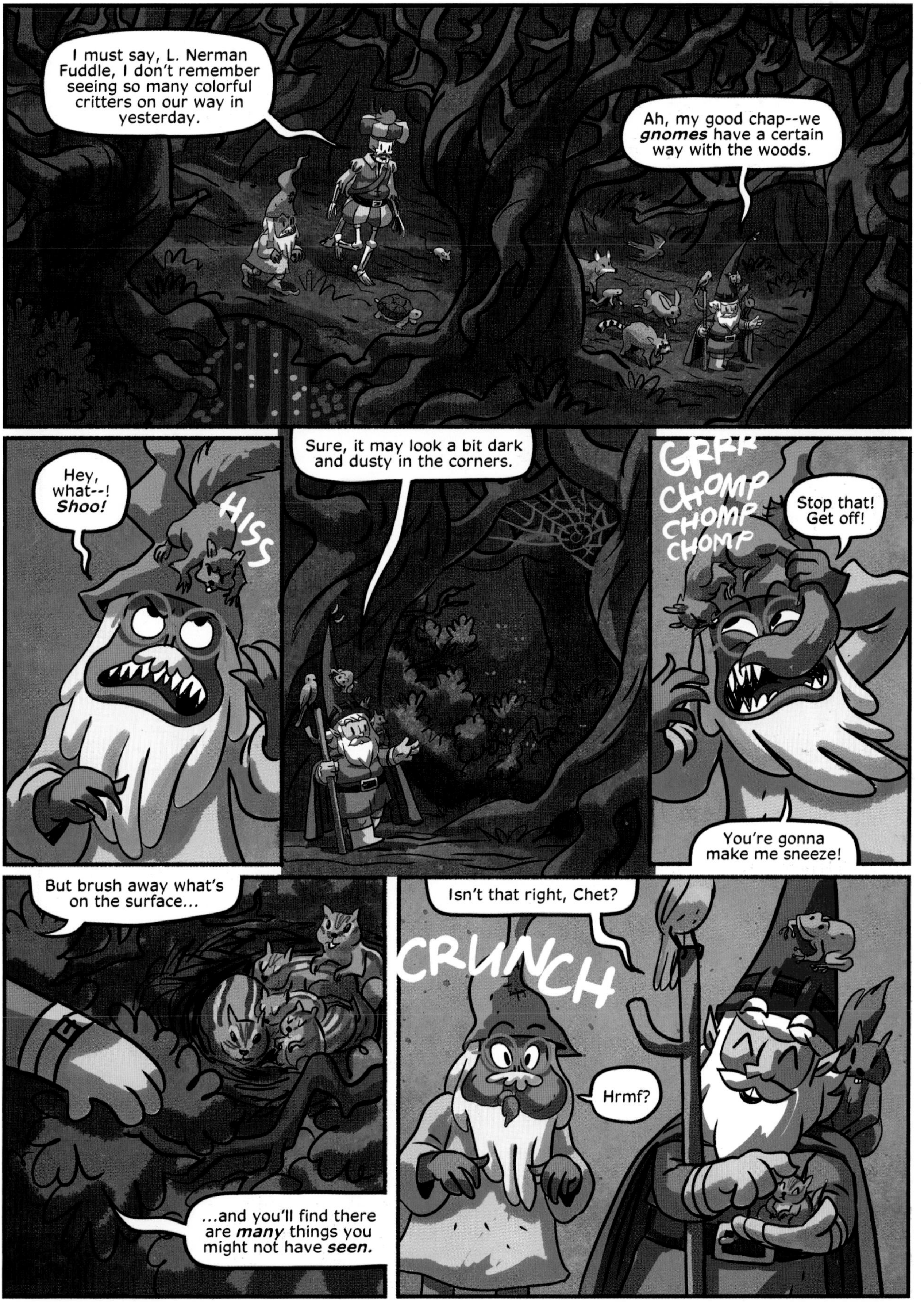

I must say, L. Nerman Fuddle, I don't remember seeing so many colorful critters on our way in yesterday.
Ah, my good chap--we *gnomes* have a certain way with the woods.
Hey, what--! *Shoo!*
HISS
Sure, it may look a bit dark and dusty in the corners.
GRRR
CHOMP CHOMP CHOMP
Stop that! Get off!
You're gonna make me sneeze!
But brush away what's on the surface...
...and you'll find there are *many* things you might not have *seen.*
Isn't that right, Chet?
CRUNCH
Hrmf?

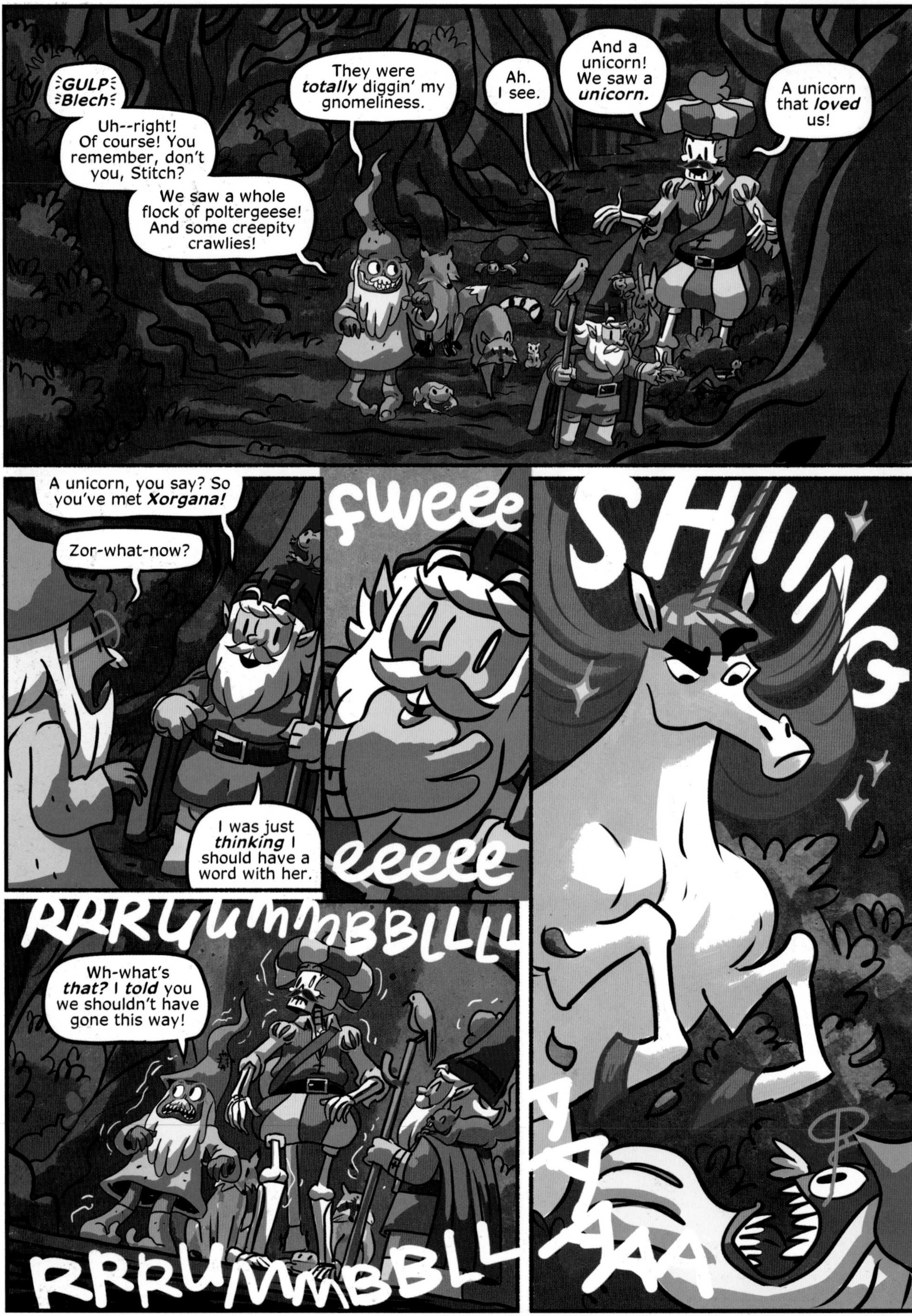
GULP
Blech
Uh--right! Of course! You remember, don't you, Stitch?
We saw a whole flock of poltergeese! And some creepity crawlies!
They were totally diggin' my gnomeliness.
Ah. I see.
And a unicorn! We saw a unicorn.
A unicorn that loved us!
A unicorn, you say? So you've met Xorgana!
Zor-what-now?
I was just thinking I should have a word with her.
fweeeeeeee
SHIING
RRRUMMBBLLL
Wh-what's that? I told you we shouldn't have gone this way!
RRRUMMBBLL
AAAAAA

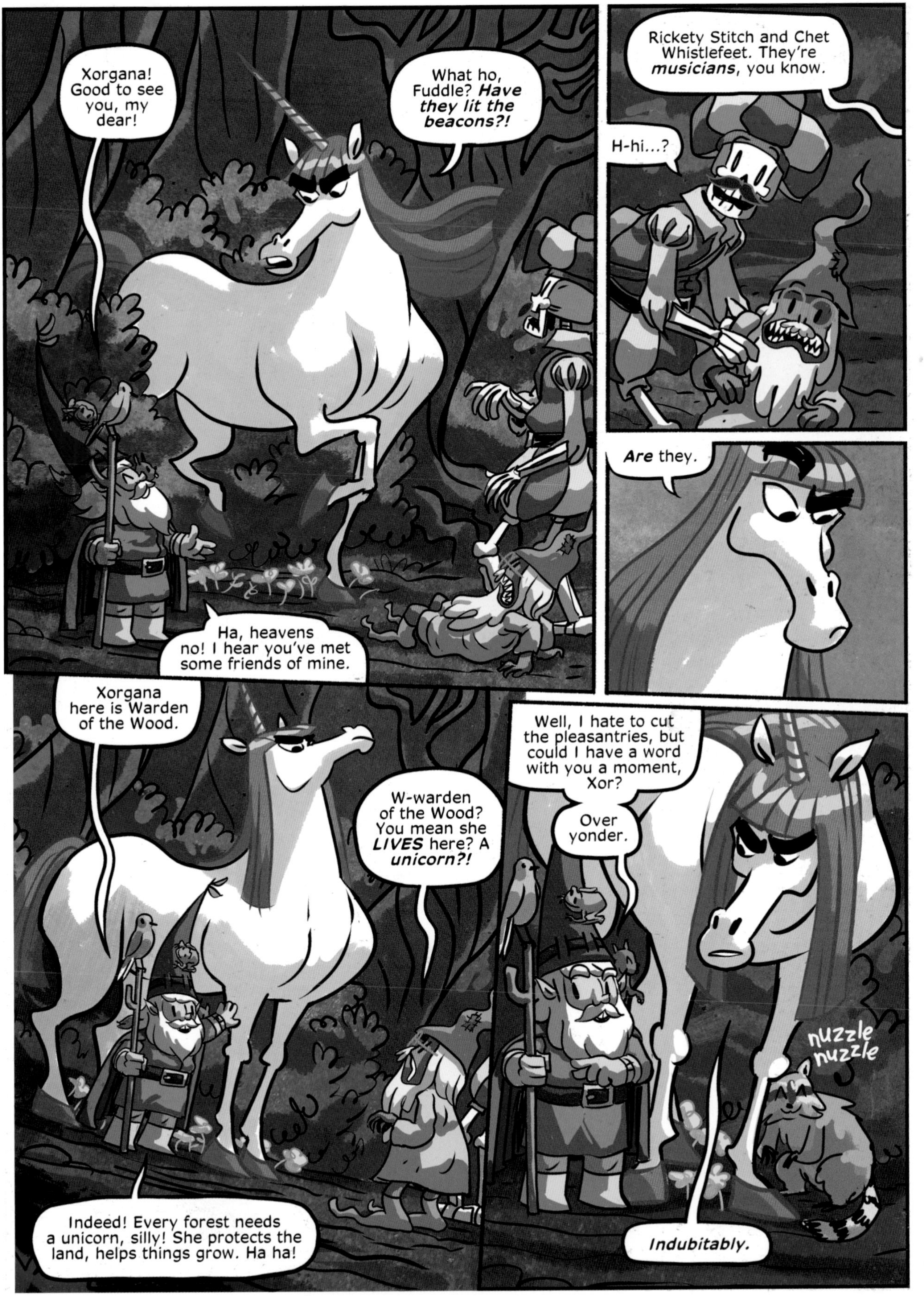
Xorgana! Good to see you, my dear!
What ho, Fuddle? *Have they lit the beacons?!*
Ha, heavens no! I hear you've met some friends of mine.
Rickety Stitch and Chet Whistlefeet. They're *musicians*, you know.
H-hi...?
Are they.
Xorgana here is Warden of the Wood.
W-warden of the Wood? You mean she *LIVES* here? A *unicorn?!*
Indeed! Every forest needs a unicorn, silly! She protects the land, helps things grow. Ha ha!
Well, I hate to cut the pleasantries, but could I have a word with you a moment, Xor?
Over yonder.
nuzzle nuzzle
Indubitably.

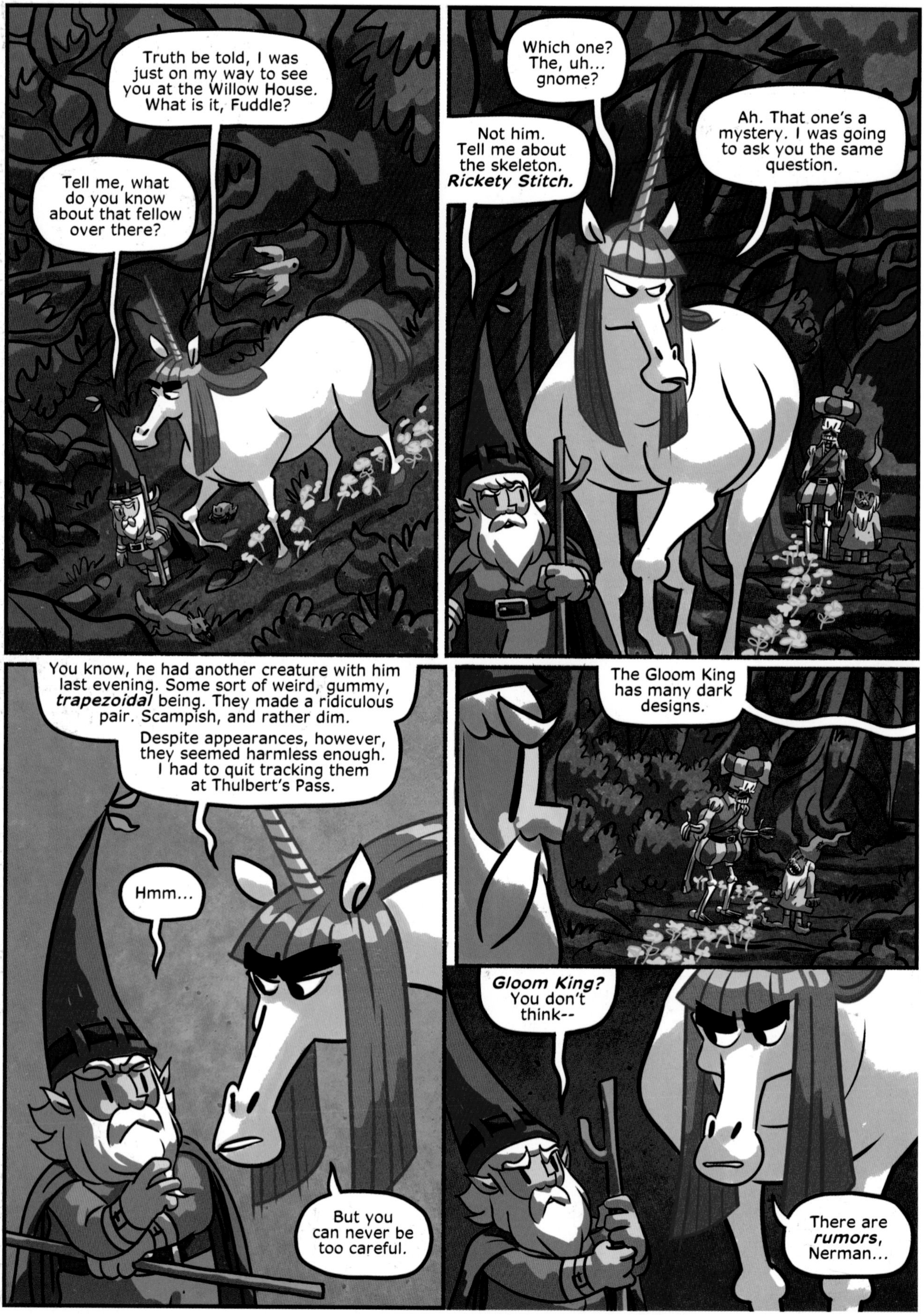
Tell me, what do you know about that fellow over there?
Truth be told, I was just on my way to see you at the Willow House. What is it, Fuddle?
Which one? The, uh... gnome?
Not him. Tell me about the skeleton. ***Rickety Stitch.***
Ah. That one's a mystery. I was going to ask you the same question.
You know, he had another creature with him last evening. Some sort of weird, gummy, ***trapezoidal*** being. They made a ridiculous pair. Scampish, and rather dim.
Despite appearances, however, they seemed harmless enough. I had to quit tracking them at Thulbert's Pass.
Hmm...
But you can never be too careful.
The Gloom King has many dark designs.
Gloom King? You don't think--
There are ***rumors,*** Nerman...

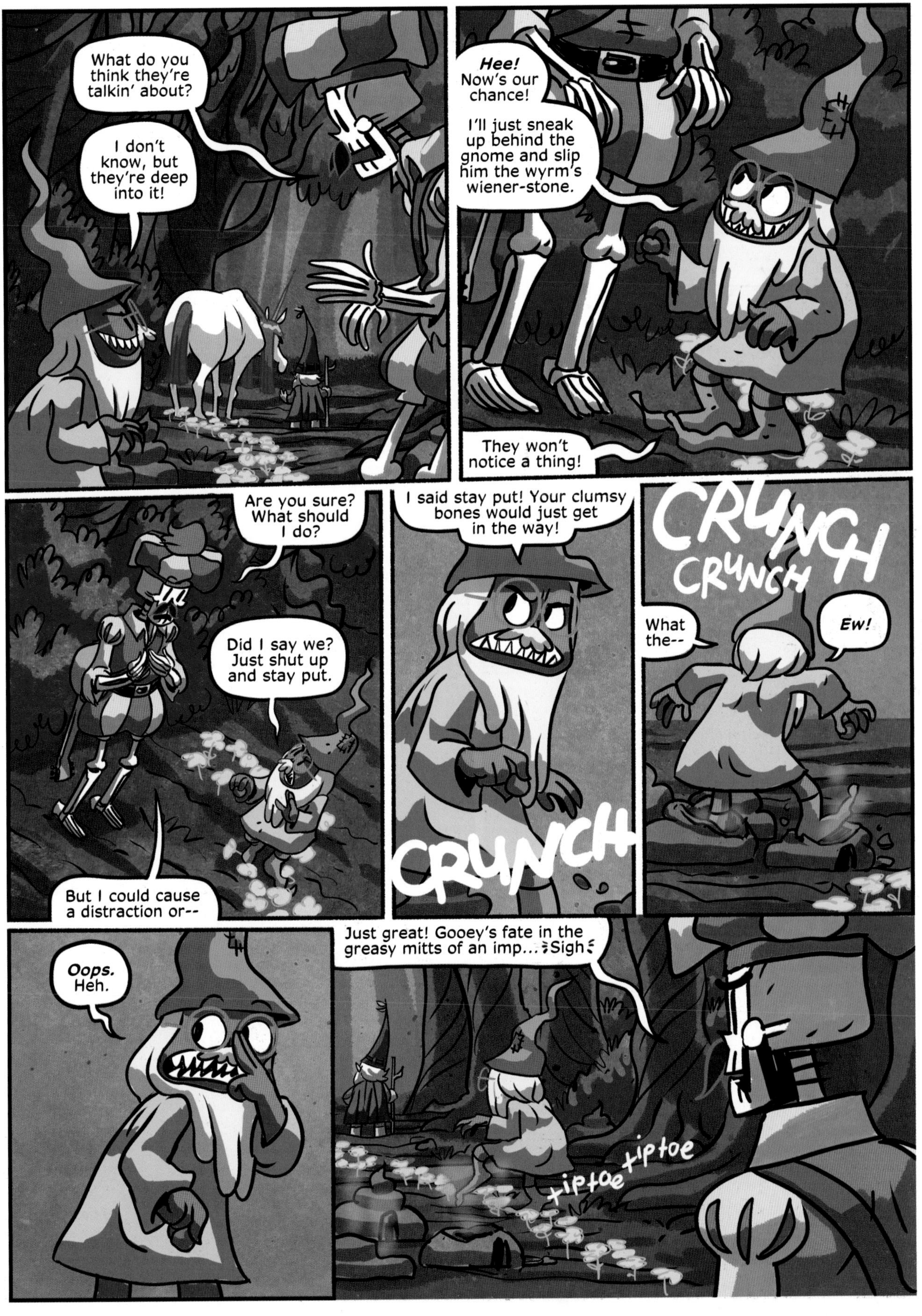
What do you think they're talkin' about?
I don't know, but they're deep into it!
Hee! Now's our chance!
I'll just sneak up behind the gnome and slip him the wyrm's wiener-stone.
They won't notice a thing!
Are you sure? What should I do?
Did I say we? Just shut up and stay put.
But I could cause a distraction or--
I said stay put! Your clumsy bones would just get in the way!
CRUNCH
CRUNCH
CRUNCH
CRUNCH
What the--
Ew!
Oops. Heh.
Just great! Gooey's fate in the greasy mitts of an imp... ⸗Sigh⸗
tiptoe tiptoe

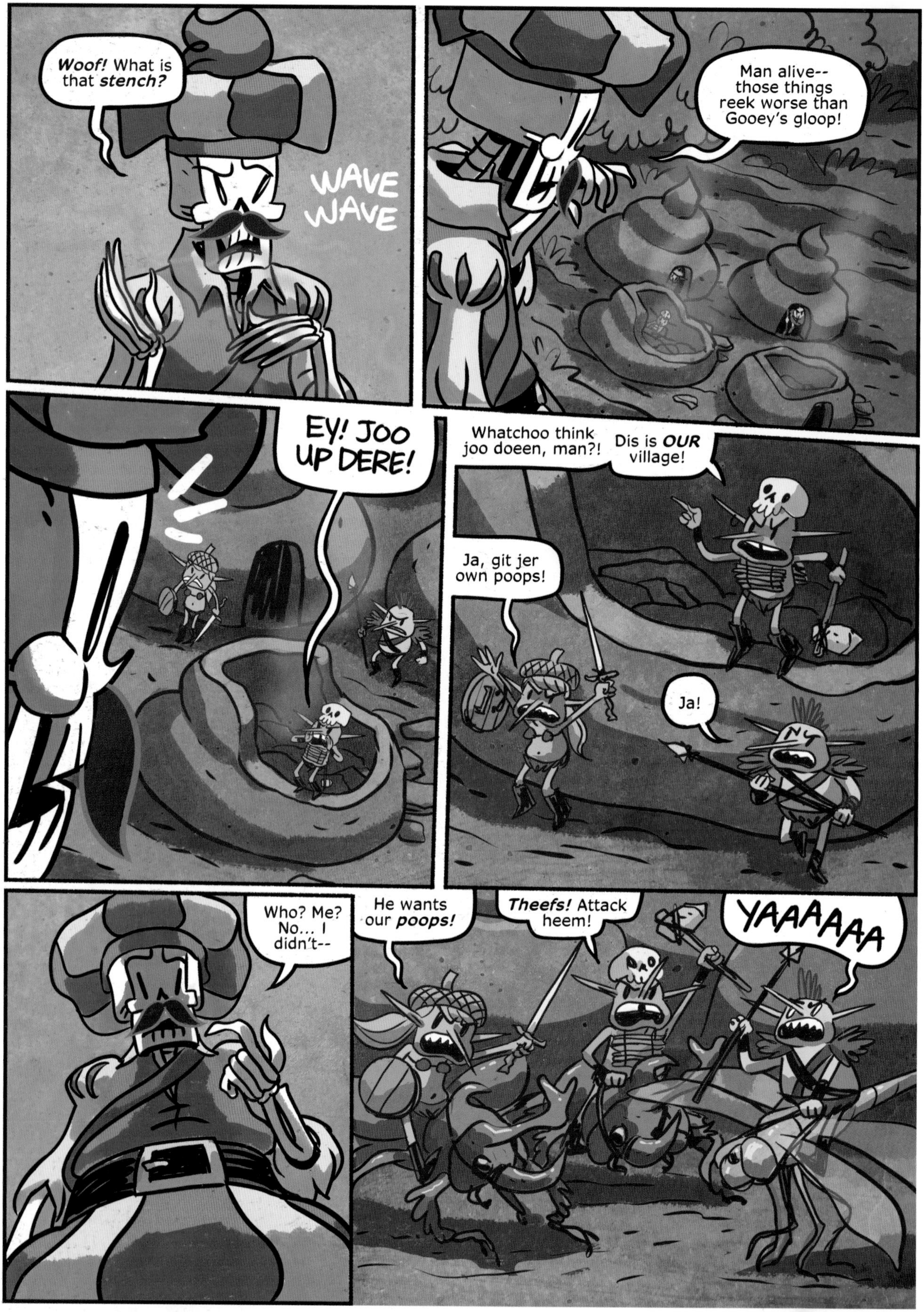

Woof! What is that stench?
WAVE WAVE
Man alive-- those things reek worse than Gooey's gloop!
EY! JOO UP DERE!
Whatchoo think joo doeen, man?!
Dis is OUR village!
Ja, git jer own poops!
Ja!
Who? Me? No... I didn't--
He wants our poops!
Theefs! Attack heem!
YAAAAAA

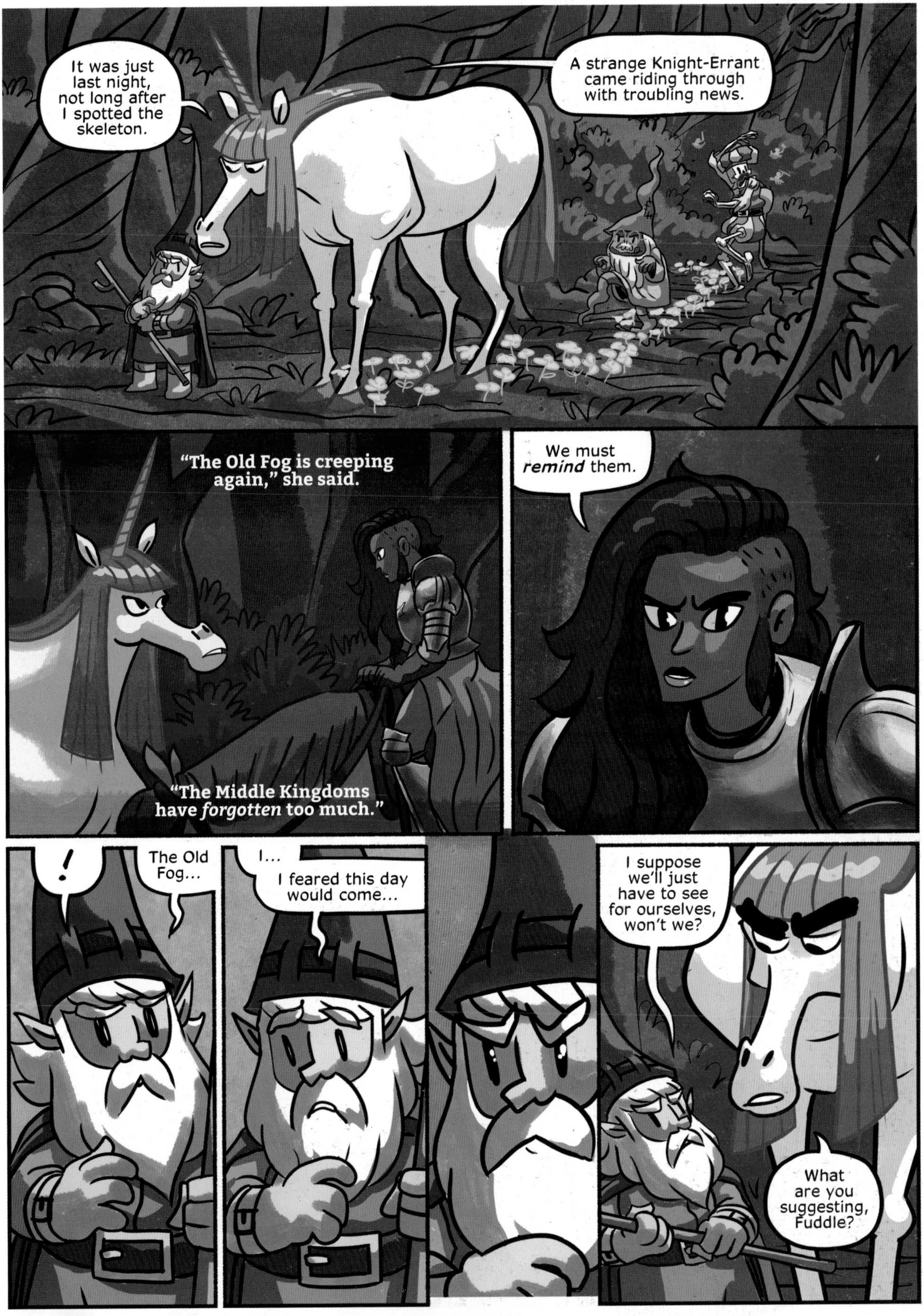
It was just last night, not long after I spotted the skeleton.
A strange Knight-Errant came riding through with troubling news.
"The Old Fog is creeping again," she said.
"The Middle Kingdoms have *forgotten* too much."
We must *remind* them.
!
The Old Fog...
I...
I feared this day would come...
I suppose we'll just have to see for ourselves, won't we?
What are you suggesting, Fuddle?

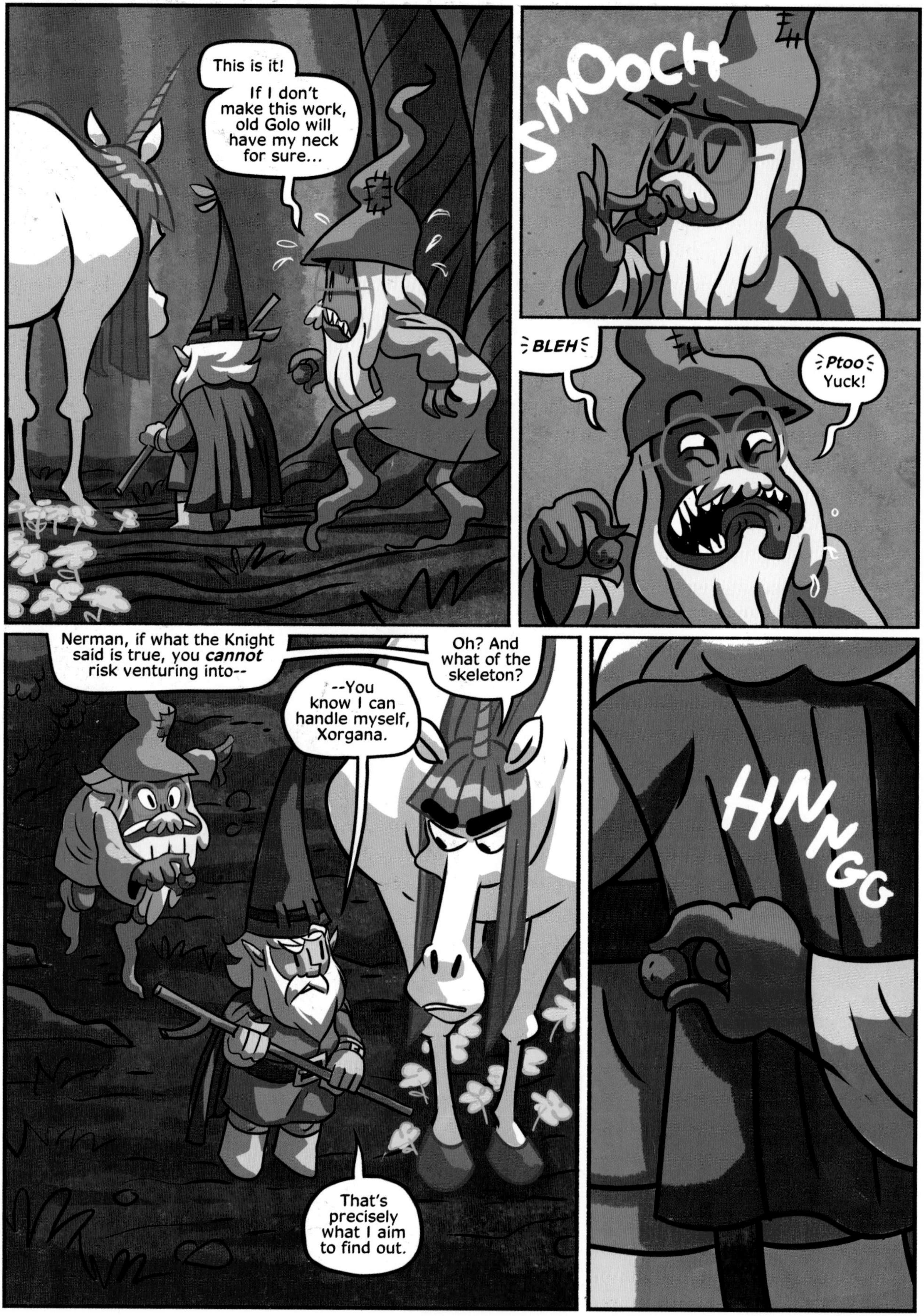

This is it!
If I don't make this work, old Golo will have my neck for sure...
SMOOCH
BLEH
Ptoo Yuck!
Nerman, if what the Knight said is true, you *cannot* risk venturing into--
--You know I can handle myself, Xorgana.
Oh? And what of the skeleton?
That's precisely what I aim to find out.
HNNGG

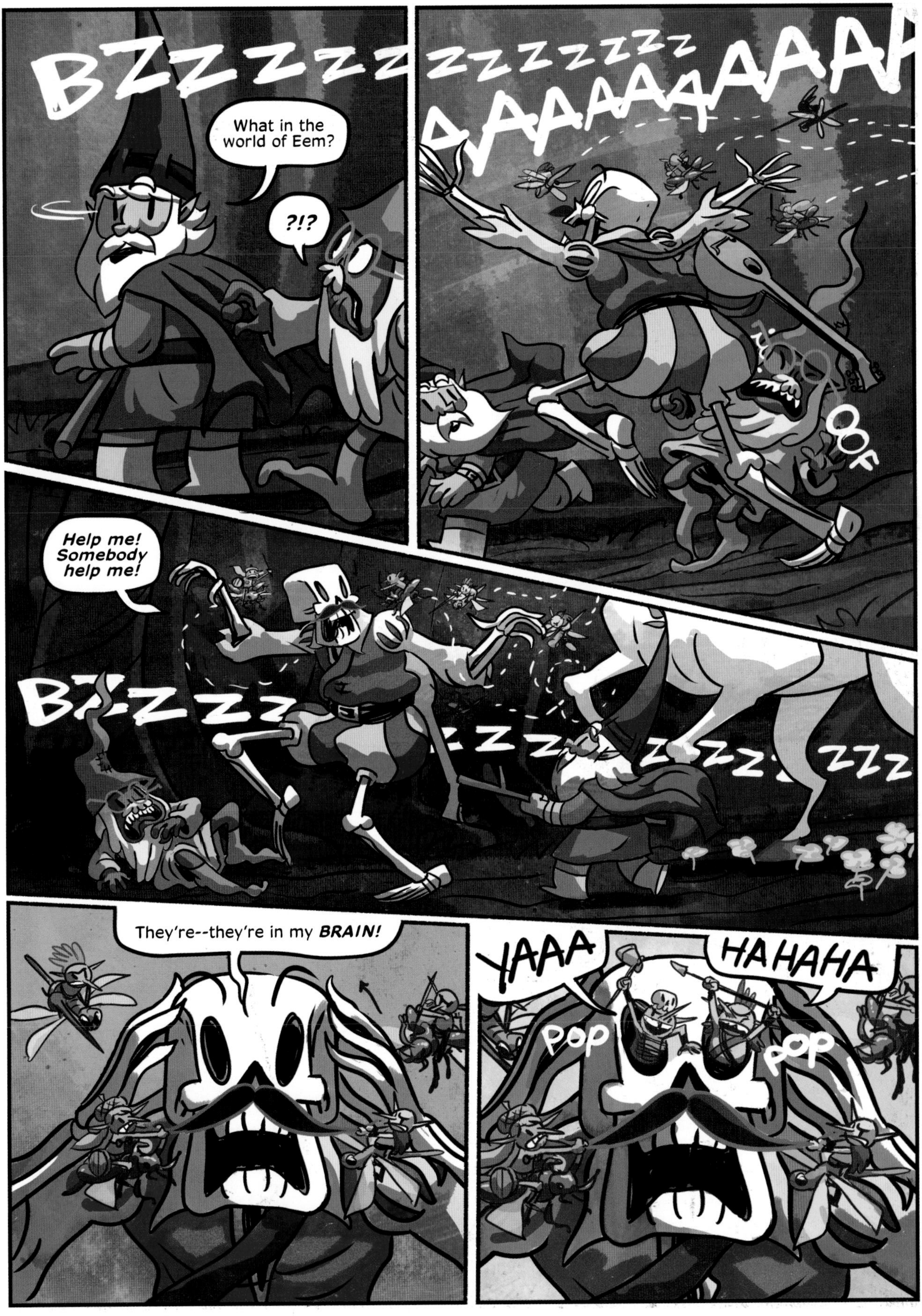

BZZZZZZZZZZZZZZZZ
What in the world of Eem?
?!?
AAAAAAAAAAAH
OOF
Help me! Somebody help me!
BZZZZZZZZZZZZZZZ
They're--they're in my BRAIN!
YAAA
HAHAHA
POP
POP

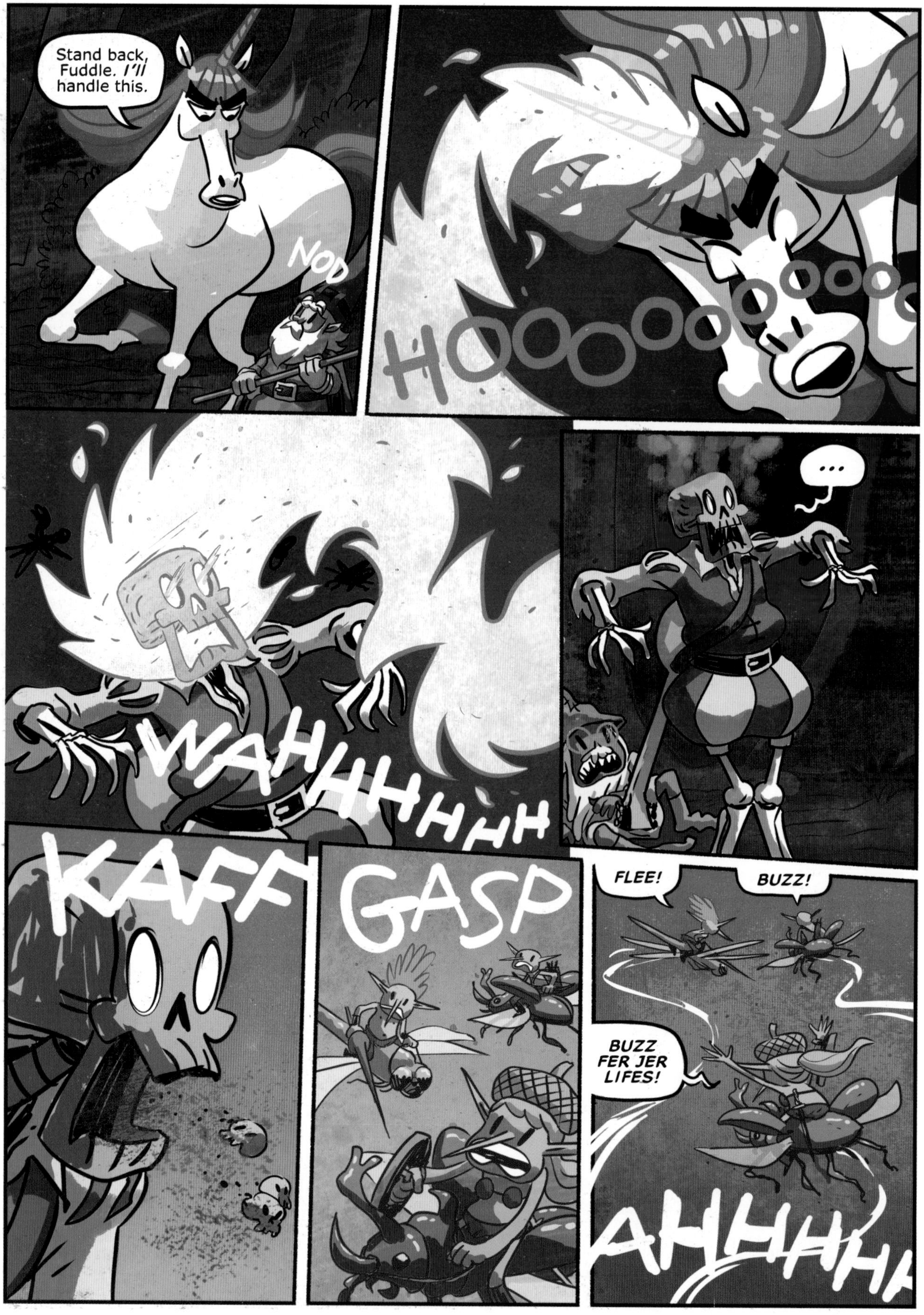
Stand back, Fuddle. I'll handle this.
NOD
HOOOOOOOOOOO
WAHHHHHHH
...
KAFF
GASP
FLEE!
BUZZ!
BUZZ FER JER LIFES!
AHHHHHH

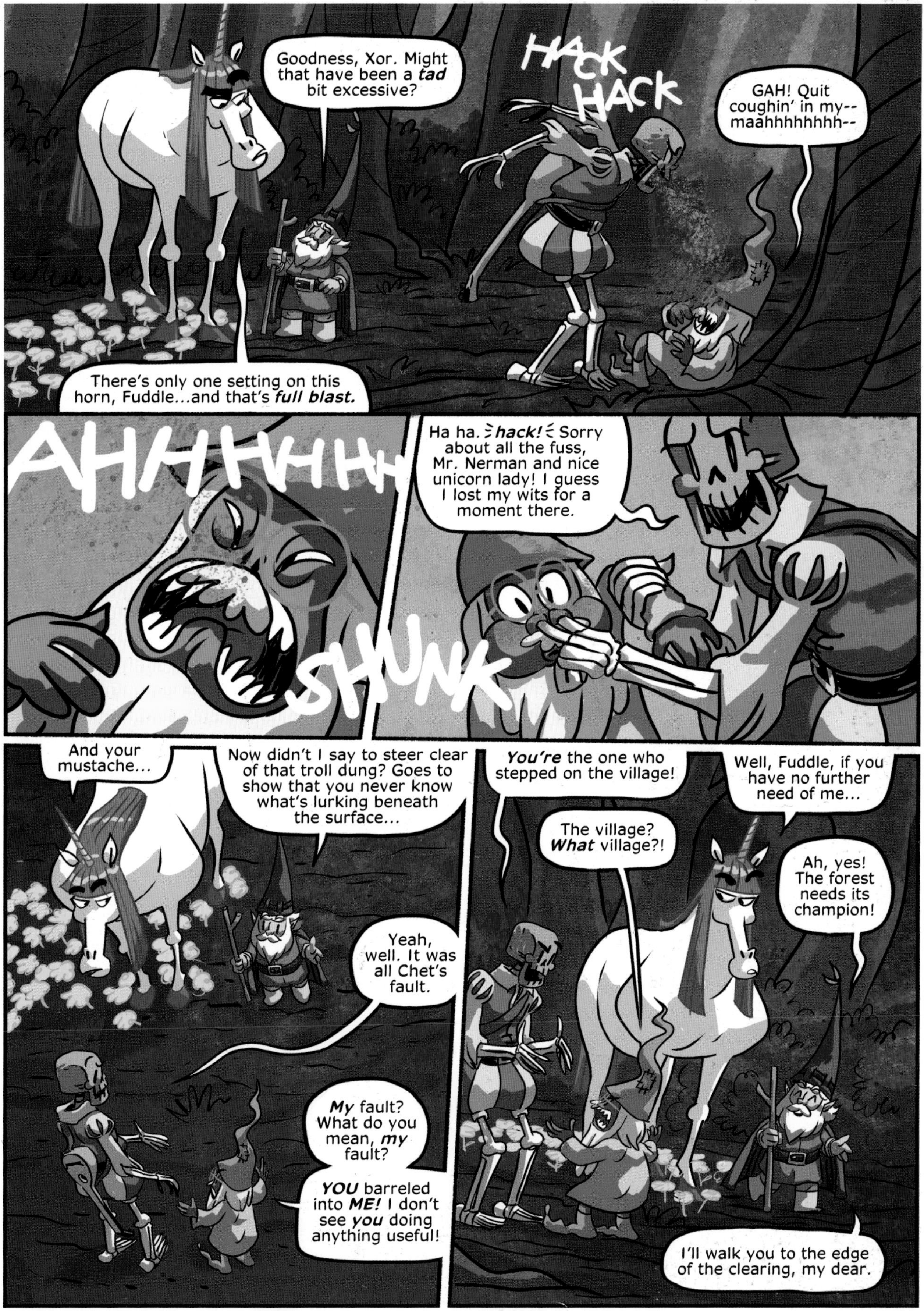
Goodness, Xor. Might that have been a ***tad*** bit excessive?
There's only one setting on this horn, Fuddle...and that's ***full blast.***
HACK HACK
GAH! Quit coughin' in my--maahhhhhhhh--
AHHHHHH
SHUNK
Ha ha. ***hack!*** Sorry about all the fuss, Mr. Nerman and nice unicorn lady! I guess I lost my wits for a moment there.
And your mustache...
Now didn't I say to steer clear of that troll dung? Goes to show that you never know what's lurking beneath the surface...
Yeah, well. It was all Chet's fault.
My fault? What do you mean, ***my*** fault?
YOU barreled into ***ME!*** I don't see ***you*** doing anything useful!
You're the one who stepped on the village!
The village? ***What*** village?!
Well, Fuddle, if you have no further need of me...
Ah, yes! The forest needs its champion!
I'll walk you to the edge of the clearing, my dear.

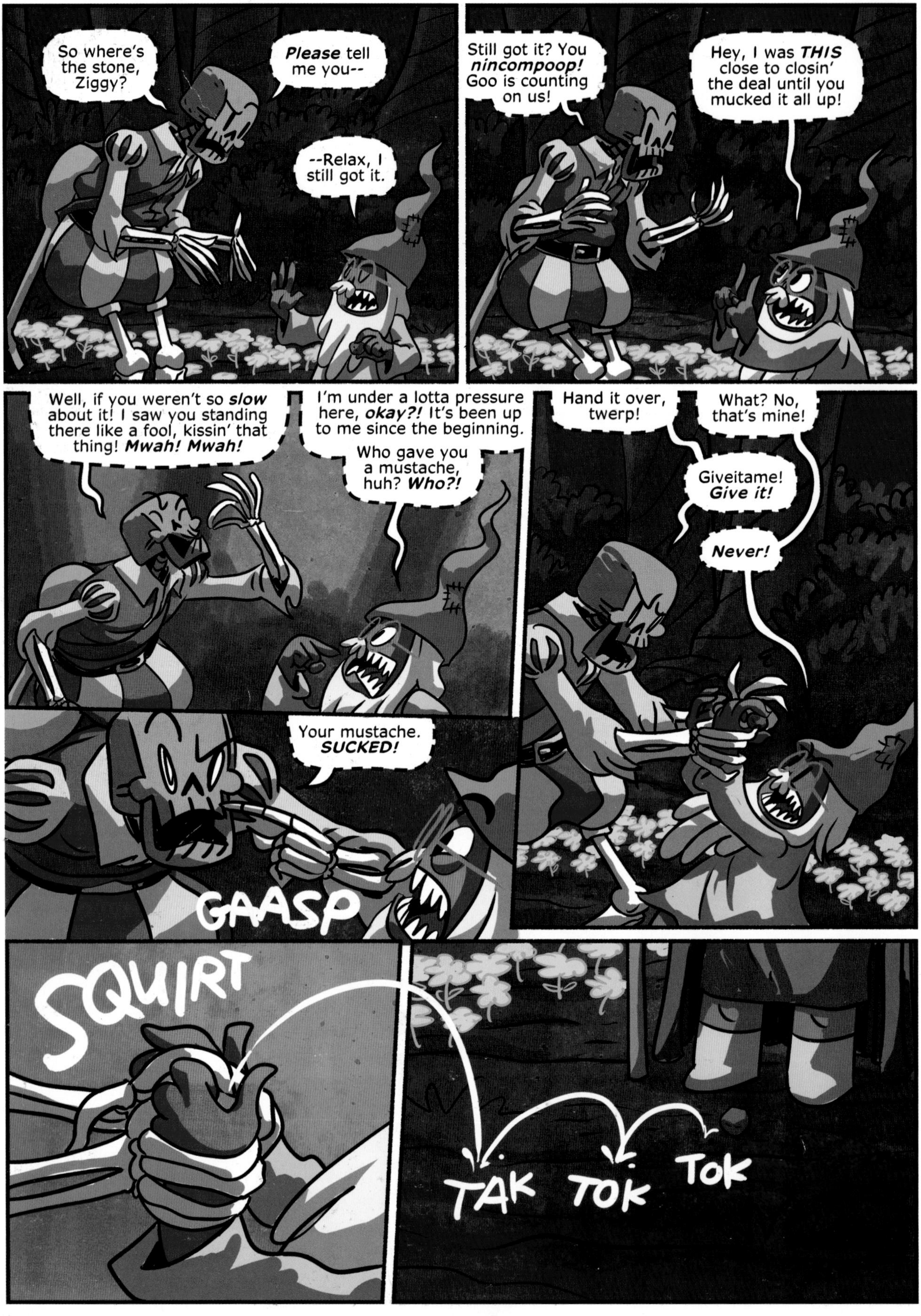
So where's the stone, Ziggy?
Please tell me you--
--Relax, I still got it.
Still got it? You *nincompoop!* Goo is counting on us!
Hey, I was *THIS* close to closin' the deal until you mucked it all up!
Well, if you weren't so *slow* about it! I saw you standing there like a fool, kissin' that thing! *Mwah! Mwah!*
I'm under a lotta pressure here, *okay?!* It's been up to me since the beginning.
Who gave you a mustache, huh? *Who?!*
Your mustache. *SUCKED!*
GAASP
Hand it over, twerp!
What? No, that's mine!
Giveitame! *Give it!*
Never!
SQUIRT
TAK
TOK
TOK

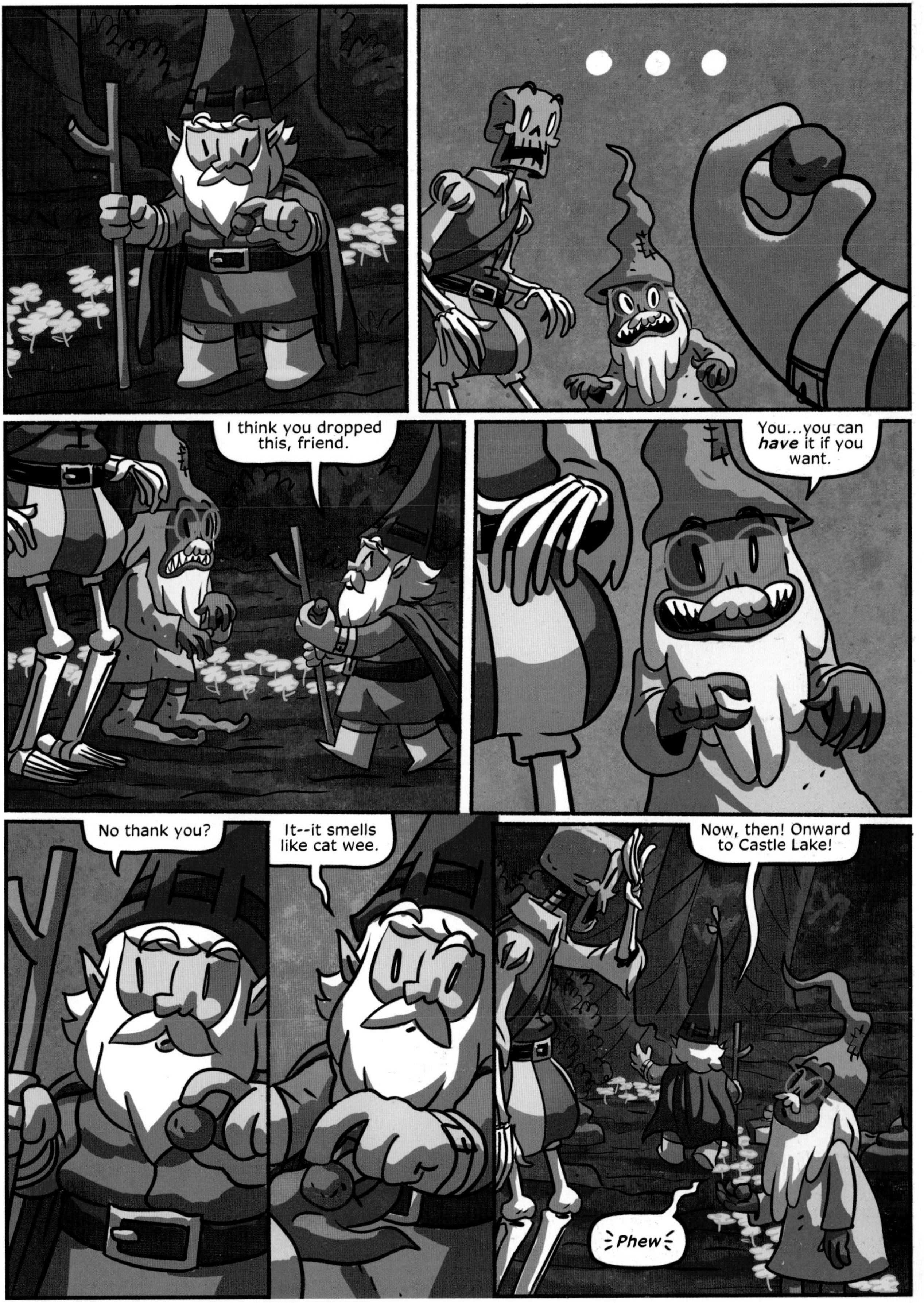
I think you dropped this, friend.
You...you can *have* it if you want.
No thank you?
It--it smells like cat wee.
Now, then! Onward to Castle Lake!
Phew

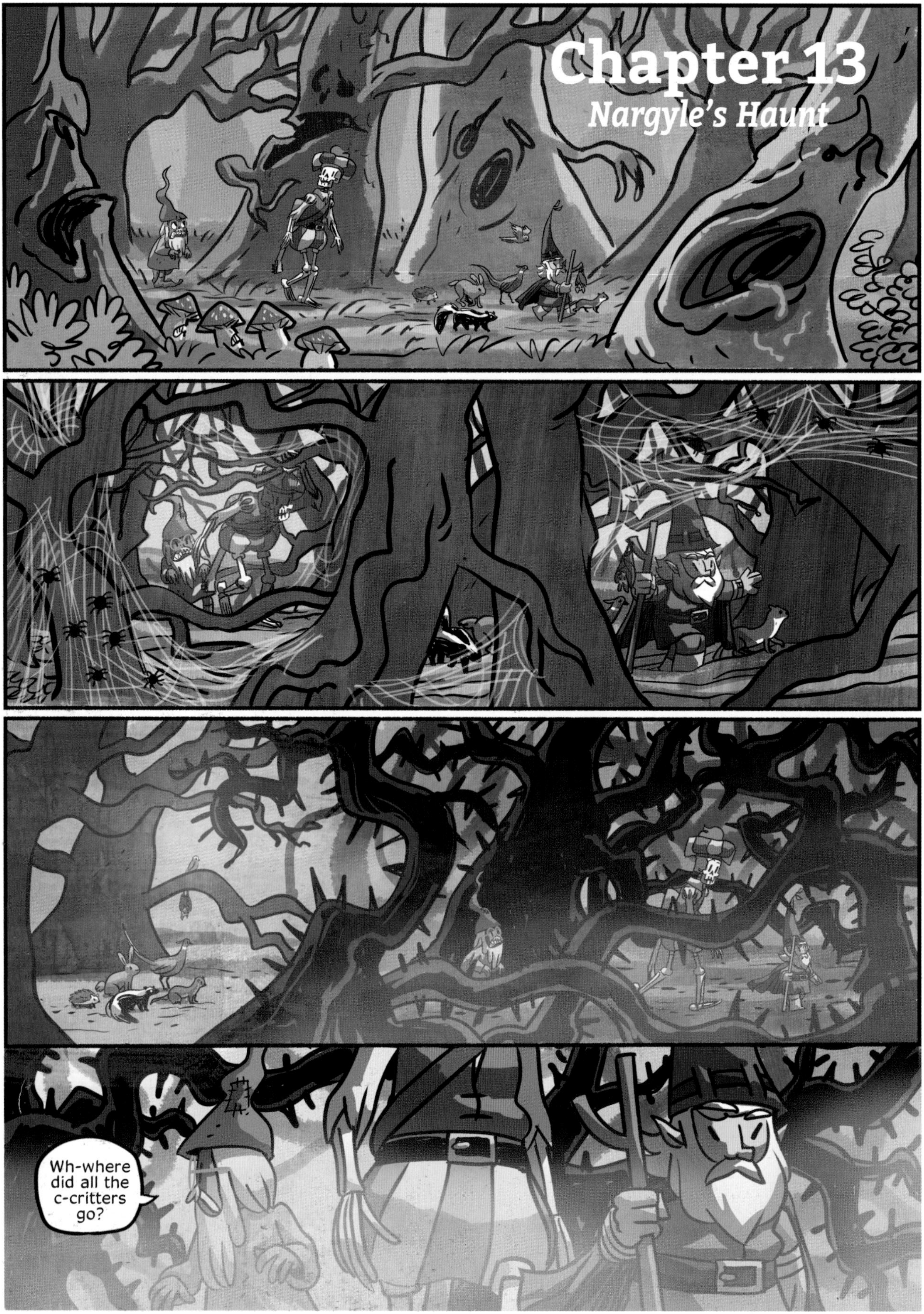
Chapter 13
Nargyle's Haunt
Wh-where did all the c-critters go?

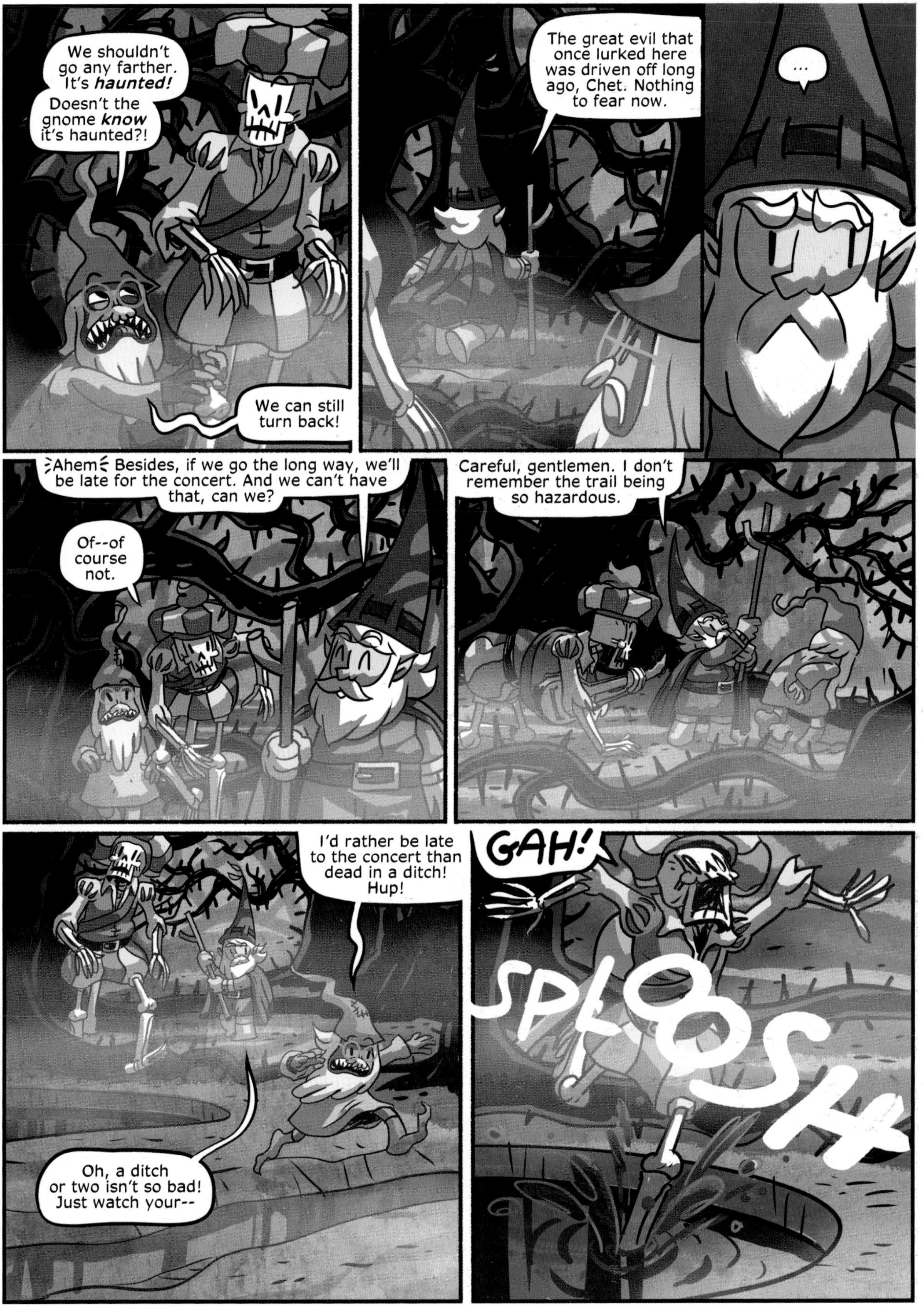

We shouldn't go any farther. It's *haunted!*
Doesn't the gnome *know* it's haunted?!
We can still turn back!
The great evil that once lurked here was driven off long ago, Chet. Nothing to fear now.
...
Ahem Besides, if we go the long way, we'll be late for the concert. And we can't have that, can we?
Of--of course not.
Careful, gentlemen. I don't remember the trail being so hazardous.
I'd rather be late to the concert than dead in a ditch! Hup!
Oh, a ditch or two isn't so bad! Just watch your--
GAH!
SPLOOSH

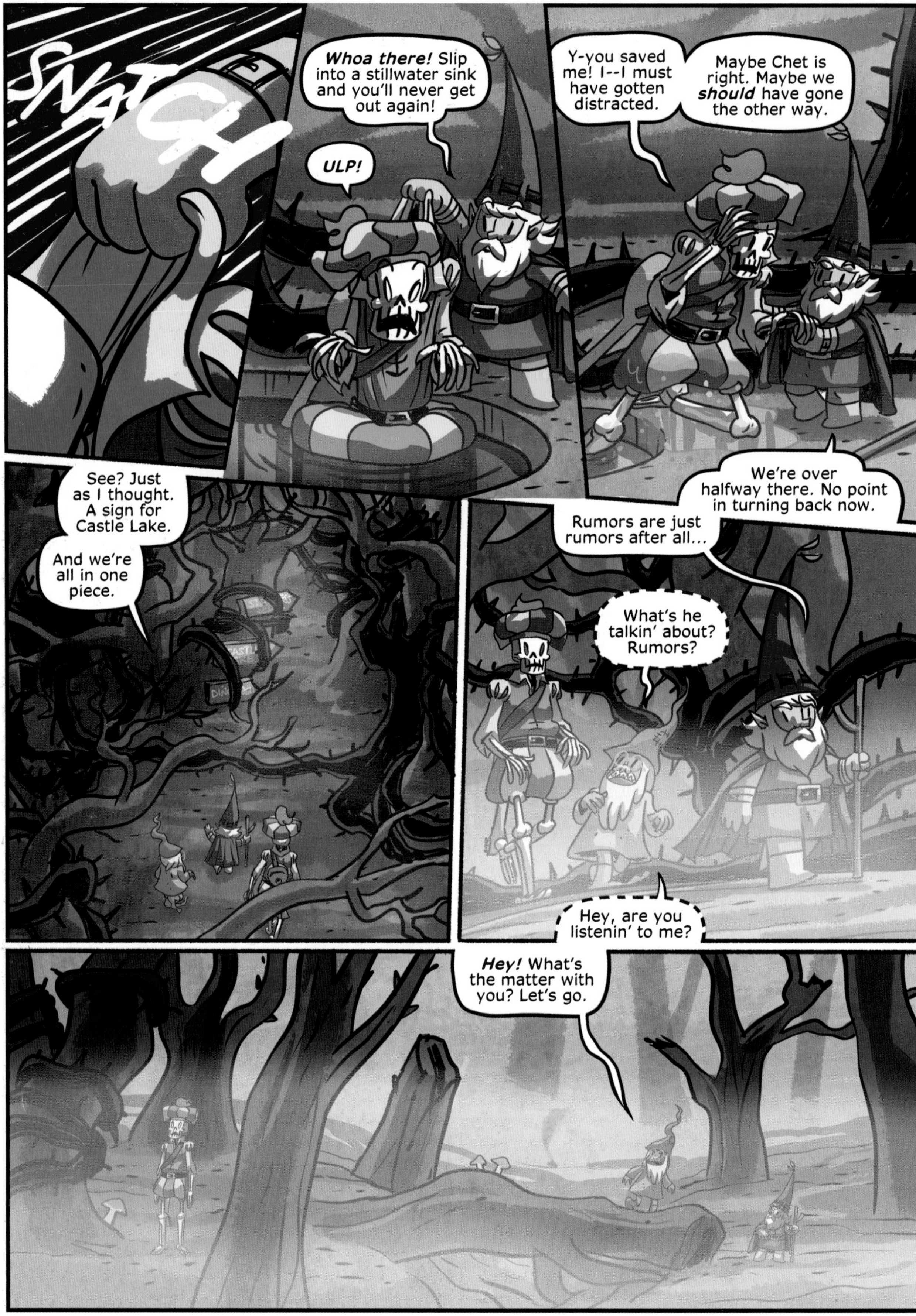
SNATCH
Whoa there! Slip into a stillwater sink and you'll never get out again!
ULP!
Y-you saved me! I--I must have gotten distracted.
Maybe Chet is right. Maybe we *should* have gone the other way.
We're over halfway there. No point in turning back now.
See? Just as I thought. A sign for Castle Lake.
And we're all in one piece.
Rumors are just rumors after all...
What's he talkin' about? Rumors?
Hey, are you listenin' to me?
Hey! What's the matter with you? Let's go.

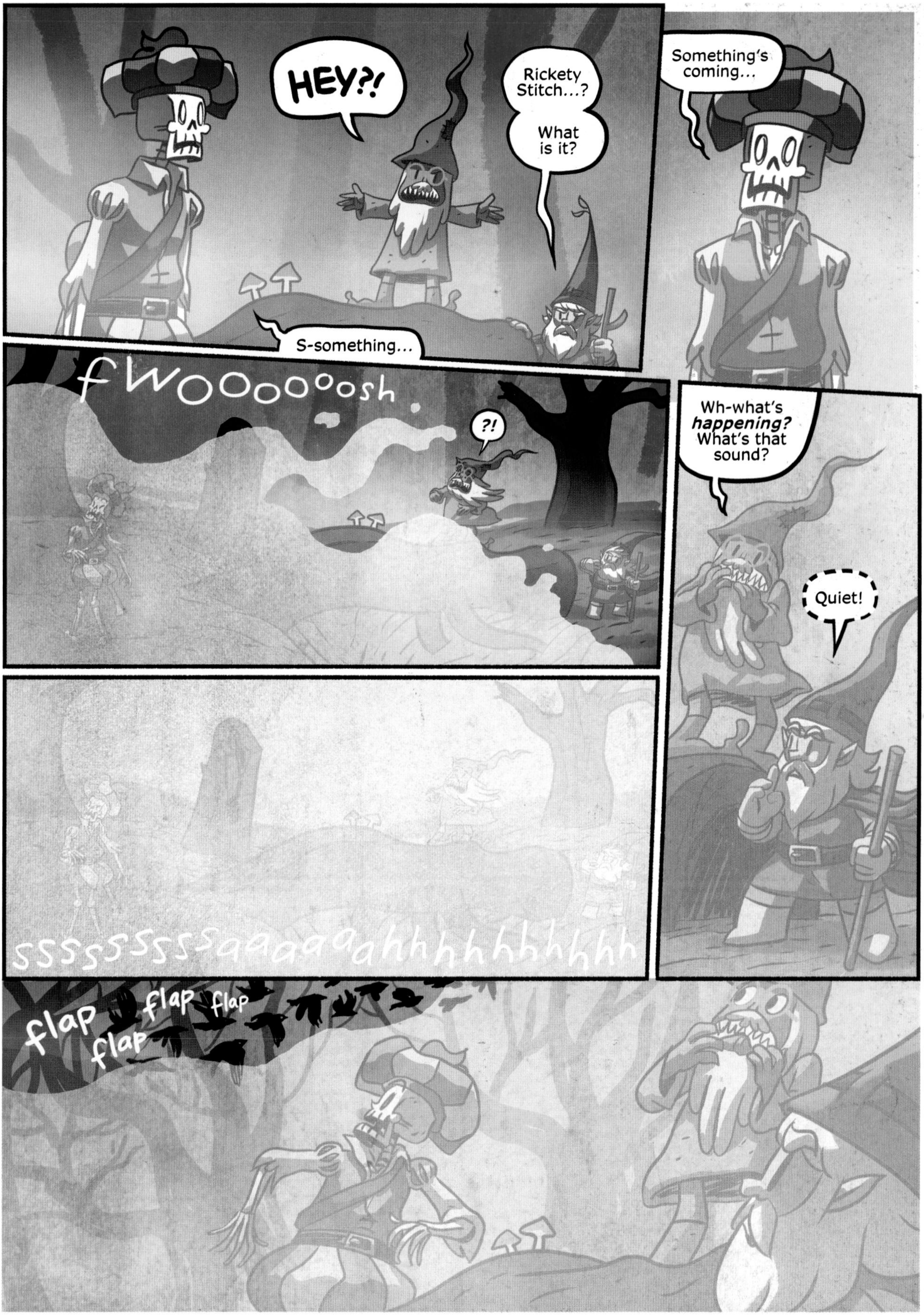
HEY?!
Rickety Stitch...?
What is it?
Something's coming...
S-something...
fWOOOooosh
?!
Wh-what's *happening?* What's that sound?
Quiet!
SSSSSSSaaaaaahhhhhhhhhh
flap flap flap flap

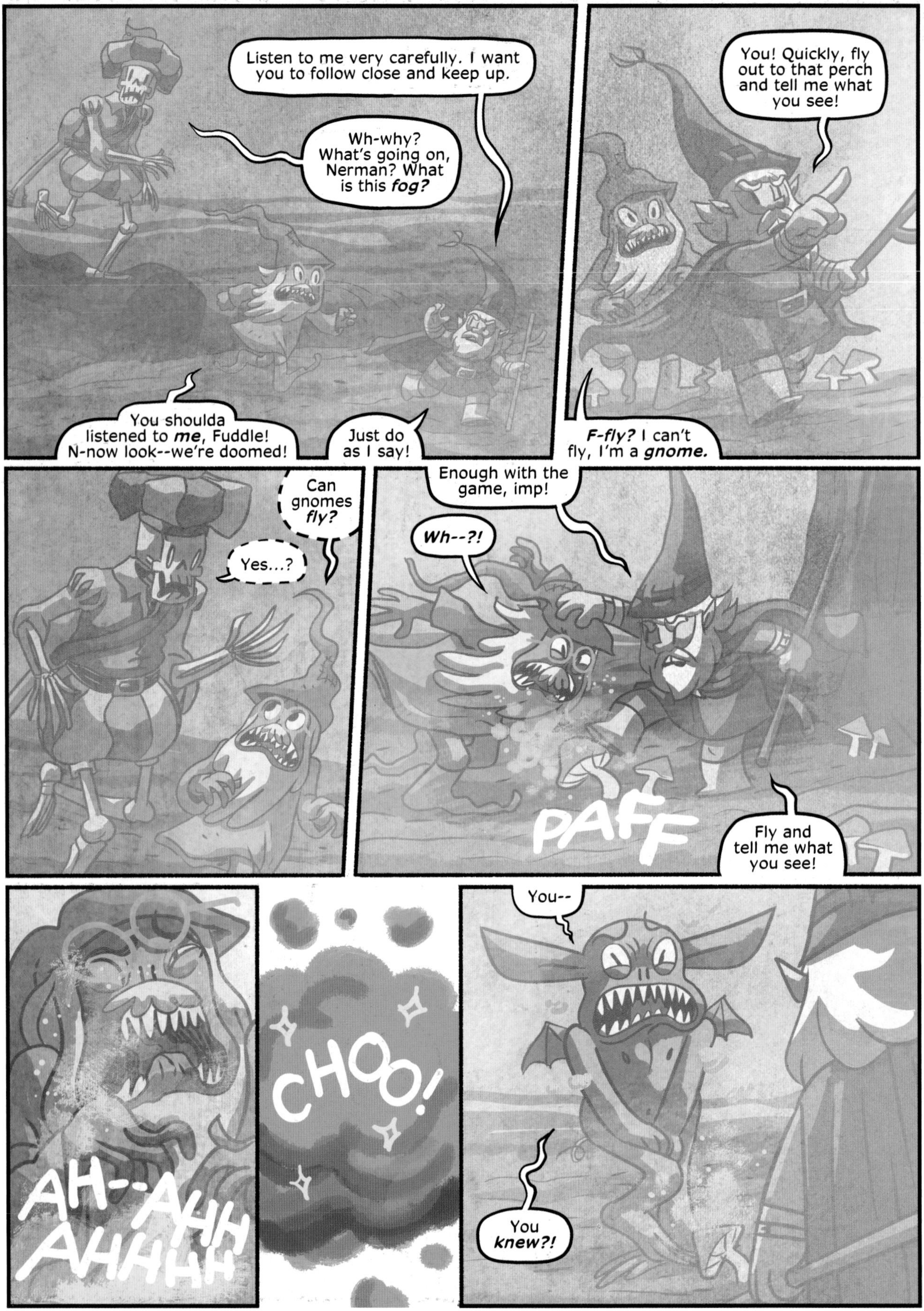
Listen to me very carefully. I want you to follow close and keep up.
Wh-why? What's going on, Nerman? What is this *fog?*
You shoulda listened to *me*, Fuddle! N-now look--we're doomed!
Just do as I say!
You! Quickly, fly out to that perch and tell me what you see!
F-fly? I can't fly, I'm a *gnome.*
Can gnomes *fly?*
Yes...?
Enough with the game, imp!
Wh--?!
PAFF
Fly and tell me what you see!
AH--AHH AHHHH
CHOO!
You--
You *knew?!*

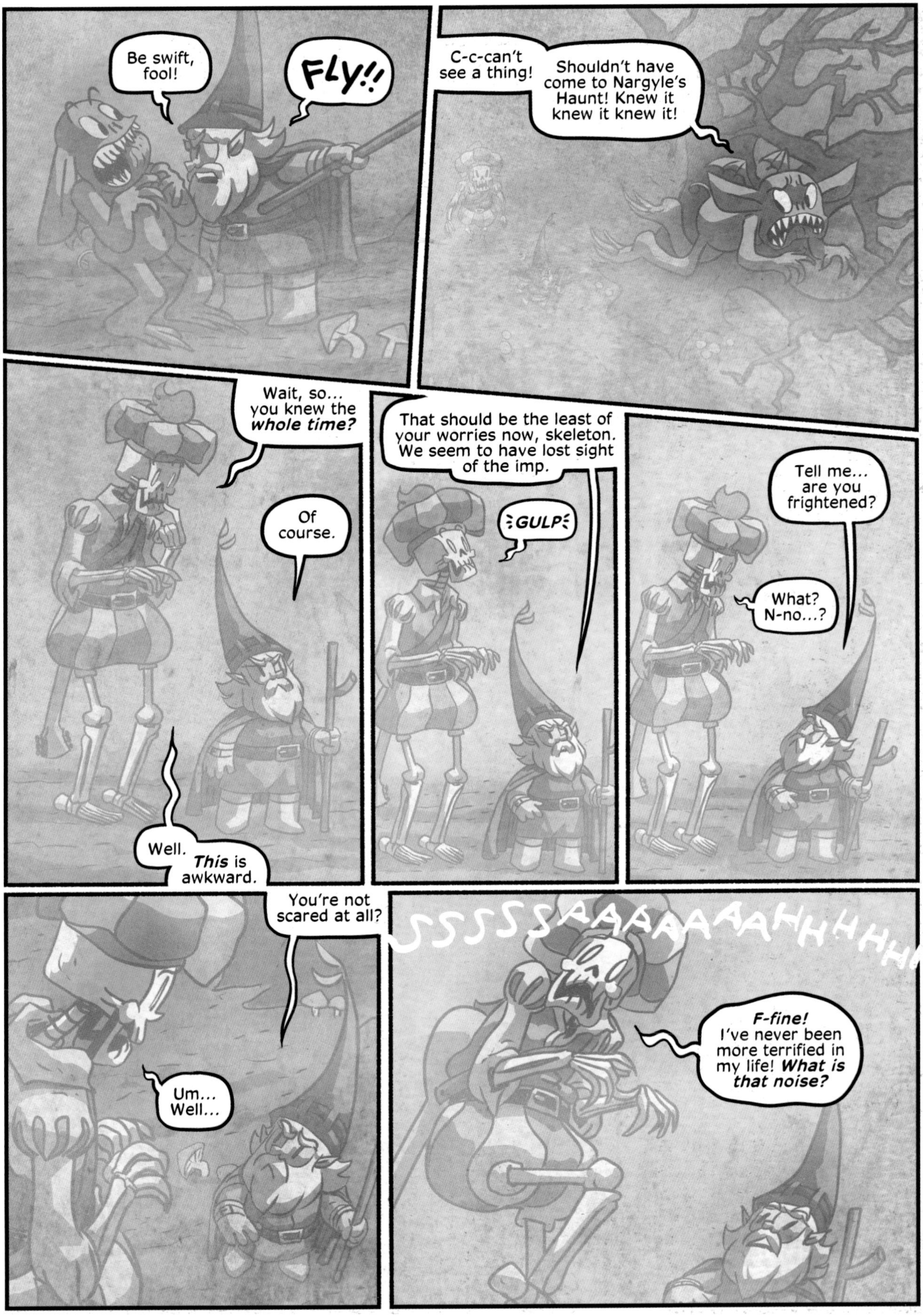
Be swift, fool!
FLY!!
C-c-can't see a thing!
Shouldn't have come to Nargyle's Haunt! Knew it knew it knew it!
Wait, so... you knew the *whole time?*
Of course.
Well. *This* is awkward.
That should be the least of your worries now, skeleton. We seem to have lost sight of the imp.
GULP
Tell me... are you frightened?
What? N-no...?
You're not scared at all?
Um... Well...
SSSSSAAAAAAHHHHHH
F-fine! I've never been more terrified in my life! *What is that noise?*

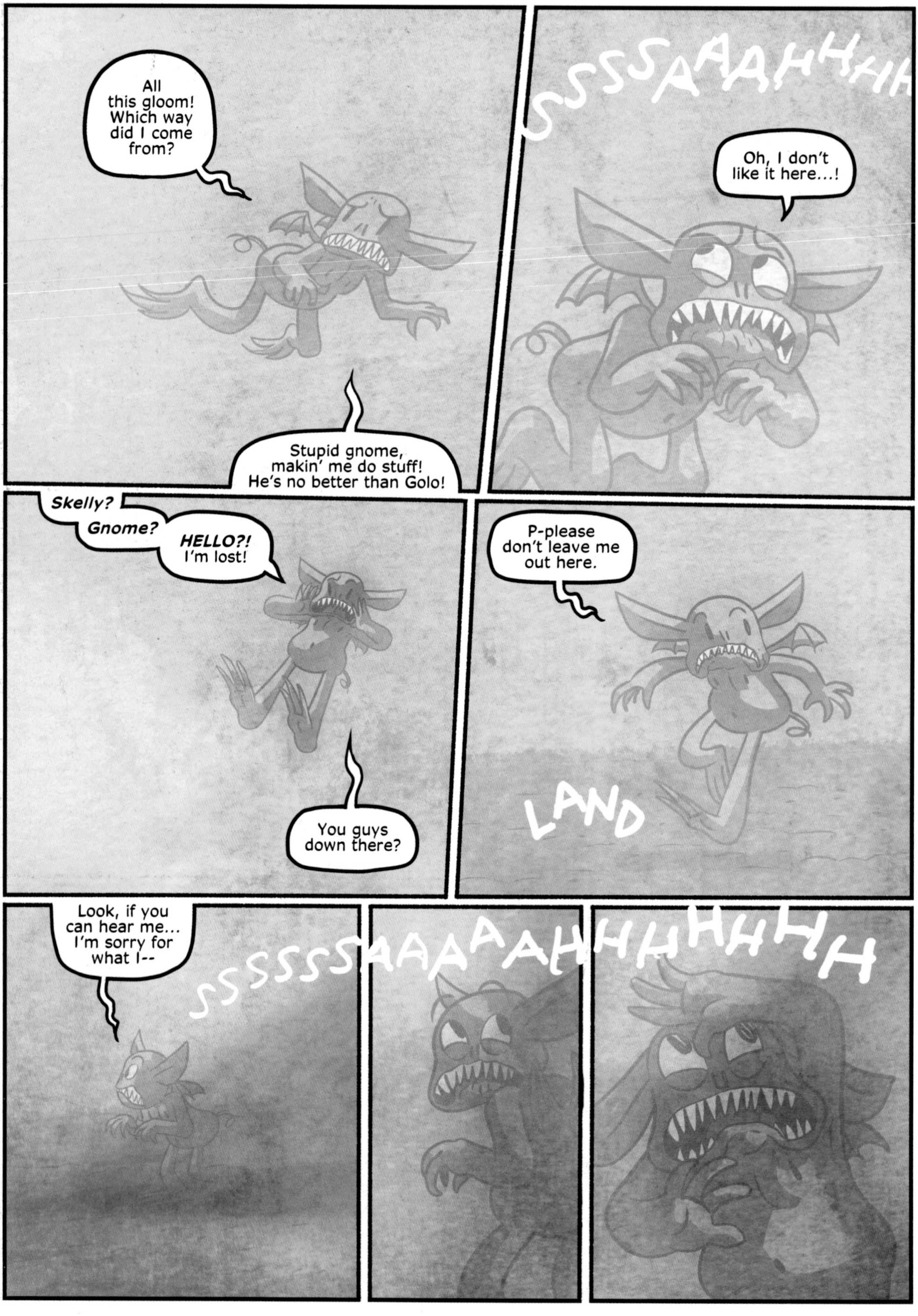
All this gloom! Which way did I come from?
Stupid gnome, makin' me do stuff! He's no better than Golo!
SSSSAAAHHHH
Oh, I don't like it here...!
Skelly?
Gnome?
HELLO?! I'm lost!
You guys down there?
P-please don't leave me out here.
LAND
Look, if you can hear me... I'm sorry for what I--
SSSSSSAAAAAHHHHHHHH

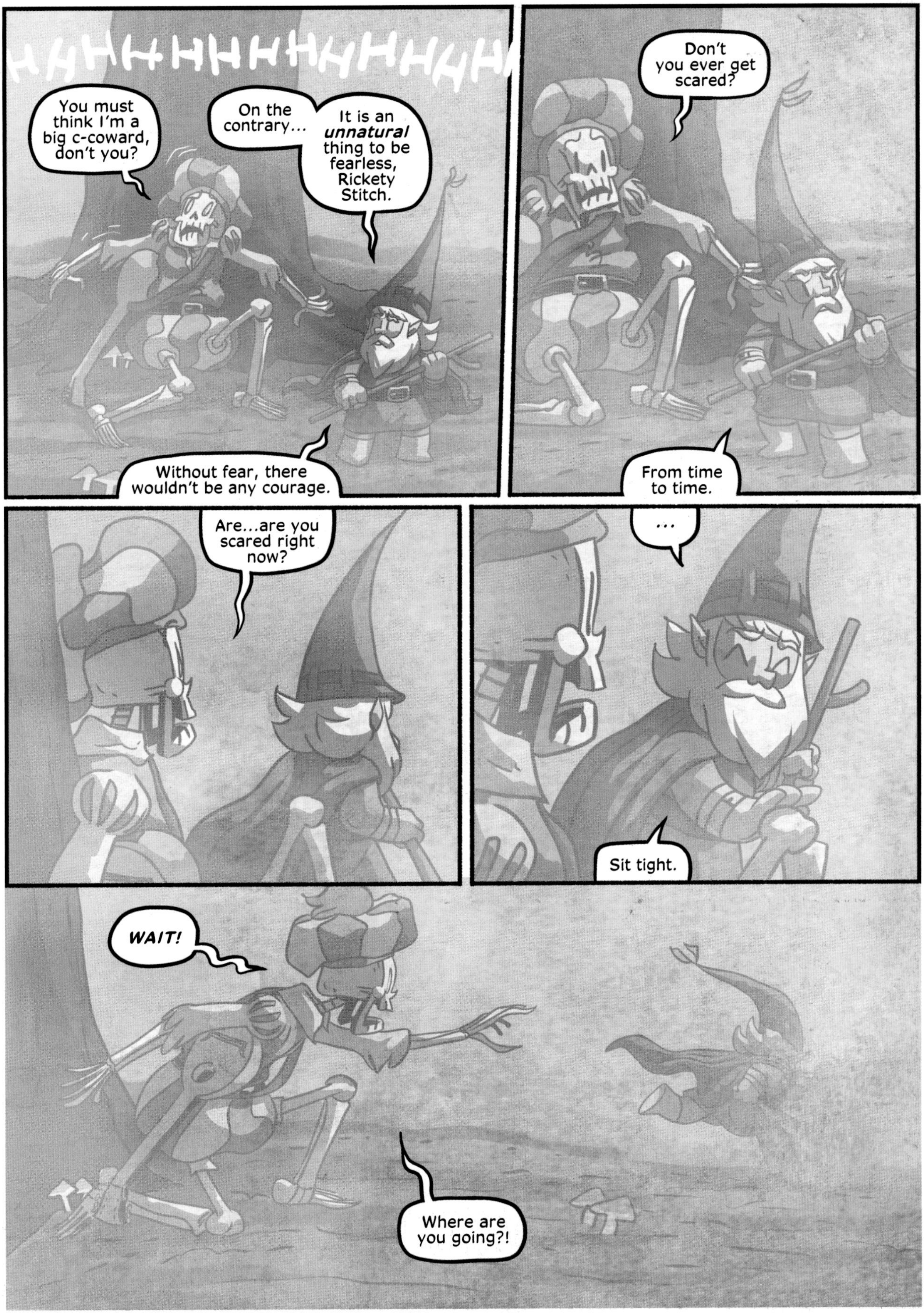
HHHHHHHHHHHHHHHH
You must think I'm a big c-coward, don't you?
On the contrary...
It is an *unnatural* thing to be fearless, Rickety Stitch.
Without fear, there wouldn't be any courage.
Don't you ever get scared?
From time to time.
Are...are you scared right now?
...
Sit tight.
WAIT!
Where are you going?!

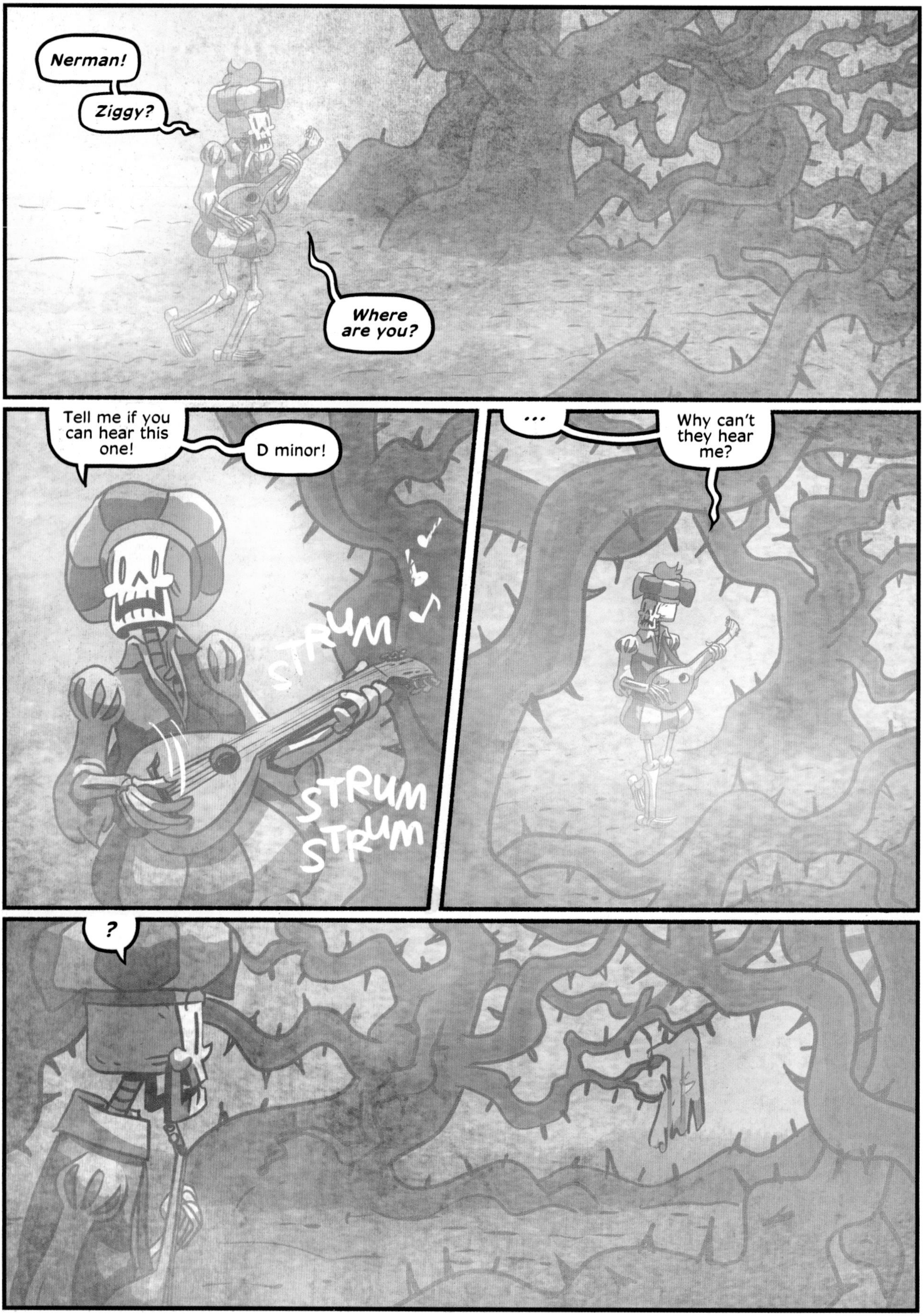
Nerman!
Ziggy?
Where are you?
Tell me if you can hear this one!
D minor!
STRUM
STRUM
STRUM
...
Why can't they hear me?
?

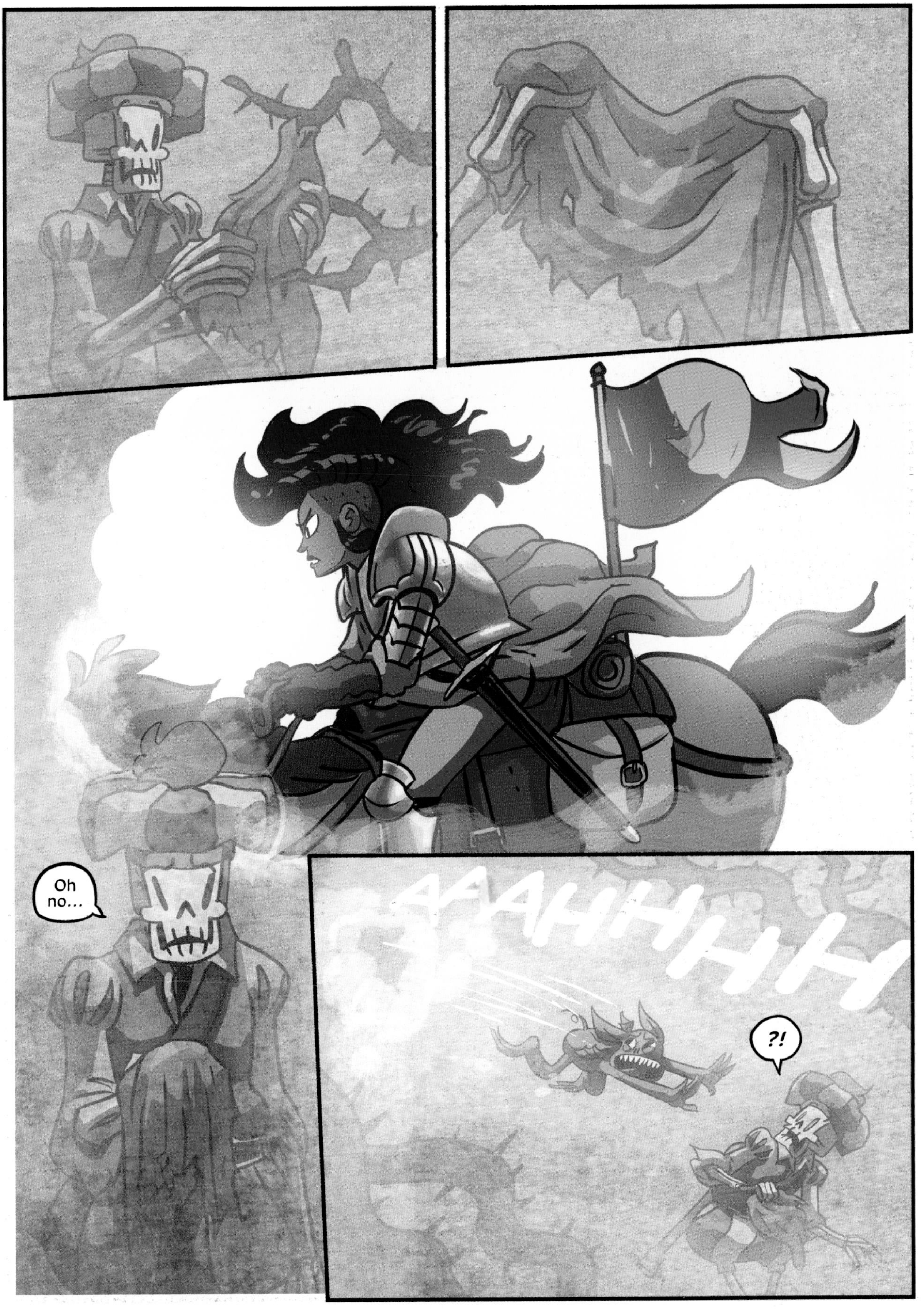
Oh no...
AAAHHHHHH
?!

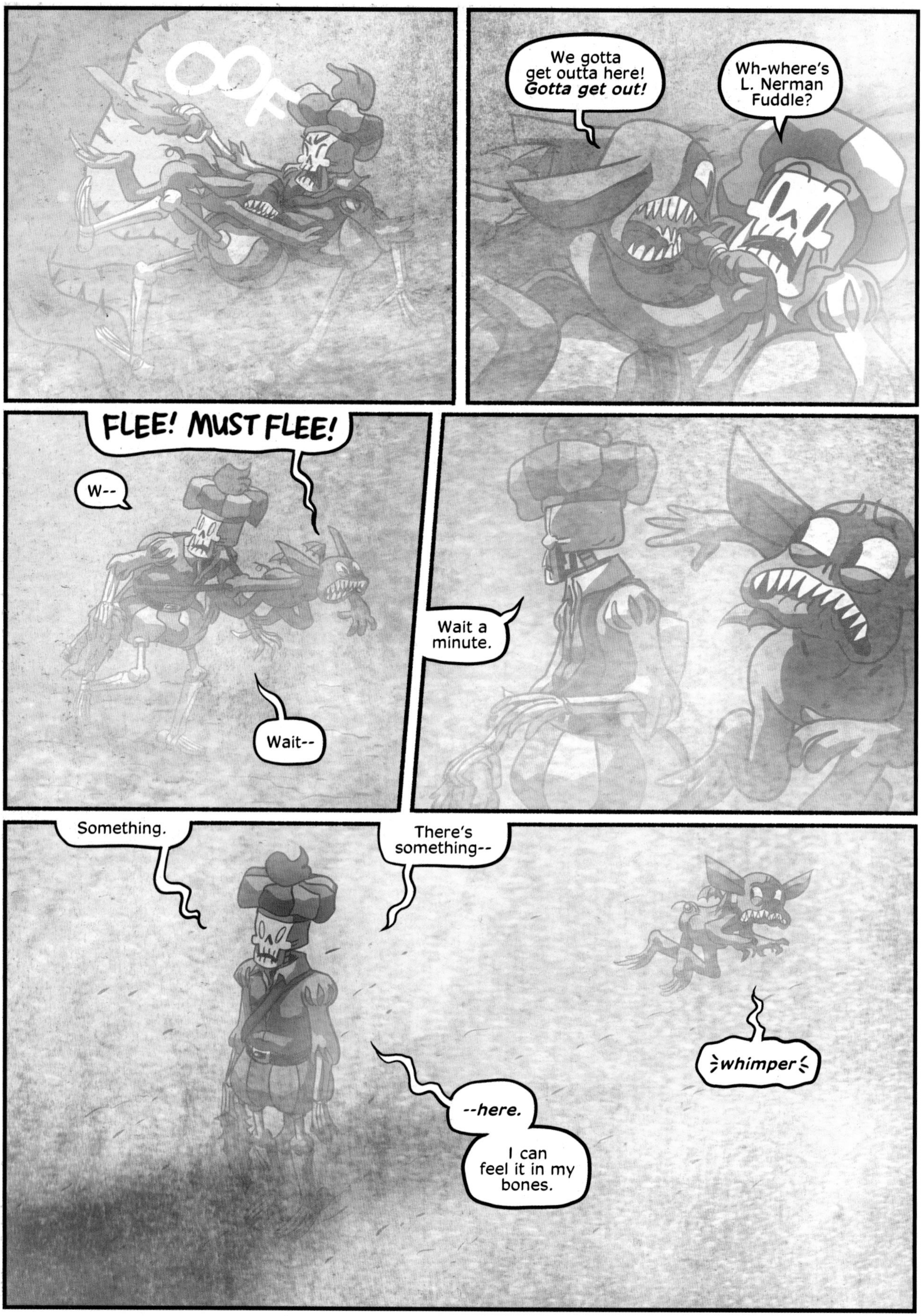
OOF
We gotta get outta here! *Gotta get out!*
Wh-where's L. Nerman Fuddle?
FLEE! MUST FLEE!
W--
Wait--
Wait a minute.
Something.
There's something--
--*here.*
I can feel it in my bones.
whimper

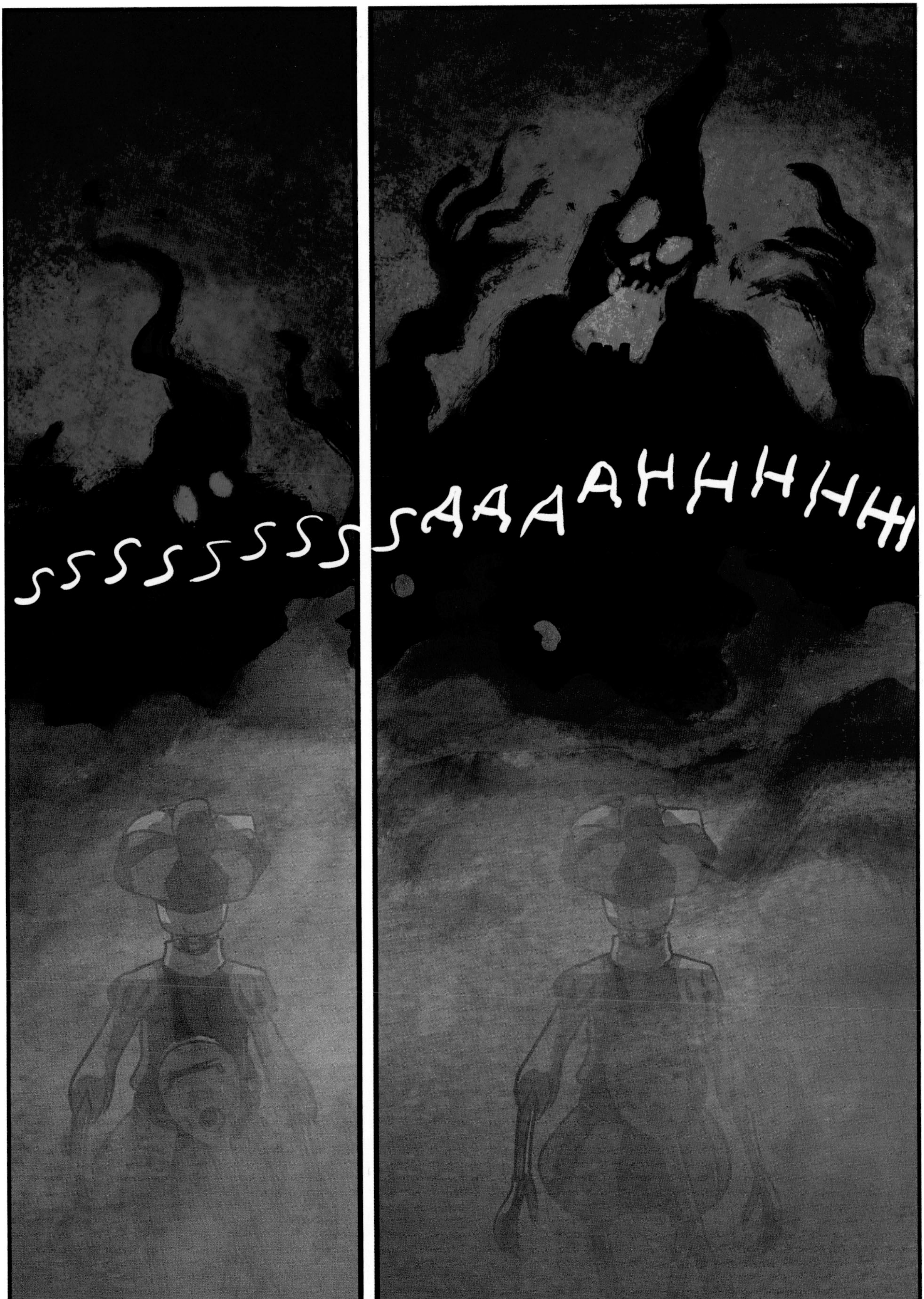
SSSSSSSSSAAAAHHHHHH

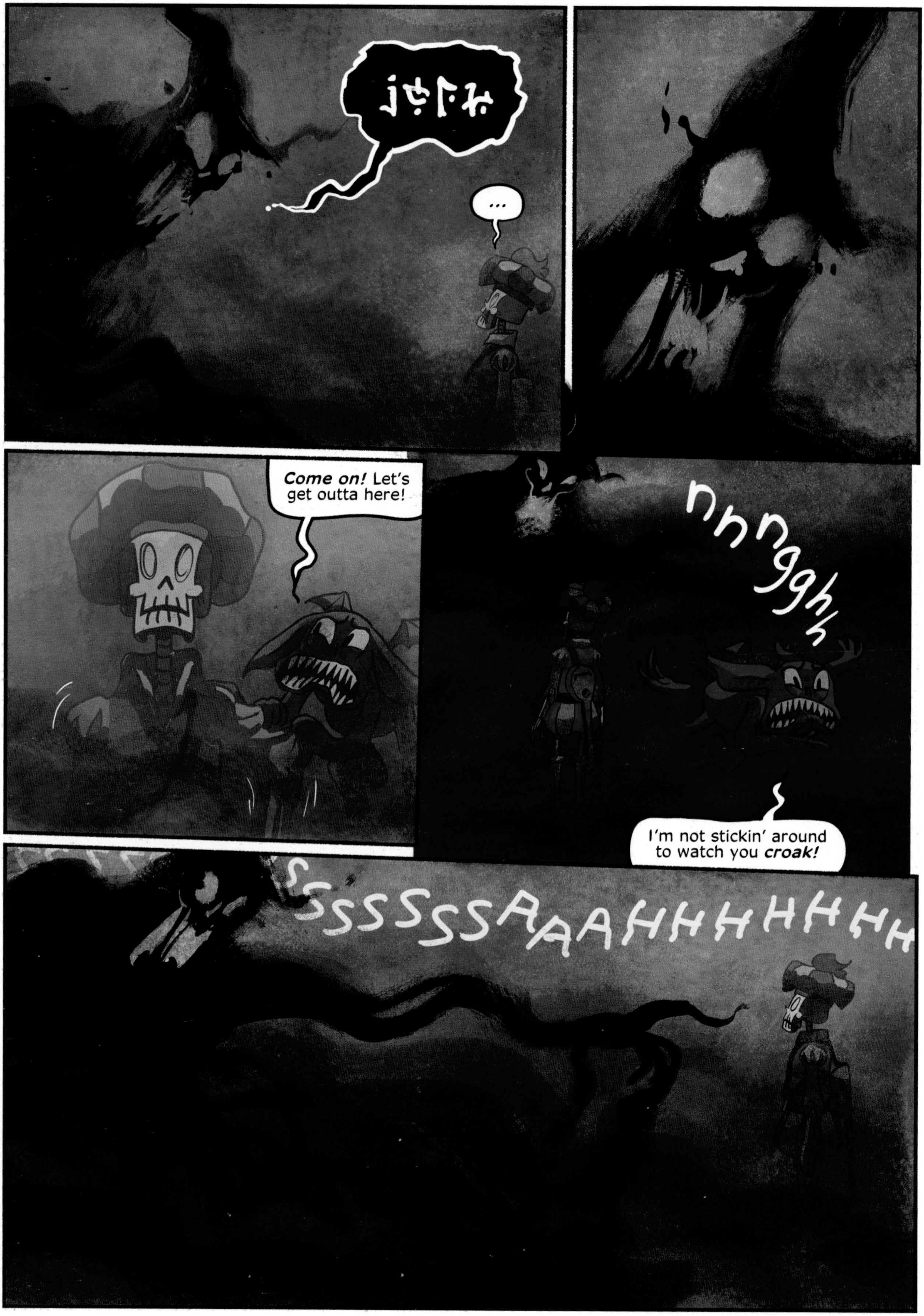
...
Come on! Let's get outta here!
nnngghh
I'm not stickin' around to watch you *croak!*
SSSSSSSAAAHHHHHHHH

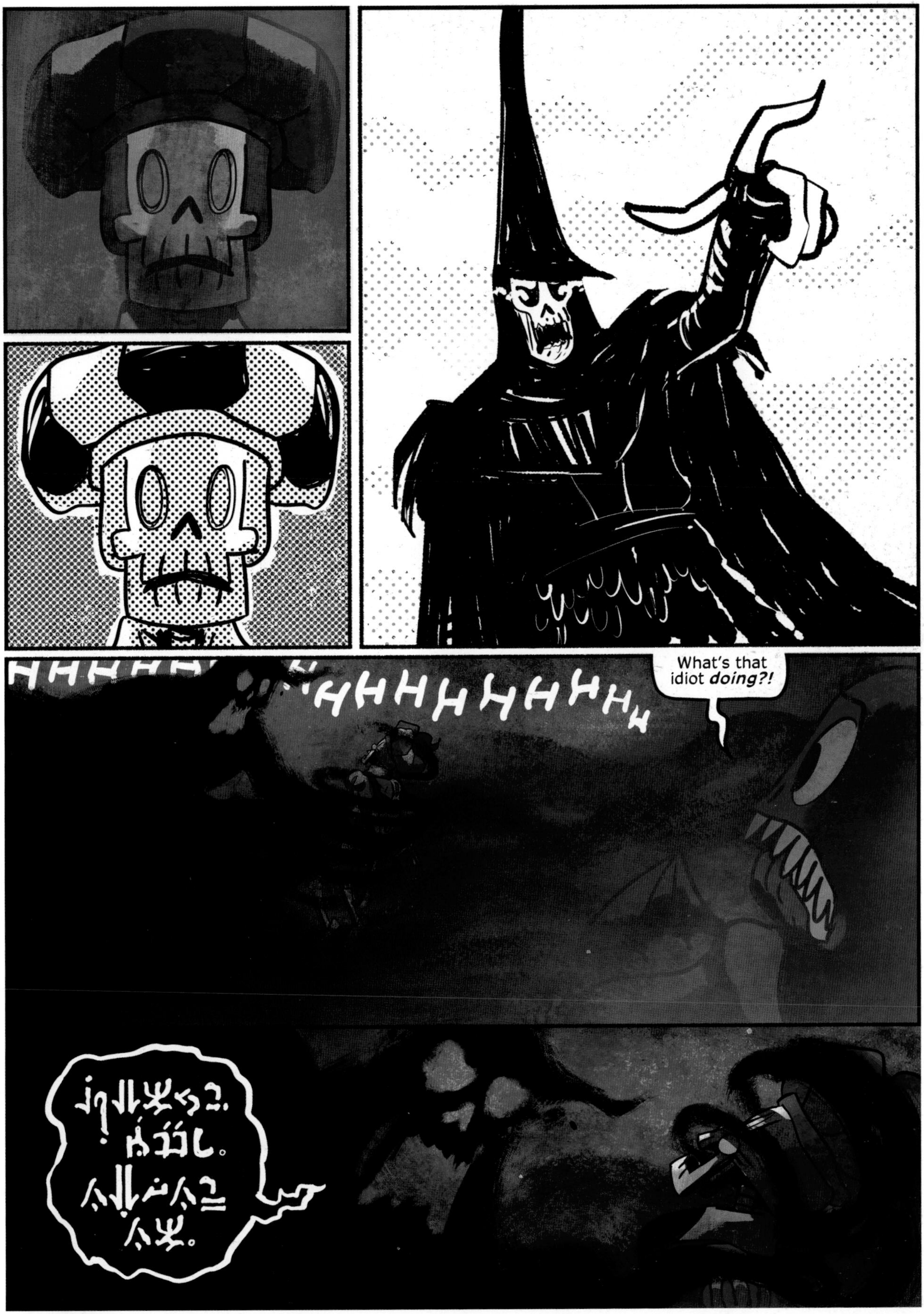

HHHHHHHHHHHHHHHHHHH
What's that idiot *doing?!*

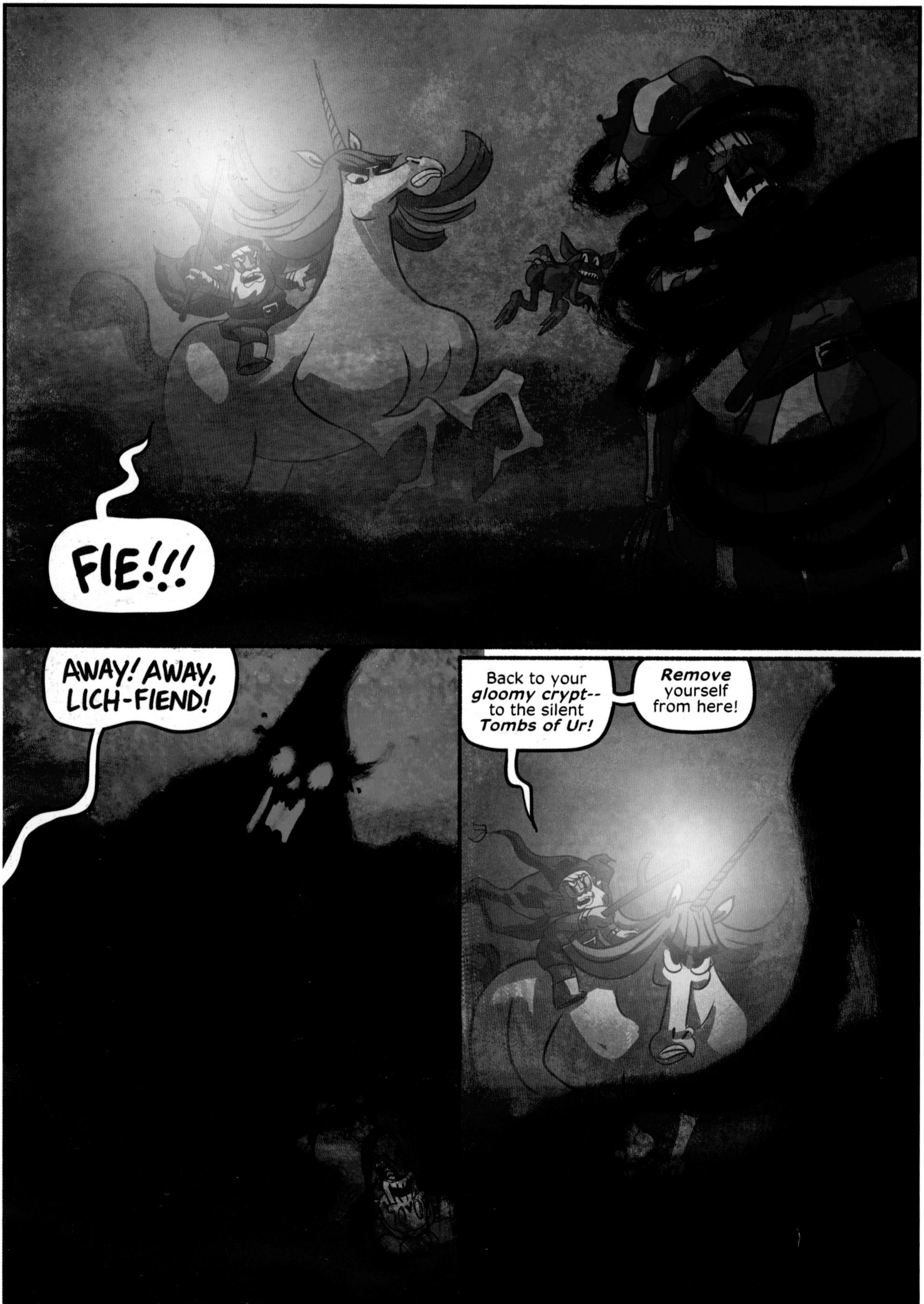
FIE!!!
AWAY! AWAY, LICH-FIEND!
Back to your *gloomy crypt*-- to the silent *Tombs of Ur!*
Remove yourself from here!

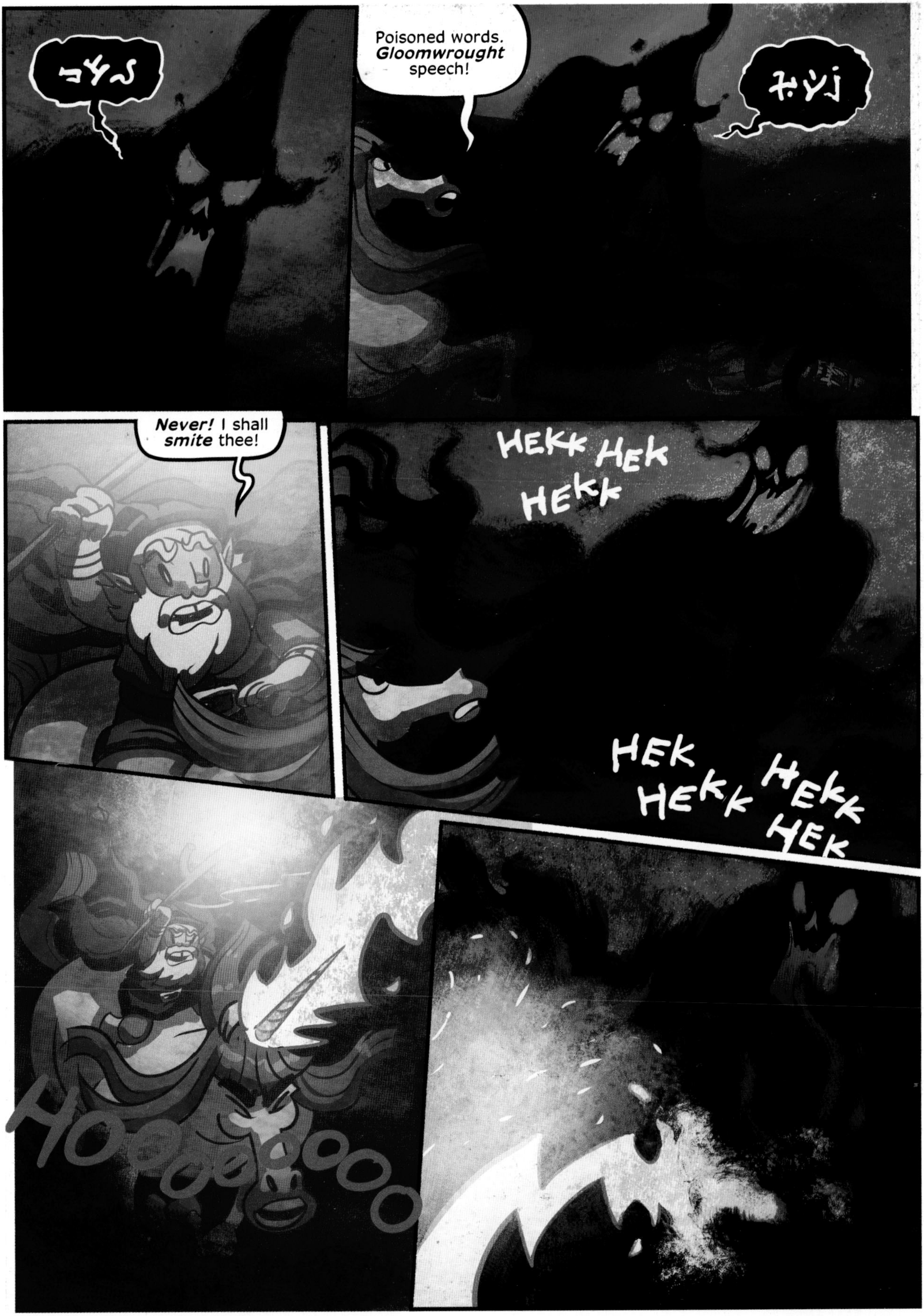
Poisoned words. Gloomwrought speech!
Never! I shall smite thee!
HEKK HEK HEKK
HEK HEKK HEKK HEK
HOOOOOOOO

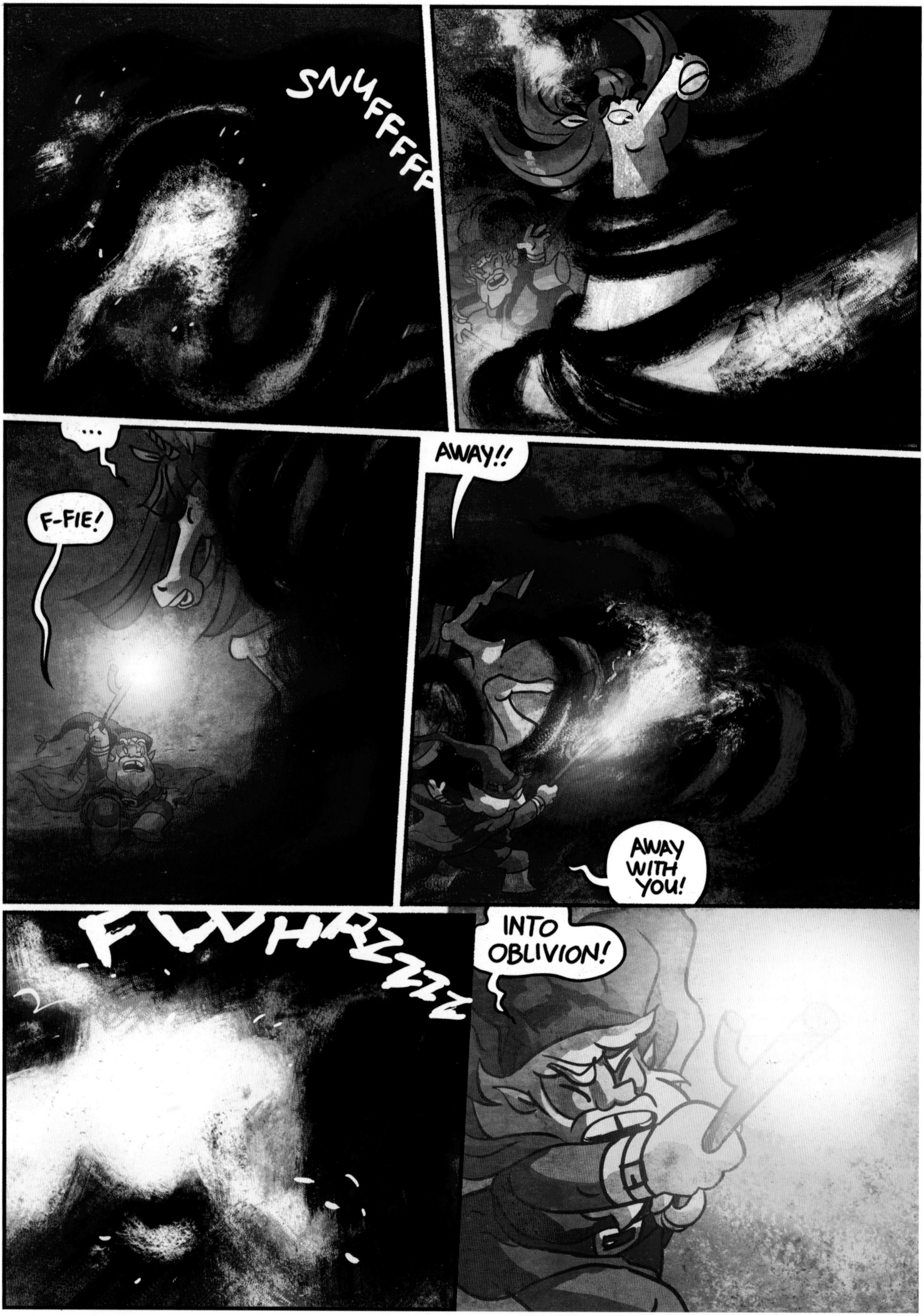
SNUFFFFF
...
F-FIE!
AWAY!!
AWAY WITH YOU!
FWHRZZZZ
INTO OBLIVION!

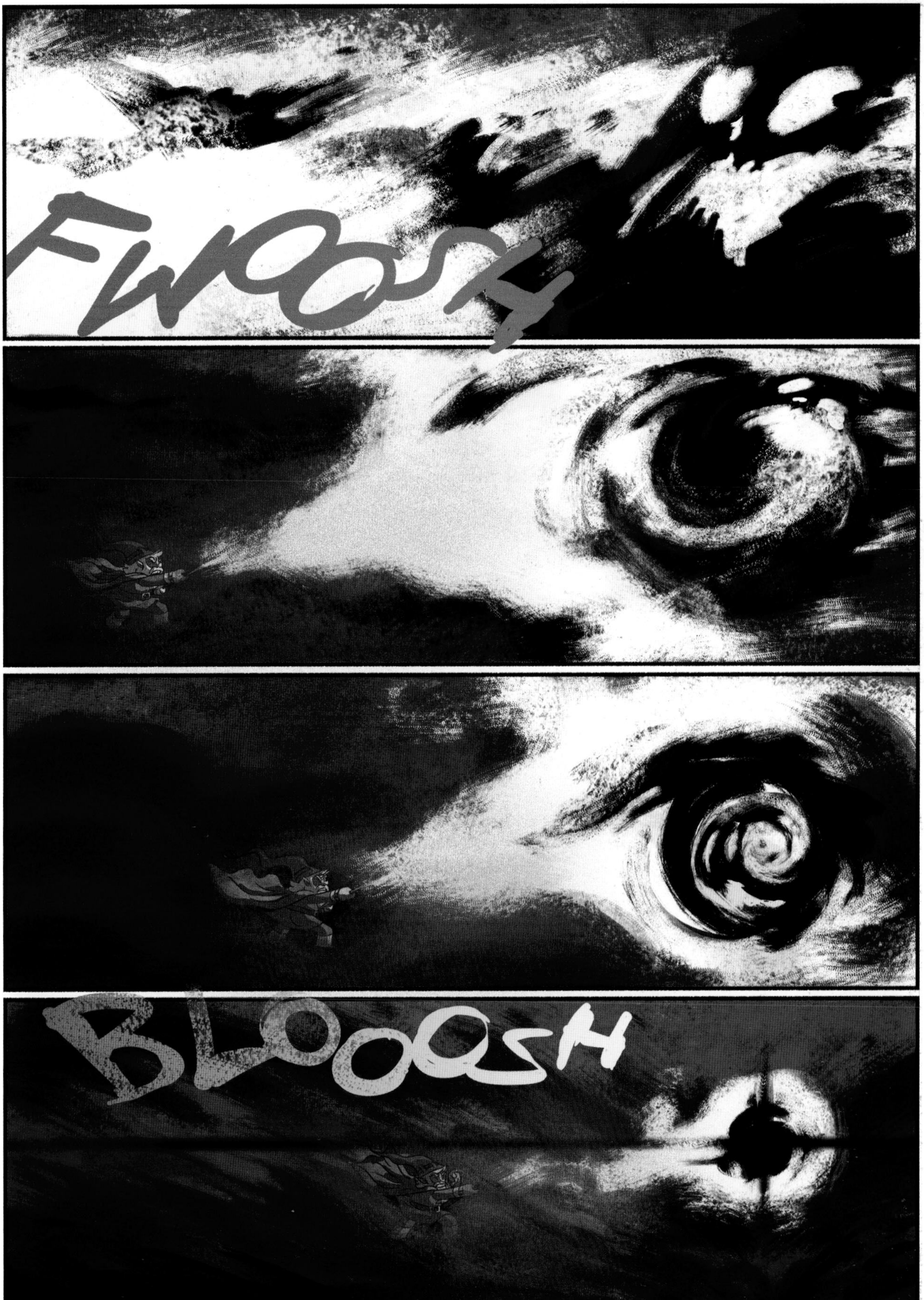
FWOOSH
BLOOOSH

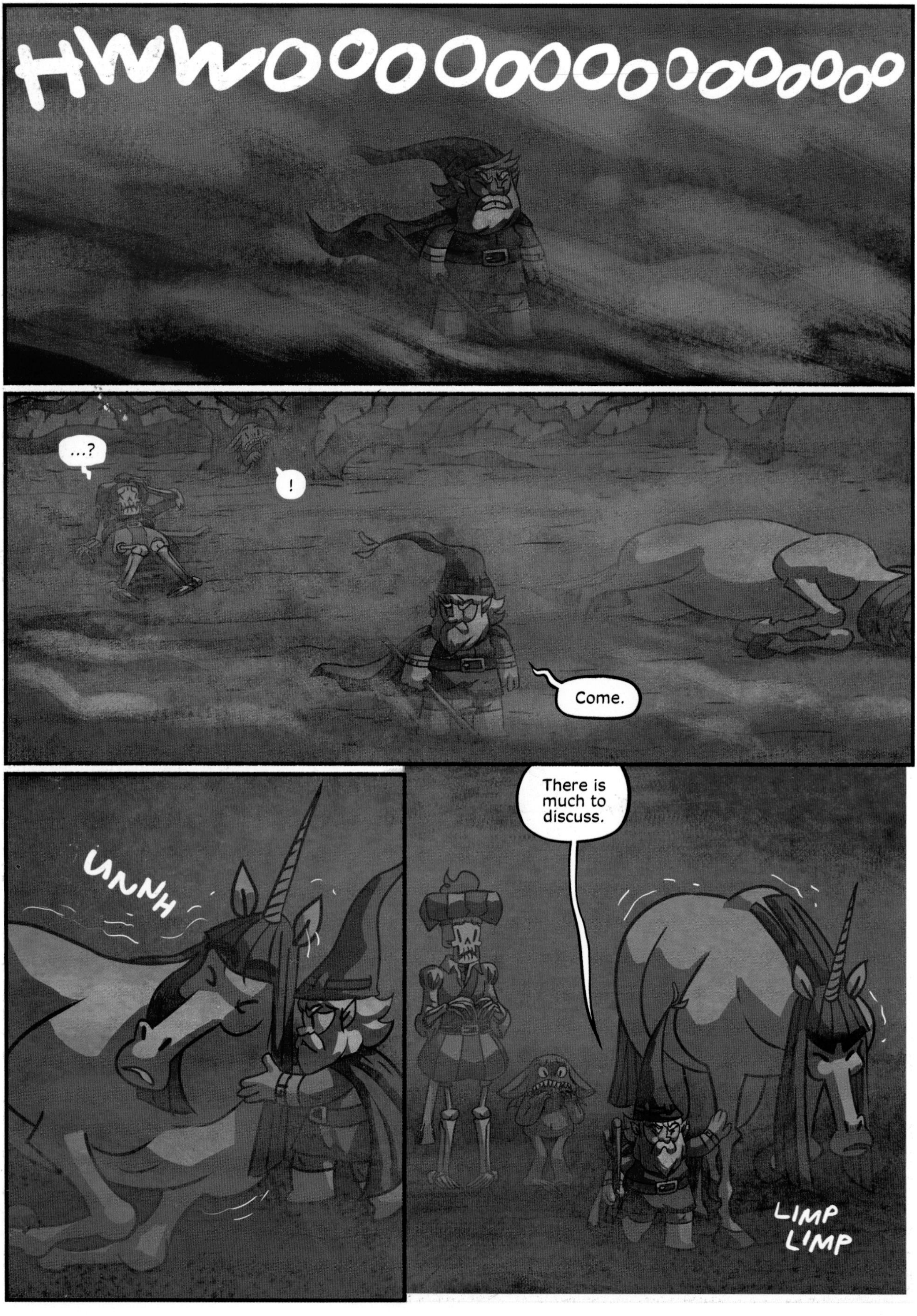
HWWOOOOOOOOOOOOOOOO
...?
!
Come.
UNNH
There is much to discuss.
LIMP LIMP

Chapter 14
The Age of Ashes

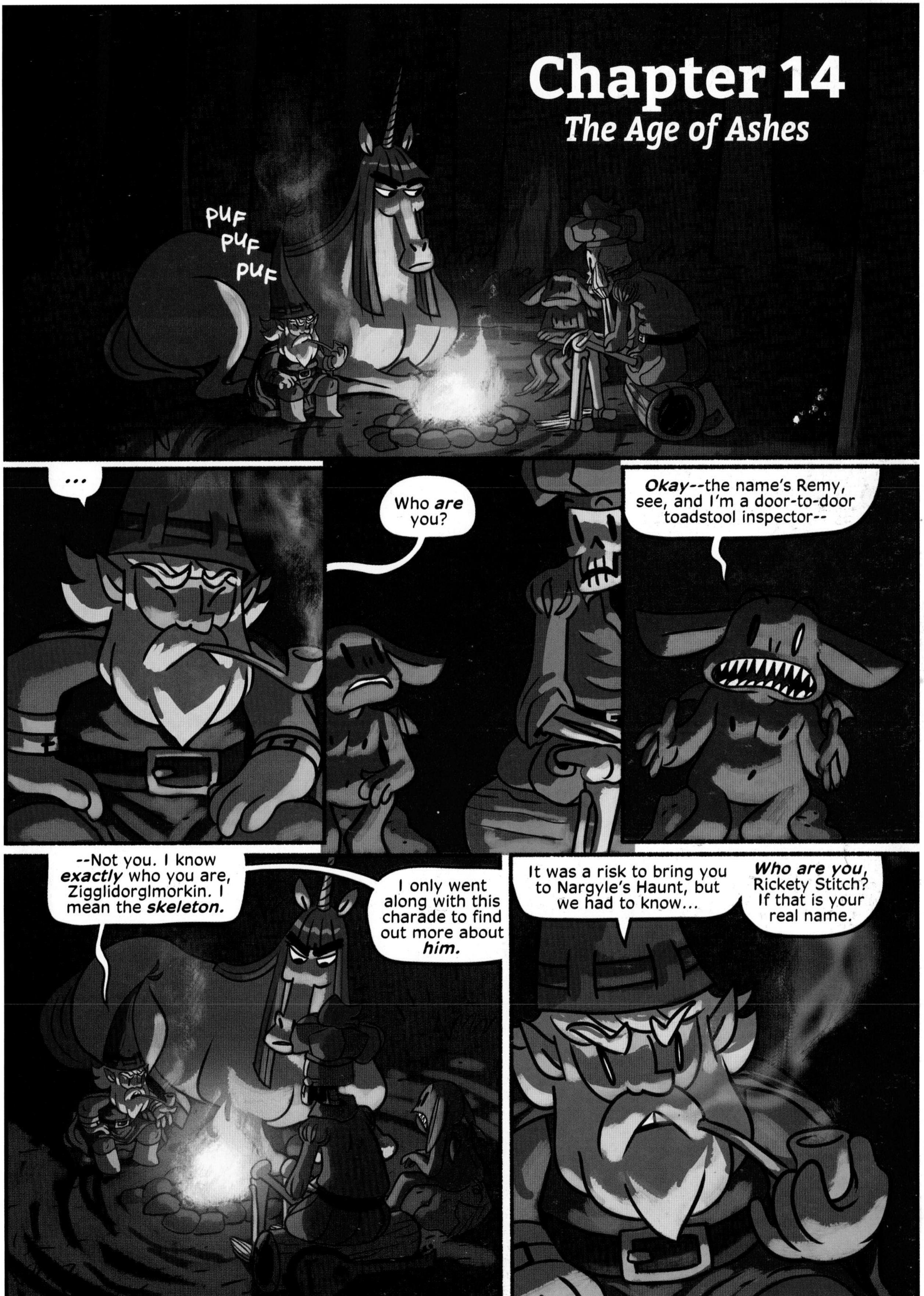

PUF
PUF
PUF
...
Who *are* you?
Okay--the name's Remy, see, and I'm a door-to-door toadstool inspector--
--Not you. I know *exactly* who you are, Zigglidorglmorkin. I mean the *skeleton.*
I only went along with this charade to find out more about *him.*
It was a risk to bring you to Nargyle's Haunt, but we had to know...
Who are you, Rickety Stitch? If that is your real name.

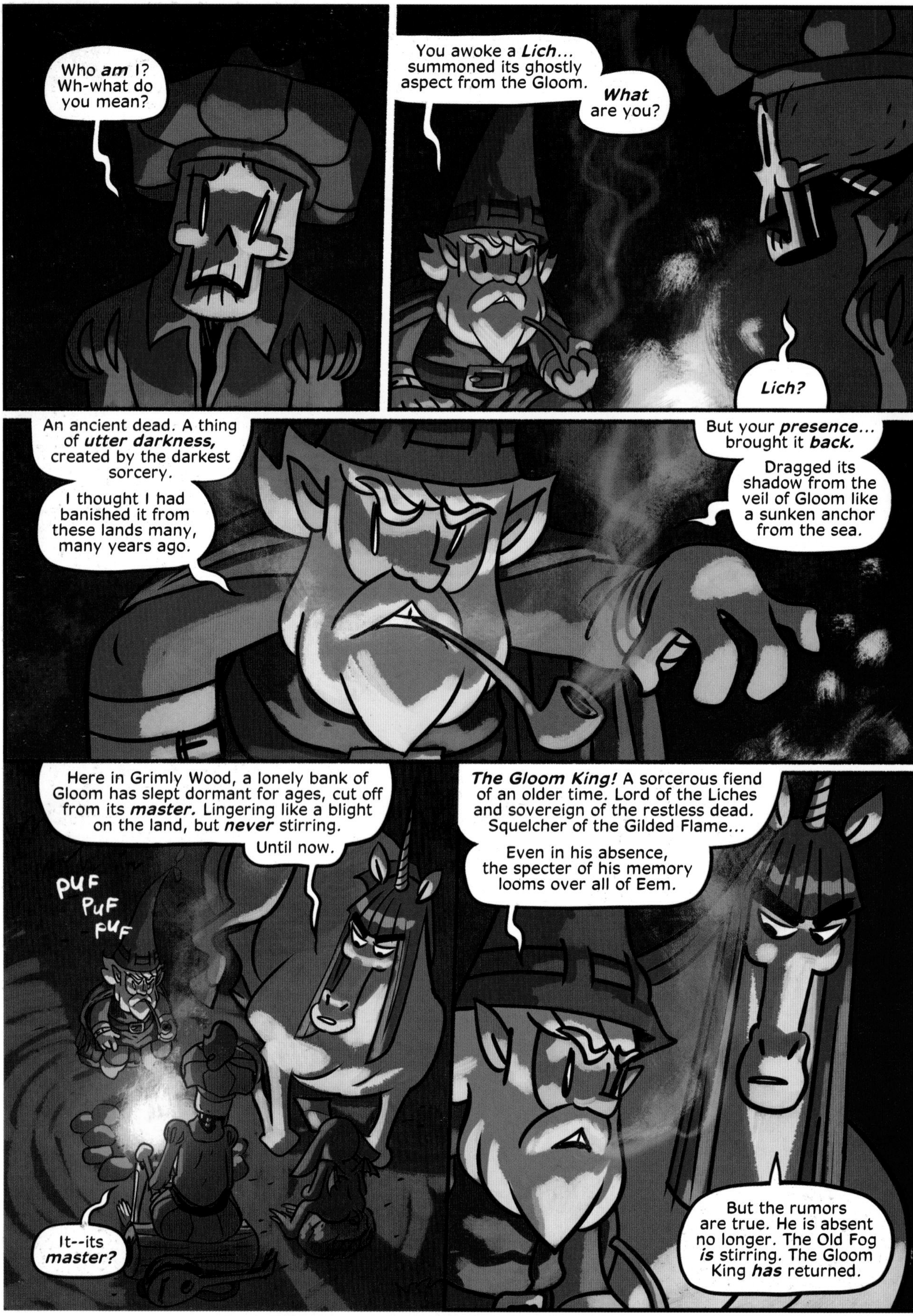
Who am I? Wh-what do you mean?
You awoke a Lich... summoned its ghostly aspect from the Gloom.
What are you?
Lich?
An ancient dead. A thing of utter darkness, created by the darkest sorcery.
I thought I had banished it from these lands many, many years ago.
But your presence... brought it back.
Dragged its shadow from the veil of Gloom like a sunken anchor from the sea.
Here in Grimly Wood, a lonely bank of Gloom has slept dormant for ages, cut off from its master. Lingering like a blight on the land, but never stirring.
Until now.
PUF PUF PUF
It--its master?
The Gloom King! A sorcerous fiend of an older time. Lord of the Liches and sovereign of the restless dead. Squelcher of the Gilded Flame...
Even in his absence, the specter of his memory looms over all of Eem.
But the rumors are true. He is absent no longer. The Old Fog is stirring. The Gloom King has returned.

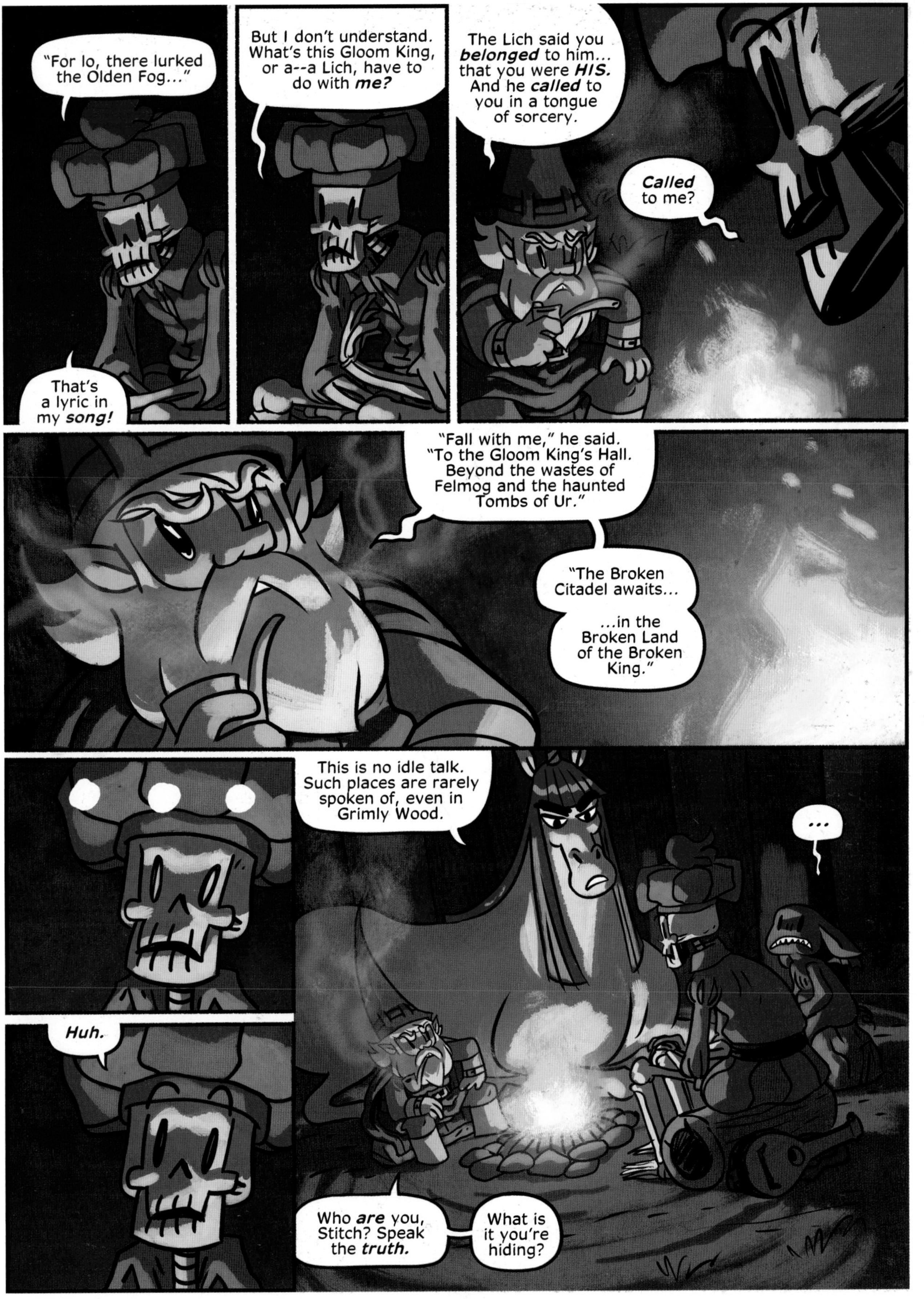

"For lo, there lurked the Olden Fog..."
That's a lyric in my *song!*
But I don't understand. What's this Gloom King, or a--a Lich, have to do with *me?*
The Lich said you *belonged* to him... that you were *HIS.* And he *called* to you in a tongue of sorcery.
Called to me?
"Fall with me," he said. "To the Gloom King's Hall. Beyond the wastes of Felmog and the haunted Tombs of Ur."
"The Broken Citadel awaits...
...in the Broken Land of the Broken King."
This is no idle talk. Such places are rarely spoken of, even in Grimly Wood.
...
Huh.
Who *are* you, Stitch? Speak the *truth.*
What is it you're hiding?

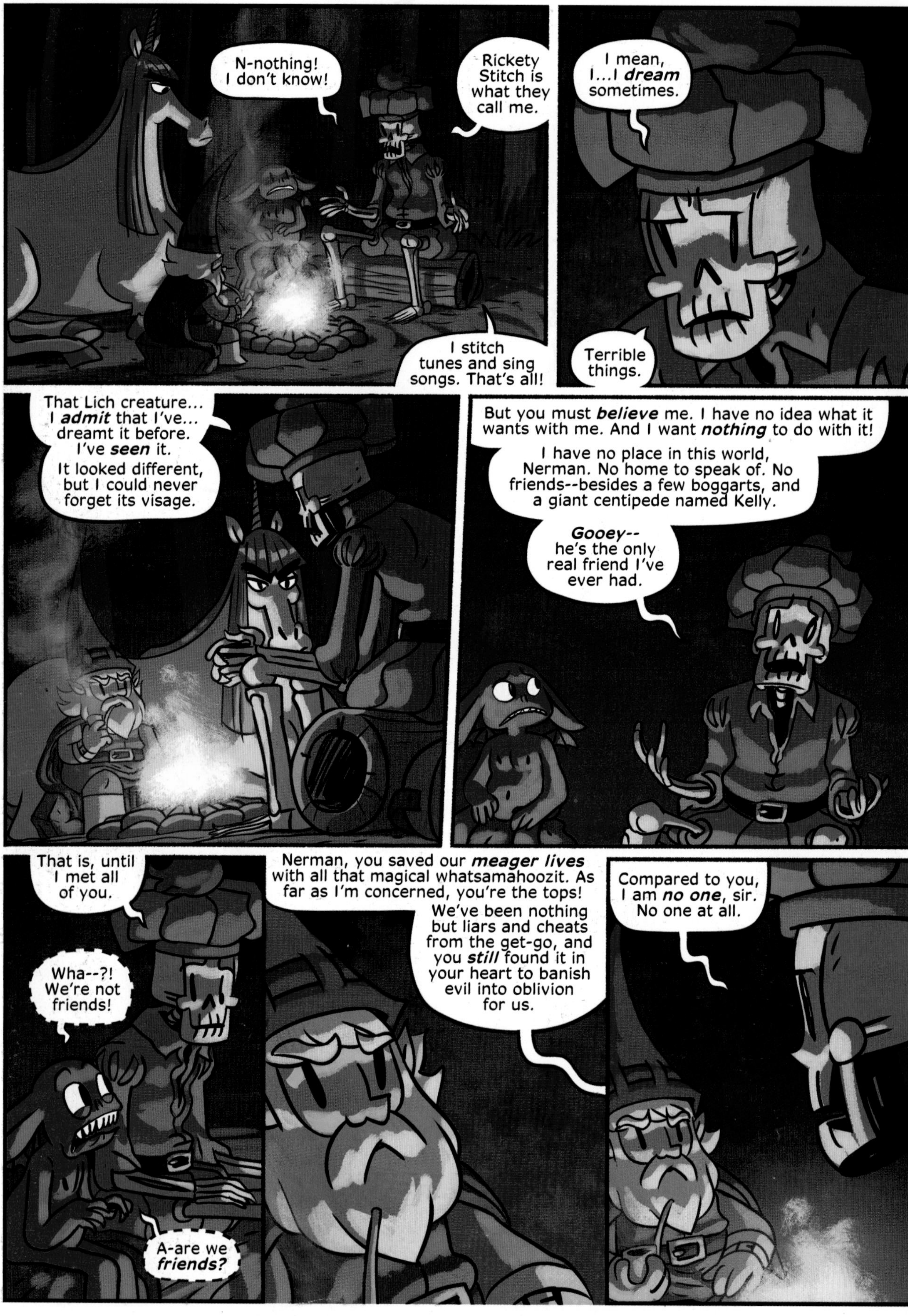
N-nothing! I don't know!
Rickety Stitch is what they call me.
I stitch tunes and sing songs. That's all!
I mean, I...I *dream* sometimes.
Terrible things.
That Lich creature... I *admit* that I've... dreamt it before. I've *seen* it.
It looked different, but I could never forget its visage.
But you must *believe* me. I have no idea what it wants with me. And I want *nothing* to do with it!
I have no place in this world, Nerman. No home to speak of. No friends--besides a few boggarts, and a giant centipede named Kelly.
Gooey-- he's the only real friend I've ever had.
That is, until I met all of you.
Wha--?! We're not friends!
A-are we *friends?*
Nerman, you saved our *meager lives* with all that magical whatsamahoozit. As far as I'm concerned, you're the tops!
We've been nothing but liars and cheats from the get-go, and you *still* found it in your heart to banish evil into oblivion for us.
Compared to you, I am *no one*, sir. No one at all.

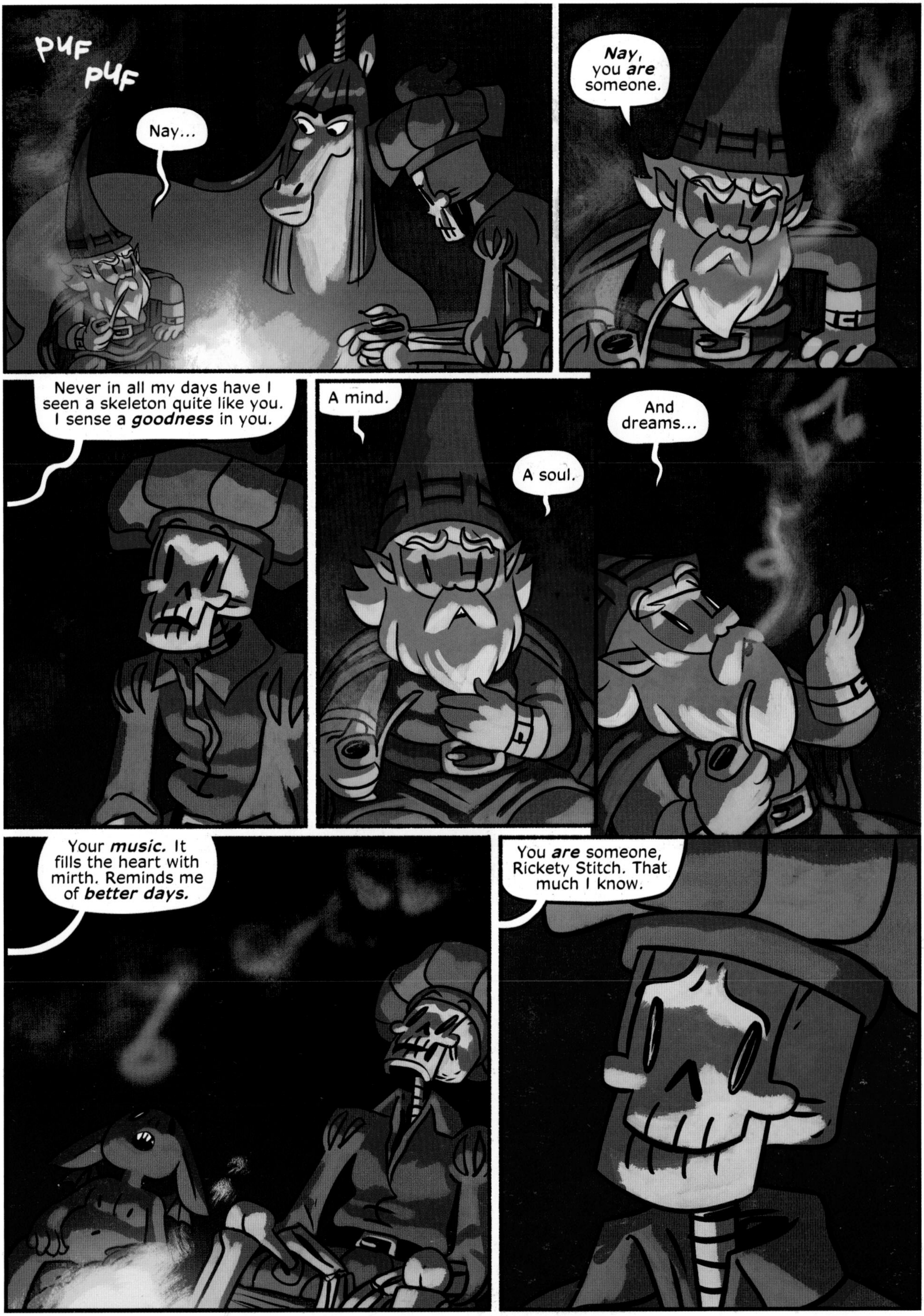
PUF PUF
Nay...
Nay, you are someone.
Never in all my days have I seen a skeleton quite like you. I sense a goodness in you.
A mind.
A soul.
And dreams...
Your music. It fills the heart with mirth. Reminds me of better days.
You are someone, Rickety Stitch. That much I know.

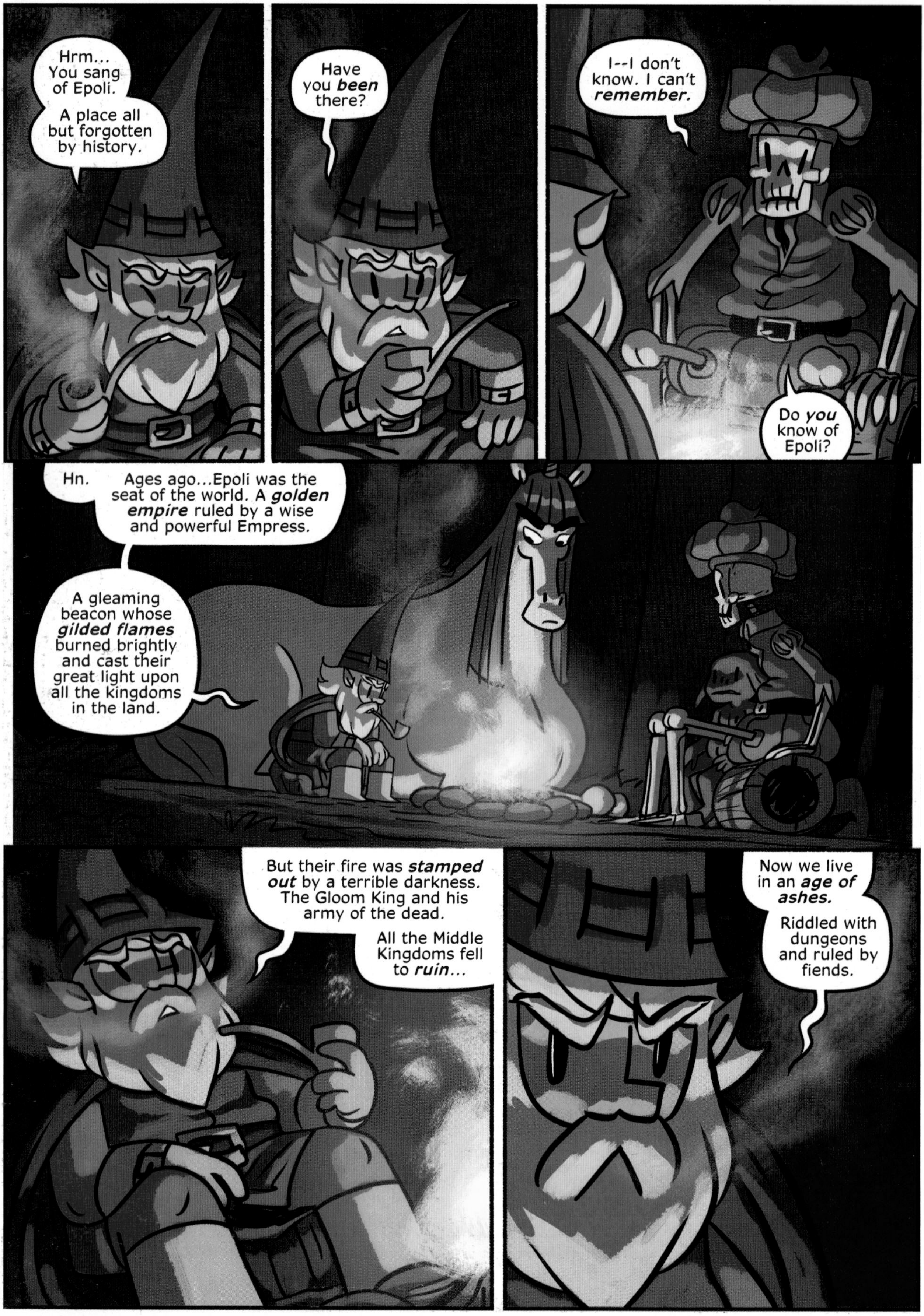
Hrm... You sang of Epoli.
A place all but forgotten by history.
Have you *been* there?
I--I don't know. I can't *remember.*
Do *you* know of Epoli?
Hn.
Ages ago...Epoli was the seat of the world. A *golden empire* ruled by a wise and powerful Empress.
A gleaming beacon whose *gilded flames* burned brightly and cast their great light upon all the kingdoms in the land.
But their fire was *stamped out* by a terrible darkness. The Gloom King and his army of the dead.
All the Middle Kingdoms fell to *ruin*...
Now we live in an *age of ashes.*
Riddled with dungeons and ruled by fiends.

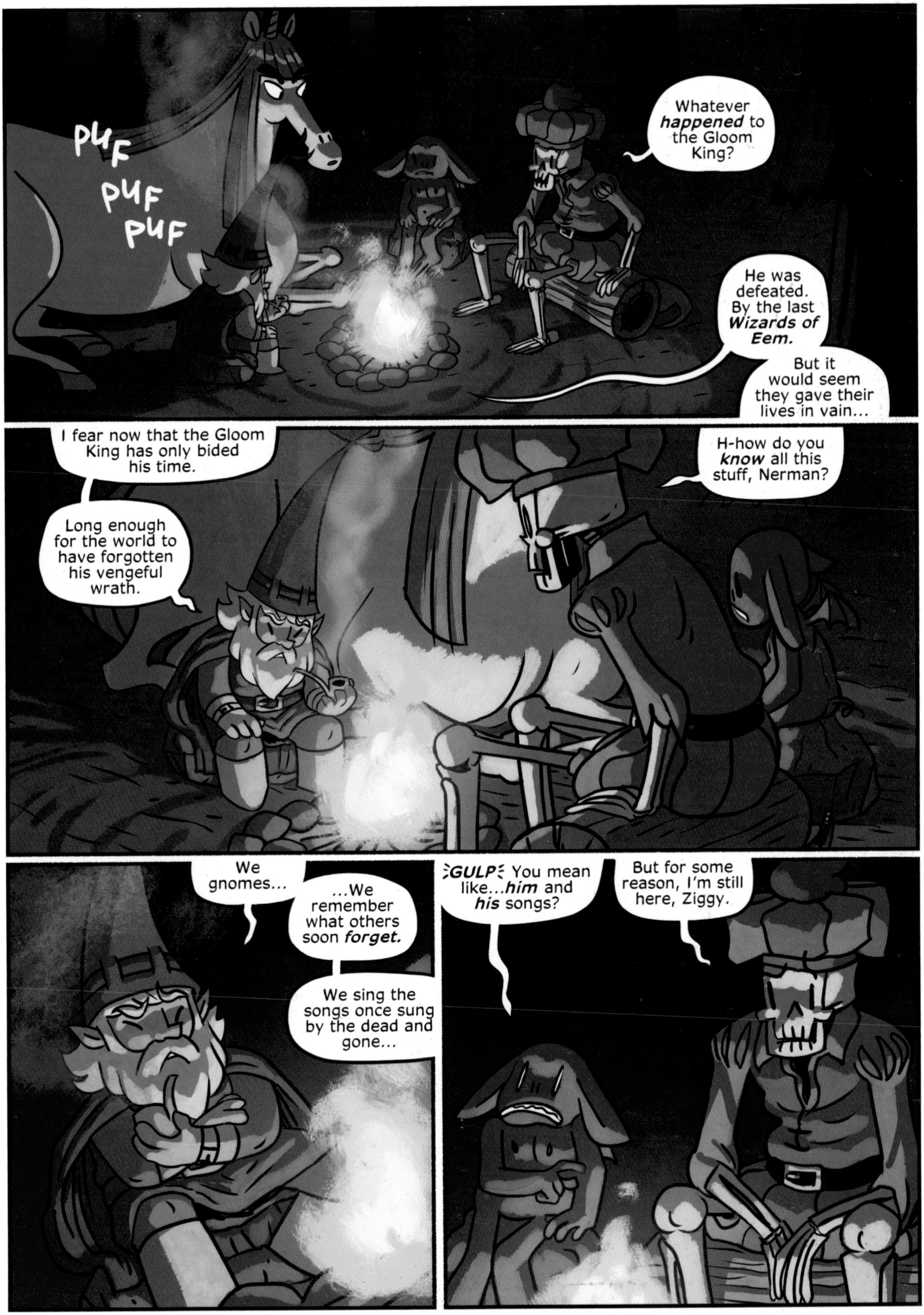
PUF
PUF
PUF
Whatever *happened* to the Gloom King?
He was defeated. By the last ***Wizards of Eem.***
But it would seem they gave their lives in vain...
I fear now that the Gloom King has only bided his time.
Long enough for the world to have forgotten his vengeful wrath.
H-how do you ***know*** all this stuff, Nerman?
We gnomes...
...We remember what others soon *forget.*
We sing the songs once sung by the dead and gone...
GULP You mean like...***him*** and ***his*** songs?
But for some reason, I'm still here, Ziggy.

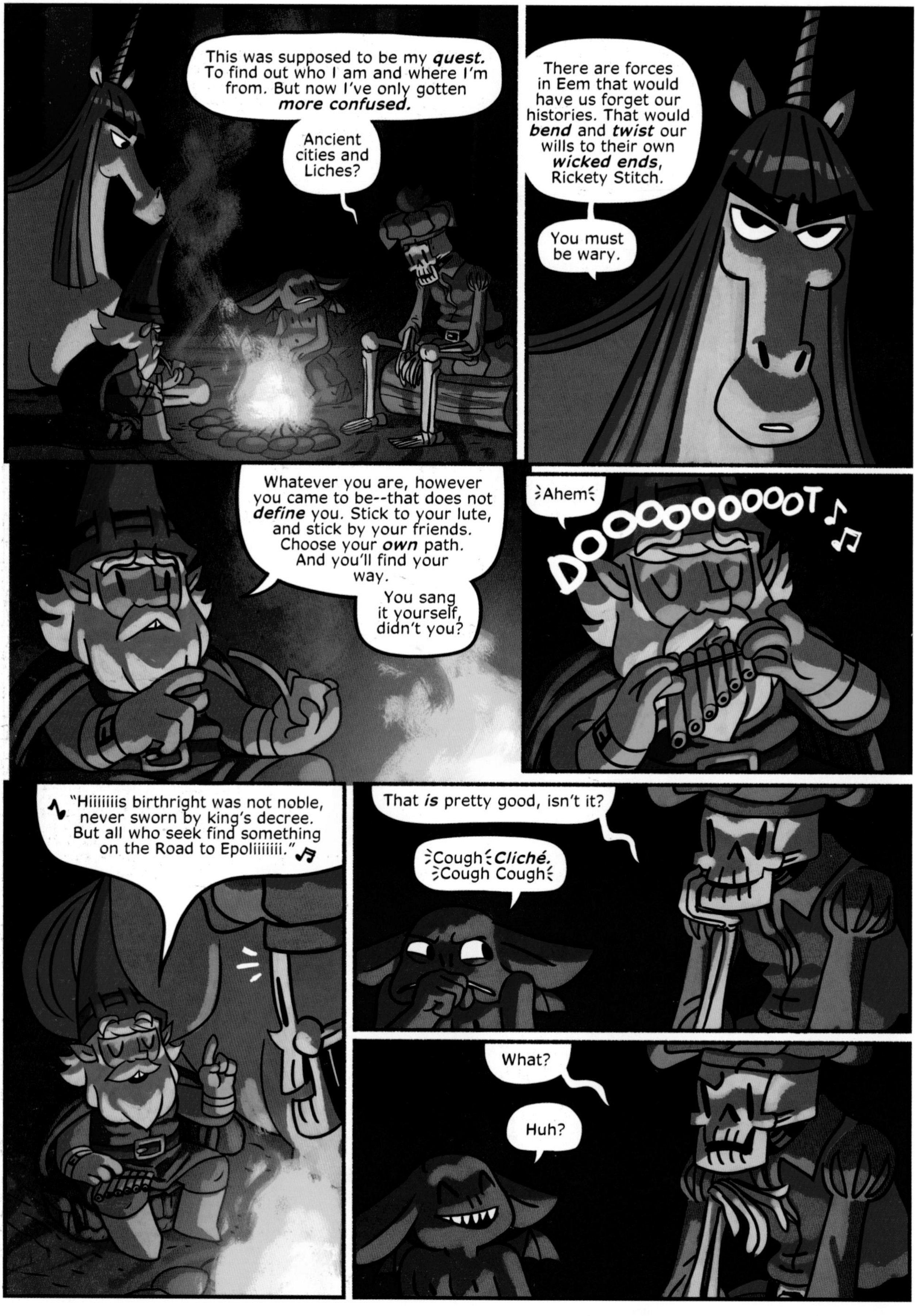
This was supposed to be my *quest.* To find out who I am and where I'm from. But now I've only gotten *more confused.*
Ancient cities and Liches?
There are forces in Eem that would have us forget our histories. That would *bend* and *twist* our wills to their own *wicked ends*, Rickety Stitch.
You must be wary.
Whatever you are, however you came to be--that does not *define* you. Stick to your lute, and stick by your friends. Choose your *own* path. And you'll find your way.
You sang it yourself, didn't you?
Ahem
DOOOOOOOOOT
"Hiiiiiiis birthright was not noble, never sworn by king's decree. But all who seek find something on the Road to Epoliiiiiii."
That *is* pretty good, isn't it?
Cough *Cliché.* Cough Cough
What?
Huh?

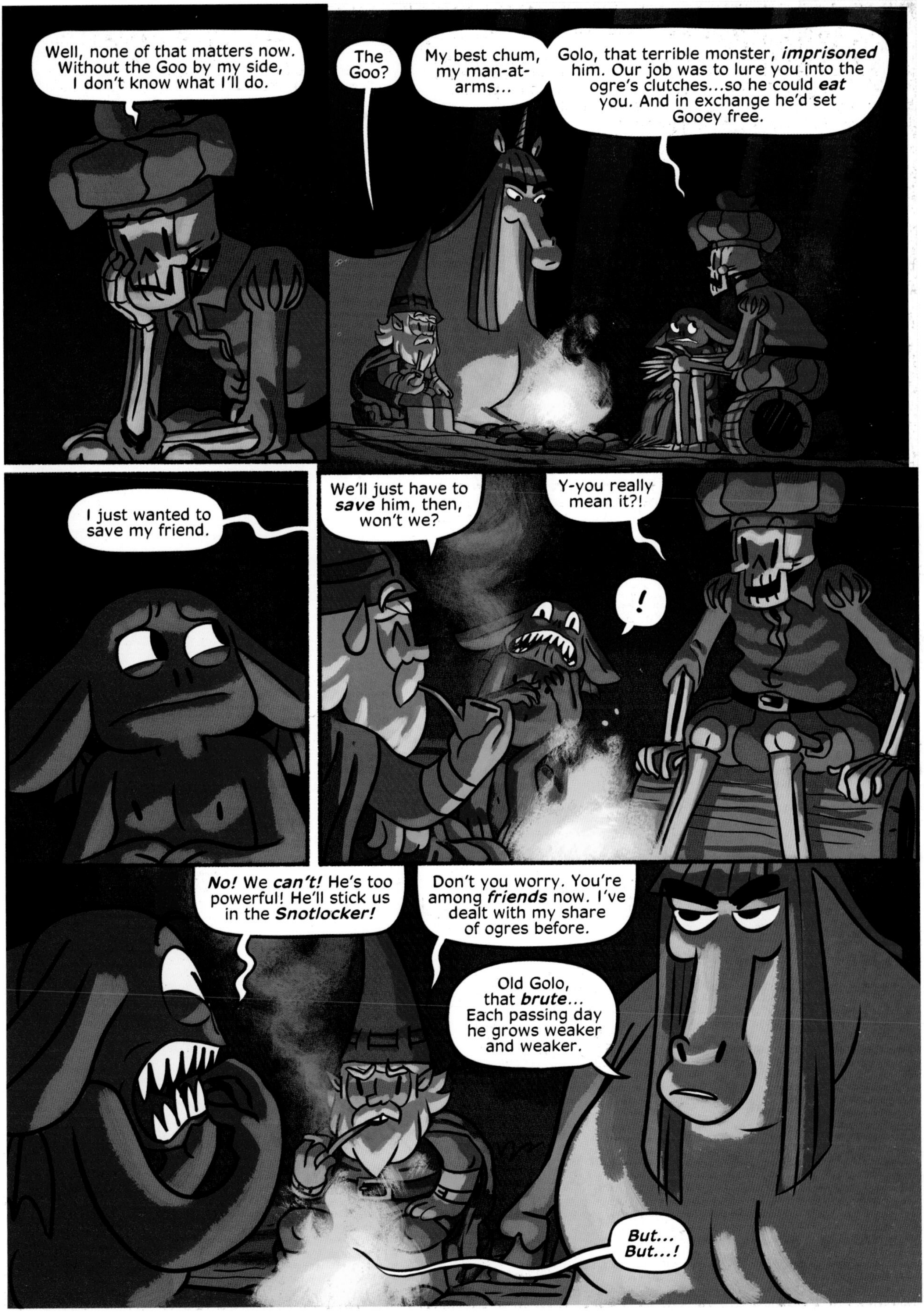

Well, none of that matters now. Without the Goo by my side, I don't know what I'll do.
The Goo?
My best chum, my man-at-arms...
Golo, that terrible monster, ***imprisoned*** him. Our job was to lure you into the ogre's clutches...so he could ***eat*** you. And in exchange he'd set Gooey free.
I just wanted to save my friend.
We'll just have to ***save*** him, then, won't we?
Y-you really mean it?!
!
No! We ***can't!*** He's too powerful! He'll stick us in the ***Snotlocker!***
Don't you worry. You're among ***friends*** now. I've dealt with my share of ogres before.
Old Golo, that ***brute***... Each passing day he grows weaker and weaker.
But... But...!

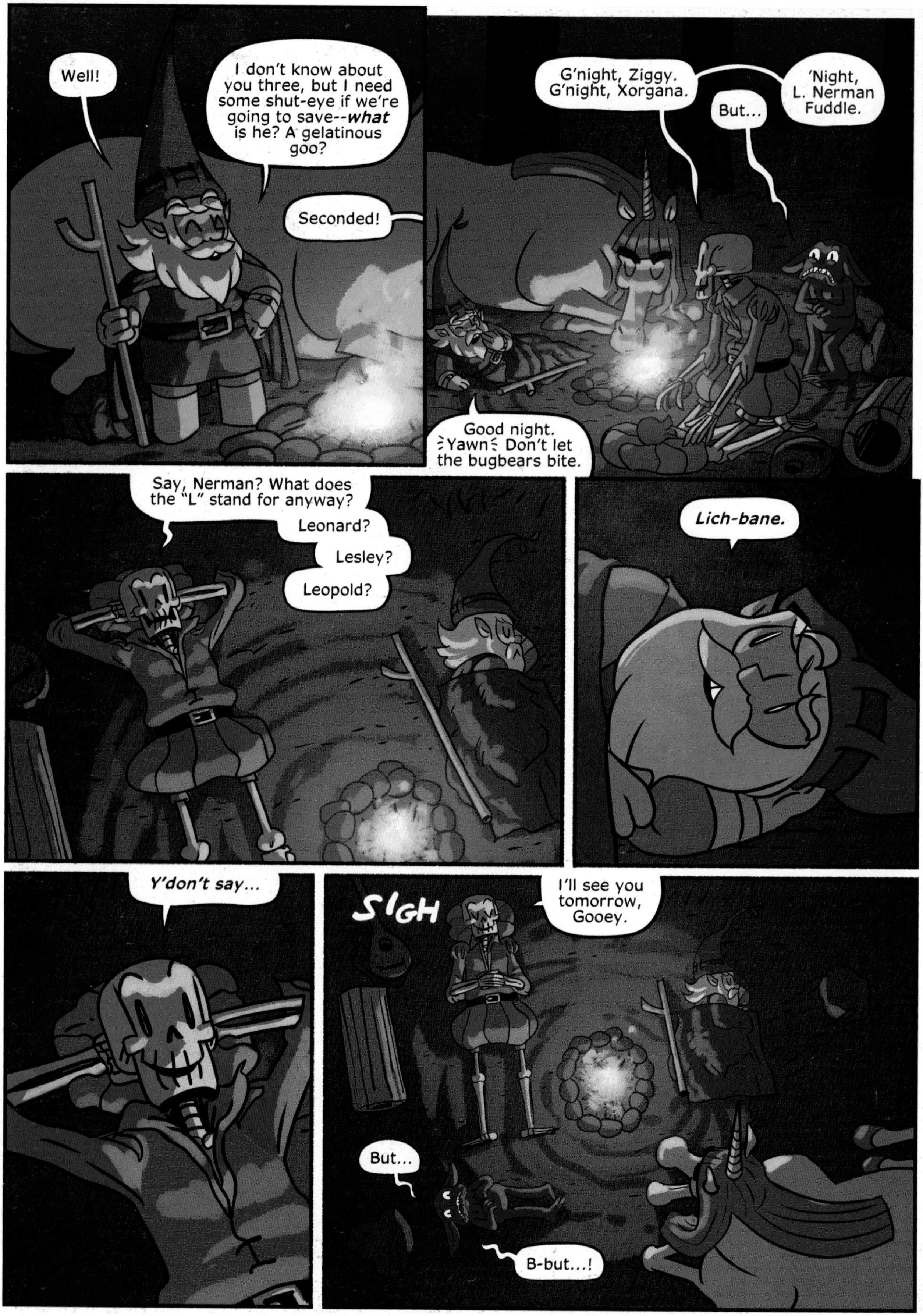
Well!
I don't know about you three, but I need some shut-eye if we're going to save--*what* is he? A gelatinous goo?
Seconded!
G'night, Ziggy. G'night, Xorgana.
But...
'Night, L. Nerman Fuddle.
Good night. ⸗Yawn⸗ Don't let the bugbears bite.
Say, Nerman? What does the "L" stand for anyway?
Leonard?
Lesley?
Leopold?
Lich-bane.
Y'don't say...
SIGH
I'll see you tomorrow, Gooey.
But...
B-but...!

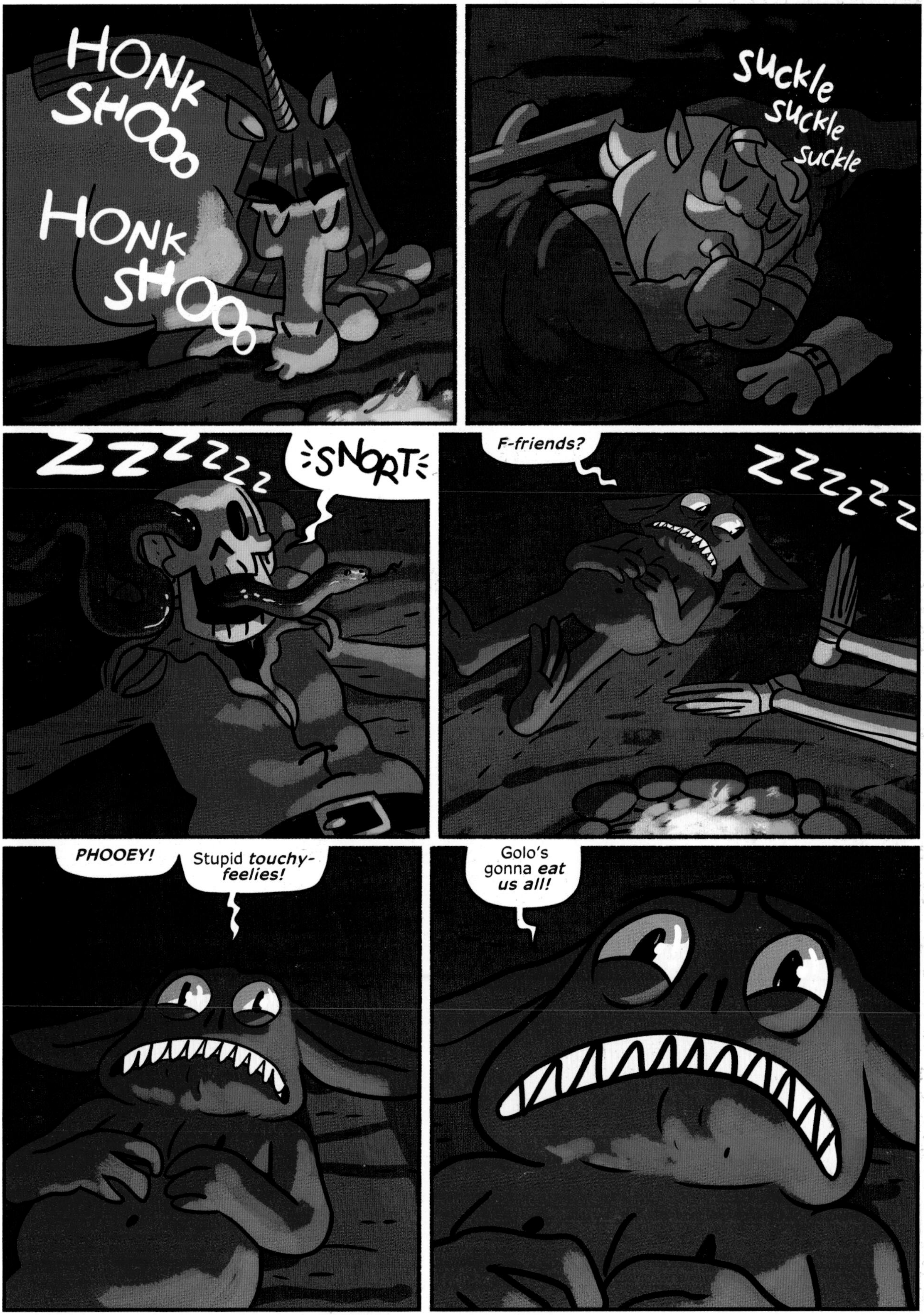
HONK SHOOO
HONK SHOOO
suckle suckle suckle
ZZZZZZZ
SNORT
F-friends?
ZZZZZZZ
PHOOEY!
Stupid *touchy-feelies!*
Golo's gonna *eat* us all!

Chapter 15
Return to the Castle

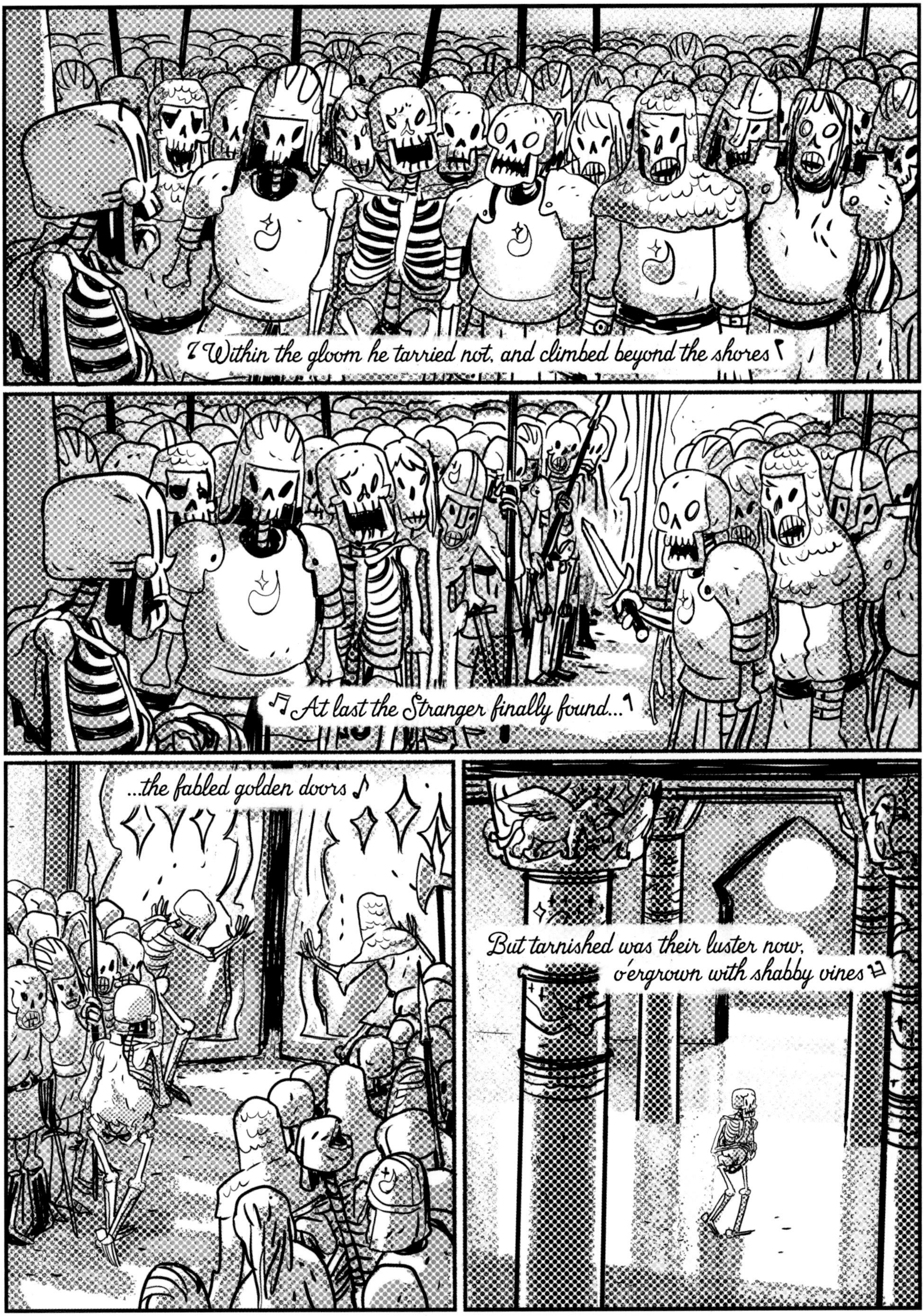
Within the gloom he tarried not, and climbed beyond the shores
At last the Stranger finally found...
...the fabled golden doors
But tarnished was their luster now, o'ergrown with shabby vines

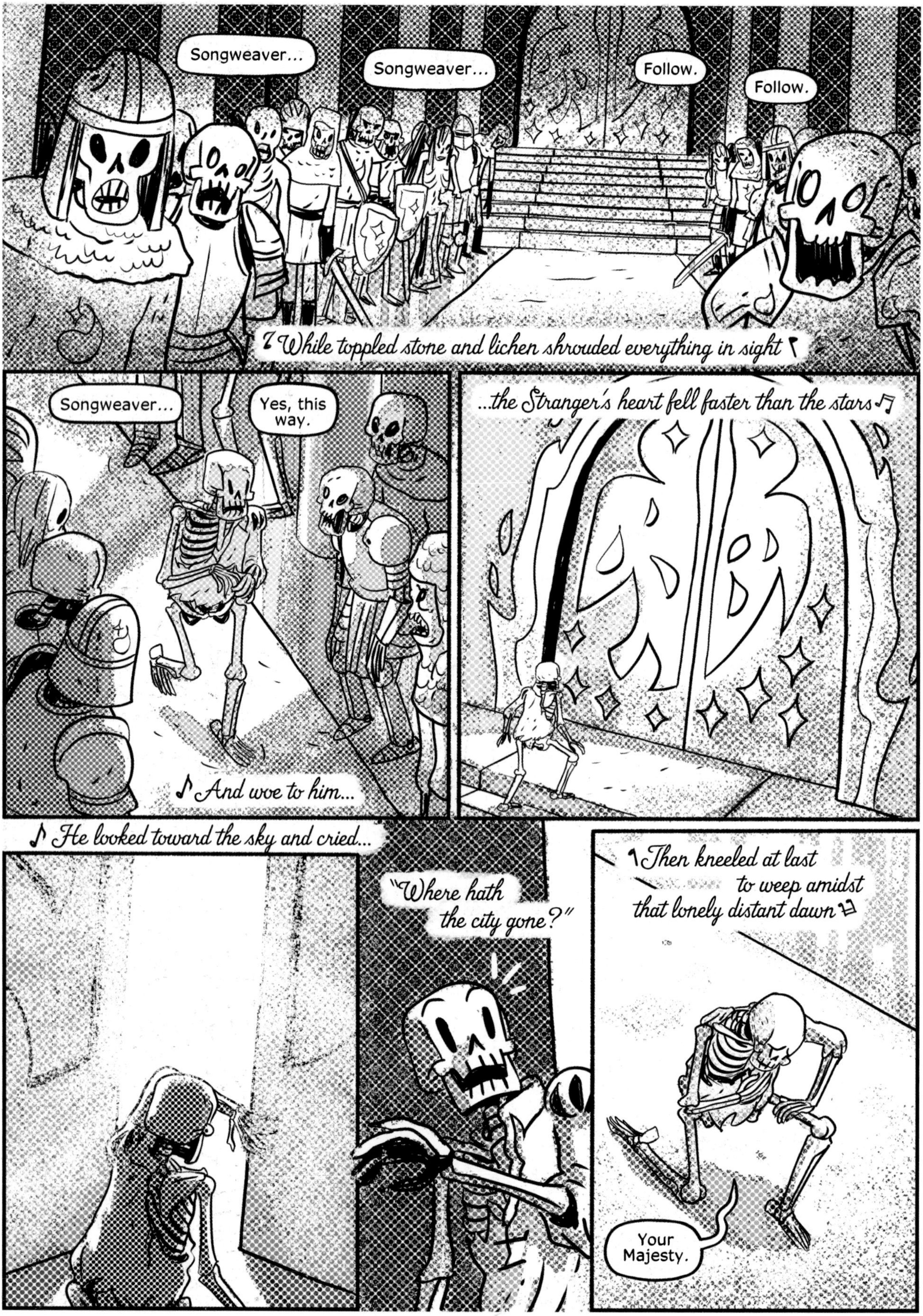
Songweaver...
Songweaver...
Follow.
Follow.
While toppled stone and lichen shrouded everything in sight
Songweaver...
Yes, this way.
...the Stranger's heart fell faster than the stars
And woe to him...
He looked toward the sky and cried...
"Where hath the city gone?"
Then kneeled at last to weep amidst that lonely distant dawn
Your Majesty.

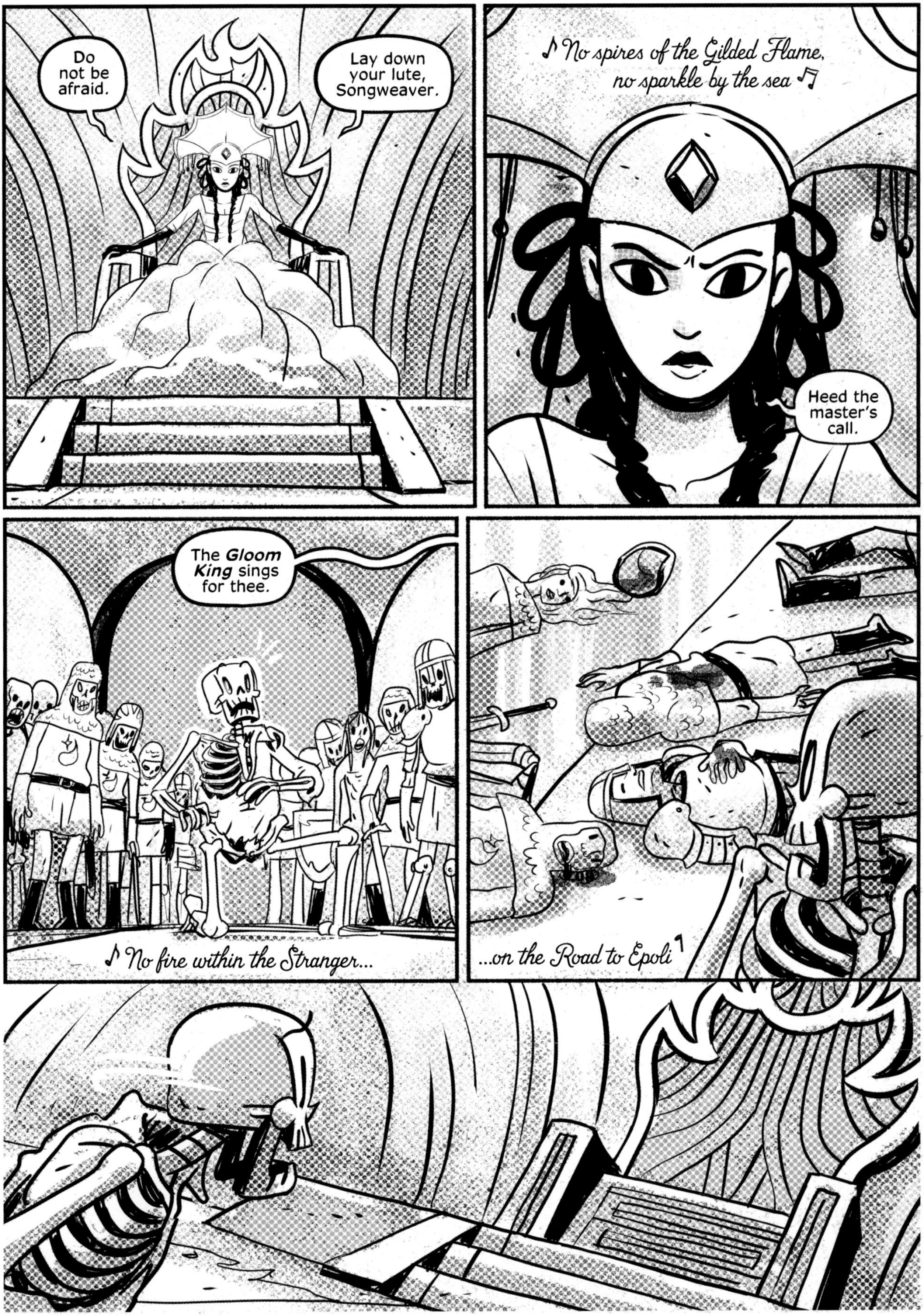

Do not be afraid.
Lay down your lute, Songweaver.
♪ No spires of the Gilded Flame, no sparkle by the sea ♫
Heed the master's call.
The **Gloom King** sings for thee.
♪ No fire within the Stranger...
...on the Road to Epoli

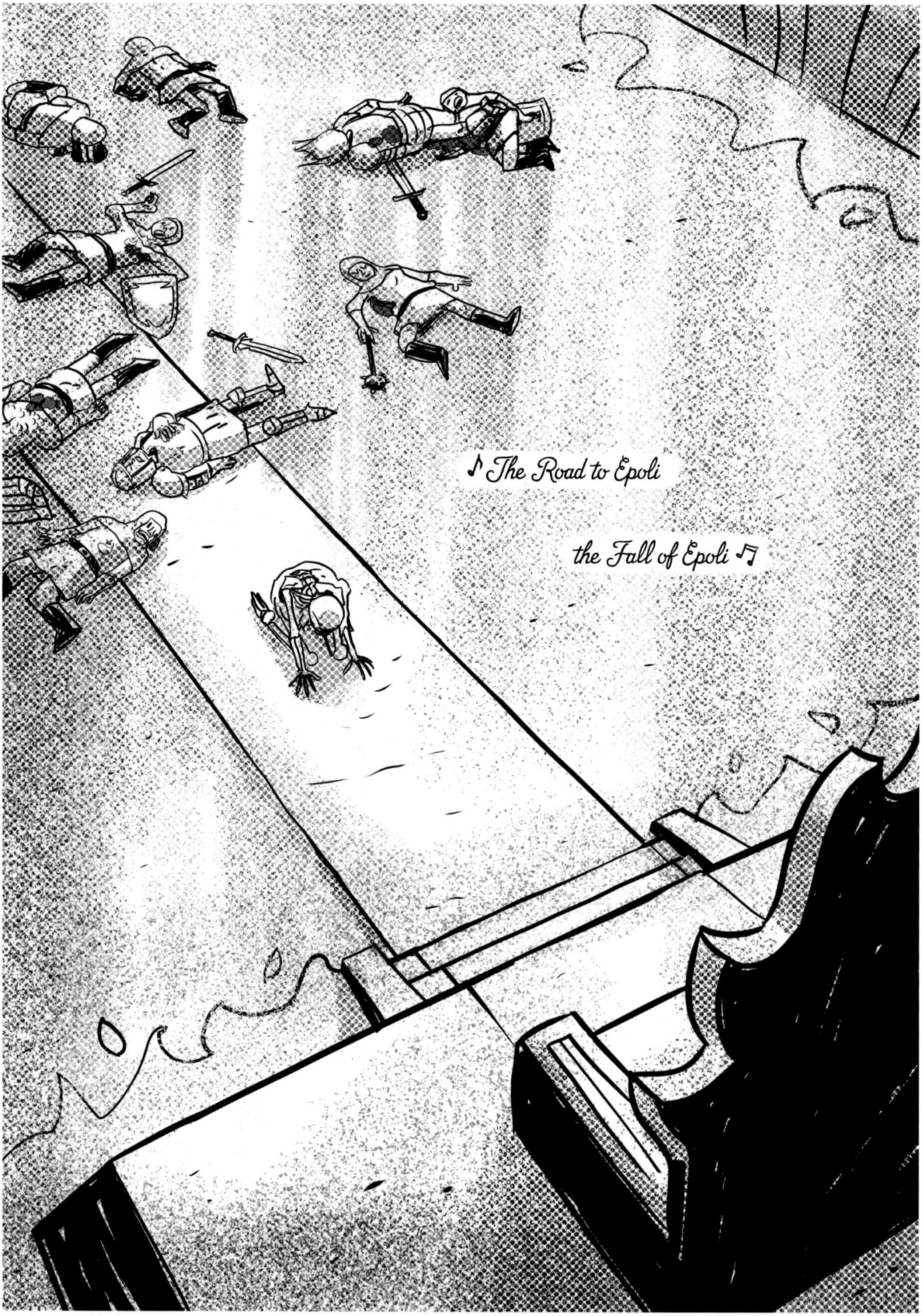
♪ The Road to Epoli
the Fall of Epoli ♫

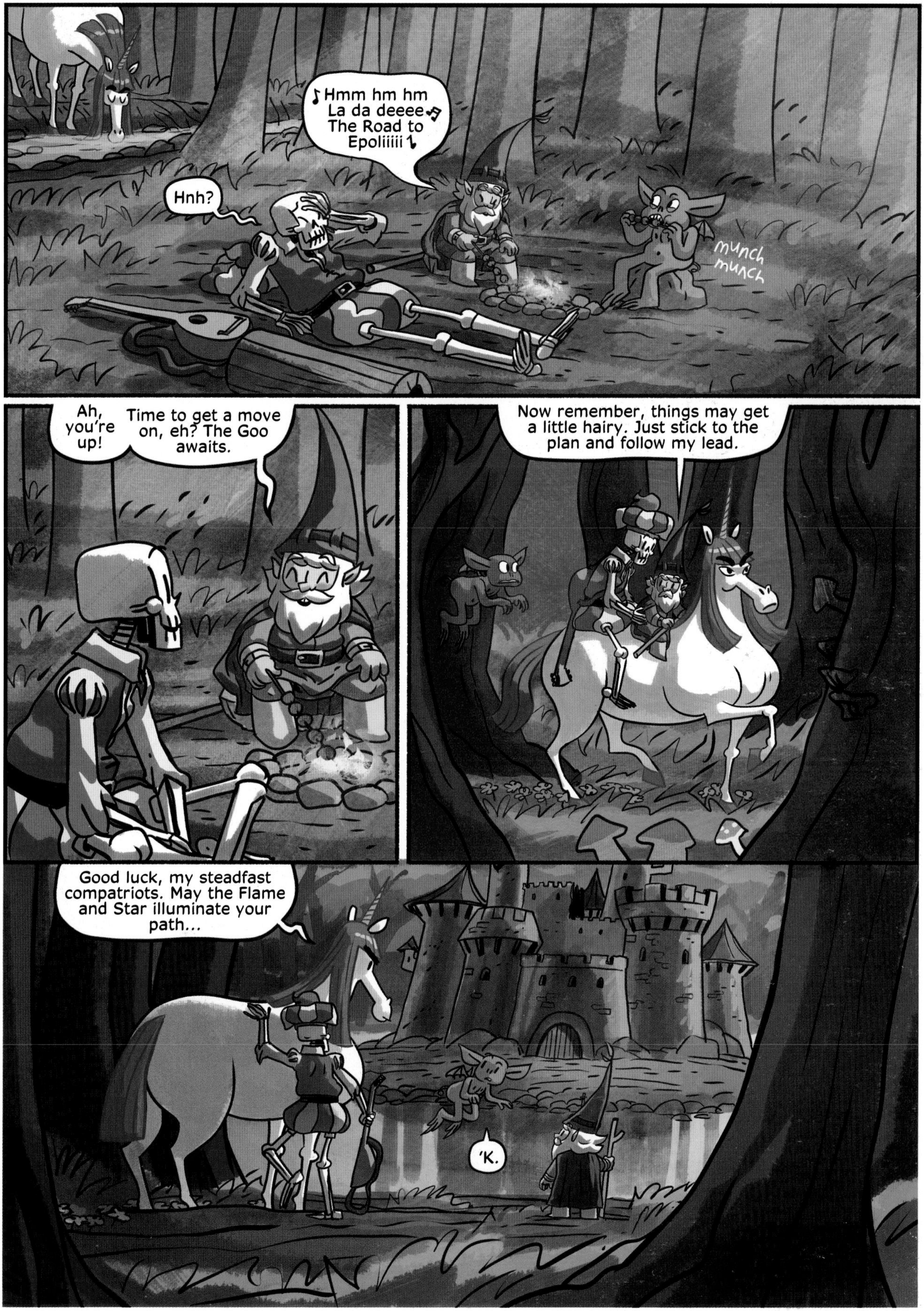

Hmm hm hm La da deeee The Road to Epoliiiii
Hnh?
munch munch
Ah, you're up!
Time to get a move on, eh? The Goo awaits.
Now remember, things may get a little hairy. Just stick to the plan and follow my lead.
Good luck, my steadfast compatriots. May the Flame and Star illuminate your path...
'K.

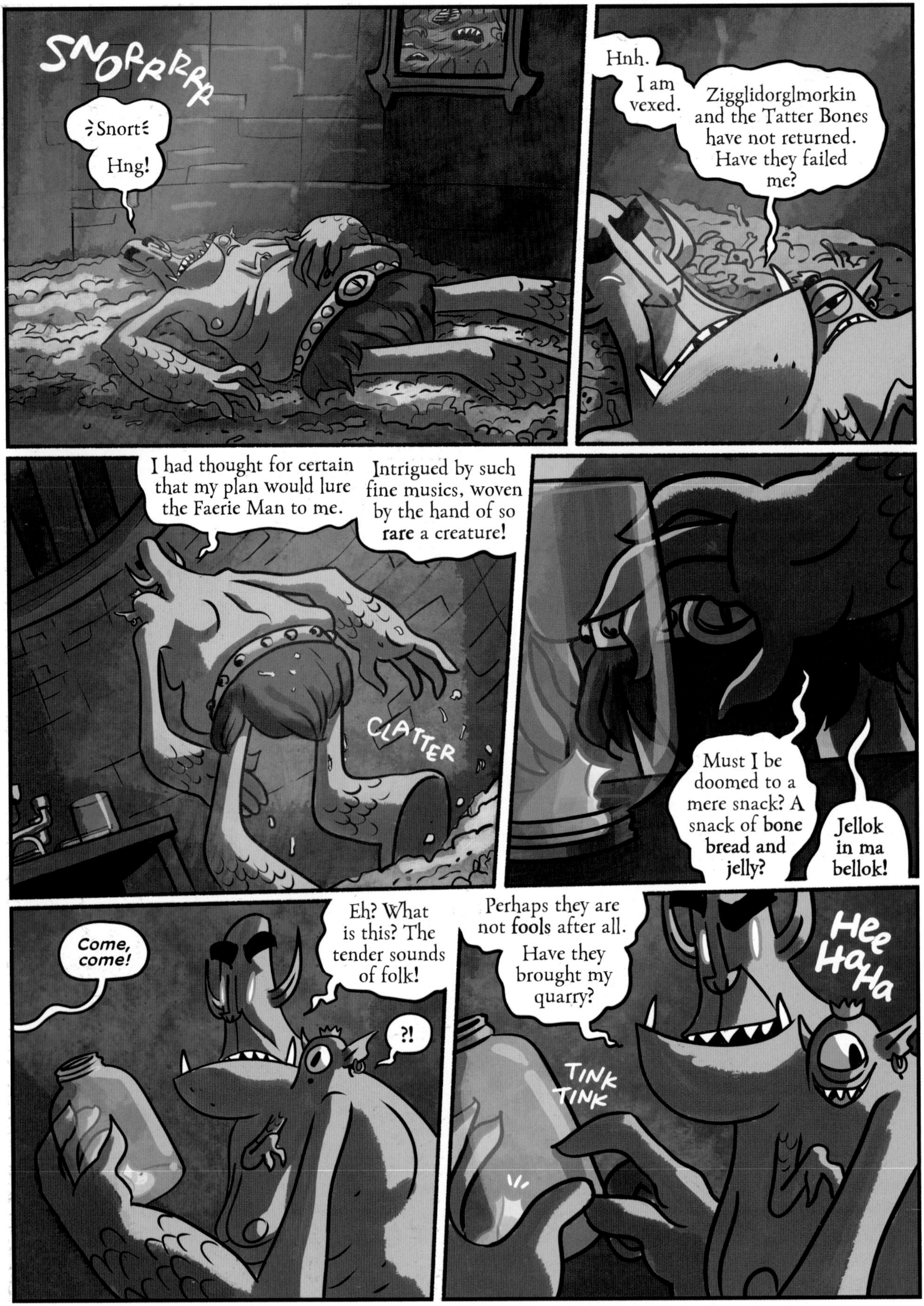
SNORRRRR
Snort
Hng!
Hnh.
I am vexed.
Zigglidorglmorkin and the Tatter Bones have not returned. Have they failed me?
I had thought for certain that my plan would lure the Faerie Man to me.
Intrigued by such fine musics, woven by the hand of so **rare** a creature!
CLATTER
Must I be doomed to a mere snack? A snack of **bone bread and jelly?**
Jellok in ma bellok!
Come, come!
Eh? What is this? The tender sounds of folk!
?!
Perhaps they are not **fools** after all.
Have they brought my quarry?
TINK TINK
Hee Haha

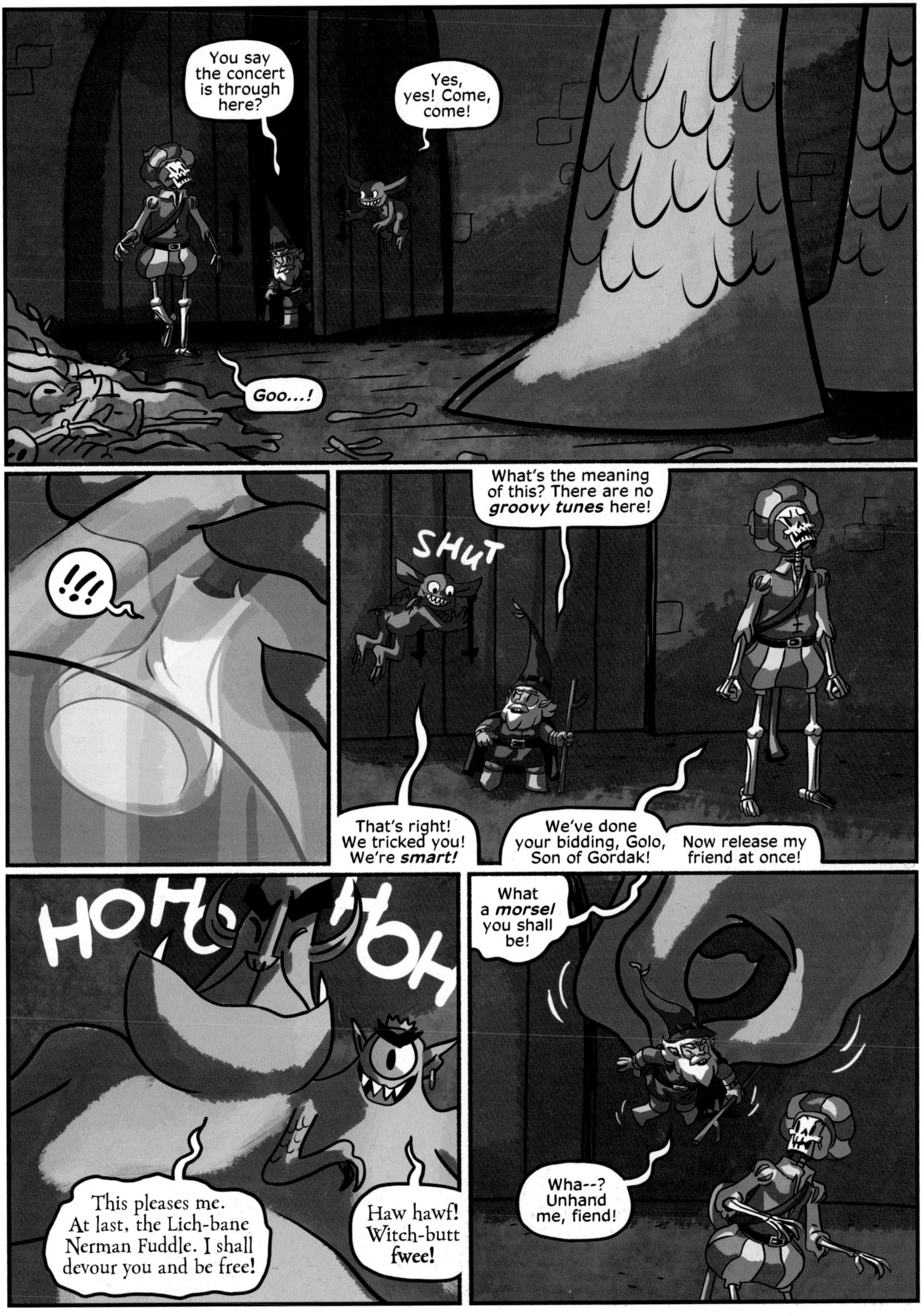
You say the concert is through here?
Yes, yes! Come, come!
Goo...!
!!!
What's the meaning of this? There are no *groovy tunes* here!
SHUT
That's right! We tricked you! We're *smart!*
We've done your bidding, Golo, Son of Gordak!
Now release my friend at once!
HOHOHOHOH
This pleases me. At last, the Lich-bane Nerman Fuddle. I shall devour you and be free!
Haw hawf! Witch-butt **fwee!**
What a *morsel* you shall be!
Wha--? Unhand me, fiend!

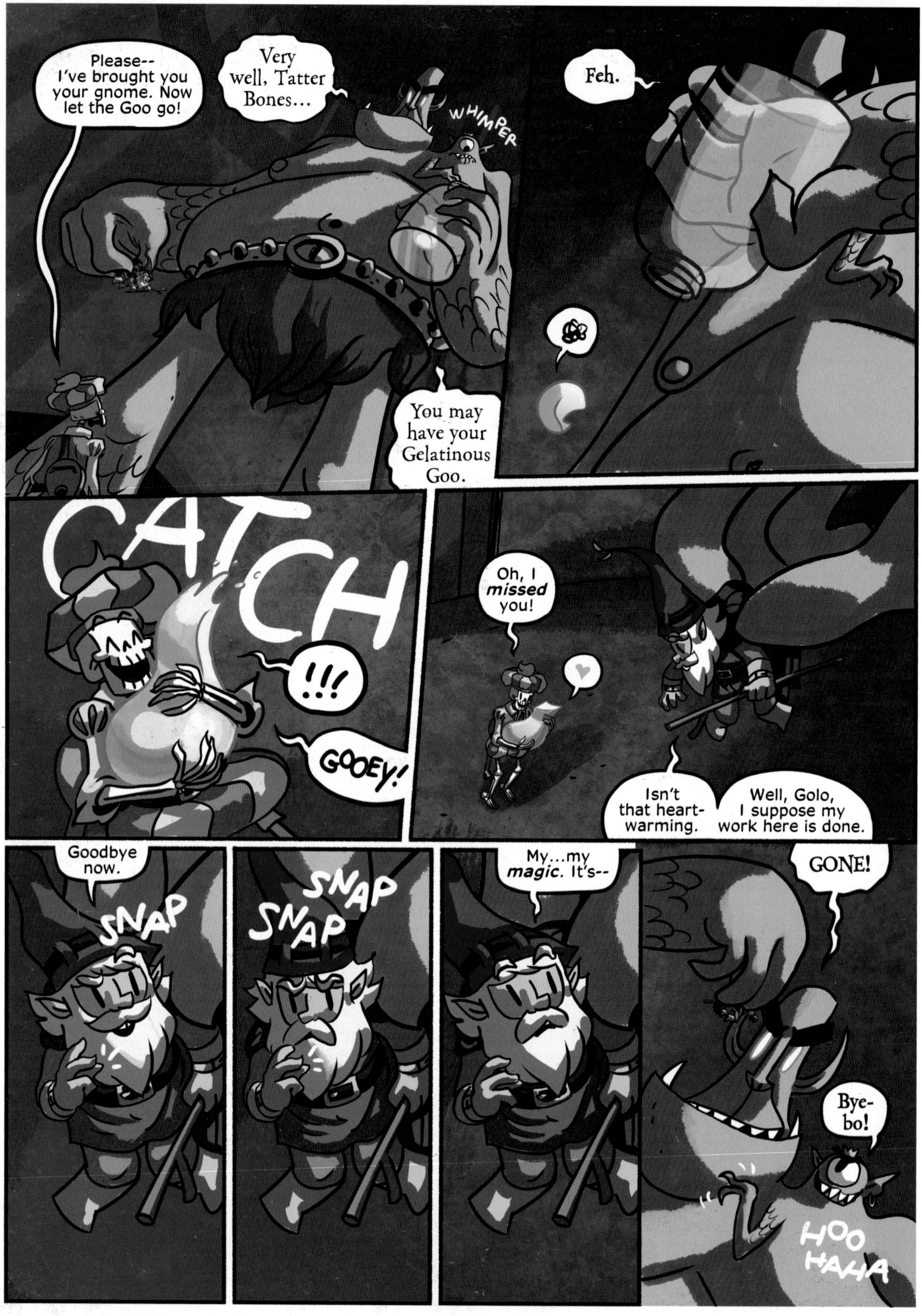

Please-- I've brought you your gnome. Now let the Goo go!
Very well, Tatter Bones...
WHIMPER
You may have your Gelatinous Goo.
Feh.
CATCH
!!!
GOOEY!
Oh, I missed you!
Isn't that heart-warming.
Well, Golo, I suppose my work here is done.
Goodbye now.
SNAP
SNAP SNAP
My...my magic. It's--
GONE!
Bye-bo!
HOO HAHA

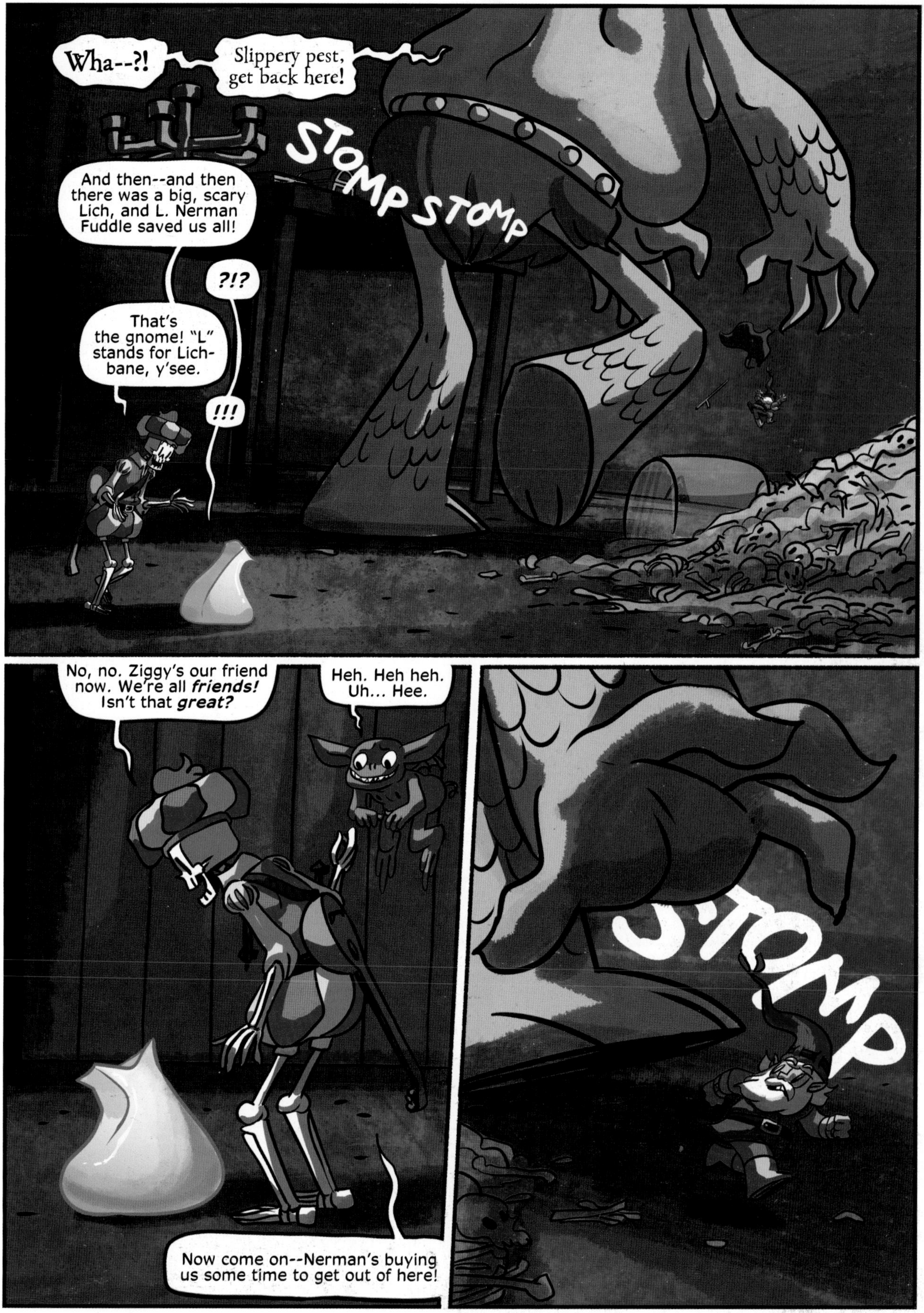
Wha--?!
Slippery pest, get back here!
STOMP STOMP STOMP
And then--and then there was a big, scary Lich, and L. Nerman Fuddle saved us all!
?!?
That's the gnome! "L" stands for Lich-bane, y'see.
!!!
No, no. Ziggy's our friend now. We're all *friends!* Isn't that *great?*
Heh. Heh heh. Uh... Hee.
Now come on--Nerman's buying us some time to get out of here!
STOMP

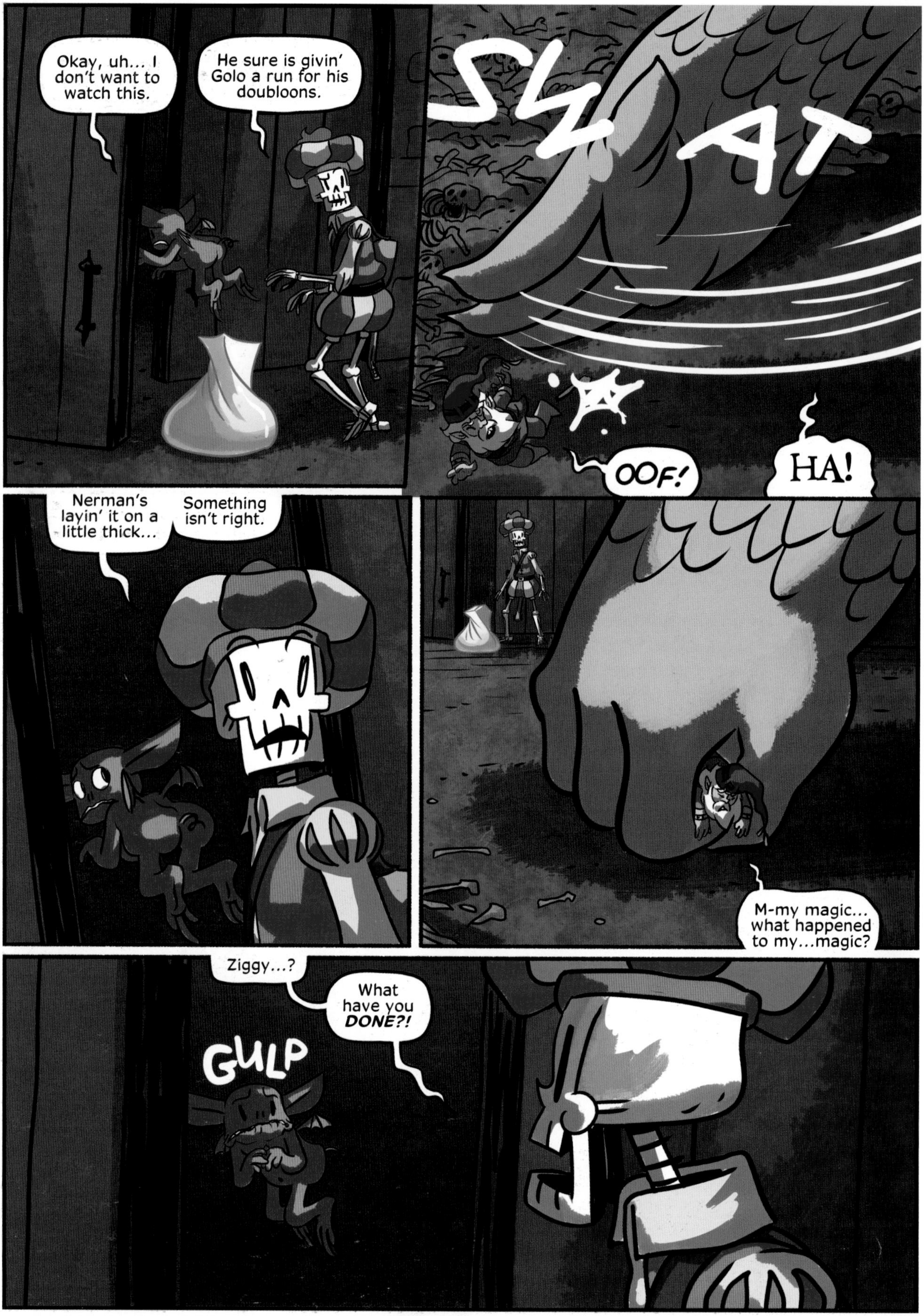
Okay, uh... I don't want to watch this.
He sure is givin' Golo a run for his doubloons.
SWAT
OOF!
HA!
Nerman's layin' it on a little thick...
Something isn't right.
M-my magic... what happened to my...magic?
Ziggy...?
What have you DONE?!
GULP

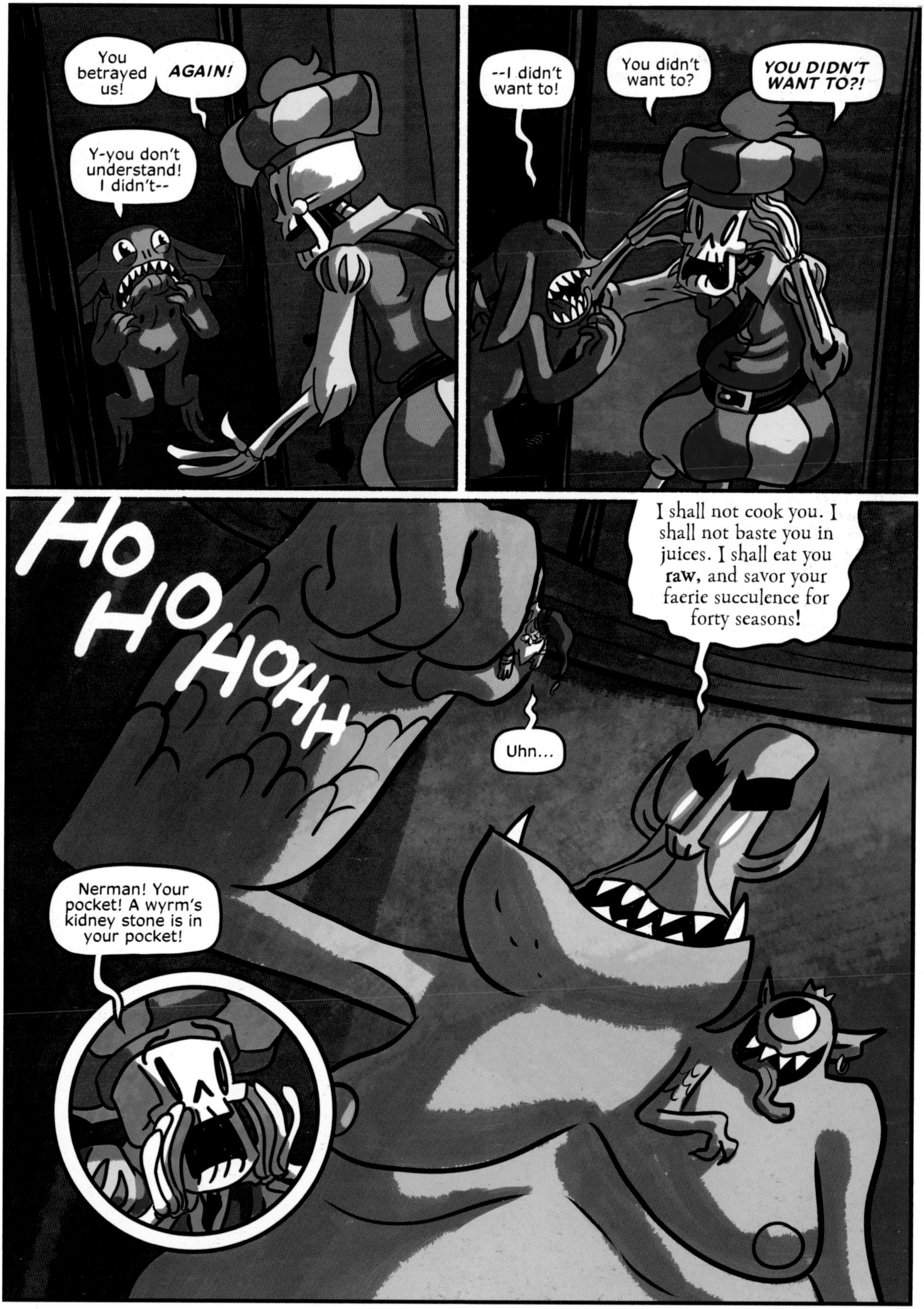
You betrayed us!
AGAIN!
Y-you don't understand! I didn't--
--I didn't want to!
You didn't want to?
YOU DIDN'T WANT TO?!
HO HO HO HOHH
I shall not cook you. I shall not baste you in juices. I shall eat you raw, and savor your faerie succulence for forty seasons!
Uhn...
Nerman! Your pocket! A wyrm's kidney stone is in your pocket!

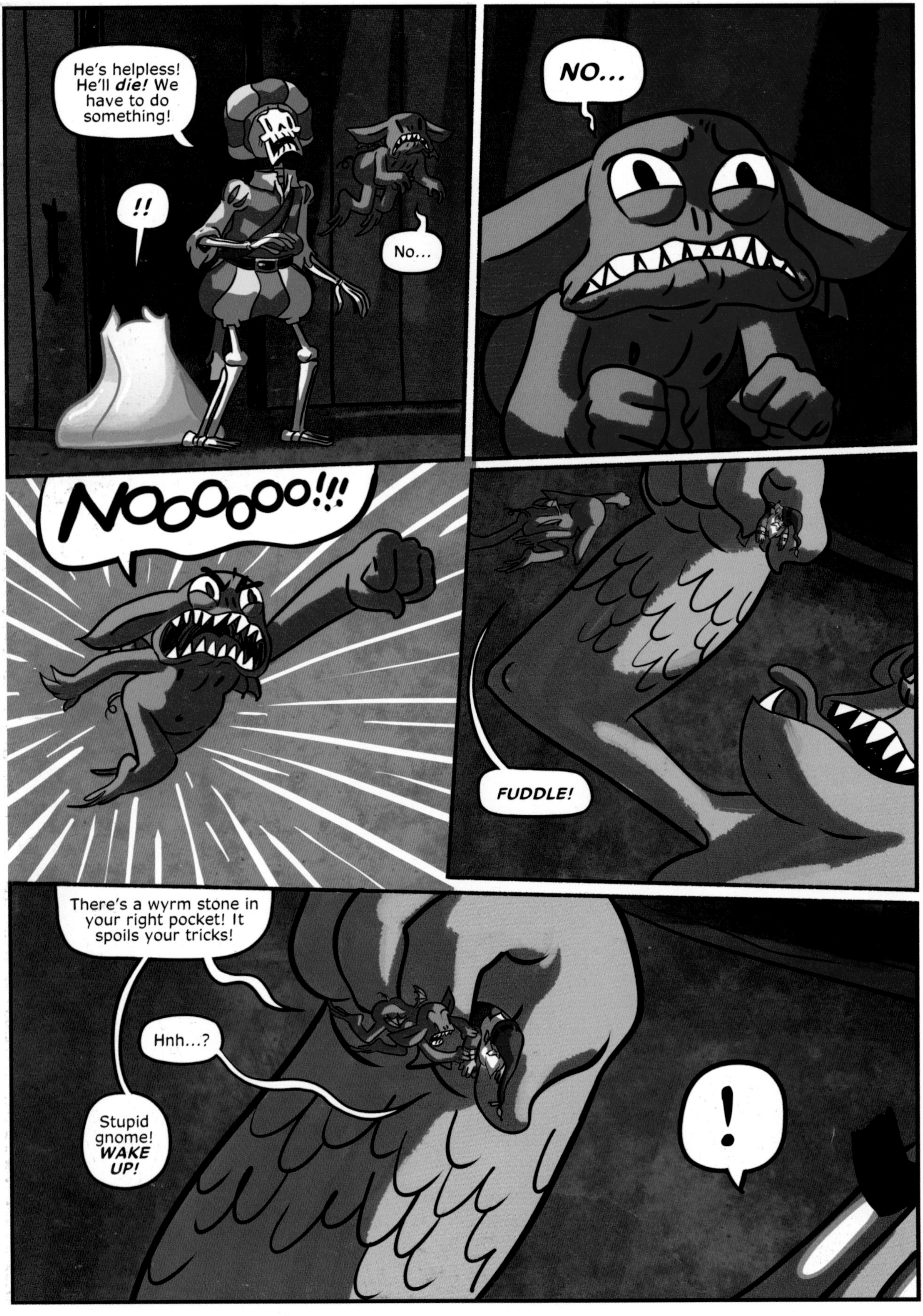
He's helpless! He'll *die!* We have to do something!
!!
No...
NO...
NOOOOOOO!!!
FUDDLE!
There's a wyrm stone in your right pocket! It spoils your tricks!
Hnh...?
Stupid gnome! ***WAKE UP!***
!

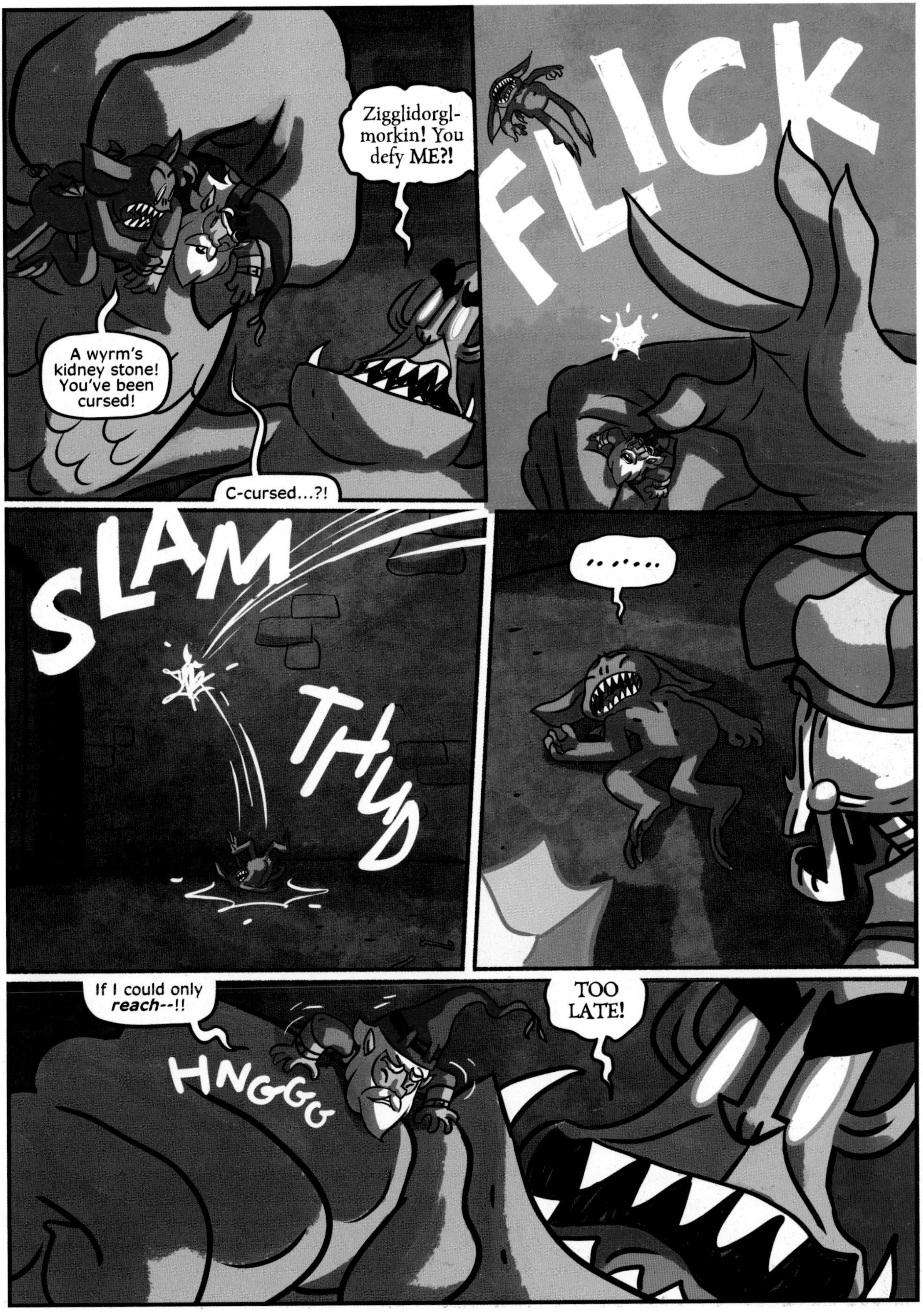
Zigglidorgl-morkin! You defy ME?!
A wyrm's kidney stone! You've been cursed!
C-cursed...?!
FLICK
SLAM
THUD
......
If I could only *reach*--!!
HNGGG
TOO LATE!

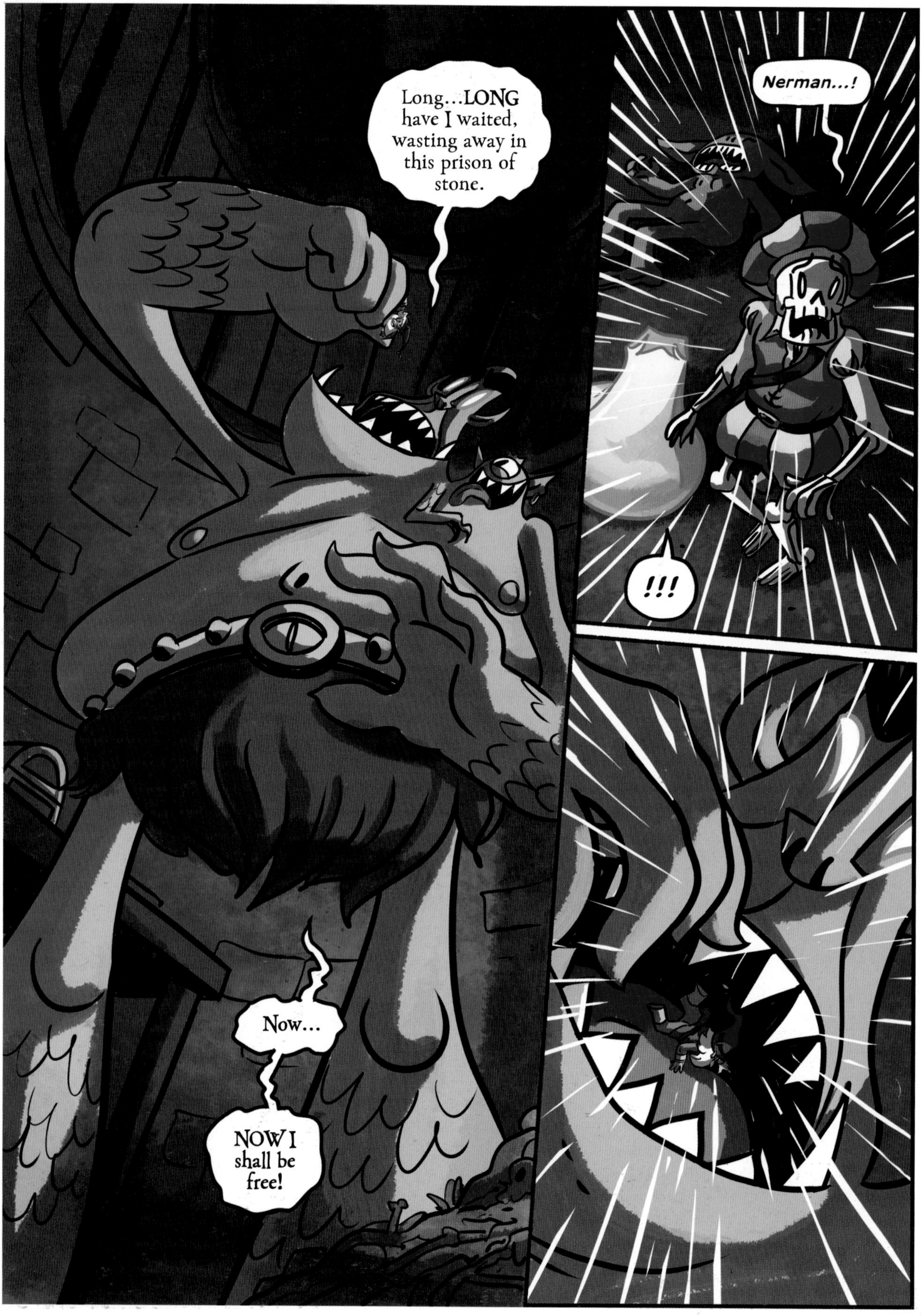
Long...LONG have I waited, wasting away in this prison of stone.
Now...
NOW I shall be free!
Nerman...!
!!!

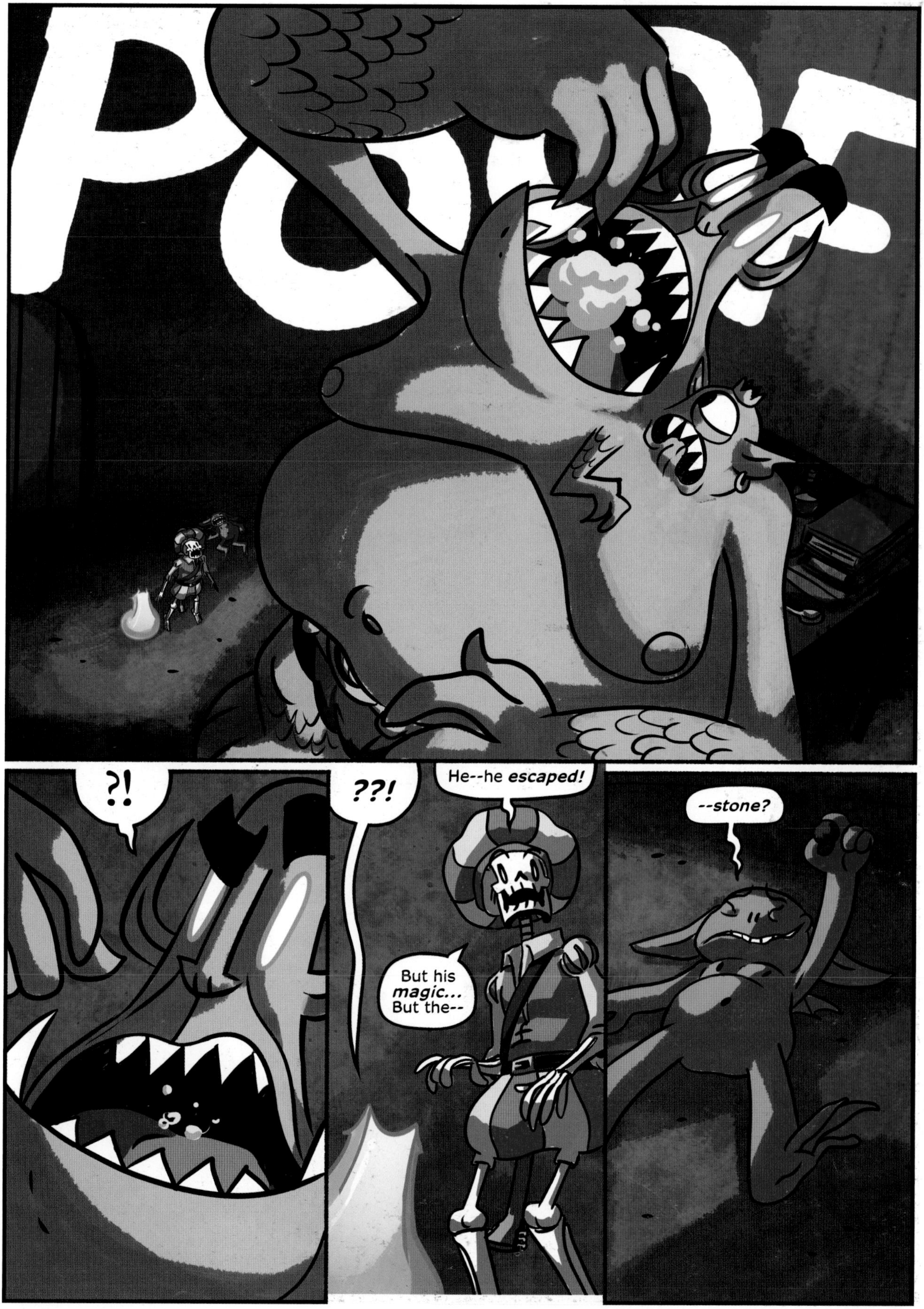
POOF
?!
??!
He--he *escaped!*
But his *magic...* But the--
--*stone?*

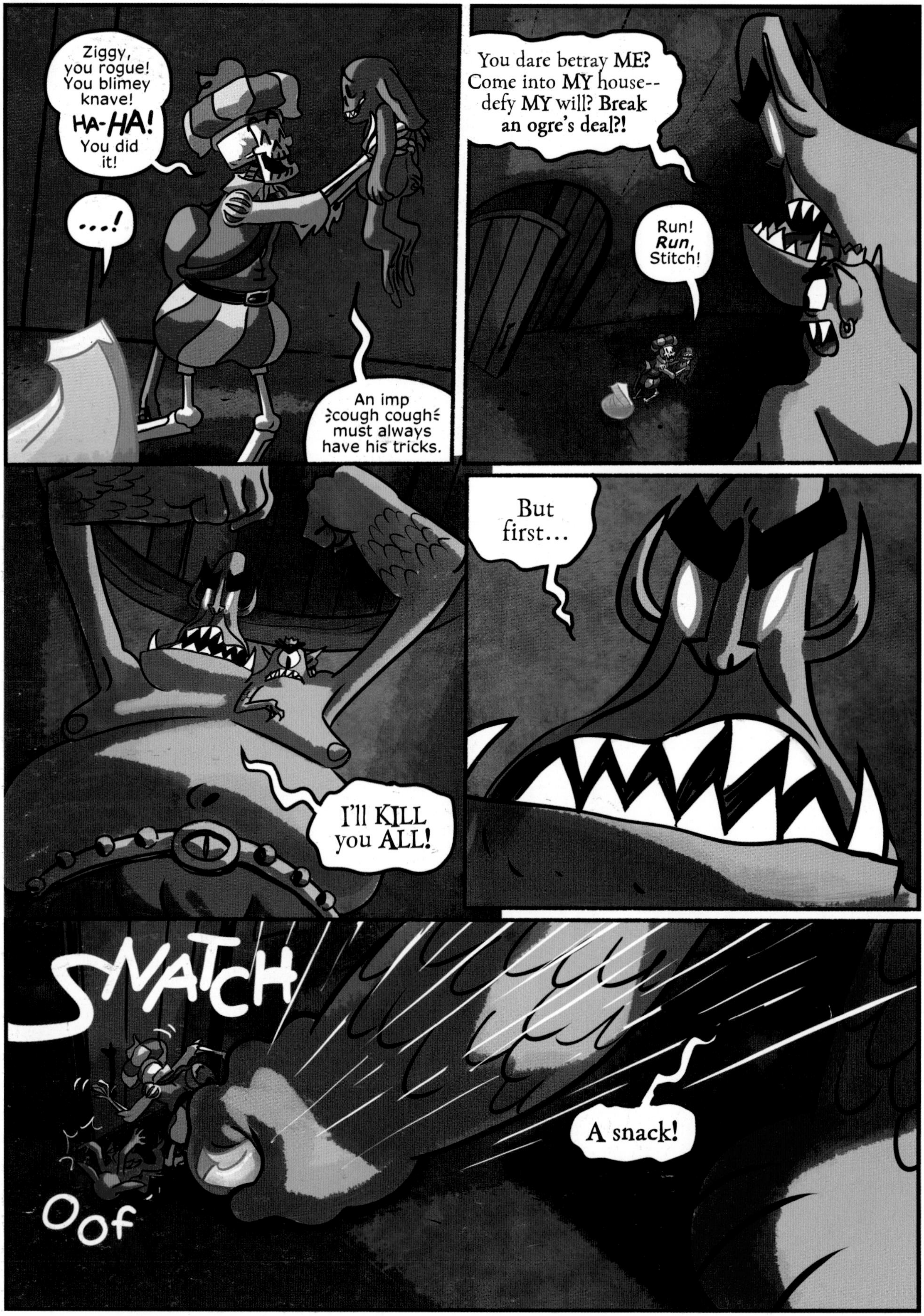
Ziggy, you rogue! You blimey knave! HA-HA! You did it!
...!
An imp ≷cough cough≷ must always have his tricks.
You dare betray ME? Come into MY house-- defy MY will? Break an ogre's deal?!
Run! Run, Stitch!
I'll KILL you ALL!
But first...
SNATCH
A snack!
Oof

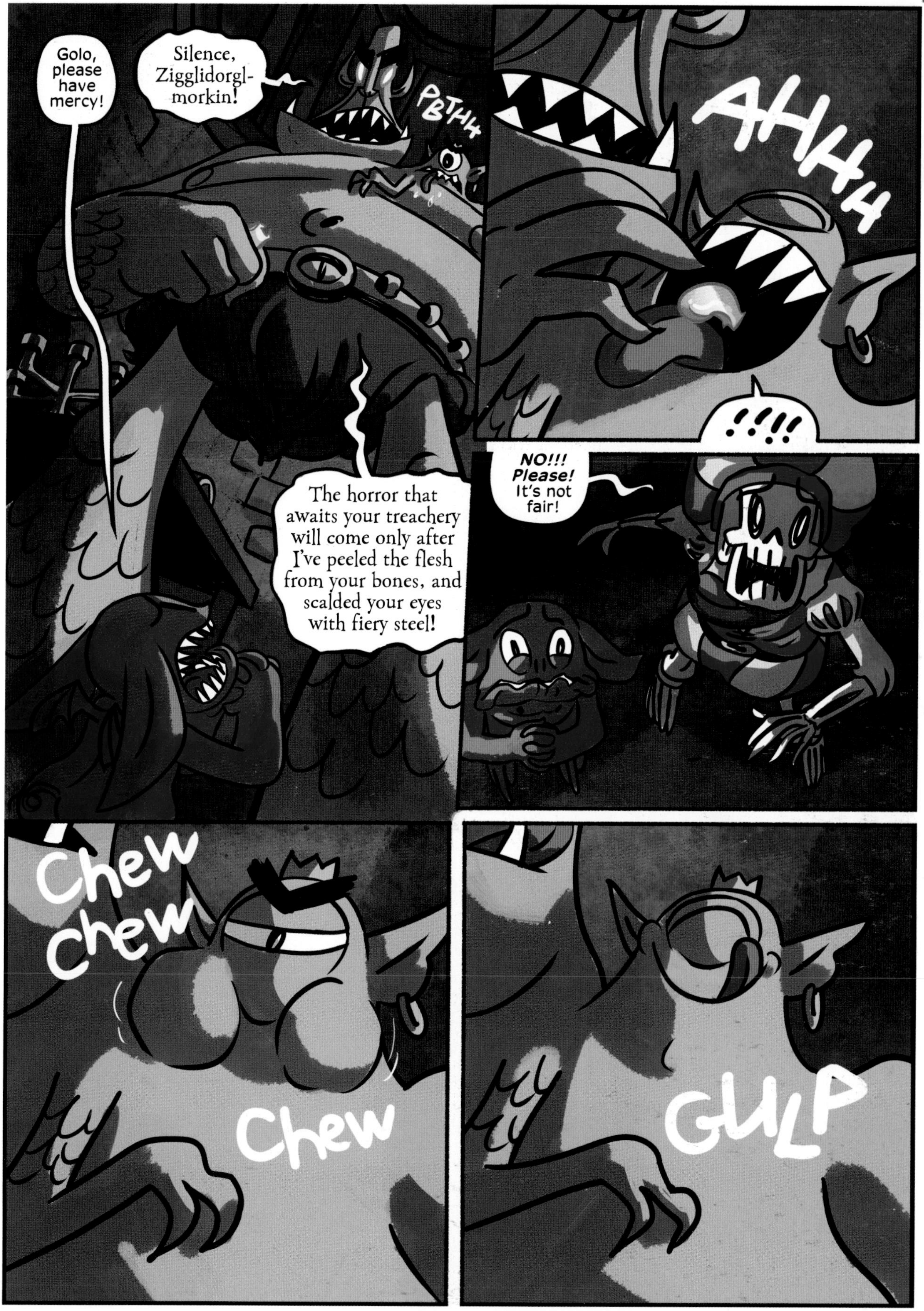
Golo, please have mercy!
Silence, Zigglidorgl-morkin!
PBTHH
The horror that awaits your treachery will come only after I've peeled the flesh from your bones, and scalded your eyes with fiery steel!
AHHHH
!?!!
NO!!! Please! It's not fair!
Chew
Chew
Chew
GULP

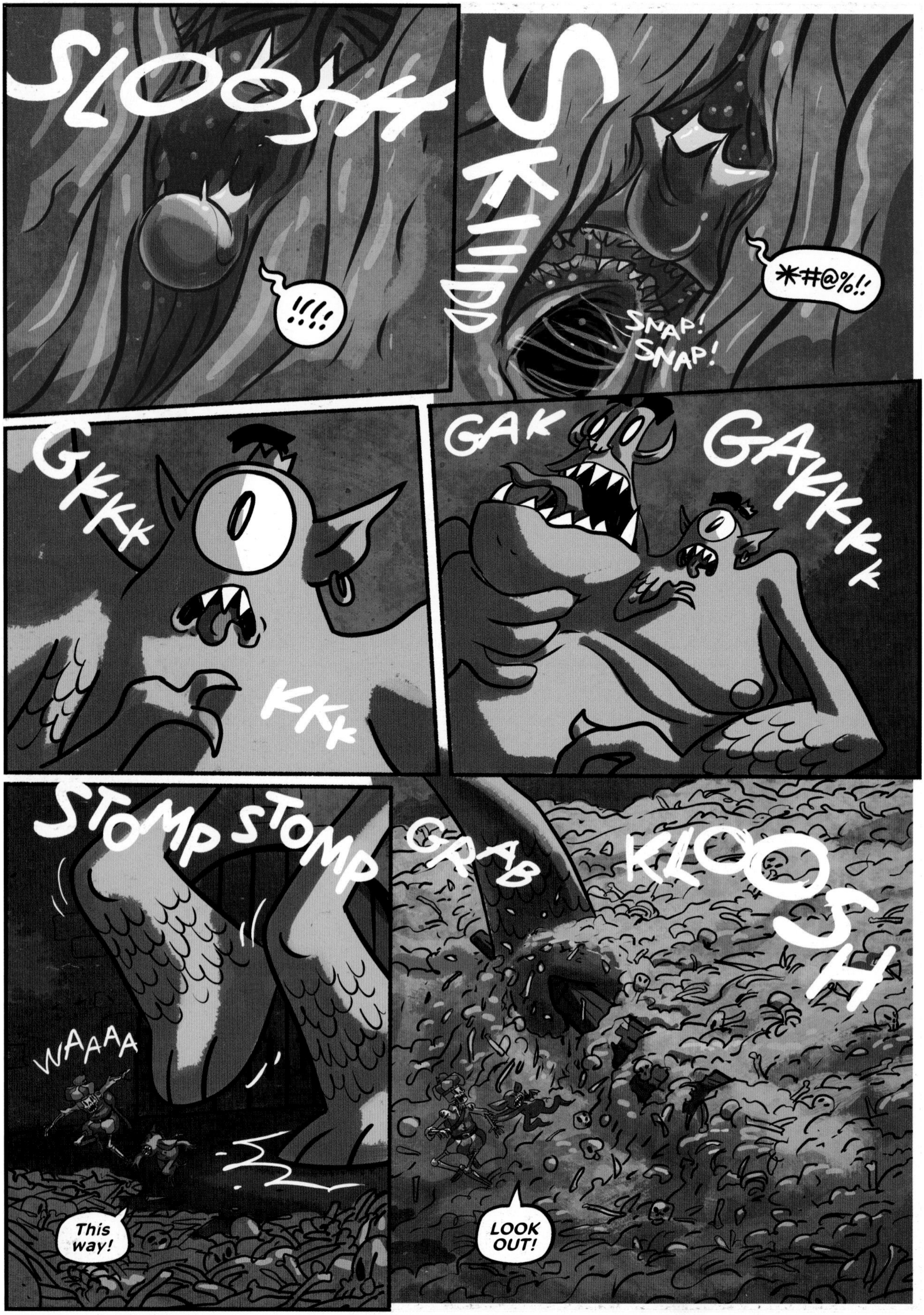
SLOOSH
!!!!
SKIIIDD
*#@%!!
SNAP! SNAP!
GKKK
KKK
GAK
GAKKKK
STOMP STOMP
WAAAA
This way!
GRAB
KLOOSH
LOOK OUT!

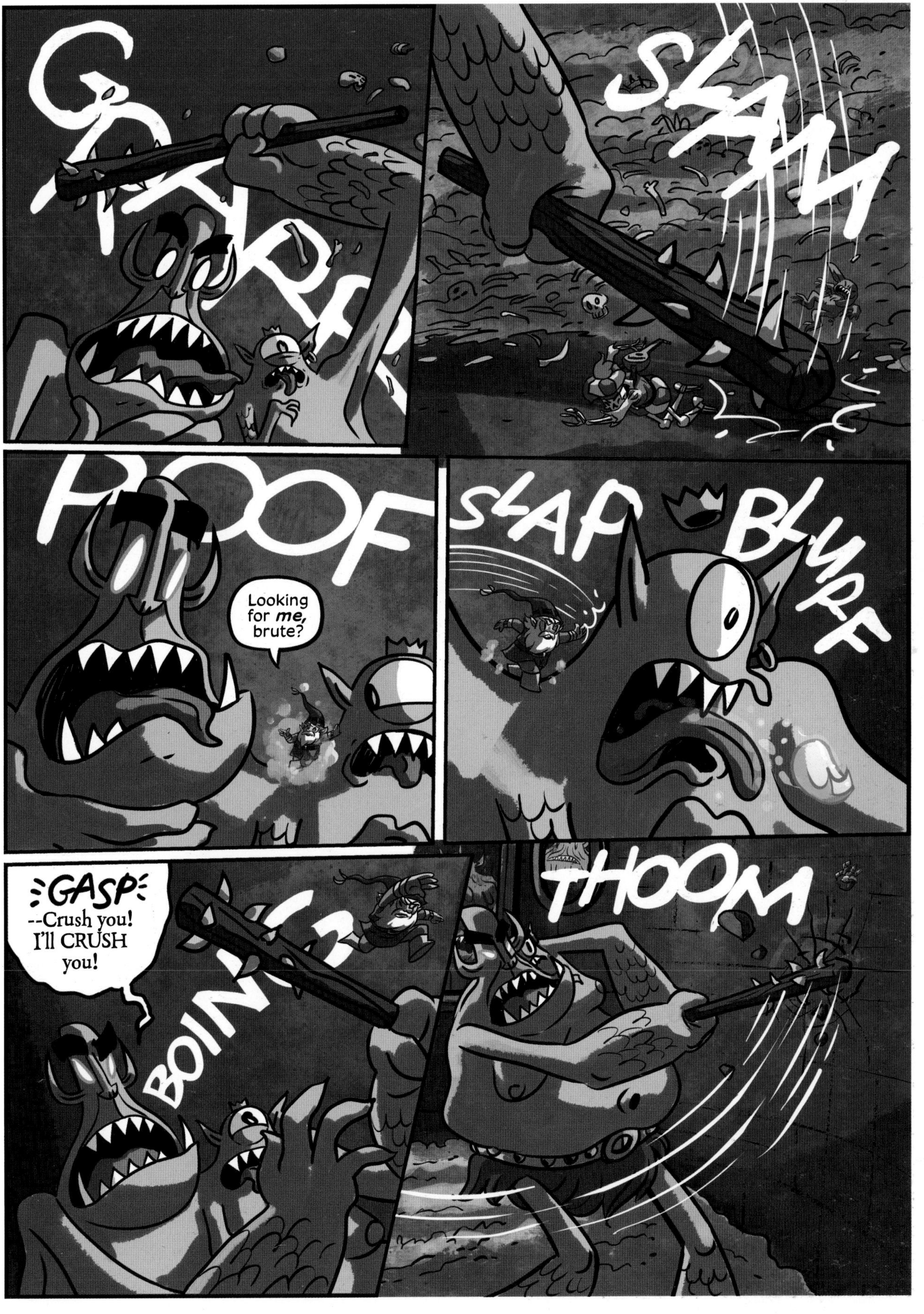
SLAM
POOF
Looking for *me*, brute?
SLAP
GASP
--Crush you! I'll CRUSH you!
THOOM

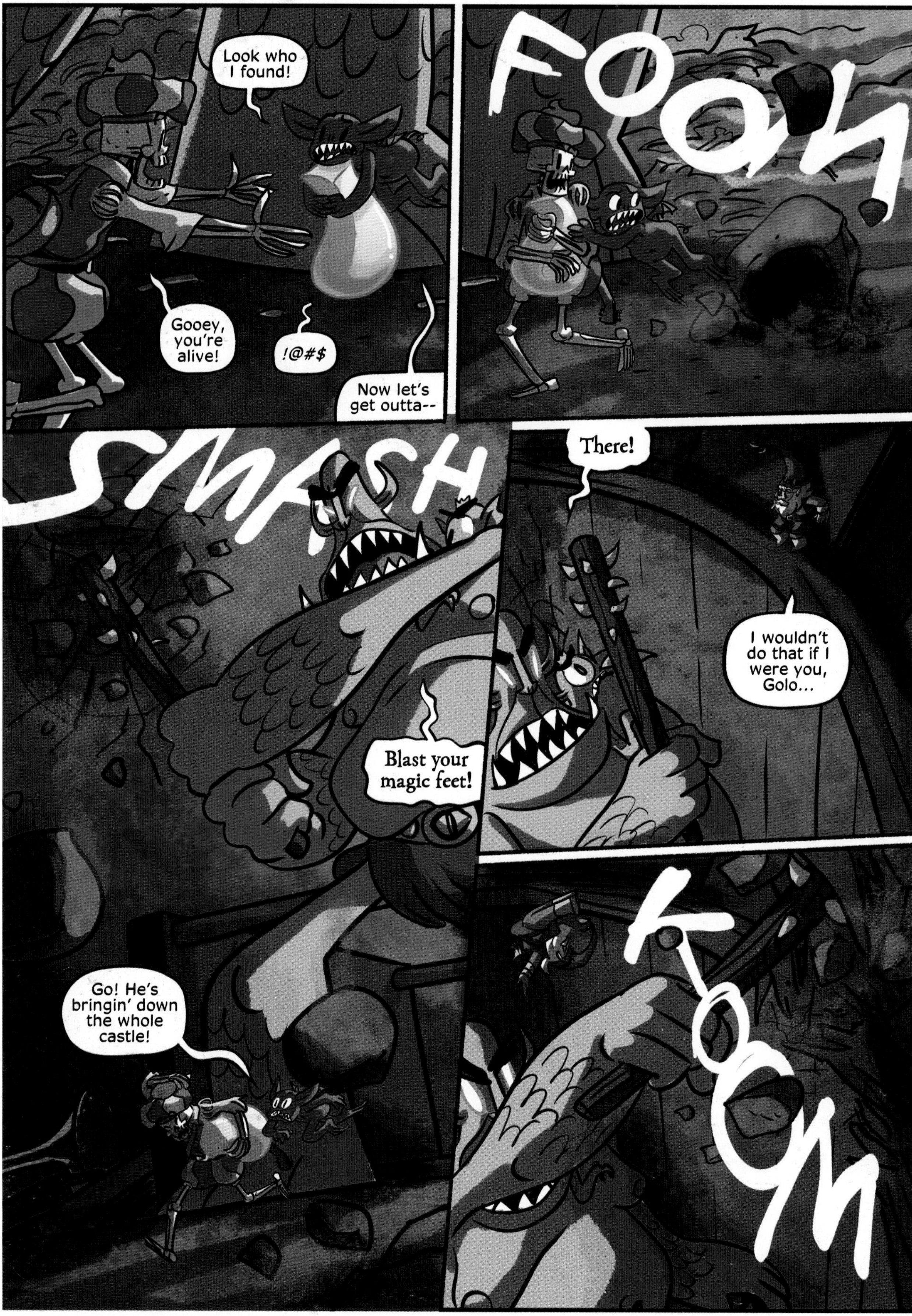
Look who I found!
Gooey, you're alive!
!@#$
Now let's get outta--
FOOM
SMASH
There!
I wouldn't do that if I were you, Golo...
Blast your magic feet!
Go! He's bringin' down the whole castle!
KOOM

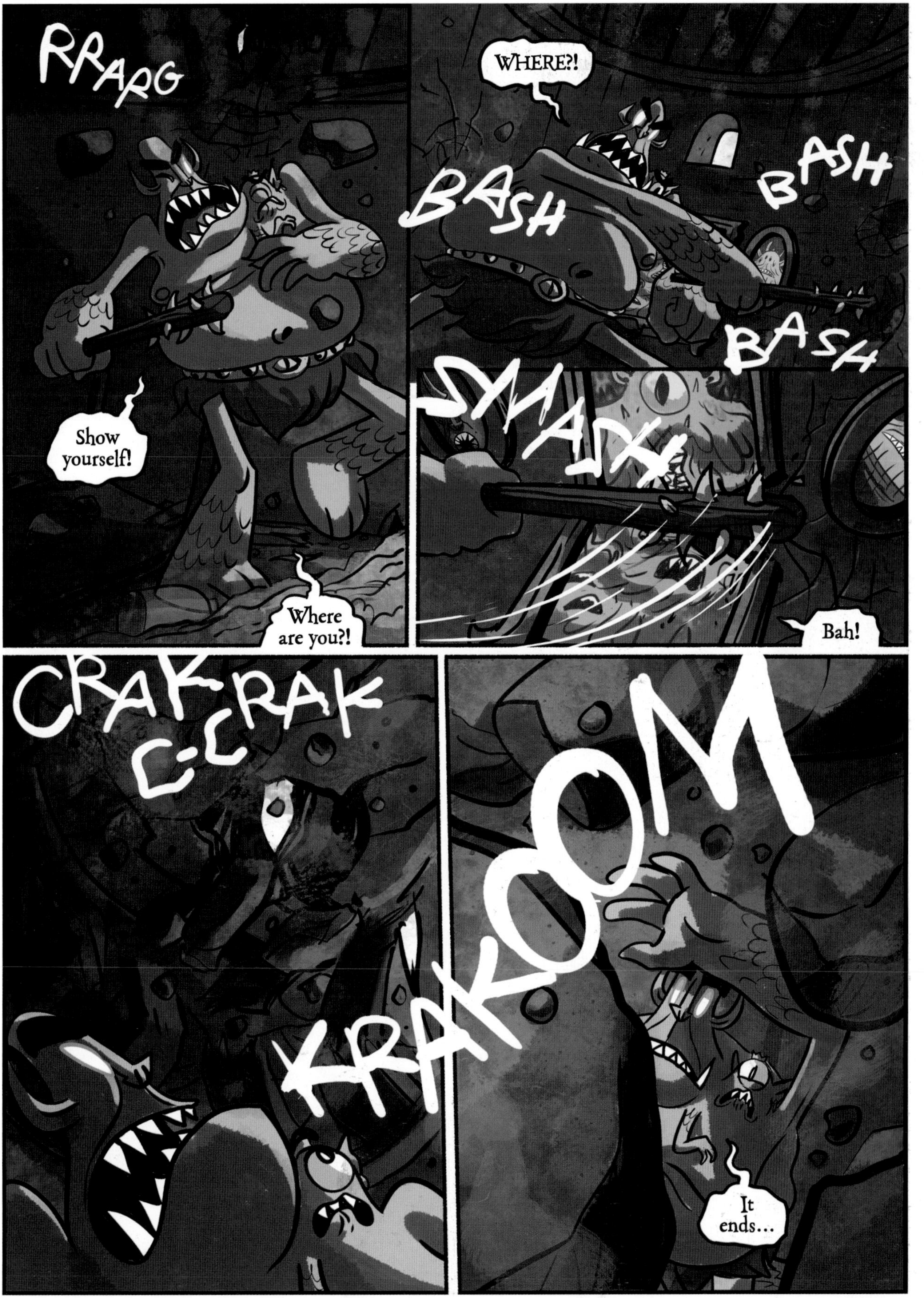
RRARG
Show yourself!
Where are you?!
WHERE?!
BASH
BASH
BASH
SMASH
Bah!
CRAK CRAK C-CRAK
KRAKOOM
It ends...

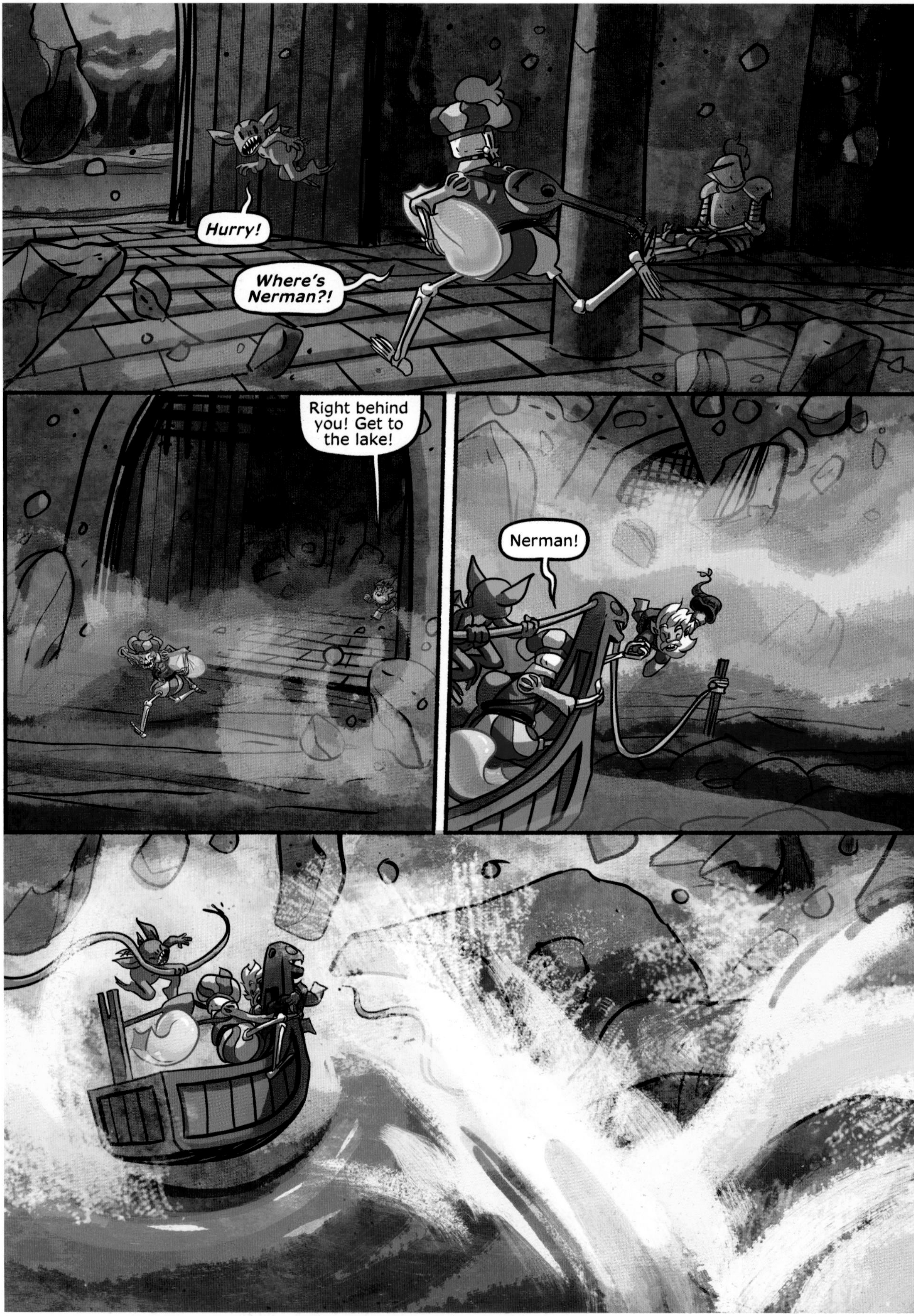
Hurry!
Where's Nerman?!
Right behind you! Get to the lake!
Nerman!

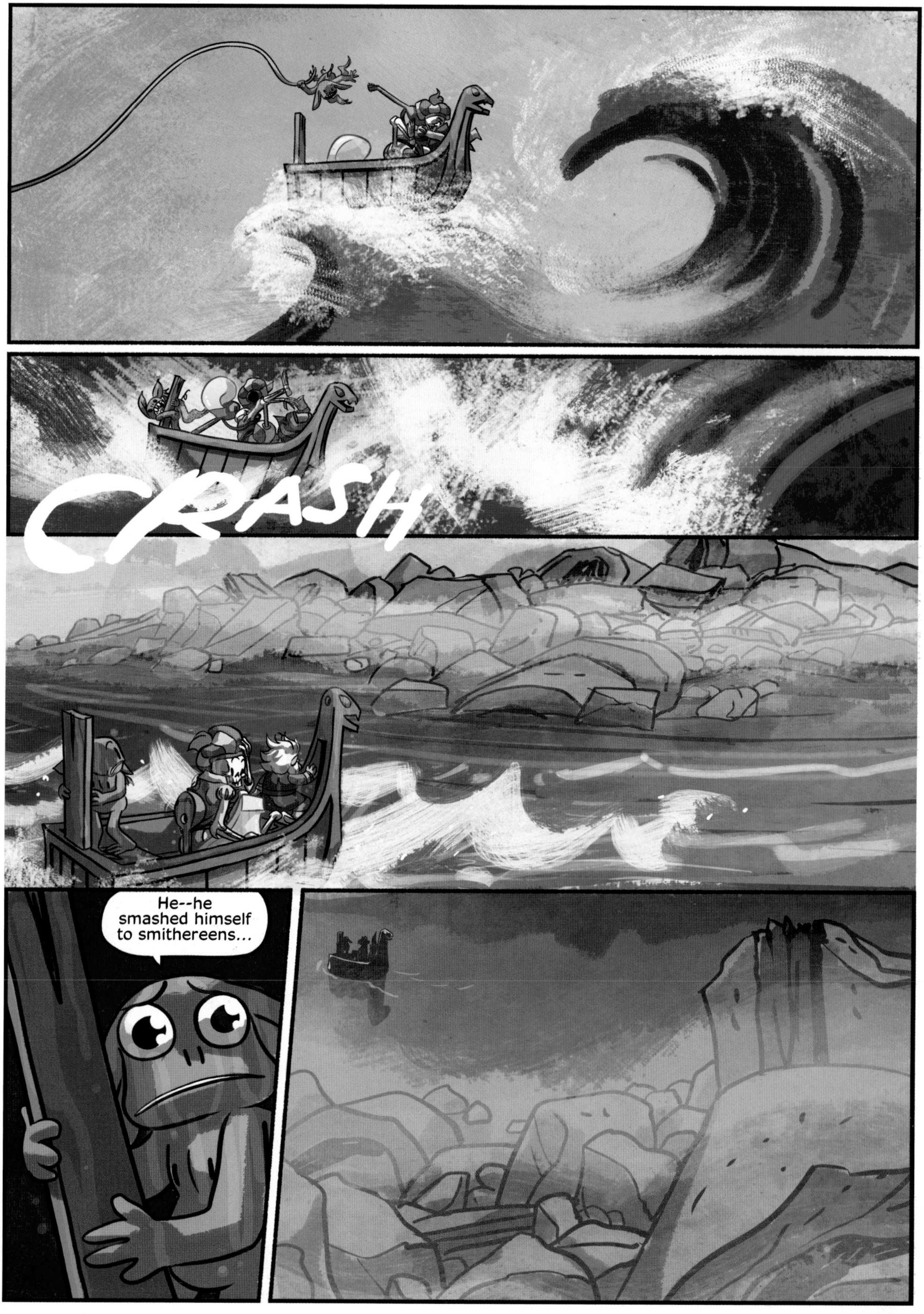
CRASH
He--he smashed himself to smithereens...

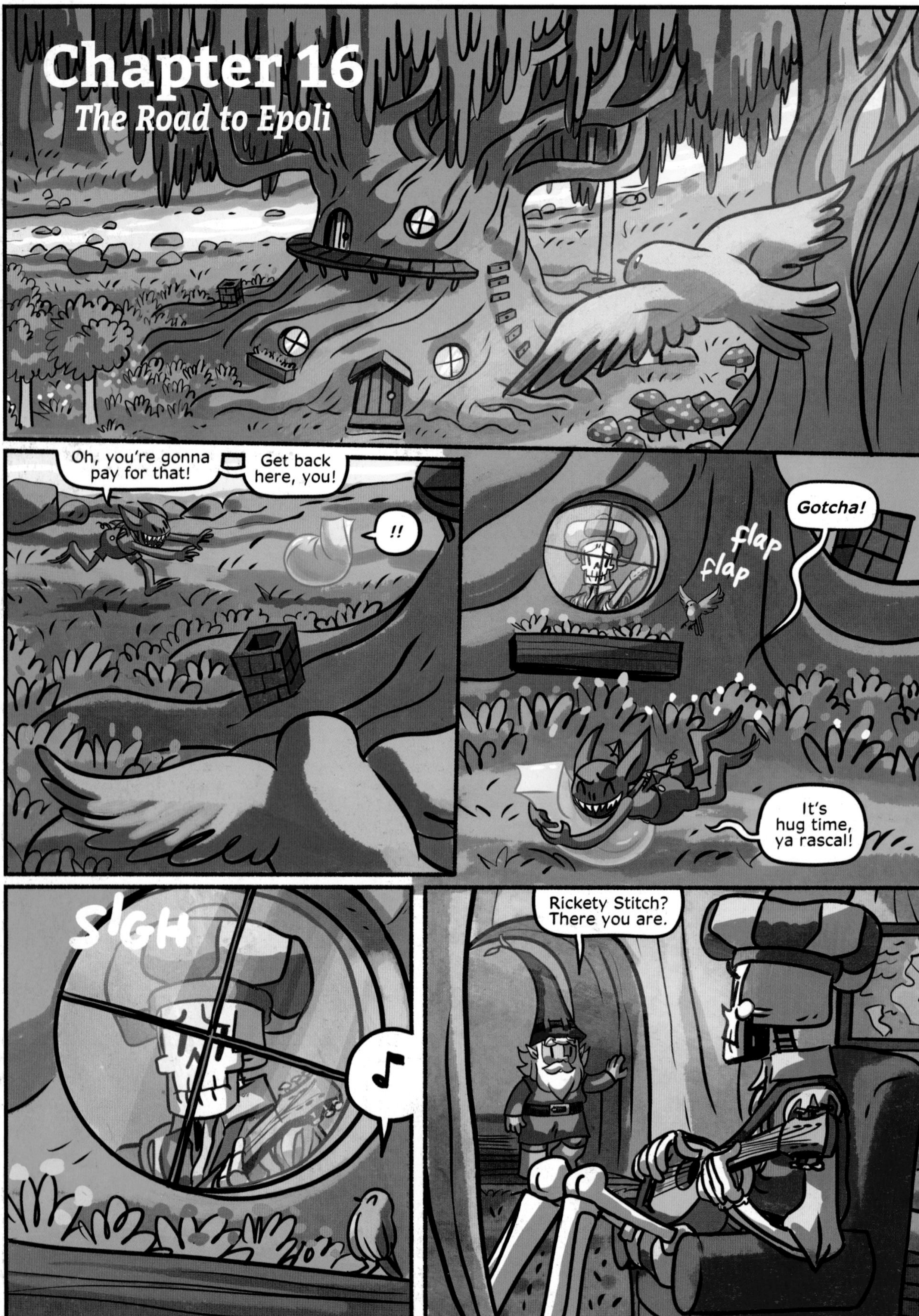
Chapter 16
The Road to Epoli
Oh, you're gonna pay for that!
Get back here, you!
!!
Gotcha!
flap flap
It's hug time, ya rascal!
SIGH
♪
Rickety Stitch? There you are.

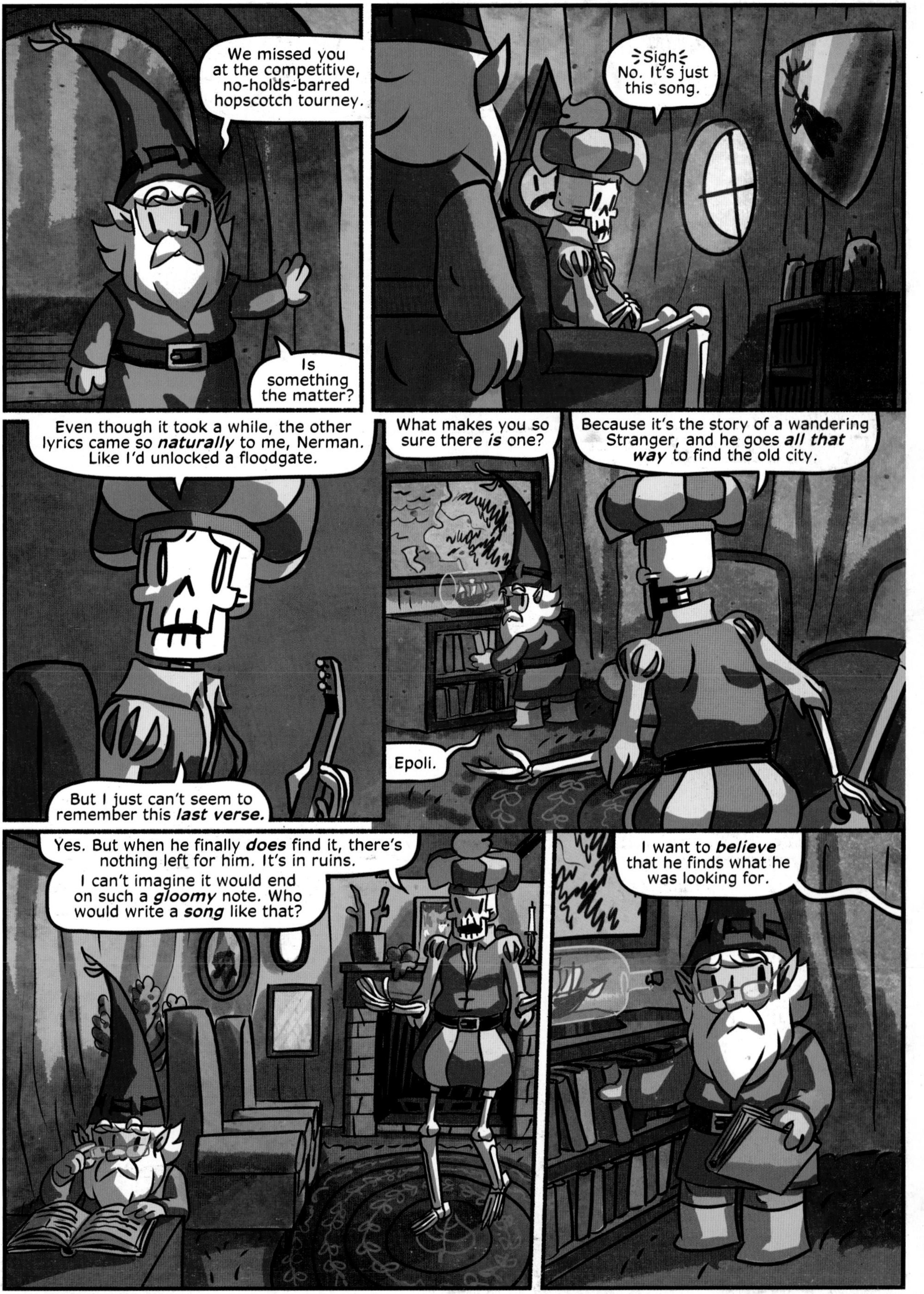
We missed you at the competitive, no-holds-barred hopscotch tourney.
Is something the matter?
Sigh
No. It's just this song.
Even though it took a while, the other lyrics came so *naturally* to me, Nerman. Like I'd unlocked a floodgate.
But I just can't seem to remember this *last verse.*
What makes you so sure there *is* one?
Because it's the story of a wandering Stranger, and he goes *all that way* to find the old city.
Epoli.
Yes. But when he finally *does* find it, there's nothing left for him. It's in ruins.
I can't imagine it would end on such a *gloomy* note. Who would write a *song* like that?
I want to *believe* that he finds what he was looking for.

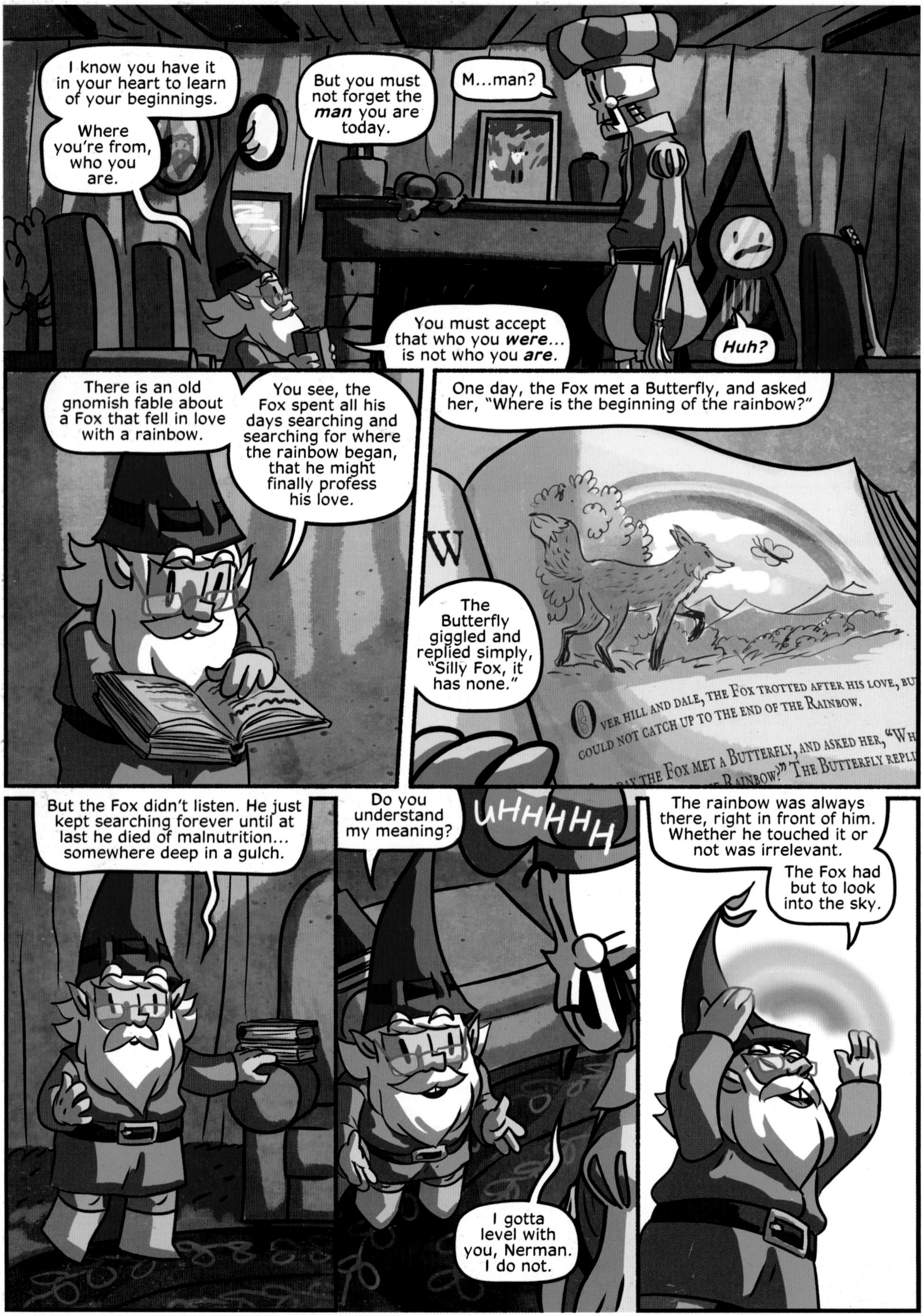
I know you have it in your heart to learn of your beginnings.
Where you're from, who you are.
But you must not forget the ***man*** you are today.
M...man?
You must accept that who you ***were***... is not who you ***are***.
Huh?
There is an old gnomish fable about a Fox that fell in love with a rainbow.
You see, the Fox spent all his days searching and searching for where the rainbow began, that he might finally profess his love.
One day, the Fox met a Butterfly, and asked her, "Where is the beginning of the rainbow?"
The Butterfly giggled and replied simply, "Silly Fox, it has none."
Over hill and dale, the Fox trotted after his love, bu
could not catch up to the end of the Rainbow.
But the Fox didn't listen. He just kept searching forever until at last he died of malnutrition... somewhere deep in a gulch.
Do you understand my meaning?
UHHHHH
I gotta level with you, Nerman. I do not.
The rainbow was always there, right in front of him. Whether he touched it or not was irrelevant.
The Fox had but to look into the sky.

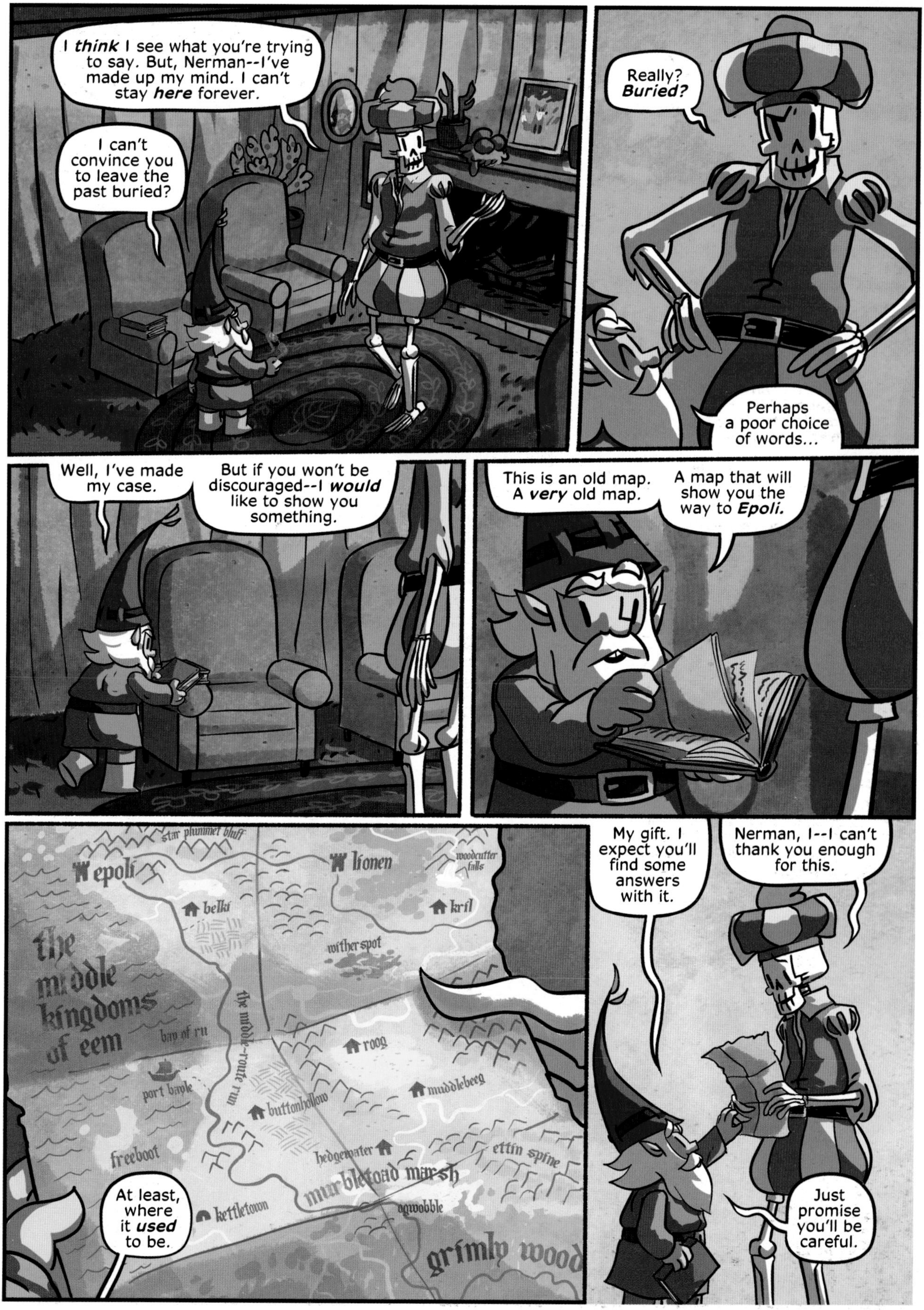
I *think* I see what you're trying to say. But, Nerman--I've made up my mind. I can't stay *here* forever.
I can't convince you to leave the past buried?
Really? *Buried?*
Perhaps a poor choice of words...
Well, I've made my case.
But if you won't be discouraged--I *would* like to show you something.
This is an old map. A *very* old map.
A map that will show you the way to *Epoli.*
star plummet bluff
epoli
lionen
woodcutter falls
belki
kril
witherspot
the middle kingdoms of eem
the middle-route run
bay of ru
roog
port bayle
muddlebeeg
buttonhollow
freeboot
hedgewater
ettin spine
murbletoad marsh
kettletown
ogwobble
grimly wood
At least, where it *used* to be.
My gift. I expect you'll find some answers with it.
Nerman, I--I can't thank you enough for this.
Just promise you'll be careful.

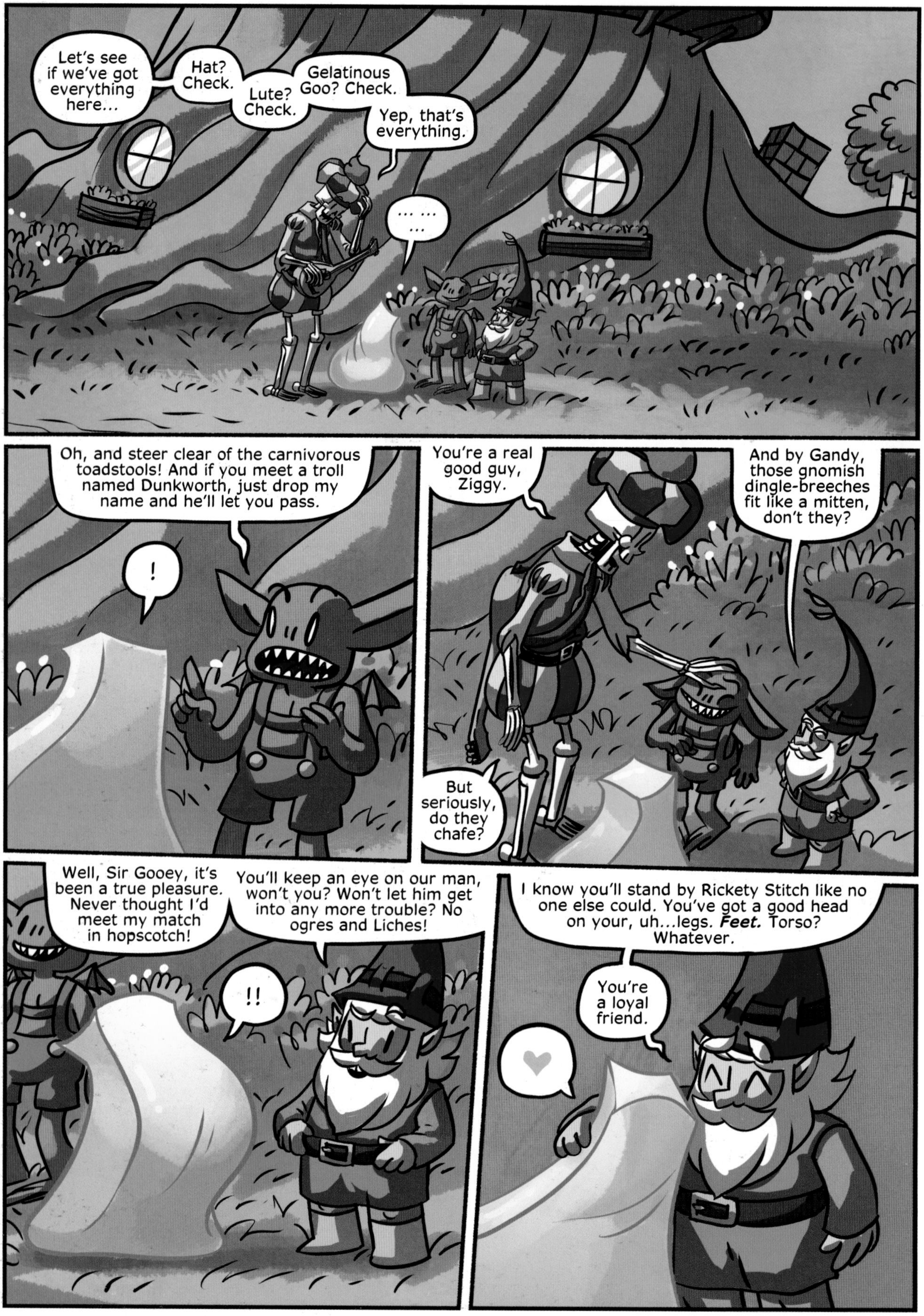
Let's see if we've got everything here...
Hat? Check.
Lute? Check.
Gelatinous Goo? Check.
Yep, that's everything.
... ...
Oh, and steer clear of the carnivorous toadstools! And if you meet a troll named Dunkworth, just drop my name and he'll let you pass.
!
You're a real good guy, Ziggy.
And by Gandy, those gnomish dingle-breeches fit like a mitten, don't they?
But seriously, do they chafe?
Well, Sir Gooey, it's been a true pleasure. Never thought I'd meet my match in hopscotch!
You'll keep an eye on our man, won't you? Won't let him get into any more trouble? No ogres and Liches!
!!
I know you'll stand by Rickety Stitch like no one else could. You've got a good head on your, uh...legs. *Feet.* Torso? Whatever.
You're a loyal friend.

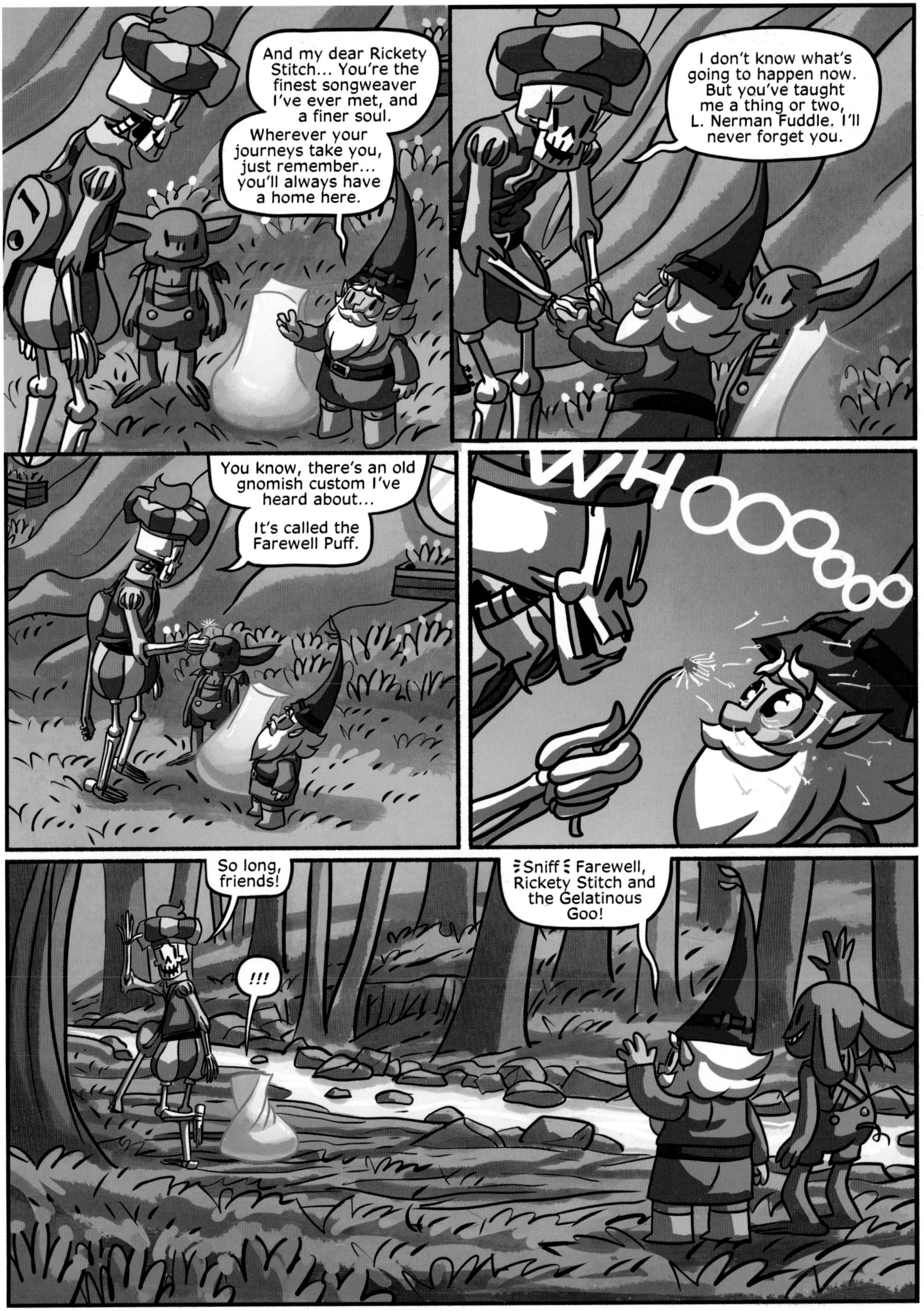

And my dear Rickety Stitch... You're the finest songweaver I've ever met, and a finer soul.
Wherever your journeys take you, just remember... you'll always have a home here.
I don't know what's going to happen now. But you've taught me a thing or two, L. Nerman Fuddle. I'll never forget you.
You know, there's an old gnomish custom I've heard about...
It's called the Farewell Puff.
WHOOOOOOO
So long, friends!
!!!
Sniff Farewell, Rickety Stitch and the Gelatinous Goo!

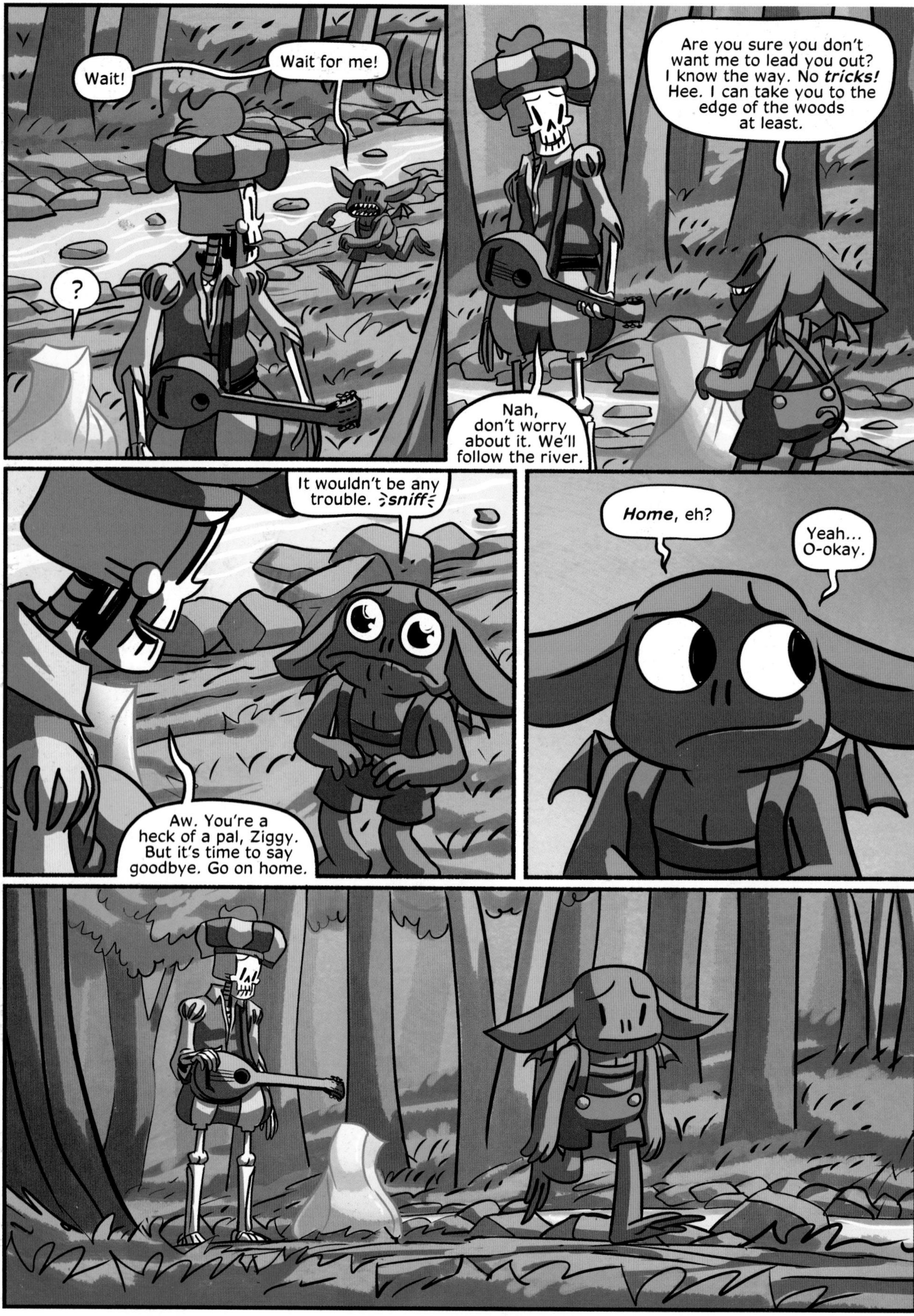
Wait!
Wait for me!
?
Are you sure you don't want me to lead you out? I know the way. No *tricks!* Hee. I can take you to the edge of the woods at least.
Nah, don't worry about it. We'll follow the river.
It wouldn't be any trouble. *sniff*
Aw. You're a heck of a pal, Ziggy. But it's time to say goodbye. Go on home.
Home, eh?
Yeah... O-okay.

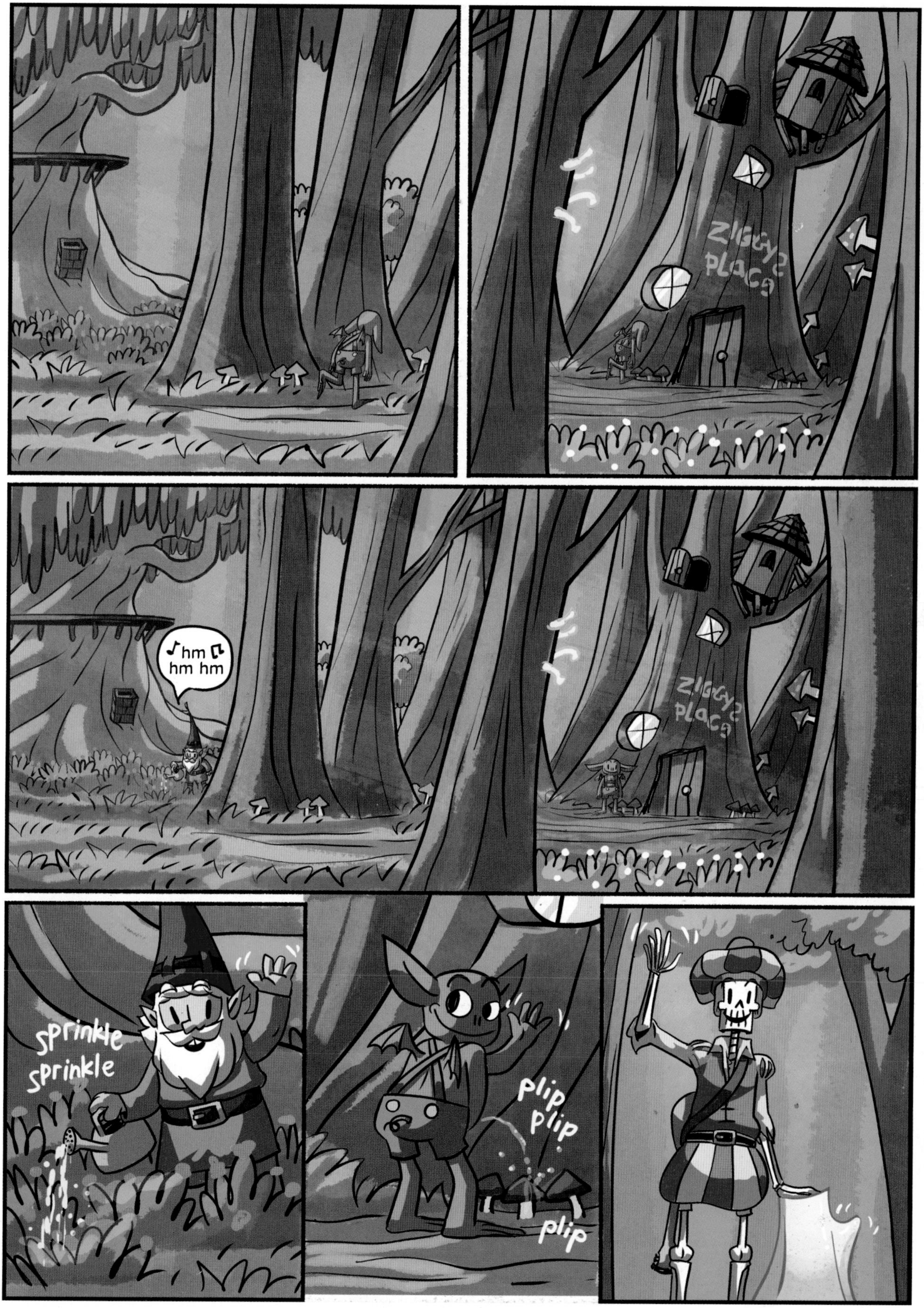
ZIGGY'S PLACE
ZIGGY'S PLACE
hm hm hm
sprinkle sprinkle
plip plip
plip

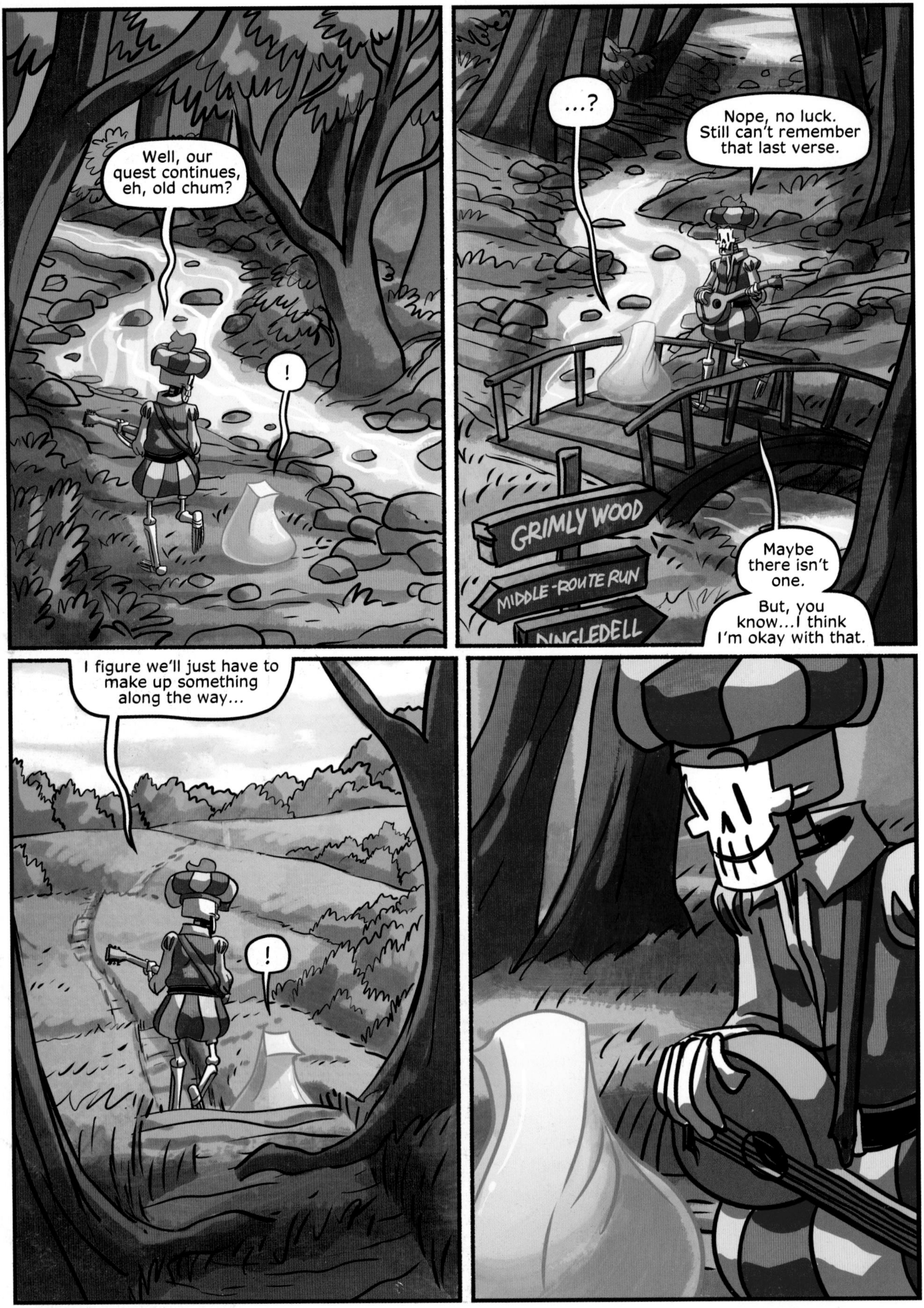
Well, our quest continues, eh, old chum?
!
...?
Nope, no luck. Still can't remember that last verse.
GRIMLY WOOD
MIDDLE-ROUTE RUN
DINGLEDELL
Maybe there isn't one.
But, you know...I think I'm okay with that.
I figure we'll just have to make up something along the way...
!

The Road to Epoli

Music written and performed by Evin Wolverton Lyrics by Ben Costa & James Parks

Upon the road the Stranger strode through fog not from the sea
O'er windswept haunts and gloomy downs of black and crooked trees
Staving fright, the Stranger sang aloud despite the dark
as wordless will-o'-wisps incanted wiles upon his heart
But though he could not see ahead, he trod forth ever on
And nevermore looked back upon the life he'd left behind
Only marching toward the golden city he must find
Away from home and hearth, his bonny bride and family
Forgotten by the Stranger on the Road to Epoli
The Road to Epoli, the Dream of Epoli

At last the Stranger wandered west past Kril and Lionen
Upon which grew the oaken vales and ash-wood Shady Glens
But where now was the warming hearth, the gold and gilded flame?
And where now were the singing saints of yesteryear's refrain?
The gray moon cast no light ahead as dusk entombed his heart
He stumbled through the darkened crypts of doubt and deep despair
And fell beneath the icy rifts of hope that brought him there
Alone and cold his burdens dampened all that he might see
Perhaps he was not meant to find the Road to Epoli
The Road to Epoli, the Flame of Epoli

O sorry-hearted traveler, just lay your head to rest
The evergreen is fading and the starlight wanes away
Like old stones set in sinking sands, so weary are your bones
Look to the Morning Light on high, look through the shrouded sky
May starlight guide you home tonight, O starlight guide you home
Though long and far you roam, upon the Road to Epoli

So lonely was the wayward road, with no one by his side
No other folk to spark the lamp, no friend to kindly guide
The crickets and the sparrow sprites went still as dusk befell
For lo, there lurked the Olden Fog a-rolling from the dells
In fright, the Stranger dropped his pack and everything he owned
He cursed himself for lacking now the footing of the bold
Like griffin-hearted champions of epic stories told
His birthright was not noble, never sworn by king's decree
But all who seek find something on the Road to Epoli
The Road to Epoli, the Heart of Epoli

The Stranger looked unto the seas, beyond the veil of night
Upon which sailed a fleet of ships, aglow with twinkling light
"Ahoy," they sang, "our silver ships draw near the Gilded Peaks"
"Below the bluffs and by the deep, the Golden City sleeps"
Then swirling mists obscured the ships and drowned the sailors' songs
The fog wove 'round the snarling crags and slithered up the sand
Like fingers on a ghostly hand, it clawed onto the land
Yet far above the shadowed shore a mighty mountain gleamed
A crown atop the sea along the Road to Epoli
The Road to Epoli, the Light of Epoli

O sorry-hearted traveler, just lay your head to rest
The evergreen is fading and the starlight wanes away
Like old stones set in sinking sands, so weary are your bones
Look to the Morning Light on high, look through the shrouded sky
May starlight guide you home tonight, O starlight guide you home
Though long and far you roam, upon the Road to Epoli

Within the gloom he tarried not, and climbed beyond the shores
The Stranger, shouting, finally found the fabled golden doors
But tarnished was their luster now, o'ergrown with shabby vines
While toppled stone and lichen shrouded everything in sight
And woe to him, the Stranger's heart fell faster than the stars
He looked toward the sky and cried, "Where hath the city gone?"
Then keeled at last to weep amidst that lonely, distant dawn
No spires of the gilded flame, no sparkle by the sea
No fire within the Stranger, on the Road to Epoli
The Road to Epoli, the Fall of Epoli

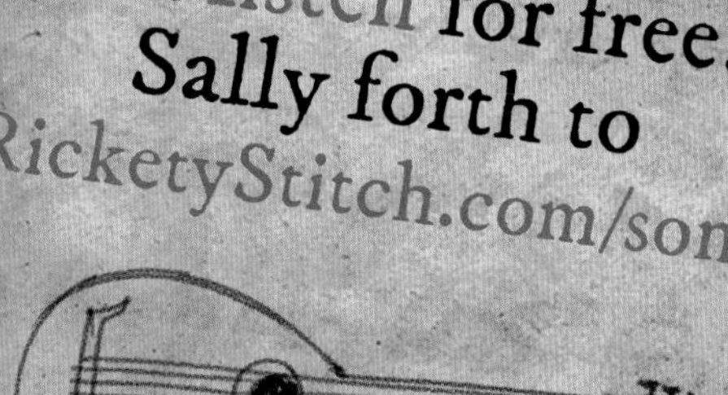

Excerpts from *The Extraordinarily Exhaustive Encyclopedia of Eem*
by P. Gandy Gandermun

Stitch

"Stitch" is the boggart pejorative term for "minstrel," or "bard," or any other sort that is engaged in the writing and performing of music. The harshness of the word itself evokes the rather crass and inelegant view that goblins and boggarts hold toward the musically inclined.

It is widely known that most goblins, boggarts, boggles, and wugs find music utterly distasteful, perceiving it as a pretentious parlor trick with little to no value. In their estimation, a stitch, like a poor seamstress, combines two things that don't belong together at all: stories and music.

Goblins, being so industrially inclined, tend to lack any deep understanding of the arts in general. This leaves few entertainment options that please them. Some examples include: public humiliation, pantomime, ventriloquism, gladiatorial games, paid inspirational seminars, and prop comedy.

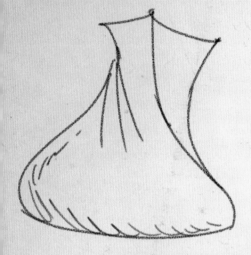

Gelatinous Goos

Coming in all shapes and sizes, gelatinous goos are sentient, subterranean jelly creatures who subsist primarily on fungi, weevils, and gemstones. They prefer to asphyxiate larger prey, such as moles and throng-worms, by engulfing the creatures within their jelly. Goos procreate through agamogenesis, spawning whilst basking in warm volcanic geysers within Eem's nether regions.

The genesis of goo society is often attributed to the Legend of the Great Goo, a mythic figure in goo history responsible for birthing the species as a whole. In the latter half of the second Kingdom of Thurf, bogril explorer Ewik Raych discovered cavern etchings that depicted an enormous goo splitting into a multitude of miniature goos, in defense against a ravenous slick of mung, a semi-sentient slime species and natural enemy of goos.

To most, goos are sought after because of their knack for gem-finding. In fact, dweorgs go so far as to enslave and sell goos throughout the Underlands. As a result, many goos have been wrested from their homes and plunged into new lives, far from their ancestral lands.

The Dungeon Era

The Dungeon Era marks the rise of the boggarts and their grand economic machine to change the fate of Eem and the trajectory of history. Vying for supremacy, the great goblin Tycoons of the Underlands—those richest and most cunning of their lot—expanded their holdings through aggressive, unchecked tunneling and exploitation of the mineral-veined earth.

However, the most prominent of the goblin entrepreneurs was not a goblin at all. No one knows who (or what) he is really, but all would agree–Orfong the Defiler changed everything. Many generations ago, Orfong devised a plan to usurp a series of dweorg mining contracts by strength of arms. And with his band of cutthroats, the wily Defiler seized control of the largest tunnel network in the Underlands, a network so vast that it undermined nearly the entire expanse of the Mucklands and as far north as Grimly Wood. It took decades to consolidate and map the network, and in that time Orfong began assembling dungeons to be rented, with the profits poured into constant expansion. Boggles and wugs were recruited feverishly, and by the thirtieth year of Orfong's mad dash for Underland control, Subterranean Pits and Lairs, LLC was born.

Soon shadowy organizations from around the world wanted in on the boom, and before long, the Dungeon Era seized the hearts and minds of an age, and consumed an obscene portion of natural resources both above and below the crust of the earth. Copycat organizations sprang up like weeds, and the abandoned structures and ruins from a grander, forgotten age were repurposed and defiled to build what is often referred to simply as Boggartdom.

In the present day, venomous executive leadership and ruthless corporate takeovers are commonplace. Shameless and invasive marketing and infamously cheap wares all lead toward a crueler society obsessed with consumption and expansion.

Gordak the Progenitor

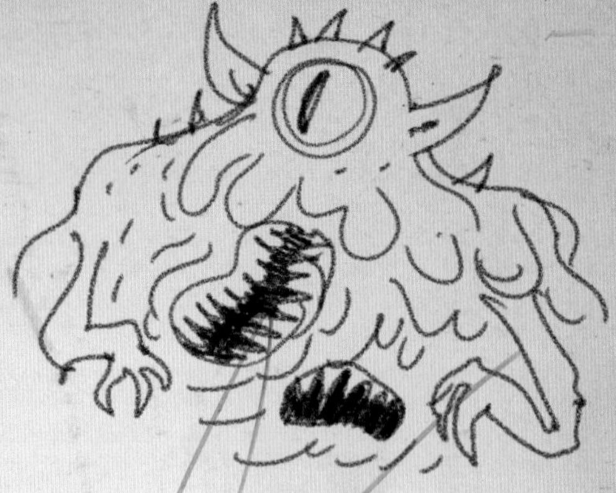

Gordak the Progenitor was once a living embodiment of the world's end. A titan and fiend, it was born of churning, primordial chaos, with flesh and bones that lurched from the thundering deep of Eem's infant core and rose in a mighty crack.

When it woke, the stars shuttered and the mountains moaned beneath the weight of her gargantuan feet. The Progenitor's tail carved rivers and valleys into the face of the earth, and her towering reach cut swaths of clouds from the sky. Its blinking eye lit the night as she sauntered over a lush and empty landscape; searching, striving, and starving for company.

Gordak wandered alone, solitary but for the lesser creatures she devoured or destroyed—until at last she settled into a great volcanic crater to birth her horrible young. Both mother and father, Gordak writhed in the bubbling froth for fifty years until at last spawning the Three Dooms—her ogre sons: Kurgonn, Oomek, and Golo.

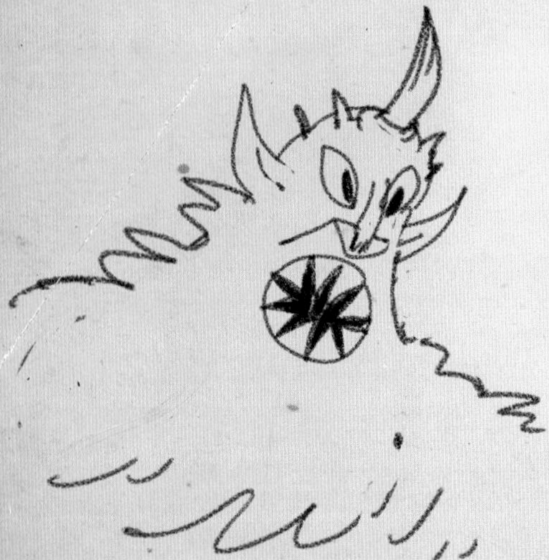

Kurgonn the Mountain Eater

The most destructive of the sons of Gordak is Kurgonn the Mountain Eater. Parted from his mother, Kurgonn's rage could not be quieted and so he thundered and he plundered and he sundered the lost kingdoms of a forgotten time.

For years the ogre wandered the Northlands, until the Mountains of Hetch sighed as Kurgonn grew fat and heavy upon the shimmering veins of precious minerals in the earth. Like a suckling babe, Kurgonn devoured the molten lead that pumped like blood from the booming deep, and his ravenousness caused terrible earthquakes that threatened the nearby Goblins of the Hob, who were once the unchallenged masters of Hetch.

Like ants, the goblins mobilized, gathering their most honored witches from every village, and marshaling a force of such magnitude, Kurgonn mistook their coming for an earthquake of his own doing. And his mistake was his *un*doing. The goblins of Hetch subdued the monstrous ogre and bound him in ghostly, witch-light chains that no amount of rage, no amount of force, could ever break. It took five years to drag Kurgonn into the Canyons of Pim, wherein even today he lies imprisoned and powerless at the shadowy bottom of that mighty divide.

Oomek the Sea Drinker

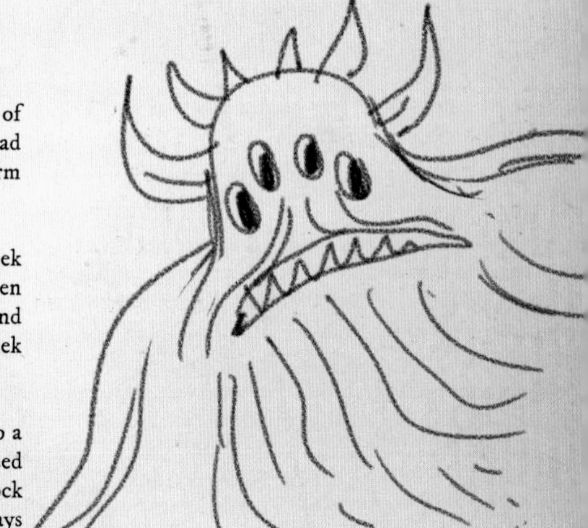

The largest of the sons of Gordak, Oomek the Sea Drinker sauntered into the briny waters of Eem to wash the sun-baked blood from his scaly body, and he never again looked back. Long had the massive weight of his shambling folds lay heavily on his bones, but when his terrible form crashed against the waves and fell into the deep, his tremendous pain subsided.

Oomek's time in the oceans of Eem as master of its roiling waters was long and rapacious. Oomek gulped and gorged upon the bounty of the sea without competition. Sailors and fishermen trembled in their tiny boats, whispering Oomek's names, the Deep Beast, the Sea Drinker. And when his four, glittering eyeballs emerged from the waters to meet their terrified gaze, Oomek would laugh and the seas would rage.

But alas, lured by the false prospect of devouring a merfolk kingdom, Oomek blundered into a volcanic fissure. As Oomek bashed and clawed his way through the rocky vent, his assault caused a super-eruption. Magma blasted from a crack in the earth, instantly cooling into volcanic rock around him. Oomek was trapped within the newly formed sea mountain, there to live out his days a prisoner, awaiting another eruption to set him free.

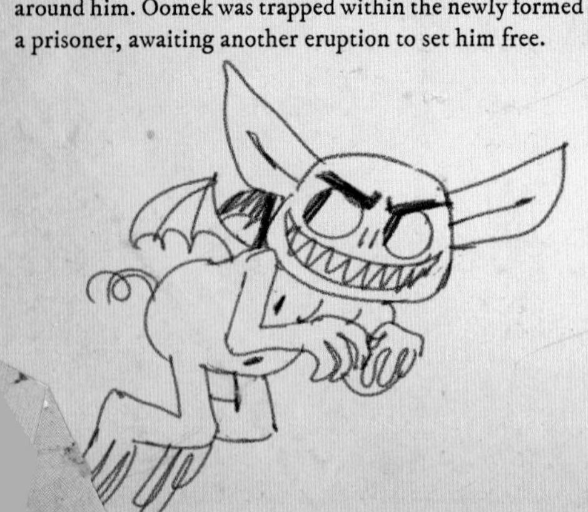

Imps

Knowing nothing more than lives of servitude, imps are diminutive, winged creatures who are bound to a master, be that a witch, or magician, or anyone else with interest in keeping magic familiars.

There are many ways to obtain an imp familiar, but the most common method is through hex magic, by casting dark dwimmers upon a wyrm's egg, and incubating it in fire for nineteen moon cycles. Approximately one out of five times, the spellcaster will end up with a baby imp; the other four times, one should be prepared to withstand a sulfurous odor so powerful and nasty it has been known to slay the young and elderly within a nineteen-mile radius. If one can survive this process, or come into the possession of an imp through other nefarious means, that imp will do the owner's bidding until the owner perishes or releases the imp from servitude.

Gnomes

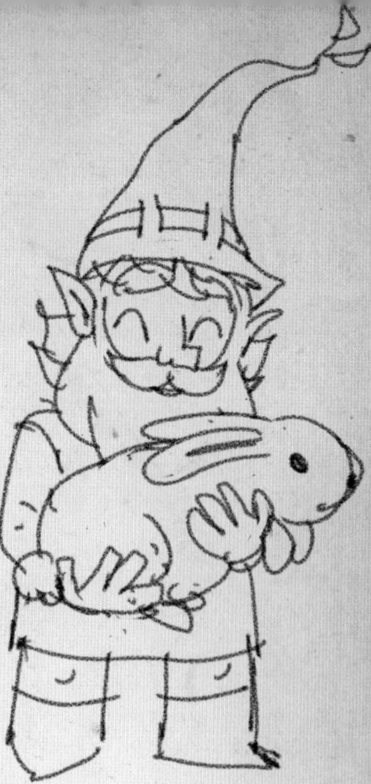

Despite their small stature and ordinary domestic lives, gnomes harbor great power. With incredible might, ability, and innate magic, gnomes make exemplary guardians of all that is right and good. But because they are remarkably unassuming, friendly folk, gnomes spend most of their simple days assisting the denizens of forests and glens. You are most likely to find a gnome tending a garden, planting a tree, or helping a fawn out of a trapjaw—but on the rare occasion that a gnome's dwimmercraft is called upon, not even the boldest fiend would dare cross paths with these wee Wardens of the Wood.

Gnome society revolves around a reverence for the quiet, ordinary things that most folk take for granted while dreaming of riches or adventure. To gnomes, riches and adventure are simply causes and effects that exist in the moments between hot tea, freshly baked bread, and the pleasures of tilling soil. Wealth has very little meaning for gnomes, though they are often wildly wealthy due to their prolonged lives. As for adventure, it is nothing to be sought after, and only something to chronicle in the lives of other folk. If there is one thing most important to gnomish culture, it is to keep the histories and tales of Eem alive: the songs, the stories, the legends of all the world's many people, which others forget in time.

While there are a handful of gnomish cities and communities sprinkled throughout the Dingledell and Eem at large—Mirth being the largest of them all—a great number of gnomes are hermits. Rather than settle down with a husband or wife to start a family, many gnomes are by nature compelled to retreat to the wilderness alone, building solitary homes for themselves so they can tend to and protect the land. This keeps the gnome population down, as they live out lives spanning hundreds of years without ever producing offspring.

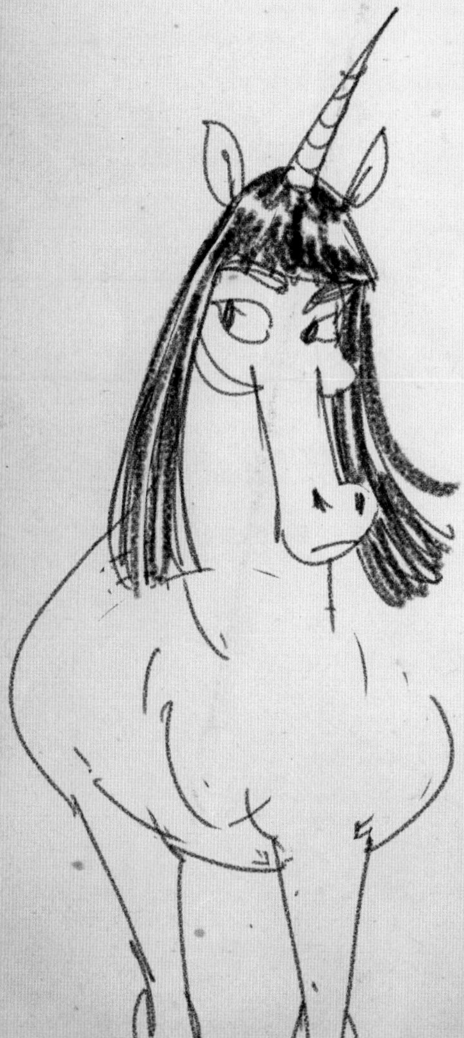

The Legend of Thalatos

The legend of Thalatos is an old one. Many eons ago, it is said a star plummeted from the heavens and split the mountain of Thalatos in two, carving a tremendous valley, which came to be known as the Gates of Thalatos, on an island called Therafin. On the western side of the valley lay the home of all unicorns, and to the east the world of Eem.

The gates were beautiful, a natural wonder of ancient stone, torn earth, majestic trees, blooming flowers, and glittering stardust. But a powerful spell from the sky hung over the gates like a great and angry cloud. For though Thalatos was beautiful, it was also deadly. No creature could pass into the valley unless their spirits were pure and their hearts devoted to preserving the natural world.

So came the first of several mystic ponies, chosen amongst the unicorns to venture into the world wide and claim their mighty birthrights as Defenders of the Sprouting Seed and Wardens of the Wood.

The first unicorn to pass into the gates was Kreldar the Ironhoof, renowned for his fiery stamp. Proud and bold were his steps as he traversed the valley evergreen. Kreldar came to a trickling rill, lush with lily pads and rife with fish, and passed through it without a thought. Then suddenly, a crack and whistle and burning light! Kreldar was struck by a meteor, pulled from the sky by the trial of deadly Thalatos. Kreldar the Ironhoof was pulverized.

The second unicorn was Shara the Nimbletail, lithe as a leaf on the wind. Cunning, she pranced to the rill's edge and leapt over it, and the fish smiled as she did. Shara then ventured farther into Thalatos, flowers bursting from hanging vines as she passed under a stony outcrop that led to the tallest peak. There she beheld the world beyond the valley, her prize. But the outcrop darkened, and venomous glowworms blinked in the dark as they descended upon her, hungry and terrible. Shara the Nimbletail suffered their bites and turned instantly to dust.

Last came Xorgana, who thanked the fish for their smiles and passed into the darkened outcrop, wherein the hungry glowworms licked their gooey mandibles. Xorgana plucked the hanging flowers and gifted them to the glowworms, who gladly accepted. In their joy and gratitude, the glowworms spun a tremendous silk bridge that led from the tallest peak to the edge of the deadly valley.

And so Xorgana passed through the Gates of Thalatos and ventured into the world of Eem. There she encountered many dangers. Glory and legend were heaped upon her name, until she came at last to a grim forest, where she is now the stalwart warden.

The Flame and the Star of Epoli

The Flame and the Star of Epoli come with a story most dear to those who still remember it. Long ago a wayward people were hopelessly lost at sea. One night, amidst the crashing waves of a terrible storm, a shining light speared through the rumbling clouds and struck land. That light was the Star of Epoli, and when it struck the earth, a brilliant flame ignited, leading the people safely to the shore, to a land that they called Eem, and to a kingdom remembered as Epoli.

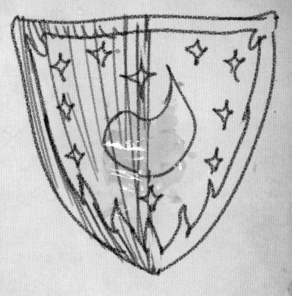

The story has many versions, but each shares the element of a falling star striking the ground and sparking a great fire. Eem's namesake actually comes from an ancient word for the light of an ember glow, or, more specifically, the "eem" of the ember.

In Epoli, stars held great metaphorical meaning because, despite the darkness of the night sky, stars burned brilliantly and seemingly forever. In Epoli, stars represented an immortal reminder to light the way, a way to home, a way to hearth, a way to new ideas that could set people free and turn enemies to friends. However, the Star of Epoli, though an important symbol, was little more than a reminder of responsibility. And though light may guide, only a fire can bring warmth to the cold. That fire is called the Flame of Epoli.

The Flame is a powerful symbol, for only mortal hands can spark a flint. And only hands can tend a fire. Upon those notions many oaths have been taken. And those who bear the emblem of the hallowed Flame and Star bring with them reminders of the light, but also flints to newly spark them.

Lich

A Lich, or Lich-fiend, is a terrible entity of necromantic horror plucked from the slumber of death and plunged into the service of its master. In ancient books of the occult, this servitude is sometimes referred to as the "Summoner's song." Differing from mindless shambling skeletons, a Lich directly possesses the will of its summoner, and is an extension of the summoner's agency and dark sorcery, making Liches incredibly powerful foes. Luckily, the processes by which a Lich is wrought have been lost to time, even among the greatest magicians of Eem (of which there are very few).

Being remarkably rare, only a few Liches have ever been referenced in any sort of history. Yet there is one common thread that ties all Liches together: every one is linked to ancient nobility. It is not known whether this nobility is a requirement of their being, or a strange coincidence—though speculation leans toward the former. Regardless, the grim irony of an innominate dead whose name once carried great weight in a forgotten world is a poignant symbol of the inevitable decay of both power and memory. To wrest a sleeping king from his ancient tomb—to carry on as a puppet of the will of a summoner—is in itself a powerful declaration of might, and a terrible insult to those that once believed themselves to be limitless in their sovereignty.

As the Ral Nok Sorcerex so enigmatically states on the subject: "Though death makes us equal, undeath ensures we are not."

The Gloom King

Eem is both a world of grandeur and a world of ghosts. From the mountains of the Broken Land to the windswept plains of Thurf, the decaying memory of the old world lingers like the embers of a dying flame. And wheresoever the haunted ruins of antiquity rest on silent hills, the stories of a once-remembered Gloom King lie fallow like remnants of a fog.

The elusive legend of the Gloom King is impossible to navigate, as there are so many different tellings and tales—mostly lost or forgotten—which loosely associate with the name and the gloomy fog common to the Northlands of Eem. Some evoke "Gloomwork" in connection to an ancient, faceless evil, and to witchcraft and dark magic. This is even true amongst both boggarts and folk living in the Southlands of Eem.

Others attribute the moniker "the King of Gloom" to old folk stories about a scheming sorcerer who, long ago, imbued the world's fog with malevolent magic to spy upon the Middle Kingdoms from faraway lands. But for what purpose it is not known, and in the end there is no proof of it. Few alive today have ever heard of the Gloom King, and fewer still know his tales.